Collateral Consequences

Best wishes.
I hope you
enjoy the read.
Keep up the good work.
It was a pleasure meeting
you George Hook

Collateral Consequences

George R. Hopkins

Library of Congress Control Number:		2008911117
ISBN:	Hardcover	978-1-4363-9059-0
	Softcover	978-1-4363-9058-3

This book is a work of fiction. Names, characters, places, and incidents are the product of the author's imagination or are used fictitiously. Any resemblance or similarity to actual events, locales, or persons, living or dead, is coincidental and not intended by the author.

This book was printed in the United States of America.

To order additional copies of this book, contact:
Xlibris Corporation
1-888-795-4274
www.Xlibris.com
Orders@Xlibris.com
56293

I wish you not a path devoid of clouds,
Nor a life on a bed of roses,
Not that you might never need regret,
Nor that you should never feel pain.
No, that is not my wish for you.
My wish for you is—
That you might be brave in times of trial
When others lay crosses on your shoulders,
When mountains must be climbed,
And chasms crossed,
When hope can scarce shine through,
That every gift God gave you might grow with you
And let you give your gift of joy to all who care for you.
That you may always have a friend
Who is worth that name,
Whom you can trust
And who helps in times of sadness,
Who will defy the storms of daily life at your side.

Anonymous Irish Blessing

I

Of one power even God is deprived,
and that is the power of making
what is past never to have been.

Agathon

MONDAY

1

Staten Island, New York

Homicide Detective Tom Cavanaugh scraped the label off the Beck's bottle he clutched in his hand. He sat alone at a table in the back of R. H. Tugs Restaurant looking out at the dark waters of the Kill Van Kull. Lights from the refineries on the other side of the choppy waters glared across at him. Monday nights were usually quiet here at this time and that was the way he wanted it. He missed his brother, but he was in Cuba. His brother had left too soon, with too many unanswered questions. Logically, Cavanaugh knew if his brother had stayed there would be more questions that he didn't want to answer. For his brother's sake, it was better this way. But he missed him.

He wished he had someone to talk to whom he could trust and be honest with. There were so many things he couldn't talk to Francesca about—at least not yet. Deep inside, he wondered if he could ever talk to her about the death of her father and the man who really killed him.

All of that would have to wait. There were other things more pressing on his mind this night.

The Inquest had been over for a week, but Cavanaugh kept reviewing the events like a kaleidoscope of horrors. It had taken longer than expected. There had been protests and demonstrations. Al Sharpton led a march outside of City Hall. The *New York Times* branded him "a reckless rogue cop" whose actions "endangered the public." TV and newspaper commentators questioned his judgment and mental stability. The witnesses' statements, the police reports, the autopsy report, the toxicology report, the photos were still etched in his mind. There had been so much confusion.

It all happened so quickly. He had stopped at the local bodega to get a cup of coffee, the newspaper, and a quart of orange juice. He was on his way home after a boring day of checking bank statements of a murder suspect and was looking forward to a shower and a grilled cheese sandwich with onions and pimentos, a diet coke, followed by a Drambuie on the rocks while he watched N.C.I.S. He would probably call Francesca and see what she was up to later. But things didn't turn out that way.

As he was pouring the coffee, two teenagers came in with guns drawn demanding everyone get down. Before Cavanaugh could turn he heard one of the teens shoot Samir, the store owner, twice. Turning he saw the other one, taller and more muscular, aiming straight at him. Cavanaugh dropped to the floor and pulled out his Colt as the teen fired at him. Cavanaugh heard glass shattering behind and a short scream as he leveled his weapon and fired four shots. Both teens fell backwards, the taller one falling into a pyramid of Campbell's soup and the chunky one crashing into the cash register and spilling a variety of sugarless gums in all directions. Three customers looked on in silence as another teen ran out the front door.

Cavanaugh rose to his feet and surveyed the damage. "I'm a police officer," he shouted. "Everyone stay calm and don't move!" Carefully, stepping around the two teens and their growing pools of blood, he looked for Samir. There behind the counter lay Samir with two bullet holes in his chest. "Somebody," Cavanaugh yelled, "call 911!"

Then he heard the scream which still haunted him in his dreams. "Maria! Maria!" Turning he saw a young woman in blue slacks and a white blouse kneeling in front of the ice cream freezer's shattered glass door beside another woman. He looked for a phone. "Does anyone have a God-damn cell phone?" he demanded. "Call 911! We need help here!"

A gray haired man in a dark suit and black eyeglasses peered up from behind the apples and oranges and flipped him his cell phone. Cavanaugh made the call moving toward the girl on the floor. She was bleeding badly from her stomach. He took his coat off and tried to stop the hemorrhaging. He couldn't hear what she was saying at first, but then he heard her say, "Help me. My baby. My baby. Help please . . . ." He looked around for the baby before realizing she was pregnant.

At the Inquest the witnesses all gave different accounts. The only undisputed facts were that both teens were dead as were Samir, Maria and her unborn child. One said Cavanaugh fired without provocation. Another alleged one of his shots had killed Samir. The family of Mrs. Maria DeFillipo was distraught. Why hadn't he protected their wife, daughter, and sister? The families of the teenagers claimed Cavanaugh fired first and never identified himself as a police officer. They insisted their sons were good boys even though they already had a long list of arrests. At the Inquest, the judge and jury of six examined all the circumstances surrounding the killings. Under pressure from special interest groups and the media, they took their time. It was the forensic report, however, which clearly showed Samir and Maria were killed with the guns from the teens. Cavanaugh's shots had all hit their targets dead center in their chests. The final verdict of the Inquest was that Cavanaugh's killings were justified. The prosecutor agreed. That was a week ago, and he had just returned to work today.

But being cleared didn't clear Cavanaugh's conscience. He still heard the screams, saw the blood, and felt the struggling fetus. He had used deadly force to stop a robbery, but had not stopped three murders. The Inquest exonerated him, but he hadn't exonerated himself.

He stared at the waters and the current outside as if waiting for an answer.

Big Paul Scamadella, Monday's bartender, came over to his table. "There's a call for you, Cavanaugh, at the bar."

"I'm not here," Cavanaugh said.

The tall white haired bartender smiled, "Suits me, but it's your partner, Goldberg. He sounds a bit anxious."

"He's always anxious."

"I think you better take it, Cavanaugh. He knows you're here, and he says it's important."

Big Paul hesitated looking down at Cavanaugh.

"What are you looking at?"

"I don't know. You look different. Are you letting your hair grow?"

"Drop dead, Paul."

Cavanaugh downed the rest of his beer and then walked slowly to the bar. "What do you want, Goldberg? This sure as hell better be important."

"It is," the voice on the other end of the phone replied. "There's been a murder. I'm at the old Staten Island Hospital. It's on Castleton Avenue, off Cebra Avenue. It's only about five minutes from where you are. Get over here right away."

"What do you mean you're on Staten Island? We work in Brooklyn. We don't work here. What the hell is going on?"

"I'll explain when you get here. All I can say is there's a dead body in a closet, and it's got your name on it—literally."

*   *   *

2

Havana, Cuba

Father Jack Bennis walked down Calle Obrapia coming from Parque Central. The park with its twenty-eight tall royal palm trees surrounding a large marble statue of José Martí, the martyred Cuban revolutionist and patriot, had become one of the priest's favorite places to listen to heated debates about baseball, to watch the reaction of locals and tourists, and to pray.

It was early evening. He wore an open white shirt, rumpled khakis, and a navy blue New York Yankee cap. He could have fit in with any of the other passersby, except for the Yankee cap and that he stood four or five inches taller than everyone else. He walked with the confidence of experience and conviction. His furrowed brow, however, showed he was troubled. He sensed someone was following him.

At the corner of Calles Aguacate and Obrapia, he turned right. The sidewalks were narrow here. There weren't many cars in Old Havana so he moved into the street. The few cars he saw were old—very old. Walking through the streets of Havana, he felt like he had stepped into a time warp and had been thrown into the 1950's. The distinctive tail fins and the sleek lines of the cars were still there, but the shiny chrome had faded and multicolored coats of paint tried to hide the rusting. Next to the peeling stucco of buildings that had not seen paint in decades, it was plain to see Havana, Cuba had not aged well.

A bicycle bell jingled, and Santiago, a gray haired sixty year old with weathered brown skin, smiled and whispered, "Buenas noches, Padre," as he rode by. Bennis tipped his Yankee cap and smiled. They were beginning to know who he was. Santiago had become a fixture in the marketplace.

Santiago sold fruit and vegetables from a small stand in the Plaza de la Catedral where Father Jack Bennis, S. J., had begun to say mass. He was the most likeable of the *pregoneros* and would sell his products in a loud, singsong, comic way which attracted all. Santiago, like most of the Cubans he met, was a good man who made the most of what he had, enjoyed a good time, and was eager to gain peace from the religion of his ancestors, which had been suppressed for a long time.

Priests were always needed, and Bennis had quickly been accepted by the people.

He had come to Cuba to do what he believed was God's work. Cuba had been wallowing in the shadows of Christianity for many years. Gradually, Castro had loosened the restraints on the Catholic Church, and, Bennis felt, the country was ripe for a new beginning.

When he left New York, Bennis took with him several numbered bank accounts Howard Stevens, an ex-C.I.A. agent who had also been his operation leader when he worked on covert missions for the U.S.A., had scattered around the world. He also took the list of Cuban contacts Vito Muscatelli, a retired mob boss, had given Stevens in return for the safe return of his grandson. Bennis knew Stevens wouldn't have any future use of these, as he was there when Stevens was shot to death.

When Jack Bennis arrived in Cuba, he met with the Archbishop of Havana and secured an assignment at the Catedral de la Virgen María de la Concepcion Inmaculada, more commonly known as the Catedral Habana or simply the Catedral San Christobal based on the belief that Christopher Columbus's body had been kept in the church for over a century. The Cathedral of the Immaculate Virgin Mary would have been a plum assignment except for the fact that it was rarely open for religious services. Except for tourists from noon to 3:00 P.M., cultural extravaganzas, and an occasional Sunday mass, the church was usually closed.

The Jesuits had started to build the church in 1748. When the Jesuits were forced to leave Cuba, the task of completing the structure fell to the Franciscans who eventually finished construction in 1777. Over the years the church fell into disuse and disrepair and became more a national monument and a social gathering place than the religious and spiritual place of worship it was originally intended to be. The Plaza de la Catedral which it faced had become a busy, noisy street market frequented by tourists with foreign cameras and deep pockets to purchase an endless array of souvenirs and other pleasures. At night, the plaza bustled with music, drink, and laughter.

Perhaps it was because of the turmoil Jack Bennis escaped from in New York, perhaps because this new assignment presented him a challenge. Whatever it was, the church with its mismatched bell towers became like a new home to him.

Father Bennis went to work quickly opening the church for 6:00 a.m. daily masses. At first, his congregation consisted of a few wrinkled old women, but gradually word spread about the smiling gringo priest and in less than two months he was saying daily 6:00 and 9:00 a.m. masses and four masses on Sundays.

His frequent walks through the city of Havana brought him in contact with many more people. As news of the tall priest spread, he quietly made inquires about the names on the list Muscatelli had given Stevens. All of them were dead or had left the country or had disappeared—all except for one—Frank Santacroce who now went by the name Francisco Santacruz.

Santacruz, Bennis learned, was a man of power and influence. The priest went so far as to invite the business man to join the new church council he was forming. Santacruz asked a few terse questions and then hung up. He never came to the church, but shortly after their conversation, Father Bennis had the occasional feeling he was being followed. Today, he was sure of it.

In the reflection of a cracked window on a 1954 Ford pickup parked in the street, Bennis noticed a man in a dark leather jacket, much too warm for the weather, hesitate at the corner behind him in the shadows of one of the porticoes jutting out from the crumbling, washed out multi-colored stucco buildings lining the street. The priest glanced across the street and spotted another man abruptly turn and disappear behind the faded blue column of another portico. He, too, was overdressed for the hot Havana weather. Both were white, and from their clothing, probably American.

Amateurs, Bennis surmised, but dangerous nevertheless. Was he becoming paranoid? Had Muscatelli traced him from his phone call to Santacruz? Had Muscatelli figured things out? Never underestimate the situation his Drill Instructor had drummed into him. He walked steadily down the street nodding at familiar faces while the two strangers continued to follow him. He casually glanced back waving at a familiar face. The two men following darted quickly into the shadows. He wasn't being paranoid. They knew he was here. This made things a lot more difficult. The seven Ps from his long ago basic training flashed back to him. "Prior proper planning prevents piss poor performance." He couldn't afford mistakes. Knowledge from his other life in covert operations kicked in. A plan began to evolve in the priest's mind. It wasn't a holy one.

* * *

3

Staten Island, New York

Police cars lined the road and a small crowd of curious onlookers had gathered outside the chain link fence when Cavanaugh got out of his car at the old abandoned Staten Island Hospital. He looked around. Goldberg, dressed in a suit and tie, was waiting for him with folded arms. Behind him loomed the crumbling remains of a three story red brick building with turrets pointing to the evening sky like inverted ice cream cones. In the dark, the building had the eerie quality of a battered medieval castle. Across the street stood the backside of a modern mosque.

"Welcome to Staten Island, Cavanaugh," a voice called to him. He turned to see a familiar face. There at the gate to the crime scene stood Officer Michael Shanley beaming like he had just hit a grand slam in the bottom of the ninth to win the World Series. "Hey, it's great to see you guys! Cavanaugh, you look a little different. Are you letting your hair grow? How the hell have you been?"

Cavanaugh's initial smile melted when Shanley moved forward, and he recognized the two police officers standing behind Shanley.

One was Officer Bill Midrasic, a cop from his precinct in Brooklyn who, Cavanaugh surmised, had probably come with Goldberg. There was no love lost between Cavanaugh and Midrasic. He knew Midrasic would like nothing better than to beat him to a pulp like he did to his wife, but Cavanaugh knew he was, like most wife beaters he met, a punk whose bark was bigger than his bite—except around defenseless women.

The police officer next to Midrasic, however, was a different story. When their eyes locked momentarily, the hostility in her eyes could be read as easily as a flashing traffic sign. Goldberg saw her reaction too and whispered, "Looks like your past is catching up with you, Tom."

Cavanaugh wanted to crawl into a pothole, but he ignored Midrasic and pretended not to see the woman whose eyes pierced his conscience like stilettos laced with hot salsa. Instead, he pushed Goldberg forward and raced to hug Shanley. "Hey! How the hell are you?" he almost shouted. "What the hell are you doing on Staten Island?"

"I live here," he said. "I transferred from the old precinct a couple of months ago. Rhatigan's here too. He lives in Rosebank."

"Wait a minute now. Where's your loyalty to Brooklyn? You guys aren't, by any chance, living together and all. I heard things like that happen on Staten Island! That's why I stay in Brooklyn like the Dodgers should have."

Shanley laughed, "Heck no. Nothing like that. I love it here. Staten Island's a great place. I live down by the ferry and walk to work every morning. It's like I died and went to heaven. You should move here."

Out of the corner of his eye, Cavanaugh noticed the woman police officer advancing slowly toward him. She had put on some weight from the last time he had seen her. She looked something like a blue snowman—except, as Cavanaugh well remembered, she lacked snowballs. Her folded arms seemed to rest on her protruding belly as her words added an icy chill to the evening air. "*Buenos noches*, Detective Cavanaugh."

"Oh, Officer Perez? I didn't see you there for the moment," Cavanaugh lied. "Allow me to introduce you to my partner, Detective Goldberg. Morty, this is Meredith Perez."

Perez and Goldberg exchanged nods.

Cavanaugh turned quickly to Shanley and said, "I hear we have a victim here. Let's get on with the show. We have a lot of work to do." The detectives followed Officers Shanley, Midrasic, and Perez into the foreboding building which now looked to Cavanaugh, as he brought up the rear, like a porthole to hell.

* * *

4

Havana, Cuba

Old stucco buildings of various fading colors guarded the narrow cobblestone street like silent wearied sentinels. Women carried bundles of produce from the markets at the Plaza de la Catedral and the shops along Calle Obispo. Music rained down on the street from apartments with open shutters and balconies with hanging wash. Bicycles weaved in and out around pedestrians and the smells of home cooked delicacies like papas rellenas and yucca rellena added to the relaxed atmosphere of a lazy evening.

But as he stopped at the corner of Calles Aguacate and Lamparilla to check for sporadic traffic, Fr. Bennis noticed his followers had closed their distance. They would want to get him before he reached the crowds in the Plaza. Abruptly, the priest turned left and then hesitated before the courtyard to an apartment house in the middle of the block until he was sure one of his followers had seen him. Then he walked nonchalantly into the three story building, passed a mother nursing her infant, two young boys kicking a soccer ball around her, and four teenagers playing upbeat Cuban music which somehow sounded to Bennis a little like an upbeat version of "Imagine There's No Heaven."

A few minutes later, the stranger in the leather jacket scurried into the building.

The priest climbed to the second floor landing and waited in the shadows. Inside one of the apartments he could smell baked beans and fried plantains cooking and hear a baby crying. But he concentrated on the steps of the stranger moving slowly up the stairs.

When the stranger reached the second landing and turned, he stopped short. There lying on the floor in front of him was the priest. Leather Jacket hesitated for a moment. That was all it took. The priest drove his right foot firmly into the man's crotch and then, springing to his feet, gave Leather Jacket a vicious head butt followed by two simultaneous bilateral karate chops to the sides of his neck.

When the stranger woke up, he was on the roof with the priest's knee firmly pressing down on his wind pipe. Below the group of teenagers assembled in the courtyard had grown and were having a vibrant Cuban jam session playing descargo music.

"Who sent you?" Jack Bennis asked politely as he eased pressure on the stranger's neck while pressing the end of the silencer of the semi-automatic Soviet made Makarov he had removed from Leather Jacket's pocket into his neck.

"No hablo ingles."

"Bull shit, José. Who sent you?"

Leather Jacket grimaced. "I . . . I don't know," he stammered.

"You are lying, and I don't like liars," Bennis said moving the Makarov's barrel to the center of Leather Jacket's forehead. "Last chance, José?"

"I . . . I had my orders . . . . I was only following orders!"

"Where have I heard that one before? What were your 'orders'?"

Beads of sweat ran down Leather Jacket's face.

"I'm not fooling, José. Speak now. It may be your last chance."

"Okay, okay, don't shoot. I was supposed . . . I was supposed to scare you—I wasn't going to shoot you . . . . I only planned to scare you . . . ."

"You're lying again. Is that two or three strikes?"

"No, no, please, no . . . ."

"This gun may be old, but it's fully loaded, equipped with a silencer, and ready for action. You don't scare people with a weapon like this, José. You kill them." Bennis hesitated, than added, "I know from experience."

"No, please . . ."

"Speak to me. I'm listening, but I'm growing impatient."

"My boss got a call from New York. Some old don or something . . . ."

"Name, please."

"I don't remember the name."

Bennis pressed the barrel of the gun deeper into Leather Jacket's forehead.

"Think harder. This isn't a Congressional hearing. Your life may depend on it. I can't recall doesn't fly here."

"Okay . . . okay. It was Macaroni or something like that."

Jack Bennis smiled, "Could it have been Muscatelli?"

"Yeah, yeah, that's it. Muscatelli."

The priest eased up the pressure on Leather Jacket's forehead and rose slowly. He leaned over and pulled the stranger up. "One more question. Did you come alone?"

Leather Jacket never hesitated, "Yeah, yeah. I came alone. I only wanted to send a message . . . ."

"Too bad, José. Didn't anyone ever tell you it's a sin to tell a lie? You just struck out." He spun the man in the leather jacket around so that he was facing the edge of the roof.

Leather Jacket tried to turn, but the priest's foot was in his back, one hand holding his jacket, the other pressing the Makarov into the back of his head.

"Make a quick Act of Contrition, José, because I have a message to send now myself. It's only a three story drop. If you're lucky, you should be able to make it with only a broken leg or two." With a quick kick to his back, the stranger toppled over the side of the building.

"*Vaya con dios*," the priest whispered as the man's screams drowned out the music below.

* * *

5

Staten Island, New York

Cavanaugh had met Merry Perez when they both worked burglary. She was young, pretty, sexy, and horny—very horny. He used to tell everyone who would listen that she attacked him like the Sioux attacked Custer at Little Big Horn. The truth was they attacked each other with a sexual passion neither had imagined. Before long they were having sex in the precinct restrooms, the equipment storage room, the locker room, the supply room, the evidence room, behind the file cabinets, on top of the portable refrigerator, on the Property Officer's desk and even beneath the Desk Sergeant's desk. Once they quietly cavorted completely naked behind a pile of file boxes while an interrogation of a suspect was taking place. And they were never caught.

No one would have ever known about their frenetic sexual adventures if Cavanaugh had kept his mouth shut. But over a few pints of Guinness at Duffy's, he would invariably succumb to boasting about his more lascivious escapades with Officer Perez to the enjoyment of the entire bar.

One particular story made the rounds of most of the precincts in Brooklyn and Manhattan. As they were engaged in what Cavanaugh termed "a mutual munchitational situation," Merry farted.

Many of the younger officers who came on the force in subsequent years would never know the true derivation of the nickname that had stuck to Meredith Perez like a garish tattoo, but they joined the others in referring to her as "Bubbles."

"Bubbles" Perez had had serious plans for Thomas Cavanaugh that included a wedding and a family. Cavanaugh's plans were different. He used to joke at Duffy's after a tour of duty with his fellow officers that there was no reason to buy the cow, if the milk was being given away for free. When he was promoted to detective, he left the precinct and Meredith Perez and never looked back, leaving Officer Perez with a broken heart, a nickname, and the reputation of a slut.

As Cavanaugh followed Shanley, Goldberg, Midrasic, and Perez up the littered stairs of the abandoned building to the victim's corpse, he felt lower than whale's shit. He had used Merry Perez, as he had used so many other women, and for some reason he was suddenly ashamed of himself. Until today, he had completely put her out of his mind, but now it all came back to him like the man who spit into the wind. Meeting and falling in love with Francesca Arden had changed him. He realized only now that he had hurt Meredith.

At the top of the stairs, he reached forward and touched Officer Perez's arm. "Merry," he started, "I'm sorry . . . ."

She pulled away abruptly. "Drop dead, Cavanaugh," was all she said.

At the end of the corridor in what had probably once been a linen closet they found what the rats had left of the victim, Crystal May. Looking at her fully clothed body crumpled in a grotesque shape, he wondered who could do such a thing to another human being. He saw Crystal's watch dangling from her partially skeletal wrist. It reminded him of a sexual game he and Merry had played together. He bent down and examined a partially chewed pierced earlobe of the victim and then looked up at Officer Perez. He wondered how much she had suffered over the years because of him. And then he looked again at the twisted body before him and wondered how much she had suffered at the hands of her killer. He closed his eyes and the lines from one of Oscar Wilde's poems about how each man kills the thing he loves began to play in his mind. The brave man kills with a sword, he thought as he rose and his knees cracked. Reaching for his little notebook, he glanced again at Officer Perez and a sinking feeling swept through him recalling another line from the poem. He sighed to himself, "The coward does it with a kiss," and started taking notes.

* * *

6

Detective Morton Goldberg filled Cavanaugh in as he examined the body and the crime scene. The twenty-eight year old full-time student at Hunter College had been reported missing by her mother six days ago. She had worked part-time at St. Mary's Hospital in Brooklyn as a ward clerk in pediatrics from 4:00 to 12:00 PM. Her husband, Robert May, was a sergeant E-5 stationed with the United States Marines Reserves in Fallujah, Iraq. Crystal had been living with her parents and her twin daughters who attended St. Francis of Assisi Elementary School. She was last seen alive leaving her Abnormal Psychology class at 10:55 AM. When Sister Mary Michael called home to report that Crystal May had not picked up her daughters, Amanda and Charlotte, who were in the first grade, Crystal's mother notified the police. Everyone who knew Crystal described her as cheerful, outgoing, reliable, and responsible.

Goldberg put the papers down, rubbed his eyes, and unconsciously straightened his tie. Yesterday, Crystal had been a missing case. Today, when her partially decomposed body was discovered in an abandoned building in the Stapleton area of Staten Island, she had graduated to a homicide.

The police initially assigned to the missing person's case had been thorough. They had searched the entire area. Her 1998 Dodge Caravan was found in the municipal parking lot a block away from Hunter College. Friends, fellow students and workers, professors, family members, and every store owner in the area were questioned. Thus far there had been no leads. And now, her masticated remains are discovered by three teenagers playing hooky from Curtis High School on Staten Island.

Cavanaugh loosened his Army desert camouflage fatigue jacket.

Goldberg showed Cavanaugh a recent photo of the victim. "Not a bad looking woman. Love that smile. What's the cause of death?"

"We don't know yet. We just got the case a little while ago. It was a missing until around 10:00 this morning."

"She's in pretty bad shape for only six days."

"No confirmation yet, but it looks like the killer smeared or poured maple syrup over her to attract the rats."

"What kind of a sick bastard would do that?" Cavanaugh grimaced. "But I still don't understand why the hell we are investigating a murder on Staten Island? This isn't our jurisdiction."

"It is now," Goldberg said tapping a file of papers against his leg. "It came from the top. We've both been assigned to the case."

"Sweet Jesus! You've got to be kidding me! Don't they have any homicide detectives on Staten Island?"

"Maybe it's because she disappeared from our precinct."

"That's B. S."

"Maybe it's because they want the best on this case for some reason."

Cavanaugh smiled, "Now that's more like it. But then why would they assign you, too?"

Goldberg continued, "Or much more likely it could have something to do with the note they found on the body."

Cavanaugh grabbed Goldberg's arm. "What note? You didn't say anything about a note. Where is it?"

Goldberg pulled back and straightened his coat jacket. He handed him a piece of notepaper wrapped in a clear plastic evidence bag. "It's some kind of sick nursery rhyme."

Cavanaugh looked at another picture of Crystal May before turning to the note. His smile faded. In the photo she was kneeling with her twin daughters by the swings in a park. Her long earrings glistened in the picture like her name. He sighed and shook his head, "What kind of person would do something like this?"

Then Cavanaugh read the words on the note, and he felt sick.

> Hey diddle diddle,
> A cat, a body, or a fiddle,
> You never know what you'll find behind a door.
> But thanks to Thomas Cavanaugh,
> There will be more.
> So while you fiddle and while you fart,
> Remember, I have just begun to start.

* * *

7

Havana, Cuba

Jack Bennis climbed, jumped and crawled over the next three building roofs until he came to the building on the corner. He jimmied the roof lock and walked down the stairs and onto a side street. He turned left on Calle Compostela and headed away from the scene which had rapidly attracted a crowd.

But then he heard the familiar jingle of the bicycle bell and recognized Santiago's voice calling to him. "Padre, *por favor*, a man has fallen from the roof around the corner. He needs you. Please help."

The irony of the situation hit Bennis immediately. What if Leather Jacket claimed he pushed him off the roof? Would anyone believe him? What if the other assassin was in the crowd waiting for him?

"*Por favor*, Padre," Santiago pleaded. "The man needs you. We must hurry."

Bennis couldn't turn away from Santiago's pleas. How could a priest refuse to help an injured man? Cautiously and reluctantly, he followed Santiago into the crowd surrounding the man in the leather jacket.

Whispers spread through the throng of people. "Make way for the priest!"

As the mob separated for him, a multitude of conflicting thoughts raced through his mind. Looking at the still body lying in the street, he asked himself, "What have I done?" and realized the man who was sent to kill him by Vito Muscatelli was no longer a threat to him or anyone else. Leather Jacket's fall had been partially cushioned when he tore through the overhanging electric wires, but his head had smashed into one of the concrete balconies before plummeting to the ground. Sparks shot and cracked from the dangling wires above as the priest knelt to give a final blessing to the man he had pushed to his death.

Lifting from the man's head a tangled woman's pink nightgown that he had fallen through on his descent, Bennis stared at a lifeless face that looked more like a squashed pumpkin. He closed his eyes in prayer—for both of them.

Suddenly, he heard a voice, "*Cuidado*, he's got a gun!" and felt a hard push from behind as a gun shot rang out. Rolling to his side, he saw the other overdressed American holding a gun and moving toward him for a better shot. Mistake, Bennis thought, bounding up and rushing head first into the stranger. The force of his head in the shooter's solar plexus knocked him backward.

With the speed of a tiger, Bennis brought his head straight up into the man's chin and then delivered two quick, powerful blows—one to the ridge of the shooter's nose and the other forcing the cartilage from his nose into the frontal lobe of his brain. The nameless man's eyes rolled back, and he crumbled to the ground.

The sounds of an approaching ambulance and the police started to disperse some of the crowd. Bennis retrieved the second assassin's weapon, a Nagant 7.62 mm revolver, and turned to leave before the questions began. But looking back at the man in the leather jacket, he saw another body.

The sirens were closer now, but he bent down to check the other body. A cold chill swept through him. It was Santiago who had pushed him aside and saved his life. But the fruit stand man, who had only tried to help, now lay dead in the Old Havana street, killed by a bullet meant for the priest.

Bennis knelt and made the sign of the cross on Santiago's forehead and then quickly vanished into the night. He would pray for him later.

* * *

8

Staten Island, New York

Cavanaugh examined the crime scene carefully. He stared silently at the mutilated body of Crystal May while scanning the area and writing notes in his little black book. He noticed one of Crystal's earrings had been ripped from her ear.

"Did anyone find her missing earring?" he asked Shanley.

"Negative."

Finally, he turned to Goldberg. "Where was the note?"

Goldberg looked over to Shanley and nodded. "It's clean," Shanley said. "We dusted it. No fingerprints."

"Where was it found?" Cavanaugh asked.

"Over there by the right side of her body near her hand. It's standard note paper. Sold at any Staples. Do you recognize the writing?"

Cavanaugh looked at the note. It was hand printed in block letters like an architect's labeling. It looked familiar, but he could have seen the same printing a hundred times before on other documents.

"Have the handwriting people had a look at this yet?"

"Negative," Shanley said.

The note was crumpled, but didn't look that old. Cavanaugh's brain was spinning. It could have been placed near the body after it was dumped here. Whoever wrote it, took his time as the letters were neatly spaced and aligned. But why did they mention him?

"What makes them think I'm the Cavanaugh referred to in the note?" he asked aloud.

Goldberg's responded, "Because you're the only Tom Cavanaugh on the force."

Cavanaugh shook his head. "This is crazy," he said. Who the hell would want to get at him this way? Who possibly could have it out for him?

He looked up to see Bill Midrasic and Meredith Perez staring at him.

"Did you question the kids who found the body about the note?" Cavanaugh asked Shanley.

"Sure did. The bastards were scared shitless when they saw the body and ran out of here and called 911. We got the call and arrived here first."

"Did they see the note?"

"Negative. They didn't see nothing except a dead body, and the rats, of course. That should teach the bastards to cut school. If I had my way . . . ."

"Well then, who found the note?"

"I did." The voice came from behind Shanley's shoulder. "I found the note," Officer Perez repeated.

* * *

9

Havana, Cuba

Jack Bennis weaved his way up Calle Compostela and then along Obispo. He passed the tiny bar La Lovia de Ora where music, song, and laughter flowed like water into the street. He turned left on San Ignacio passing O'Reilly's Bar heading toward the music and crowds in the Plaza de la Catedral. He passed La Bodegatta del Medio, said to have been Hemingway's favorite place to drink a mojito.

But he kept walking. He passed the large monument to General Maximo Gomes, the Dominican hero of the Cuban Independence movement. He passed the remains of the Tacon Prison and the Park de los Martines built in memory of those who suffered in the infamous prison.

He headed for Avenue Antonio Maceo and the Muro de Malecón, the jetty wall. Here he stopped, looking out into the starry night over the dark waters which crashed against the jetty wall. Behind him the voices of the night diminished. Occasionally, he heard the laughter of youth as they drove their cars splashing through the sea's overflow on the street, or the seductive rhythmic beat of Cuban music, or the calls of the *jineteras* luring the foreign tourists in their brightly colored spandex outfits that looked like they had been spray painted on them. But he surrendered himself to prayer—prayer for Santiago, for Leather Jacket and his accomplice, and for his brother, Thomas Cavanaugh, back in New York.

As he prayed, he tried to come to some understanding of who he was and what he had become. His mind traveled back through his training to be a Jesuit, through his experiences as a covert assassin for the government, to what he had done in New York, to his childhood and his mother. Maybe, he reasoned, it was the right thing to leave New York and his brother Thomas and come to Cuba. Wherever Jack Bennis went, it seemed he brought more harm than good. Still, he prayed that he would see Thomas at least one more time.

* * *

10

Staten Island, New York

When Goldberg, Cavanaugh, Shanley, Midrasic, and Perez left the crime scene, they had to walk through a mixed crowd of reporters and curious neighbors. Two large satellite dishes with bright spotlights sprung from a CBS van and an ABC Eyewitness News van giving the appearance of daylight. Cavanaugh recognized Dave Slattery from CBS, Pablo Guzman from NBC, and beat reporters from the *New York Post*, the *Daily News*, and the *New York Times*. He put his head down and tried to hide behind Shanley.

"These guys make me sick," he whispered to Goldberg.

"It's their job, Tom. I'm sure they don't like it any more than we do," Goldberg answered as a reporter thrust a microphone into his face and a barrage of questions flew at them from all over.

"Do you have any leads on who did it?"

"How long has she been dead?"

"Have her parents been notified?"

"Did you know the victim, Detective Cavanaugh?"

"What's the significance of the poem mentioning you, Detective Cavanaugh?"

"Can we get in there to take some pictures?"

"Who found the body?"

Suddenly, Cavanaugh stopped. "Hold it. Who told you guys about a note? Who told you guys the victim was female?" he demanded.

"What exactly did the note say?"

"Do you think this is a serial murderer?"

"When can we get a copy of the note?"

Cavanaugh turned to Goldberg. "Something's wrong here. How did they find out about the note? Who leaked it to the press?"

A microphone was pushed into Cavanaugh's face as a 300 pounder with a nose like Rudolf the red-nosed Reindeer's with miniature moon craters, almost shouted, "Clayton Shaffer, 1010 WINS. How does it feel to have a killer mention your name in a nursery rhyme left by a dead body?"

Cavanaugh suddenly grabbed the mike and turned to the WINS reporter and said, "How would it feel to have this microphone shoved up your fat ass!"

* * *

II

Though the wisdom or virtue of one can very rarely make many happy, the folly or vice of one man often makes many miserable.

Samuel Johnson

TUESDAY

11

Brooklyn, New York

In the morning, Cavanaugh stopped by Steve's Barber Shop for a haircut he didn't really think he needed and for local gossip only a barber like Steve knew. He never bothered to learn Steve's last name. He knew it began with an I and ended with an I, and to Cavanaugh that meant it was Italian. Words ending in A, I, or O and spaghetti were Italian. He never bought into the idea that spaghetti came from China. Spaghetti was Italian and Steve, his barber, whatever his last name was, was Italian. It didn't really matter. He liked Steve and spaghetti.

In his hands he held a stack of mail he hadn't opened from the week before. Steve's father was reading the *New York Post* when he entered the small shop. "Is your son in today, or is he on another trip to Aruba or the Bahamas?"

The white haired man in his early 90's looked up and motioned with his head, "He's in the back on the phone."

"Thanks," Cavanaugh said as he climbed into Steve's chair and started to flip through his mail. Mementos of recent trips to the Caribbean adorned the mirror in front of him. Tonic and water lined the counter in what were once full bottles of Chivas Regal, Grand Marnier, and Drambuie. Cavanaugh knew it was against the health code, but he didn't mind and neither did Steve's other customers. A health inspector had cited Steve once, but obviously Steve had managed to work things out and the bottles were back again.

Steve's father looked up from the paper and said, "I see you made the papers again."

Cavanaugh shrugged. "You can't believe everything you read in the papers."

"Says here you threatened a reporter and that you are involved in some murder on Staten Island."

"Like I said, Pop, you can't believe everything you read in the papers."

"Says here you belted the bastard."

"Don't believe it even if the bastard did get blood all over my jacket!" Cavanaugh said pointing to his sleeve of his beige Army camouflage jacket.

Steve's father smiled and went back to the paper.

"Hey, pal, how are you doing?" Steve said coming out of the back room and placing his hands on Cavanaugh's shoulders. "Didn't I just see you a week or so ago?"

"You got me, Steve. I'm here for a trim and some info."

Steve whipped a large black apron around Cavanaugh and fastened it behind his neck. "Actually, I'm glad you stopped by," he whispered. "There's some talk on the street about you. I think you should know."

"I can always trust you, Steve," Cavanaugh said opening a bill from Con Edison.

"Somebody is after you."

"Who?"

"Can't say for sure, but whoever it is, is a psycho."

"Speak to me."

Steve picked up his scissors and started to clip away as he spoke. "Whoever it is plans to taunt you a bit before he goes after you in person. A real psycho."

"The taunting has started already. But why?"

"Don't know. Somebody you offended over the years . . . ?

"Oh, great! It would be easier to number those I didn't offend."

"I wish I could help you more, but you need to watch your back. Whoever it is, is a real nut job."

Cavanaugh looked down at the small clumps of hair dropping on the black bib. He was getting gray. He was getting too old for this crap. Maybe it was time for him to pack it in.

Suddenly, he stopped going through his mail when he came to a letter. It was from Havana, Cuba. Steve clipped away while Cavanaugh read. The letter was from Cavanaugh's half-brother, John Bennis. As he read, Steve continued to talk, but Cavanaugh didn't hear him. The letter recounted a little about life in Cuba, but he picked up a note of fatalism and loneliness in the words. It was as if John were saying good-bye, as if he were planning on doing something that was very dangerous.

"Let me ask you something, Steve," Cavanaugh said interrupting the monologue.

"Shoot, pal. What do you have?"

"How do I get to Cuba?"

Steve shook his head, "That's what I like about you. You are a real nut job, too! Cuba? You got to be f—ing kidding me!"

"Cuba, Steve. Focus. How would I get there?" Cavanaugh's eyes locked onto Steve's in the mirror.

"Easiest way I know is take a plane out of Mexico. You don't need any clearance. I have a lot of customers who fly there regularly."

"What about Toronto? That's closer."

Steve scratched his head with his scissors. "Yeah. That probably works too, but there may be some more paperwork involved there though. The beauty of that is you could drive to Toronto and then hop a plane. Yeah. That would work, too."

"Thanks, Steve," Cavanaugh said looking at his watch. He was late again, but he couldn't leave the barbershop without following a long established ritual he and Steve had. "And oh," he added, "did you hear the one about the blonde who was riding down a country road in Texas when she accidentally runs over a little rabbit."

Steve stopped and leaned forward. "No. Go ahead. I'll stop you if I heard it."

Cavanaugh knew he wouldn't stop him even if he had heard it a million times before, so he went on. "The blonde jumps out of the car and is frantically jumping around and crying when another car pulls up. The guy comes over to the blonde and asks her what happened. She points to the bloody limp body of the little bunny rabbit and starts screaming that she killed it. The guy tells her not to worry, goes into his car and comes back and sprays something on the rabbit. With that the rabbit jumped up and hops off down the road. Every fifteen feet or so, the bunny turns around and waves at them. The blonde can't believe her eyes. 'How did you do that?' she asks. He says, 'I'm a barber. I just used hare restorer. It says right on the label, 'Restores life to dead hair, adds permanent wave.'"

Steve hesitated a moment and stared at Cavanaugh in the mirror. Finally, Cavanaugh said, "Get it—hare, like a rabbit, hair restorer?"

Steve just shook his head. "That is probably the worst joke I have ever heard."

"When you have to explain them, they usually are," Cavanaugh said and then added, "Alright, one more and then I really have to go. A man walks into a barbershop for a shave. While the barber is foaming him up, the man tells him the problem he has in getting a close shave around the cheeks. 'I have just the thing,' the barber says and takes a small wooden ball from a drawer. 'Just place this between your gum and your cheek.' The guy puts the ball in his mouth and proceeds to get the closest shave he has ever gotten. After a few strokes, the guy mumbles, "And what if I swallow this thing?' 'No problem,' says the barber, 'Just bring it back tomorrow—like everyone else does!'"

"Now, that's disgusting," Steve said. "I just hope I can remember it."

Cavanaugh looked down at the gray hair on his bib. Somebody is out to get me. My brother is in trouble. I'm getting old. And I'm sitting here telling stupid jokes. I must be out of my mind.

"Thanks, Steve," he said rising from the chair and giving him his business card. "Keep me informed about my new friend if you hear anything else. Okay?"

"You got it, pal," Steve said as he rang up a price on the ancient cash register and pocketed his tip. "And," Steve added, "try to stay out of the papers will you, pal?"

* * *

12

Havana, Cuba

Jack Bennis knew he couldn't return to his small room in the back of the church—at least until it was safe. They would definitely be looking for him there. He needed to find another place to live. He needed a place where he could think and plan how he could stop the "hit" Vito Muscatelli had put on him. Finding another apartment, however, wasn't that difficult. One just had to be careful. He needed an apartment in a bed and breakfast or a private home. Cuban laws allowed home owners to rent rooms, apartments or houses. By renting a private room the rent went directly to the person or family, not to the government which owned practically everything else. A "casa particular," as it was called, was a good way to help a home owner whose average income was around $40.00 a month and, at the same time, it would allow Bennis to keep his head low. A hotel would have put him straight on Muscatelli's radar. The added fact that Cuban law did not permit native Cubans visiting foreigners in hotels might be another problem. He needed mobility. A "casa particular" was what he looked for.

Asking discreetly around, Bennis was recommended to Diego Velasquez, a full professor at the University of Havana. The University of Havana is the oldest university in Cuba and has fifteen colleges and fourteen research centers in different fields. But Dr. Velasquez's current wages as a biology professor were less than twenty dollars a month. He supplemented his teaching salary by working in the pharmacy at Miguel Enriquez Hospital. After meeting with Bennis, Velasquez offered the priest a small room for more money than he made on both jobs.

Jack Bennis quickly settled in.

But Santiago's death haunted him. The nightmares and the headaches of the past returned. Innocent people weren't supposed to be hurt, but they always were. Looking through the broken shutters of his room, he watched two elderly Cubans playing a game of dominoes in the shade of a huge Blue Mahoe tree. He remembered stacking the dominoes upright when he was young and how he and his little brother Tommy would tap one and watch the dominoes fall one after the other in intricate paths.

He reached into his pocket and pulled out the semi-automatic Makarov pistol he had taken from Leather Jacket. A worn set of rosary beads were entwined around the gun. Unthreading the beads, Bennis realized his life was like a game of dominoes. One thing had led to another and then another and then another. It had been like this for years. He tried to do the right thing. But then he saw things that shouldn't be. He tried to fix things that others were afraid to touch or unable to accomplish. Laws, he always felt, were made to serve man, not to bind him. If evil flourished in spite of laws, then he tried to stop the evil—one way or another. Laws never bothered him. They didn't bother the evildoers, why should they hinder him?

Fingering the small beads around the barrel of the gun, he unconsciously started to pray the "Hail Mary." Images flashed before him. "Hail Mary, full of grace, the Lord is with thee, blessed art thou amongst women . . . ." His mother's face smiling at him as she prepared eggs and bacon over the gas stove in the railroad flat in Brooklyn for Tommy and him before they walked to school. Makeup trying to hide the black eye his step-father had given her. " . . . and blessed is the fruit of thy womb . . . ." Tommy, the homicide detective who turned away from God; Jack, the soldier who thought he could turn to God by becoming a priest, but who continued to find himself in the killing zone.

He stared at the gun in his hand. "Holy Mary, mother of God, pray for us sinners now and at the hour of our death."

* * *

13

Brooklyn, New York

Lieutenant Bradley wanted to see him. Cavanaugh knew this meant trouble. Lieutenant Thomas Bradley was new to the division. Young, efficient, intelligent, he knew the rules. No one had tested him—yet.

The fat reporter had swung at Cavanaugh after his remark. In the ensuing scuffle the press had a field day taking pictures. And when the 1010 news reporter came out of the fracas with a bloody nose, Cavanaugh expected more trouble. And he was right.

First the shootings in the bodega, then the Inquest, then the note, now this. Things were falling apart.

"What is it, Lieutenant?" Cavanaugh asked.

"Shut the door and sit down," Bradley commanded.

Cavanaugh felt like he was in the principal's office again.

"I'll get to you about last night later. First, however, I have here a complaint about you harassing Patrolman Bill Midrasic."

"Bill Midrasic? I saw him last night at the crime scene, but I haven't spoken to that ass hole in over a month!"

Bradley read from a paper in his hand. "It says here you threatened him a month ago."

"Oh, Lieutenant, this is ridiculous! I met his wife in the supermarket about a week before the bodega thing. I went to grammar school with her. Maureen had a black eye and both her wrists were bandaged. I asked her what happened, and she said she didn't want to talk about it. I prodded a little because we were good friends back then. She was my eighth grade dancing partner. She finally told me that Midrasic got drunk and beat her up. She was crying and all. She made me promise not to say anything. I gave her the number of the National Domestic Violence Hotline."

"What did she do?"

"I don't know."

"What did you do?"

"The next time I saw Midrasic I took him aside and told him I would personally beat his ass in if he ever touched his wife again."

Bradley folded the paper and put it in a folder. He leaned back in his chair and folded his arms. He waited as if trying to put distance between Bill Midrasic and the turmoil caused by Cavanaugh's confrontation with the press.

Finally, he leaned forward and spoke. "What's with this bullshit at the crime scene last night? Are you trying to single handedly take down the whole New York Police Department? You can't go around shooting teenagers, threatening fellow officers, and beating up reporters and expect the department to support you. You seem intent on not only giving the department a black eye, but giving the ACLU jurisdiction on police investigations . . . ."

"Hold on, Lieutenant, give me a break. That guy started it last night. He asked me a stupid question, and I answered him. He started it. I didn't."

"The way I hear it you threatened to shove his microphone up his fat ass."

"He was a jerk. He was looking for it."

"You broke the bastard's nose for God's sake!"

"I'm not saying I didn't do it, Lieutenant, but all hell broke loose. The bastard attacked me with his microphone. I tried to defend myself. The next thing I know there are hands all over the place grabbing, pushing, punching. It was a mad house."

Bradley threw the *New York Post* front page at him. "Look at him. His nose is bleeding, his shirt is ripped, he's a frecking mess!"

"Lieutenant, all I can say is, 'Go to the videotape.' There were so many cameras there they'll show you what really happened."

"Do you really believe they are going to show that bastard swinging his microphone at you on the Six O'clock News? You'd have a better chance being a snowball in hell."

Cavanaugh looked at his hands. "Look, Lieutenant," he said pointing to his jacket, "the fat bastard even bled all over me."

"Outstanding. You have evidence of his bleeding on you. Beautiful."

"Lieutenant, the video they were taking will show I didn't start the fight!"

"Cavanaugh, no one wants to know the police actually need to defend themselves from time to time. Somehow it doesn't amount to newsworthy material!"

Bradley snatched the newspaper and walked around the desk. He scratched a small scar over his left eye and hesitated, staring straight down at Cavanaugh. Then he reached for a wood carving on his desk. Cavanaugh couldn't read it from behind, but when the Lieutenant turned it around and faced it toward him he could clearly read the attached letters. They spelled, "BULLSHIT."

The Lieutenant leaned on the side of his desk. "Cavanaugh, it's all bullshit. You know it and I know it, but the public doesn't know it. They believe the bullshit because it's what they hear, it's what they see, it's what they read. You can't let these guys get under your skin. They're having a field day with it."

He placed the wood letters back on the desk. "Do you understand what I'm saying to you? We have to cover each other's backs, but there's a limit to how far we can go. You are over that limit. You need to control yourself. Think before you speak."

Cavanaugh looked up. "What do you want me to do, Lieutenant?"

Bradley rubbed his eyes. "Stay out of the press. We will handle it from here. Avoid reporters like they had an infectious disease." He threw the paper in the trash and added, "Now get the hell back to work, but remember this isn't the Thomas Bradley Police Department. It's the New York City Police Department and there's only so much I can do."

"Thanks, Lieutenant," Cavanaugh said heading for the door.

"Oh, one more thing. Speaking of infectious diseases have them check that blood on your jacket. You never know . . . ."

"That's okay, Lieutenant. I'm not worried about it."

"Turn it in to forensics, Detective. That's an order."

* * *

14

When Cavanaugh returned to his desk, Goldberg was studying another report. He looked up and commented, "Have you seen the papers yet?"

"I try not to read them. But apparently everyone else does."

"You get more press then Britney Spears."

"I think I'm beginning to feel like she does, too." He looked at the papers in Goldberg's hands. "What's new on the case?"

"The handwriting analysis came back. Nothing conclusive, of course, but it's interesting."

Cavanaugh settled into his chair. "So, what's it say?"

"Apparently, people who print tend to put up a barrier to keep others from getting to know them."

"Oh, give me a break! I print and everyone knows me."

Goldberg sighed and continued. "A lot of men print, but the analyst feels it may have something to do with keeping their insecure feelings hidden from the world. They want to appear confident to those around them while hiding their inner-most feelings."

"Oh, boy, more psycho-babble. It's probably a female handwriting analyst. Do you think any of this is really going to help us find the killer?"

"The printing slants a little to the left, again indicating the writer is keeping his emotions hidden, overcompensating for his true feelings. It could mean the writer has experienced a traumatic event in his life or a severe illness and therefore turns his thoughts and feelings inward."

Cavanaugh started doodling on the paper in front of him. "BULLSHIT. BULLSHIT. BULLSHIT . . . ."

"The writer may be confused about who he is and be having trouble stabilizing himself. The printing of all capital letters is also significant . . . ."

Cavanaugh stared at what he had written. It was printed and in all capital letters.

"He is into control, but he is hiding behind a mask. He is afraid to have people know the 'real' him. When the tension rises he could lose control . . . ."

Cavanaugh looked at the blood stains on his sleeve. "You're making this shit up, aren't you, Morty?"

"No. I'm not. You can read it for yourself. It says the writer tends to talk and judge more than he listens. Although neat, he is likely moody, has a sharp tongue, is short on patience, and may be considered insensitive by others."

Cavanaugh stared at Goldberg. Finally, he put his hands up and said, "Morty, that could be describing me!"

Goldberg smiled, "Yes, and it could be describing most of the cops, male *and* female, in this station house and all over the country. The writer more than likely tried to disguise his handwriting anyway, but it does give us a bit of knowledge about the killer."

"Oh, it's a great help. He has multiple personalities. He isn't what he appears to be. And he is losing control. That's a great help. I could have told you that before I saw the body in the closet."

"Or," Goldberg added, "*he* just might be a *she*."

Cavanaugh plopped down in his chair and murmured, "More bullshit!"

* * *

15

Cavanaugh distrusted modern technology. Although he had one, he refused to carry a cell phone. The handwriting analysis was just another example to him of pretentious bureaucratic waste. Nothing beat good old fashion police work. It was labor intensive, boring, but fruitful. Blood, sweat and tears beat electrodes and circuit chips any day. After another hour poring over the other detectives' reports, he remembered the Lieutenant's order to get the blood on his jacket tested and went down to the lab to drop it off. When he returned he was tired and ready to pack up and go home. "I've had it for today, Morty. If anything comes up, give me a call."

Goldberg looked up. "Where's your coat?"

"Aren't you perceptive, Detective? You would think you were my mother. It's a long story, but it's in the lab. It's not that cold out anyway. Did I ever tell you I'm a strong supporter of global warming? See you in the morning."

If Cavanaugh's mother had known how things would have worked out for him, she might have more appropriately picked "Impetuous" for his baptismal name instead of Thomas. Over the years he came to almost realize his impulsiveness, but he enjoyed living in the moment. Wasn't that what it was all about? Or was it?

Leaving the precinct, he had a lot on his mind. His job sucked. The Inquest was icing on the cake, but now the murder with the note. Who was the nut case out to get him? The writer of the note might be a female. "Bubbles" Perez found the note. Could she be involved in planting the note to get back at him?

Or could the son of a bitch Bill Midrasic have planted the note? It would be just like the sneaky low life to pull a stunt like that.

And then there was his brother in Cuba. He was in trouble. Cavanaugh felt it. His instincts screamed at him that his brother was in trouble, and he always trusted his instincts.

He decided he needed to walk home to clear his head. He left his car parked in the "Police Only" parking spot he had crawled into the morning and began his long trek up Third Avenue. It was early afternoon and the wind whipped around him like an angry lover.

Walking into the wind his thoughts wandered like they did when he was a kid listening to Father Sheehee's sermons in church. Sometimes then he would close his eyes and pretend to pray while his thoughts jumped from a stickball game with Johnny McGrath, Bernie Flynn, and Jimmy Ward to fantasizing about Faith Raymond's bodacious boobs. And just when his adolescent body started to respond to his visions of Faith, by some sixth instinct, his mother would invariably jab him in the ribs with her missal.

Crossing 68th Street, he saw another nail salon. Why were there so many of them? They had cropped up like crabgrass on nearly every block. Why did women spend so much time and money to have their nails done? And then there were their toes, too. What kind of people would work on cleaning, rubbing, scraping, painting toes? And why were most of them Asian or Russian? Was this the way the next global war would be won? Slowly and subtly from the toes up? Or were those Asian girls who arrived in vans and were picked up in vans, actually indentured slaves? Someday he imagined going into one of the nail salons and having his toes painted. He smiled wondering what Goldberg and Francesca would think about that.

At the next corner he darted across the street against the red light. He smiled to himself thinking about how pedestrians stopped for red lights in San Francisco. New York was different, so different. Yet, on his visits to San Francisco he never met a native San Franciscan. They all seemed to have migrated there like lemmings waiting for the inevitable earthquake that would topple them into the San Andreas Fault.

Block after block, he forced his mind to wander and his body to fight the cold. He didn't want to think about his brother.

The familiar flashing green shamrock on O'Flaherty's Pub caught his eye. Next to nail salons, Cavanaugh theorized, saloons must rank high on the list of the most prolific private enterprises in New York. Each bar, it seemed, catered to a different crowd. There were singles bars and gay bars. Some lured the rich and famous, some lured the eager and gullible. Some were for the young, hungry, and horny, some for the older, sadder and lonelier. Sanitation workers, construction workers, accountants, Wall Street executives, African Americans, Cubans, Puerto Ricans, it made no difference, they all sort out a watering hole for themselves. The odd part of the equation was that most of the bars had Irish names. Another example of ethnic stereotyping, Cavanaugh thought, as he stopped in front of O'Flaherty's.

O'Flaherty's was a cop bar. After a long tour of duty, it was the place many would stop before heading home to their private cliff dwellings in the city or their manicured lawns in the suburbs. It had a long mahogany bar and private booths the length of the bar. In the back were an assortment of tables and chairs, a pool table, a juke box which only played music from the fifties and sixties, and a fireplace burning real logs. There was a TV in every corner of the place showing sports events or CNN news with captions running across the bottom of the screen. Dim lighting, sawdust, and the smell of stale beer added to the ambiance of O'Flaherty's.

Years ago, Cavanaugh had to research this place when investigating a couple of anonymous tips about Final Four and Super Bowl Lotteries and possible IRA gun fund raising. He knew about the lotteries as did most of the cops in the city who participated in it. The lotteries were not about to stop even though the best Cavanaugh had ever done was to get to the final eight.

All the bartenders and waiters and waitresses in O'Flaherty's had Irish brogues. The kitchen staff was all Chinese. The owner of O'Flaherty's was actually a Jewish businessman named Arnold Krivitsky who ran a group of strip joints on Long Island. All the money Krivitsky made from O'Flaherty's went to his lawyers, his two ex-wives, child support, and a penchant to play the ponies. What little was left went to Krivitsky, and that was so little that he usually stayed on Long Island in one of his clubs and left the management of O'Flaherty's to a tiny leprechaun from Australia known to all the patrons only as Dr. Bob.

Cavanaugh saw Dr. Bob behind the bar when he entered. Down the length of the bar he spotted Foxell and Clarke from robbery, Roland and Balossi from narcotics, and Ward, Coco, and Stavola from vice. Bill Midrasic was with them. Midrasic glared at Cavanaugh like a former Marine POW watching a Jane Fonda interview in Hanoi. Cavanaugh nodded and focused on a few young faces he recognized as cops but had never seen before. They were hiring kids now, he thought.

"G'day, mate. What will it be?" Dr. Bob asked. Everyone was "mate" to Bob. It was easier than remembering names. "Looks like you're drinking with Pat Malone again," he added.

Cavanaugh looked down at the diminutive bartender whose chest was on line with the top of the bar and nodded. He knew enough Australian to know "Pat Malone" meant he was drinking alone.

"Cheer up, mate. Life is grand. My bookie Denny just called to tell me My Precious Mary came in first in Philadelphia Park today," Dr. Bob volunteered. "Paid seven to one."

Cavanaugh nodded and said, "Give me a cold draft beer."

"Sorry, mate, the taps are broken," Dr. Bob replied wiping the bar with a dirty dishtowel.

"What the hell is this? A conspiracy? Nothing's going right for me!" Suddenly, Cavanaugh remembered the handwriting analysis. Short on patience. Could lose control. Hiding behind a mask. Afraid to let people know the real me. Was that why he lashed out at the 1010 news reporter? Was that why he was so scared to commit to a meaningful relationship? What really mattered in his life? It wasn't the job. It was people. Two people in particular. Francesca and his brother. He needed to concentrate on what was important.

"I've got a new Bavarian beer you might like, mate."

Cavanaugh placed both hands on the bar and looked down at Dr. Bob. "Would you by any chance have any Cuban beer?"

"Don't be a wanker now, mate. You'd be in the bloody wrong place for that. We don't sell bloody Communist beer here!"

"Thanks. That's good to know," Cavanaugh smiled. "Mind if I use your phone," he added throwing a buck on the bar.

Dr. Bob snatched the dollar like a frog would a fly. "The dog and bone's at the end of the bar, but just don't take all night on it."

Cavanaugh made a quick call. "Fran, how would you like to go to dinner with me tonight at Tugs?"

* * *

16

Havana, Cuba

Diego Velasquez liked Jack Bennis immediately. Velasquez lived alone, his wife having died in childbirth over twenty years before. It had been a long time since he had had someone he could talk to and share a drink with.

That first night the priest moved into the apartment, Velasquez invited him to share a bottle of Cuban rum with him. Bennis accepted hoping to learn more about the area and the people. After a couple of glasses of Havana Club, the professor spoke freely; never realizing the priest was leading the conversation, but not sharing anything about himself.

By the third glass of rum, Velasquez was describing the deplorable conditions he observed in the hospital he worked in. There were broken windows, dirty toilets, holes in the floor, a lack of medicine, patients' clothing hanging out the windows. He told of one family who used a wheelbarrow to get their grandfather to the hospital as there were no available ambulances.

Bennis savored the smooth aged rum and commented, "But I read how Cuban medicine has advanced and how your hospitals are modern, clean, and efficient."

"Sí," Velasquez replied slurring a bit, "some of that is true, but those hospitals are for the tourist and the rich and famous. Castro was very shrewd. He realized the U.S. embargo would hurt tourism, so he catered to tourists from other countries. Now we have famous people coming to Cuba for our free health care. It is estimated that over 20,000 Venezuelans had their sight restored thanks to Cuban doctors. The World Health Organization praised the high scientific and technological level of the Cuban pharmaceutical industry. When the Argentinean soccer star Maradona needed surgery, he came here to Cuba. When your Michael Moore brought the American 9/11 responders here they received excellent treatment."

"But why do you complain about the health care system you have?" Bennis asked.

"Because I see it every day. The good care goes to the tourists, but the Cuban people do not receive the same care."

Velasquez poured himself another glass of Havana Club. "In my hospital I have few supplies. If you go to a local pharmacy for something as simple as aspirin, you will probably be sent to one of the hotels. It would make you sick to see what the common Cuban goes through in some of our hospitals. Many patients have to bring their own towels, bed sheets, and pillows or they would have to lie down on filthy blood, urine and feces stained mattresses. There are roaches and flies all over the hospital."

Bennis took another sip of his rum, but remained silent.

Velasquez drained his glass. "You doubt me, Padre? You, like your doubting Thomas in the Bible, think these things are figments of the imagination? Come with me tomorrow, Padre, and I will show you of what I speak."

Bennis stood and placed his glass on the table next to him. "It is late, my friend, and we still have much to talk about, but I am tired."

Diego Velasquez staggered to his feet and extended his hand to Bennis. He smiled, "You are right, Padre, but will you come with me to see for yourself what I speak of?"

Jack Bennis shook the professor's hand and smiled, "Of course I will."

* * *

17

Staten Island, New York

"What are you staring at?" Francesca asked. You look like you're in a trance?"

Cavanaugh sat at a table by the window looking out at the tug boats as they glided smoothly up and down the Kill Van Kull in the dark waters of the night. His once frosted glass of Becks remained untouched as he stared past the realities of the dark waters. He jumped at the sound of Francesca's voice, but recovered quickly.

"Did you know during World War II, FDR got together some of the top brains in the world and one of the things they experimented with was hypnosis?"

The woman across from him wasn't amused. She tossed her long red hair to one side and her sparkling green eyes rose toward the painted white tin ceiling.

"Don't change the subject, Tom. You do that all the time. It's a disgusting habit."

Cavanaugh thought briefly about a few other disgusting habits he had, but decided not to go there. "Have you ever been hypnotized, Fran?"

She nodded. "As a matter of fact, yes. My grandfather used to bring a mesmerist to our birthday parties. We had a lot of laughs."

Cavanaugh sighed and reached for his beer. He looked at her yellow cashmere sweater in the dim light of R.H. Tugs Restaurant. "Your grandfather, Vito Muscatelli? He probably would have."

"And what does that have to do with anything? You just don't like him!"

God, he thought, she was beautiful when she got angry. "Hypnotism is not a joke, Fran, and your grandfather is a crook!"

"Let's not go there, Tom. He's old and in a nursing home. It's a gorgeous night. But where are you? Since we got here you keep staring out the window and drifting off as if you are thinking about something else. You're here, but you're not here."

He tightened his grip on the glass and brought the beer to his lips. "Did you know that a shark is the only fish that can blink with both eyes?"

"Please stop it with your inane trivia. Do you want to just take me home now because it's obvious you don't want to be here?"

"No," he snapped as he took a gulp of his beer. "No. I want to be here . . . with you. It's just that I have something on my mind."

"So?"

"So what?"

"So what is it you have on your mind? You didn't drag me all the way to Staten Island to look at tug boats and tankers go cruising by in the night. Or did you?"

Cavanaugh looked down at the glass in his hand and then at the elaborate ceiling fans above them. "No. I like this place. I thought you would too. I used to come here to think. By myself. When things got crazy on the job, I'd come here, have a hamburger and a couple of beers and look at the tugs. Somehow it relaxes me to watch the ships fight the currents and go smoothly by with no apparent effort." He hesitated a moment and then added, "I wish life were like that."

"Well, you and I both know it's not. So what's on your mind?"

He sipped the Becks and savored its taste. He avoided looking Francesca in the eyes, but he could feel her green eyes boring in on him like laser beams.

"Fran," he began as he took a long gulp of beer, "there's a lot about me you don't know."

She waited.

A waitress interrupted their silence. "Are you ready to order yet or should I give you a little more time?"

Cavanaugh fumbled looking for the menu. Francesca said simply, "We're not ready yet. Thank you."

Cavanaugh drained his glass. "Can we have another round?"

"Not me," Francesca replied, "I'm fine."

The waitress smiled a Disneyland smile and left.

"So what's going on, Tom? You've been staring off into space since we got here. It's as if you are in a trance or something."

"Did you know women blink nearly twice as much as men?"

"Stop it, Tom. We've been through a lot together. Can you talk to me about what's bothering you, or not? Is it the Inquest? It's over. They cleared you. It was just a big waste of the public's money."

Cavanaugh looked at his now empty glass and then turned toward the choppy waters outside the window. It was true they had been through a lot together. He was one of the homicide detectives assigned to investigate the death of her father. In the course of his investigation, her husband was also murdered and one of her brothers arrested. And he had fallen in love with her.

"No. It's not that. Although, I guess, that's part of it. It's about my brother. I got a letter from him. I think he's in trouble." Cavanaugh held back. There was so much he couldn't tell her now—maybe ever. "It's a long story. It gets very complicated. But I think he's in Cuba and I was thinking of going down there to talk to him."

Francesca suddenly reached over, grasped his hands, and pulled him to look at her. "Are you crazy? You can't go to Cuba! It's off limits. It's one of those restricted countries you can't go to. And besides, you're a New York City cop!"

"I'm thinking about taking a little 'vacation,'" he said softly.

"They'll never let you do that. And what about us? You're just going to up and leave? Have I used up my fucking usefulness to you already? Is that it?"

This time he grasped her hands. "No, Fran, no. It's not like that. I've never felt this way before about anybody. You know that."

"Then why are you leaving?"

"I told you. It's my brother. Once I get things straightened out with him, I'll be back."

A huge tanker blocked out all the lights on the piers and tanks across the water in Bayonne, New Jersey.

Francesca shook her head, pulled her hands away from him and folded her napkin. "Somehow, I think I've heard this one before, but never with the exotic forbidden country scenario thrown in there. If this is a brush off, lover boy, you've got an elaborate imagination. Why don't you just come out and say it? I'd have more respect for you if you did."

He looked at her and their eyes locked. "This is no brush off, Fran." He hesitated and then blurted out the words he had always been afraid to say, "I . . . I love you."

She just stared at him for what felt like a sixty second commercial for nothing. He felt tightness in his chest. He had never said the words before and meant them. He was a barge adrift in unfamiliar waters. He had never felt so vulnerable. The customized Colt ACP in his shoulder holster didn't help. He sat motionless like a naked skinny dipper caught in the spotlight of a patrol car.

"Are you ready to order now?" The waitress with the painted smile was back again with Cavanaugh's beer. He started to reach for the glass when Francesca touched his hand and held it. "No," she said, "just bring us the check. We're leaving."

Cavanaugh's mouth dropped as she loosened her grip. "Finish your beer, lover boy. We're going back to my place."

His smile lit up her eyes even more. "But I'm telling you one thing right now," she added quickly, "if you're going to Cuba, honey, I'm going with you."

"No. No. You can't. It might be dangerous. You don't know what this is all about. I can't let you come with me."

"No arguments." She lowered her voice and continued, "You see, stupid, I love you, too, and if you think I'm going to let you slip through my life without a fight, you're wrong. 'Life for me ain't been no crystal stair,' in case you didn't notice. You say you love me, and I love you. And I'm still climbing. I'm going with you."

The first grade homicide detective who had been involved with more murderers and drug dealers than all the Hollywood actors, directors and producers combined struggled for something to say. "But . . . ," he started.

"No buts. Do you speak Spanish?"

"No, but . . . ."

"I do," she smiled. "Have you ever been in Cuba before?"

"No, but . . . ."

"I have. My grandfather took me there a few times when I was younger. It's a great place to visit, but you wouldn't want to live there."

"Fran, listen to me, please. This could be dangerous. I'm not quite sure where my brother is. He may be in some serious trouble."

"Tom, you are going to need someone with you who speaks the language. You are going to need someone to show you around. You are going to need someone you can trust." She reached out and held both of his hands tightly. "Plus," she said simply, "I love you and want to be with you."

Cavanaugh never finished his beer and left a rather large tip because he never waited for the check. In the morning, as he looked at Francesca sleeping beside him, he smiled and didn't regret over tipping the waitress with the perpetually happy face. Still in the back of his mind, a fear gently gnawed at him, lurking like a fart beneath the covers. With or without Francesca, his plan to go to Cuba to find his brother might not be a very good idea, nor a very safe one.

* * *

III

The truth that makes men free is, for the most part,
the truth which men prefer not to hear.

Herbert Agar

WEDNESDAY

18

Havana, Cuba

In the morning Jack Bennis washed his face and looked in the mirror. He had become a Jesuit to help people. His past experiences had brought him in contact with the Cuban people. He knew the Castro regime and the U.S. embargo had hurt the people. But they were a resilient, strong people. They endured a police state, food rationing, and a lack of many conveniences.

Fidel Castro had brought them problems, but he had also in a strange way empowered them. The rich no longer controlled their lives. Medical services were available to all. Once the affluent imported more American cars than any other country. Today, the American made cars of the 1950s still ran in the streets of Cuba. Because of Cuban care and pride, these cars outlived their brothers and sisters in the United States by four and five times. Education was available for everyone. Unlike in New York from where he had come, in Havana Bennis did not see homeless, crime, or drug addiction. But he also did not see any overly rich people either. Was that such a bad thing, he wondered.

One day Fidel Castro would die. He had already passed the powers of government over to his brother, Raúl. Perhaps the man who had received a Jesuit education would return to God on his deathbed. Perhaps not. A new Cuba would soon rise. Buildings would be restored. Stucco would be repainted for the first time in decades. Broken shutters would be fixed. New cars would run on Cuba's roads. People would experience a new found freedom. Money would pour in and new businesses would spring up.

Jack Bennis wanted to be a part of the new revolution. He wanted this new revolution not to lose sight of the only thing that made sense to him—a belief in a Supreme Being, a belief in God. He didn't care what people called this Supreme Being. He felt this belief gave people a moral compass, a hope, a reason to work together and help each other.

He had seen what was happening in the United States. People objected to the word "God" used in any public arena. Prayer was not allowed in schools. Religious symbols were not permitted to be displayed on public lands. The Ten Commandments were no longer spoken about. People who practiced their religions—whatever they may be—were suspect. They were called "fanatics" or "evangelists" and feared or mocked. He saw the moral fabric of America wearing away rapidly. He didn't think it was an accident that violence, pornography, divorce, crime, and greed dominated the headlines and the news shows. History recounted how the Roman Empire's collapse came from within. Now it was happening to his native country. He had tried to help by eliminating two top mob bosses the police were unable or unwilling to stop, but now he had become the hunted.

He knew some would call him a vigilante, some an assassin, some a cold-blooded killer, some a nut case, but in his heart he believed he was a crusader, a prophet, an optimistic pragmatist. He hoped he could start a movement in Cuba that would spread. Christianity had done it in the past. Without the bells and banjos of self-absorbed political clerics and bureaucrats, he wanted to help start a grassroots movement that would be more powerful and more peaceful than any other movement the world had ever known.

Going back into his small room, he picked up two of the items he had left on the night table the night before. He looked at the gun in one hand and the rosary beads in the other. But maybe they were right, he thought. And the headache came back again. Maybe he was a "nut case."

* * *

19

Brooklyn, New York

Wednesday morning Morty Goldberg arrived at the station house early as he usually did, only to be briefed about another murder victim found on Staten Island. The victim's name was Luca Andrassy. Her body had been found the previous afternoon in the woods along Manor Road by members of the Susan Wagner cross country track team. Initially, the police thought she had been a hit and run victim, but after sending her to the Seaview morgue, they found she had been murdered the same way Crystal May had.

Around 3:15 the previous afternoon, five students were laughing loudly as they ran through the weed-choked grass along Manor Road and started to cut through the woods toward the Richmond County Golf Club. One of them saw something sticking out from the weeds and went to investigate. At the sight of the dead woman's body, he screamed and the frightened boys raced back to the school to call 911.

Local police from the 122 Precinct arrived around 3:45 P.M. Luca was fully clothed, dressed in a dark blue short-sleeve button-down shirt, tan polyester pants, black stockings and black dress shoes. Her navy blue trench coat had been thrown over her face. There was no evidence of a sexual attack. Her purse was found at the scene with several hundred dollars in cash. Some animals, possibly rats, had bitten into her face and legs.

After the coroner arrived, the body was transported to the Seaview morgue. Despite the fact that her body was lying over 15 yards from the road and her face had traces of maple syrup on it, her death originally was treated as a traffic fatality because of the multiple injuries to her arms and legs. As soon as the autopsy report came in, however, the cause of death was changed to homicide. In addition to indicating Luca Andrassy had eaten a vegetable meal shortly before death, it also showed her throat had been cut clear through to her spinal column. The coroner listed the official cause of death as partial decapitation, massive hemorrhaging, and shock. Each of her wrists had been dislocated.

Laboratory analysis of the injuries to Crystal May, the missing student found in the abandoned building on Staten Island the previous day, Goldberg recalled, indicated similar injuries and the same cause of death. This time, however, pieces of hair had been found on her clothing. Perhaps, Goldberg thought, the killer is getting sloppy.

* * *

20

Havana, Cuba

Diego Velasquez insisted Bennis eat breakfast with him before heading by bicycle to the hospital. He had prepared ham *croquetas*, a smoky creamed ham, shaped in finger rolls, lightly breaded and then fried. Velasquez also placed buttered and toasted *tostada* on the table along with *café con leche*, a strong, espresso coffee with warm milk.

"Diego, you are too good to me," Bennis said. "I must confess, however, I don't usually eat breakfast."

"But you should, Padre. Breakfast is good for you. In my case, living alone all these years, I have come to believe what that British writer Frances Bacon said, 'A bachelor's life is a fine breakfast, a flat lunch, and a miserable dinner.'"

Bennis laughed. "In that case, Diego, I will cook dinner tonight."

They talked while breaking the *tostada* into pieces and dunking them in the *café con leche*.

"When I was a boy in America, my mother used to cook eggs and bacon in the morning for my brother and me," Bennis commented as he stood and brought his cup and dish to the sink. "I think that was when I first learned the difference between 'involvement' and 'commitment.'"

Diego Velasquez finished his coffee and joined the priest at the sink. "I do not understand, Padre. What do you mean by that?"

Bennis smiled. "The difference between 'involvement' and 'commitment' is like an egg and bacon breakfast. The chicken was 'involved' but the pig was 'committed.'"

The professor laughed, "That is a very good one. I will try to remember it for my classes."

The priest cautioned, "Remember it when we visit the hospital today. We live in strange times, my friend, and one has to be careful about what one says and does."

As they rode through the narrow streets of Havana toward Miguel Enriquez Hospital, Jack Bennis thought about egg and bacon breakfasts, involvement and commitment, Santiago, and his brother.

* * *

21

Brooklyn, New York

When Cavanaugh finally arrived at the station house, he carried two large cups of black coffee from the 7/11 on the corner. "Here you go, partner," he said placing a cup on the papers Goldberg was studying. "How's my favorite Jewish detective doing this morning?"

"Be careful," Goldberg replied lifting the coffee from the papers. "You are late."

"It's a beautiful day and I had to walk. I left my car here yesterday."

"*Meshuggener*!"

"Morty, did I ever tell you how I love it when you speak Jewish?"

"For the umpteen-millionth time, it's not Jewish, it's Yiddish!"

"Relax, buddy. You need to loosen up a bit. By the way, did you know iguanas, koalas and Komodo dragons all have two penises?"

"We've got another one," Goldberg said ignoring his question. "Same M.O. as Crystal May." He sat at his desk studying the little information they had received on the victim.

Over the course of the next several hours, they accumulated a mountain of details. The victim's name was Luca Andrassy. She was 25 years old, approximately 5 feet 6 inches tall and weighing 165 pounds. Her hair was dark brown. She had been attending the College of Staten Island as a part time student. Friends and fellow students on Staten Island described her as having a sweet disposition and as being a very shy, soft-spoken girl. A neighbor told how they used to do each other's hair and nails and Luca always liked messing with her hair as she did hers. She had been the former Walton High School Homecoming Queen when she had lived in the Bronx.

But there was another side to Luca Andrassy, too. Before moving to Staten Island, she had been known as "Loquita" and was known to have gang connections. Since moving to Staten Island, according to her family and close friends, she had been trying to break these connections. But they were hard to break. A lot of hostility existed between her and her former gang members. In addition, she still had problems with some old rival gang members due to some previous activities in the Bronx where she was reportedly known to take money in advance for sex from her clients and then run away before performing the acts.

Five nights before, she had last been seen at a bar on Forrest Avenue talking to a man no one had seen before. She left the bar around 1:30 A.M. walking with this man in the direction of her home. She never got there.

* * *

22

Havana, Cuba

When they reached the hospital, Diego Velasquez paused before leading Bennis into the massive white concrete building in front of them.

"Please, Padre, try to understand. I teach genetic biology at the University. There we have the best equipment you can imagine. Our students have gone on over the past few years to treat thousands of patients with asthma, high blood pressure, diabetes, cancer, heart disease, and senile dementia. The research we do there is vital to our country. We have cryogenic laboratories, ultrasound equipment and other state-of-the art medical technology."

Bennis looked up at the open windows of the hospital in front of him. Some were broken; some had clothes hanging out of them.

"Why I am telling you this is because what you are about to see is quite different. It is not a pretty picture you are about to see."

The priest patted Velasquez on the back. "Come, Diego. Let us see your hospital. Trust me, my friend; I have seen many unpleasant sights in my life."

When they entered the building they were met by a tan skinned nurse in a white uniform. Her black hair was pulled back and tied in the back by a blue ribbon. She smiled at Diego and than looked inquisitively at Jack Bennis.

"Buenas días, María Izabelle," Velasquez said. "This is a friend of mine, Padre Jack Bennis."

María Izabelle looked Bennis up and down like she was judging a beauty contest and replied in Spanish, "He doesn't look much like a priest."

Bennis smiled and answered, "And what does a priest look like?"

"You speak Spanish?" María Izabelle said in perfect English.

Bennis smiled again, "And you speak English. We are even."

Diego interrupted, "I have brought my friend here on an unofficial visit to show him our hospital."

"That may not be a good idea," she said.

"Relax, María Izabelle, we can trust him," Diego said moving past her and leading Bennis down the hall.

"You are naive," she said following after them.

Walking down the dimly lit corridor, Bennis felt and heard an occasional crunch under his feet as he stepped on a roach. Looking into small hospital rooms, he saw electric wires dangling from the ceiling and Che Guevara posters plastered to pealing walls. The bathrooms were even dirtier than Diego had described. The many spots on the walls in patients' rooms turned out to be resting flies.

At one room on the second floor, Bennis saw a statue of St. Anthony of Padua. In a corner of the room lay a dark skinned man he had seen in the Plaza de la Catedral selling produce next to Santiago's stand. The man wore a string of red and black beads around his neck. There was a slight odor of coco butter in the room.

"I recognize that man," he said. "May I go in and talk with him?"

Nurse María Izabelle responded quickly. "He won't talk to you."

"Do you mind if I try? I won't be long."

Diego nodded and María Izabelle folded her arms and remained stationed at the door.

Jack Bennis walked over to the man in the bed and said in Spanish. "Good morning. My name is Father Bennis. I think I have seen you in the plaza selling vegetables."

The man swatted a fly away from his face. "You are the American priest I have heard them talk about?"

"I don't know what they said, but I am an American priest."

"Why have you come here?"

"I want to help. Is there anything I can do for you?"

"No," he replied. "Go away and leave me alone."

The female voice at the door commented, "See. I told you."

Bennis ignored the words and moved to the table next to the man and examined the statue there. "I see you have a strong devotion to St. Anthony of Padua . . . ."

"I have a devotion to Eleggua and . . . ."

Bennis nodded. "I see. You are a Santerían?"

"Yes. Now go away. Your Christian beliefs have corrupted the Yoruba beliefs of my ancestors."

The priest pulled up a chair and sat down. He leaned over and read the name on the chart hanging from the bed. "We are not really that far apart, Manuel. Basically, we believe in the same things. I believe in one God and so do you."

"Your people oppressed my people when they came here as slaves. You forced them to accept Christianity."

"But your people kept the beliefs of their own faith and melded them into the Christian religion. You kept the traits of the Catholic saints and matched them up with the qualities of your orishas."

The little black man tried to sit up in his bed and a group of flies scattered about the room. "How do you know so much about Santería ?"

"I don't really know that much. I just know that you and I are searching for the same things. The name we call our God is immaterial. He is the same God. A Frenchman may call a book *livre,* while a German may call it *buch.* It makes no difference. It is still a book."

"You speak strange for a Catholic priest."

Bennis stood and walked to the window where a group of brightly colored ceramic bowls rested. Flies buzzed around the bowls which contained honey, aguardiente, tiny bits of smoked fish, powdered eggshells, toasted grains of corn, and what smelled like cocoa butter. "I see you have bowls on your window sill. Are they to summon the powers of your orisha?"

"Do not mock my faith, padre. I am a sick man, and I need help from beyond."

Bennis moved back to the chair and pulled it closer to the bed. "Manuel, I do not mock you. You and I both need help. Some people need spiritual help and some need physical help. Tell me about your beliefs and hopefully we can help each other."

* * *

23

Brooklyn, New York

Interviews and reports took up the major part of the morning and afternoon. Toward the end of the day, Cavanaugh and Goldberg compared notes on both Crystal May and Luca Andrassy. They were both young women who were attending college. Both suffered similar injuries. Both were found on Staten Island. Both had maple syrup smeared over their faces. Both were found by high school students. But they were from vastly different backgrounds. One was the married mother of twins, the other single with possible gang ties. One was covered by rats when first found. Rodents had gnawed on both bodies. Forensics was checking the traces of hair found at the latest crime scene.

"Well, what do you think?" Cavanaugh asked.

"I don't see any connection with the victims," Goldberg said. "We might be looking at a serial killer here."

"He obviously tortures his victims, but there is no sign of sexual abuse."

"There is one other difference between the two murders," Goldberg offered.

Cavanaugh answered, "Yeah, the note. There was no note on the Andrassy woman."

"None that was found, at least."

"What do you mean?"

"It's windy out there and starting to get dark when they found her. A note could get blown away."

"Has anyone been looking for a note?" Cavanaugh asked.

"Not that I know of," Goldberg admitted. "Initially, they thought it was a traffic accident."

"Well, then what the hell are we waiting for?"

Goldberg looked out the window. "It's dark out there now. Can't it wait till the morning?"

"It could be blown away by then," Cavanaugh stated. "We can't afford to wait till morning." He reached for the phone and called the 122 precinct and explained the situation. They agreed to send some people out to re-check the crime scene. They told him it may take some time. It was a busy night. There had already been two accidents, one on Hylan Blvd. and another on the Staten Island Expressway and a robbery at the Staten Island Mall. He told them to put a rush on it, that the order came straight from the Mayor's Office.

Goldberg rolled his eyes and started to re-read the files on both victims.

Both detectives spent the next three hours poring over the same reports looking for something—anything that might give them a clue. The only thing they came up with after a pot of coffee and a few trips to the men's room was that both women were missing an earring—the left one. It could just be a coincidence, but neither believed in coincidences.

After three and a half hours, the phone rang. It was Shanley. "Hey, Cavanaugh, you were right! We found another note."

Cavanaugh motioned to Goldberg who picked up the extension phone. "Well, don't keep us in suspense all night, Shanley, what does it say?"

Shanley hesitated, "Well, I don't know . . . ."

Goldberg interjected, "It's okay, Officer Shanley, tell me what it says. You can forward it through channels later. We need this information now."

Shanley remained silent.

"What does it say, Shanley?" Goldberg demanded.

Shanley slowly read the note into the phone,

> The rats crawled in little Miss Luca,
> And the rats crawled out.
> They chewed her guts, then spit them out.
> Where was Tommy Cavanaugh?
> Didn't I tell you there'd be more?

Goldberg buried his head in his hands. Cavanaugh straightened up and asked, "Where did you find the note?"

"It was in the tree under which the body was found."

"Who found the note?"

"I just told you. We did."

"No, Shanley, listen carefully. Who exactly found the note?"

Shanley thought a moment and then replied, "Bubbles . . . . Officer Perez found the note."

* * *

24

When news of the second note reached him, Bradley summoned Cavanaugh and Goldberg into his office. He told them to have a seat and then calmly closed the door and came back to sit on the edge of his desk. Pictures of his wife and sons adorned his desk as well as the wooden carving.

"Gentlemen, I will get straight to the point. What the hell is going on?"

"What do you mean, Lieutenant?" Cavanaugh asked.

"Don't bull-shit me, Cavanaugh! Two female bodies show up with messages on them mentioning you? The Chief is on my ass. The Mayor is on his ass. And I'm going to sit on your asses until we get some answers."

Goldberg straightened his tie. "We haven't found a connection yet, Lieutenant, but we are working on it. We checked the files for similar M.O.'s. Both had similar injuries, both bodies were found on Staten Island . . . ."

"Tell me something I don't know, Goldberg."

Cavanaugh stared straight ahead.

"It may not be anything, but both victims were missing an earring."

"Have you run that through the F.B.I., N.C.I.S., and INTERPOL?"

Goldberg looked over at Cavanaugh who seemed to be in a trance. "Lieutenant, we," he hesitated, "we didn't think you wanted to involve the F.B.I. in this."

"Two women have been brutally murdered and a note naming one of our detectives has been found on the scene of both crimes. I want this bastard stopped and stopped soon. I don't care what it takes or who has to get involved!"

Bradley moved over to Cavanaugh. "Detective, are you with us?"

Cavanaugh looked up. "Yes, sir."

"Then tell me what the stupid nursery rhymes have to do with you!"

Cavanaugh took a deep breathe. "I wish I knew."

"Bull-shit!" Bradley shouted. "You are involved in this somehow Cavanaugh and I want to find out why and how."

"Lieutenant, I have no idea. I never saw the victims before. I just got back from trying to recover from the Inquest and all this breaks out. I don't know what to say."

"Are you losing it, Cavanaugh? Is that what I hear? Because if you are maybe it's time to put in your papers . . . ."

Cavanaugh looked down at his hands and murmured. "Maybe."

Before Bradley could reply, Goldberg interrupted. "We did find some unidentified hair on the last victim. We are running that through the lab now."

"Maybe it will lead us somewhere," Cavanaugh added.

Bradley stared at him. "Yeah, maybe." He went to the door, opened it, and commanded, "Now get back to work and keep me informed."

* * *

25

When Goldberg and Cavanaugh got back to their desks, Goldberg asked, "What was that comment 'Maybe' all about?"

"Morty, a lot's going on in my head right now. I'm thinking of taking a break for a while."

"You are in the middle of a murder investigation, *meshuggener*. Have you lost it?"

"Maybe I have. I don't know."

Goldberg leaned over. "What's bothering you, Tom?"

"A lot of things. I keep thinking about the Inquest and the death of Maria DeFillipo. If I hadn't ducked, she'd still be alive. Now she and her baby are gone. I have nightmares over it . . . ."

He rubbed his hand over his eyes. Goldberg listened.

"And then there's Francesca. I really like her, Morty. More than anyone else. It's a damn good feeling. I never felt this way before. But we put away her brother for murder and her father was a real bad guy until he was murdered . . . ."

Cavanaugh looked up at Goldberg. Neither blinked. They understood something they weren't going to talk about.

"And then, there's my brother." Cavanaugh scratched his head. "He's in Cuba now. I've gotten a couple of letters from him. I think he's in some kind of trouble . . . ."

Goldberg straightened his tie again. "It wouldn't surprise me."

"Morty, he's my brother!"

"Okay, okay, I won't go there. Maybe if we concentrate on these murders a little more, it will get your mind off these things at least for a little while. Where do we go from here?"

Cavanaugh looked him straight in the eyes. "Staten Island," he said. "We need to question Officer Perez."

"Hold on, Tom. Why do you want to do that?"

"You know damn well why. She's the one who found both notes. She has good reason to hate my guts. Believe me, I am not looking forward to another trip to Staten Island, and I am definitely not looking forward to questioning her, but it's something we have to do."

"Do you know what you are getting yourself involved in?"

"No."

Goldberg looked at his watch. "You don't want to go there now, do you?" he asked.

"No. Let's take the ferry over there in the morning. The 120 Precinct is right at the foot of the ferry in St. George." Cavanaugh reached into his desk drawer and took out a brush to straighten his hair. "And that's another thing I want to know. How did Perez find the note at the scene of the second body? It was found in the 122 Precinct. She's assigned to the 120."

Goldberg shook his head and grabbed his coat. "Meet you in the morning at the ferry."

* * *

26

Staten Island, New York

Vito Muscatelli sat in a brown leather lounging chair by the window gently petting the velvety soft coat of the pixie-like cat nestled in his lap. The room smelled of dried urine like the rest of the nursing home, but the old man and his Devon Rex cat didn't seem to notice. The cat purred and closed its eyes. Vito admired the unusual range of color and pattern in his little friend.

He didn't respond when the phone rang and Gestas, his huge attendant-body guard answered it. "It's for you, Mr. Muscatelli," Gestas whispered as he brought the phone to his boss.

Of course it's for me, the old man thought as he snatched the phone from Gestas with one hand while still cradling the precious little cat with the big ears and wide eyes.

"Papa, this is Francesca. I'm going to Cuba."

"What?"

"I'm going to Cuba with a friend, and I may need your help."

The old man looked at the phone as if it were a *New York Times* crossword puzzle. "Why you want to go to Cuba?"

"My friend is looking for his brother. You remember him. He was the detective who caught the man who killed Daddy. His brother is the priest who said the mass at Daddy's funeral."

Vito Muscatelli looked out the window at the Verazzano Bridge in the distance. It was a clear night, and it looked cold outside. In the nursing home, however, the heat was oppressive, but the old man did not notice as he pulled the blanket on his knees closer to him while still cuddling his cat.

He remembered Detective Thomas Cavanaugh. And he remembered his brother, the priest, too. The news reports all indicated that Cavanaugh and his partner, a Jewish detective named Morton Goldberg, had killed Howard Stevens, the man who they said had killed Vito Muscatelli's only son, Rocco, and murdered the old man's best friend and business associate, Carmine Anthony Malentendo. Despite the fact that Stevens' fingerprints were on the murder weapon, Vito Muscatelli never believed the stories. He had a gut feeling, and he always trusted his gut.

Stevens had kidnapped the old man's grandson and tried to blackmail Vito into giving him names to contact in Cuba who could get him to see Fidel Castro. Shortly before Stevens was shot to death by the police, Vito had sent him a list of names. Recently, the old man learned someone in Havana had tried to contact some of the people on the list. The description of the person, he realized immediately, matched that of the priest who had mysteriously vanished after the shooting of Stevens. The police were satisfied that the case was closed, but not Vito Muscatelli. His gut told him differently. If the priest were now in Cuba, Vito knew he must somehow have been involved in the deaths of his son and his friend. Vito Muscatelli knew what he had to do.

"Papa, will you help us contact people down there who could help us find his brother?"

"Francesca, did this Detective Cavanaugh ask you to call me?"

"No, Papa. He doesn't even know I'm doing this."

"Why you want to go with him? Could be dangerous."

"That's what he said, Papa, but I want to go with him."

"You should stay here."

Francesca's voice rose. "Forget it, Papa! I've been through this with him. I'm going! Are you going to help us or not?"

Vito Muscatelli's feeble arm trembled, but his brain spun like a roulette wheel. He needed time to plan this. The priest, he concluded, was a marked man. He had already sent people to get rid of him. In some way, he felt the priest had something to do with his son's death. And the priest's brother was a cop, and cops were always expendable. Right now he thought of Cavanaugh and his brother as walking dead men.

"Papa," Francesca's voice interrupted his reverie. "Papa, will you help me or not?"

"*Fa bene*, Francesca. I help you. Give me a little time. You come here tomorrow afternoon, visit your grandfather. I give you help."

"Thank you, Papa. I love you."

"I love you, too, Francesca. *Cioa*."

As he hung up, Vito called to his personal attendant who looked more like a WWF wrestler than a nurse. "Gestas, get me that doctor what's his name who hypnotize. We use him before. Get him. I need talk to him."

"Mr. Muscatelli, sir," the attendant asked, "do you mean Dr. Benevento?"

"*Sì*. Benevenuto. That's the guy." Vito clutched his hands together and squeezed. "I want him here tomorrow morning. I need him."

Gestas cracked his knuckles and didn't ask any questions as he turned and started to leave the room. He would do as he was told. Vito Muscatelli knew that Gestas's brain was the one part of his body he never exercised. Vito liked it that way.

"Oh, and Gestas," the old man called, "one more thing." Vito shook his blanket and the limp body of his Devon Rex rolled onto the floor. "Get me another cat. This one's dead."

* * *

27

Havana, Cuba

That night, Jack Bennis prepared dinner for Diego Velasquez as promised. It had been a long day, but his conversation with Manuel gave him new energy. Throughout the preparation, images flashed before him of the frail vegetable man with his black and red beads around his neck and the flies circling around the room while cockroaches crawled along the floor and up the walls. And yet Bennis marveled how Manuel's indomitable spirit and faith permeated the room.

Scurrying around the kitchen like a squirrel, the priest prepared foods he had purchased in the afternoon at the market in the Plaza. When they finally sat down to dinner, Diego found a meal before him he had not experienced in years. For an appetizer, Bennis prepared a fruit dish of papaya and pineapple slices with guanaban. The main course consisted of Cuban pork chops covered in a paste of crushed garlic, oregano, and cumin sprinkled with a dash of sherry, allspice, salt and pepper, and side dishes of rice, eggplant and pineapple ratatouille, tamales and plantains.

Diego opened two bottles of Castillo del Morro Gran Reserva Tinto, a fruity, dry red Cuban wine blend of Cabernet Sauvignon and Merlot. Bennis questioned the need for two bottles of red until a knock on the door announced they had another visitor, María Izabelle Melendez, the nurse from the hospital.

In the hospital, María Izabelle had been reserved, formal, and even hostile toward the priest. Dressed in a loose white nurse's uniform with a wrinkled apron with her folded arms, she could have been a member of the kitchen staff or a matron in a prison ward. But the woman he saw now wore a tight, red, low cut dress, high heels, and a warm, inviting smile. Her face shone like a golden orb and her azure eyes lit up the room. She was beautiful.

"Welcome, María Izabelle," Diego said greeting her with a warm embrace and a kiss on both cheeks. "I am so glad you could come."

Bennis cleared his throat and wiped his hands on his trousers. "I didn't realize we were having another guest for dinner, Diego . . . ."

"María Izabelle is not a guest, my friend, she is family. She was my wife's sister. I thought the three of us could share a meal together tonight and talk freely about your impressions of Miguel Enriquez Hospital."

During the meal, Bennis guarded his remarks about the hospital, but found himself coming back to the subject of Manuel frequently.

"Does he have many visitors?" the priest asked.

"No," María Izabelle said looking straight into the priest's eyes. "You are the only one I have seen him talking with. What were you two talking about so much? He really seemed to enjoy your visit."

"As I did, too. We discussed religion mostly. I am intrigued with Santería. As it is a closed religion, few know anything about it."

Diego poured another glass of wine for himself. "They are a cult of devil worshipers if you ask me! They practice voodoo and sacrifice animals while they dance around to the beat of drums. I would stay away from him, Padre, if you ask me!"

"Everything is not the way we think it is, Diego. Santería does not practice voodoo or worship the devil as some people believe. They actually do not believe in the devil. Their belief system is not like ours, good versus evil, or God versus the devil. They believe all things have positive as well as negative aspects, and that nothing is completely good or completely evil. The way they see things, everything has different proportions of both good and evil."

Bennis hesitated for a moment and then turned to Diego and María Izabelle. "To a Santerían," he said, "no action is all wrong or all right, but can only be judged within the context and circumstances in which it takes place. So, to them, each of us is made up of both positive impulses as well as negative or destructive impulses. In their religion, the focus is on each person striving to develop good character and doing good works. Good character is doing the right thing because it is the right thing to do, not out of fear of burning in hell or as a way of seeking the rewards of heaven, but simply because it is the right thing to do.

"There is a simplicity and beauty to their belief system in that all human beings are seen as having the potential of being good people even though they have the potential to make evil choices. The universe, they believe, is benevolent and forgiving."

"But they do sacrifice animals," María Izabelle insisted. "I have seen the charred remains of the chickens they have killed."

"At certain times, Manuel told me they do kill chickens. He told me, however, it was rare and that it depends on the situation. But they eat the chicken after it has been killed and cooked. Don't we do the same thing, but in a different way?"

"Perhaps, but we don't drink the blood of the chicken."

"And at the holy sacrifice of the mass, don't Catholics believe we drink the blood of Christ?"

Diego laughed raising his glass and toasting the priest. "Jack Bennis, you must truly be a Jesuit because you can logically argue truth into fallacy and fallacy into truth. It is a special gift to make one think of other ways of looking at things."

Bennis clicked his glass with his host and María Izabelle. "Please," he added, "don't dress me in another's robes. Understand I may be a priest, but I am just a man, a man with feet of clay like all of us."

Diego laughed again and rose to open another bottle of wine.

María Izabelle leaned closer to Bennis and whispered another toast to him. He smelt the sweet perfume she wore which blended in with the bouquet of the wine that intensified her violet, ruby-red lips. Their eyes locked. Her lips moved slowly as she stared at him, "I must confess, Padre, I have always liked men with feet of clay."

* * *

IV

There are people who eat the earth
and eat all the people on it,
like in the Bible with the locusts.
And other people who stand around
and watch them eat it.

Lillian Hellman

THURSDAY

28

Whitehall Street Ferry Terminal, Manhattan, NY

It was the first time Morty Goldberg had ridden on the Staten Island Ferry. He took his badge out at the ferry terminal to flash to avoid paying a transit fare, but Cavanaugh politely pulled him back and said, "You can put that away. It's free."

"How can that be?"

"It just is. Relax."

When they boarded the "Andrew J. Barberi" at Whitehall Terminal, Detective Goldberg morphed into a tourist. He stood on the starboard side of the ferry and watched with the eyes of a curious child as they sailed past Governor's Island, Ellis Island and the Statue of Liberty. Cavanaugh sat quietly looking up at his partner. He didn't want to spoil his enjoyment by telling him the ferry they were on was the same one that went out of control in 2003 and rammed a concrete pier at the St. George terminal in Staten Island killing eleven passengers and injuring more than thirty others.

After ten minutes of Cavanaugh's total silence, Goldberg looked over at his partner and commented, "I've never heard you so quiet. What's up?"

Cavanaugh's early morning euphoria had vanished. That handwriting analysis came back to him. He had to tell his partner. They had been through much together. He deserved Cavanaugh's honesty. "I'm thinking of taking off for a while, Morty."

"I thought we went through that," Goldberg said.

"No. I have to try to find my brother. I need to talk to him."

"You're what?" Goldberg eased himself into the blue plastic chair next to him.

"I've got a few weeks coming to me and some overtime. If I need more I'll just take it."

"But why?"

There was only one way to get this done, Cavanaugh realized. He had to dive into the icy water. "I got a letter from my brother the other day. He's in Cuba. I've decided I'm going to see him."

"Are you completely *meshuggener*? You can't go to Cuba. There's a U.S. embargo on travel to Cuba."

"I think my brother may be in trouble, Morty, or about to get himself into some trouble. I've got to see him and talk to him."

"Hold on, Tom. I don't understand this. You don't see your brother for twenty years. He shows up for a few days a couple of months ago and then disappears again and now you are thinking of leaving your job to go to Cuba to find him?"

"I've made up my mind, Morty."

"Well, make it up again, Tom. You can't go. Cuba is a restricted country."

"There are ways."

"You're not a journalist. You're not going on official government business. You're not going to do professional research. You're not going to attend a conference. You're not going for educational reasons . . . ."

"I'm going, Morty."

"They'll never give you permission."

"I'm not going to ask permission. It would take too long. I'm going by way of Canada."

"Listen to reason, Tom. You can't go. If they find out, you'll lose your job, your pension, and everything else, plus you could be fined a lot of money and imprisoned for up to ten years."

"He's my brother, Morty. A lot has happened to him that I don't know, and I want to find out. If he is in trouble, I've got to help him. If I'm right, he could get himself killed."

"What are you talking about? Your brother is a priest."

"You know damn well what I'm talking about. You bailed him out with the Muscatelli murder." Cavanaugh reached into his jacket pocket and pulled out a worn letter. "Here, Morty, read his last letter."

Goldberg took the letter and started reading.

"Morty, my brother's a good man," Cavanaugh began. "He might be a little mixed up because of all that training and stuff he went through in covert operations with the C.I.A., but basically he's a good man. I can't let him do what I think he plans to do."

Goldberg's eyes slowly worked their way down the pages of the letter. Suddenly they froze as he focused on the final sentences of the letter. He looked up at his partner. "This is nothing!" he exclaimed. "He doesn't say anything specific . . . ."

"Did you read that part where he quotes from an epistle of St. Peter? 'Who indeed can harm you if you are committed deeply to doing what is right? Even if you should have to suffer for justice's sake, happy will you be.'"

"You are reading too much into this, Tom."

"Remember Howard Stevens. He was determined to kill Fidel Castro."

"Stevens is dead. I know. I shot him."

"My brother took the list of names Muscatelli sent Stevens who could get him close to Castro. He also took Stevens' briefcase with money he tried to bribe my brother with to help him assassinate Castro."

"Tom, you are nuts! He wouldn't do that!"

"Look at the postmark. It's from Havana."

"No. This is crazy. He can't be serious . . . he wouldn't."

"You don't know my brother like I do," Cavanaugh said firmly. "He doesn't say it exactly, but if you read between the lines, I think he would. I think he's going to try to kill Castro."

"This is insane. He doesn't say that. You must be wrong."

"Maybe, you're right, but I'm not about to take that chance. He's my brother. I have to talk to him. Whatever is happening down there, he's in trouble. I just know it. I can feel it. I've got to help him. Isn't that what brothers are for?"

* * *

29

Staten Island, New York

"Mr. Muscatelli? Dr. Benevento is here to see you."

The old man sat in his recliner staring out the window at the Verazzano Bridge in morning sun. Traffic was at a standstill both ways. Vito wondered how much the toll on the bridge had risen and tried to recall the names of his "associates" who had disappeared into the bridge's pilings thanks to his providing them with a unique if unexpected mausoleum.

"Mr. Muscatelli, sir," the huge attendant approached the old man and spoke a little louder. "Dr. B. is here to see you, sir."

Vito turned and said quietly. "*Bene*. Send him in and wait outside."

When Dr. Anthony Aloysius Thomas Benevento entered the room, he rubbed his hands, checked his gold Rolex watch, and then readjusted his wireless eyeglasses. He wore a silk double-breasted charcoal gray Armani suit which was tailor made for him twenty-five pounds ago. His cheap toupee was slightly askew making him look like a pregnant man on chemotherapy.

Vito Muscatelli spoke without moving from the window. "Sit down. This won't take long. And stop checking your watch. I have a job for you."

"Yes, Mr. Muscatelli," the doctor said as he unconsciously checked his watch again. There were beads of sweat forming under his wig and starting to ooze out. "I . . . er . . . I have a legitimate practice now, Mr. Muscatelli."

The old man swung the chair around. "Shut up!" he snapped like a crack of ice. "When I call you, you come. *Capise*?"

The doctor stared at the eyes of the man in the chair and shuddered. They were the eyes of death, cold, penetrating, final. He pulled over the hospital chair in the corner and obediently sat down.

"You still know how to hypnotize?"

The doctor smiled. He had just published a paper in *The American Journal of Medicine* on the benefits of hypnosis in pain relief and would soon have another published in *The American Psychological Journal* on a ten year study of hypnosis in treating smoking and obesity. Perhaps, this "job" would not be as bad as he had initially thought it might be.

"Yes. Yes, I do. In fact I just had an article . . . ."

"Shut up and listen. I want you here tomorrow when my granddaughter Francesca visits. I want you hypnotize her. You can do this?"

"Yes. Yes. Of course. I used to hypnotize them when they were young. Remember? But why? What . . . ?"

"I want you to plant a thought in her head that when she hears my voice on the telephone, she will do exactly what I tell her to do. *Capise.*"

The doctor rubbed his Rolex watch, but did not look at it. He wanted to know why, but he had been here before. The less he knew, the better he would be. He knew Francesca as a child and had successfully hypnotized her many times before. But he also knew, depending upon what the old man wanted his granddaughter to do, there was no such thing as a sure thing in hypnotism. He knew what Vito Muscatelli wanted to hear, so he lied.

"Yes. Yes. Of course, Mr. Muscatelli, I can. I am very good at hypnotism. In fact, I recently gave a talk at Columbia about subliminal perception in auto- . . . ."

"Spare me. Just be here tomorrow when Francesca come."

"Yes. Yes, Mr. Muscatelli," the doctor agreed. He had come a long way since he was on-call to do whatever Vito Muscatelli wanted. He had earned a reputation for himself he was proud of. The frail man in the chair had helped him along the way, but now he was weak and sick. Dr. Benevento was not accustomed to being told what to do. He thought it prudent to add, "I could lose my license if . . . ."

Vito's eyes narrowed and his voice shattered the doctor's arrogance like a rock through a plate glass window. "You could lose your life if you don't. *Capise?*"

Dr. Benevento nervously scratched his head further dislodging his toupee. "Yes. Yes, Mr. Muscatelli," the doctor whispered and rose to leave.

Suddenly, Vito reached out and grabbed the doctor by his tie and pulled him close to his face. There was a rattle deep in the old man's throat and spittle flew up into the doctor's face. "You do as I tell you, or else. *Capise?*"

"Yes. Yes, Mr. Muscatelli," the doctor stammered as he felt the icy grip on his necktie loosen. Dr. Benevento straightened himself and removed his spit flecked eyeglasses as he moved quickly toward the door. "I *capise*."

When the door closed behind him, Dr. Benevento stopped to clean his eyeglasses and thought to himself, "I only wish that I did not *capise*."

* * *

30

Staten Island, New York

It took less than an hour to reach the St. George Ferry Terminal on Staten Island and walk the short distance to the 120 Precinct. Most of the way, they had argued about Cavanaugh's plans to find his brother in Cuba. At one point in their, at times, heated discussion walking up the steep hill to the station house alongside the home for the New York Yankees' minor league team, the Staten Island Yankees, Goldberg finally lifted his hands and shouted, "*Aroysgervorfench verter*!"

"And what the hell is that supposed to mean?" Cavanaugh asked.

Goldberg ignored the question and walked on in silence.

"Did I ever tell you, Morty, how much I hate it when you speak Jewish?"

"It's not Jewish. How many times must I tell you? Jewish is a religion. Hebrew is a language," Goldberg said and then added, "but that wasn't Hebrew. It was Yiddish!"

"Whatever. But what does it mean? What did you call me now?"

"Nothing. I just realized I was talking to the wall and my words were wasted arguing with you. You refuse to listen to reason so there's no sense in my trying to talk you out of your crazy idea."

They were both tired and frustrated when they finally walked up the steps to the 120 Precinct and asked the Desk Sergeant for Officer Meredith Perez. The Desk Sergeant put down the chocolate cream donut he was devouring to check the duty roster. His name tag read, "Gelding."

"You're out of luck, guys," he said wiping some of the chocolate off his mouth with his sleeve. "She ain't here."

"Well, where is she?" Cavanaugh asked.

The Desk Sergeant leaned toward them. "You're the guy that was in the paper, ain't you?"

Cavanaugh moved closer. "I asked where Police Officer Meredith Perez is?"

"You think you're hot shit, don't you, Detective? Well, your shit doesn't float around here. Understand, Mr. Hot Shot Detective?"

Cavanaugh started to respond, but then remembered the handwriting analysis and Lieutenant Bradley's warning. He backed away and took a deep breath.

Goldberg spoke. "We'd like to see the Duty Officer."

The Desk Sergeant took another bite out of his donut. "I'm afraid you'll have to go back to wherever you guys came from and call to make an appointment."

Cavanaugh turned and started walking toward the Squad Room.

"Hey," Gelding shouted and started choking on the donut. "You can't go back there," he said as pieces of half chewed donut spewed into the air.

"Watch me," Cavanaugh said.

A tall, thin lieutenant with a booming voice suddenly appeared. "What seems to be the problem?" he asked calmly.

Goldberg and Cavanaugh showed their badges while Gelding continued coughing behind them. "We came to see Officer Meredith Perez," Goldberg said. "We'd like to ask her some questions concerning the deaths of Crystal May and Luca Andrassy."

The lieutenant escorted them into an office. "My name is Bob Ryan," he said. "I apologize for Officer Gelding. He gets a bit high strung at times."

"Maybe he should change his name," Cavanaugh suggested.

Ryan ignored the comment and continued. "We'd all like to help you, but I am afraid Officer Perez did not report to work today."

"Is she sick?"

"I don't know. We called her home, but there was no answer. I think you know her partner, Officer Shanley. He went over to her apartment, but again no answer."

"Has she done something like this before?" Goldberg asked.

"No. She is a good officer, and frankly I'm a bit worried about her."

"If you don't mind, Lieutenant, could you tell us why Shanley and Perez were at the crime scene last night? The response team should have come from the 122 Precinct, not the 120."

"There were a couple of major traffic accidents yesterday and a robbery in process in a jewelry store on New Dorp Lane when the call came in to re-check the scene. Apparently, the Mayor's Office put a priority on it so we dispatched some of our people."

Goldberg and Cavanaugh looked at each other. Finally, Cavanaugh spoke. "Would you mind if my partner and I went over to Officer Perez's house to have a look?"

"No problem, Detective. I'll have Officer Shanley drive you over."

* * *

31

Havana, Cuba

When Jack Bennis visited the hospital the next day he brought with him a number of items in a large plastic bucket which he balanced on the handlebars of his bicycle. María Izabelle greeted him with a smile. Her nurse's uniform seemed cleaner and more form fitting this morning and Bennis could smell the tell-tale strands of Chanel #5.

"Buenas días, Padre Bennis," she beamed.

"Buenas días, Señorita," he said bowing slightly and removing his baseball cap with his free hand.

"I had a great time last night," she said.

"That makes two of us—no three. I think Diego had a good time, too, that is until he passed out."

María Izabelle giggled like a school girl. "You are so bad!"

"Yes," he admitted, "I am, but I have work to do now. How is Manuel doing today?"

"I haven't checked his chart yet today. Come let us visit him." Walking down the corridors, María Izabelle checked the contents of the plastic bucket Bennis carried with him. She saw rags, brushes, cleaning agents, disinfectant, soap, and shaving cream among other things.

"What are you doing with those things, Jack?" she asked.

"I did some shopping this morning. It wasn't that easy, but I ended up 'borrowing' some items from the Hotel Palacio OFarril and the Hotel San Miguel. Diego was right. The local stores didn't have much on their shelves, but the hotels which cater to the tourists miraculously did. I plan to do some work today, starting with Manuel's room."

When they reached the room, María Izabelle touched his arm and whispered, "Be careful."

He smiled, "I will try."

Suddenly, at the door she reached up and gave him a gentle kiss on the cheek, then turned and hurried down the hall.

The three patients in the room observed the interaction and smirked. Bennis felt his face flush. Manuel sat up in his bed and teased, "You look like a hot tamale."

Bennis reached into the plastic bucket and produced three cups of *café con leche* from under the rags. "Buenas días, my friends, I thought you might enjoy a bit of real coffee this morning instead of the muddy water they usually serve."

After distributing the coffees and some *tostadas* from a local bakery, Bennis started to work cleaning the room. He scrubbed the floor and walls and counted forty-seven confirmed cockroach kills. He secured some of the dangling overhead wires to the ceiling with duct tape as a temporary measure until he could come back with the proper equipment. He dusted and washed the beds and all the furniture and strategically hung fly paper by the window. And then he addressed himself to the patients in the room. He gave each of the men a needed shave and bathed them from head to toe with the soap he had "borrowed" from the hotels. Manuel and a younger man in the corner by the window had severe bed sores which he treated with special ointments.

When he finished with Manuel's room, he worked his way down the hall. The nurses and doctors, if there were any assigned to the floor, never appeared. Perhaps, he thought, María Izabelle had managed to keep them away to avoid a confrontation.

At noon, he left for an hour and when he returned he brought new, clean bed sheets and linens for all the patients on the floor. Along the way, he lost count of cockroach fatalities and replaced the strips of flypaper three times. Before he left, he gave each patient a special blessing and promised to return.

Pedaling back to his room, he knew that some of the patients were dying, but he also knew that he had given each of the patients on that floor a glimmer of hope and a spiritual boost. All in all, he concluded, it had been a good day—until the shot rang out.

* * *

32

Staten Island, New York

"I'm worried about her," Shanley said driving along Richmond Terrace and the waterfront. "This isn't like her. Bubbles is a good cop. She's real thorough and it's like she took a special interest in this case."

Cavanaugh sat in the passenger seat of the police car staring out the window.

"What do you mean?" Goldberg asked from the back seat.

Shanley ran a red light narrowing missing a Ford Explorer. "I hate those SUV's they're all over the place. Why would anyone need one of those gas guzzlers with the price of gas what it is?"

"What do you mean she's taken a special interest in this case?" Goldberg repeated.

"It's like she's obsessed with the case ever since she found the note." He glanced over to Cavanaugh. "I think she's still got the hots for you."

"Since when did you become Dr. Bill?" Cavanaugh snapped.

"It's Dr. Phil," Shanley corrected.

"Whatever. Just drive the stupid car, will you? Where does she live anyhow?"

"She rents an apartment in Mariners' Harbor. It's not the best neighborhood, but the owner is a retired detective."

After a few blocks, Shanley asked, "Anything turn up about the last victim?"

"We did find some hairs on the victim," Goldberg said. "They are checking them now."

"Yeah, we heard about that, but they might only be animal hairs," Shanley volunteered. "Those woods are full of rats, possums, raccoons, and even a few deer."

"We'll see," Cavanaugh said. "Now would you kindly get us to her place without all the talk?"

Shanley checked Goldberg in the rear view mirror. "Kind of touchy, isn't he this morning?"

Goldberg simply nodded.

When they finally pulled into the driveway of the narrow two-story colonial house, a tall man with thinning white hair opened the front door. The house was located on a 40 x 150 ft. lot and had a white plastic picket fence running along the front and sides. Two large neatly trimmed azalea bushes guarded the front door. Like most of the houses in this high crime area, the house was built in the 1930s, but the clean, beige aluminum siding and the manicured lawn indicated it was well kept.

The white haired man approached the officers quickly. "What can I do for you fellows?" he asked. "My name is Mike Keane."

Keane extended his hand and gave a strong handshake to each of them. "I retired from the job about ten years ago. What's up?"

Cavanaugh spoke first. "We are looking for Officer Meredith Perez. Would you happen to know where she is?"

"Merry goes in and out of here all the time. I don't keep a tab on her, but I think she should be at work today."

"That's the problem, Mike," Shanley said. "She didn't report for work today."

"Could we possibly have a look at her apartment?" Goldberg asked.

"Wait a minute, guys. Merry's not involved in anything now, is she?"

"We just wanted to ask her a few questions," Cavanaugh said.

"We're kind of worried about her," Shanley added. "It's not like her not to show up for work."

"We could get a warrant, Mr. Keane, if you wish, but we are trying to save some time."

Keane reached into his pocket and pulled out a set of keys. "Don't get your balls in an uproar. I'll let you in, but don't mess up the place."

They thanked Keane and they all walked around the side of the house to a separate entrance. There Keane opened the door and stepped back as Cavanaugh, Goldberg, and Shanley entered.

The room was neatly, but sparsely furnished. On a desk by the window an empty Dennino's Pizza box rested next to two empty Diet Cokes. It was the walls of the small room which drew their immediate attention. All around the room taped to the paneled walls were newspaper clippings and pictures of the recent crime scenes. Reading the clippings, Goldberg noticed they all concerned Cavanaugh. Some were about the shooting in the deli, some were about the Inquest, some about the recent murders. The clippings were from the *New York Times*, the *New York Post*, the *New York Daily News*, and the *Staten Island Advance*. He even picked out obituary clippings for Maria DeFillipo.

Cavanaugh noticed a paper pad on the desk next to a half eaten piece of pizza similar to the paper the notes were left on.

Cavanaugh and Goldberg exchanged glances.

Shanley stared and simply said, “Holy shit!”

* * *

33

Brooklyn, New York

That night, Francesca Arden ate a grilled chicken salad with Caesar dressing she had picked up at Antonio's Pizza Palace after a fruitless day of shopping at Lord and Taylor and Bloomingdales looking for clothes for her trip to Cuba. She had been very young when she had visited the secluded beaches of Arroyo Bermejo Beach when she and her family visited with her grandfather. They had stayed at Hotel Breezes Jibacoa even though children under fourteen were not allowed. Wherever her grandfather went, people seemed inclined to break the rules. She was too young to question. All she knew was that she loved the catamaran trips and the snorkeling around the coral reef, and the beautiful white sands.

She was tired now and decided to take a warm bath. As she was unbuttoning her blouse, the phone rang. Francesca was what she would call an organized disorganized person. She kept everything, but did not always put things back in the same place. She found the portable phone under Sunday's *New York Times* Book Review which was covering the hair blower in the bathroom.

"Hi, Fran. It's me. How are you doing?"

"Tom, I just got home from shopping for something to wear in Cuba. It's warm down there, you know."

There was a moment of silence before Cavanaugh's voice continued. "I've been thinking, Fran. Maybe it's not a real good idea for you to come with me. It's not going to be like a vacation. I don't know how long it's going to take me to find my brother. And it could be dangerous."

"I thought we'd been through all that last night, Tom."

On the other end of the phone, Cavanaugh sat with his third bottle of Sam Adams larger staring at the muted televised game of the Knicks losing another to the Shaq. He wasn't watching the game. Crystal May, Luca Andrassy and Meredith Perez were on his mind.

"Fran," he began slowly, "I'm no good for you . . . ."

"What are you talking about?" She wanted to look in his eyes and see him. He wanted the safety and security of space between them. He didn't know if he could say what he needed to say face to face with her.

"I realized something today. Something about me . . . . I'm not a nice guy. I've done a lot of things I'm ashamed of . . . ."

Francesca sat on the toilet bowl and gripped the phone tighter. Her voice rose as she removed her blouse. "Wake up! We have all done things we are ashamed of. That's life. We fall. We pick ourselves up and we try again."

"No. You don't understand. I don't want to hurt you."

"What are you talking about? What happened today? You weren't like this last night?"

Cavanaugh took another slug of Sam Adams, but he didn't taste the award winning barley and hops. He hoped the alcohol would anesthetize the depression he was sinking into. It didn't.

"Two women have been killed. Both brutally murdered. The officer who found the notes mentioning me I used to date." He paused and started to tear the label off the bottle with his index finger.

Finally, Francesca asked, "And . . . ?"

"And I realized," Cavanaugh said, "I . . . I probably hurt the woman I dated as much, if not more, than the killer hurt the dead women."

Francesca's eyes widened. "Did you beat her?"

"No. No, Fran. Nothing like that. We were both consenting adults and I didn't abuse her physically, but I did use her and worse than that I told stores about her that I shouldn't have."

"Were the stories true?"

"Yes, but they were private things. Things I shouldn't have shared with others." He added, "I was a jerk."

"Did you love her?"

"No, but I think she loved me. That made it worse. I took advantage of her."

Cavanaugh heard only silence on the other end of the phone. Now he wished he could see her face.

"Fran, I love you, and I don't want you to be hurt by me. I've never felt this way about anyone before, and I don't want to lose you. But I'd rather lose you than hurt you."

Francesca Arden's emotions were spinning like a yo-yo. How could he do that to another person? Why is he telling me this? How do I feel about him knowing this piece of information? Does this change the way I feel about him? Should it change the way I feel about him?

"Fran, are you still there? I wouldn't blame you if you hung up. I'm a creep, and I don't deserve someone like you."

Still silence from the other end of the phone line.

"Okay," he finally said. "I understand. I'm sorry. I had to tell you because I want to change. Since I met you things have been different. I don't know why. It's like life has a whole lot more meaning when you love someone. I guess I was never lucky enough to love someone before. Thanks. I'll give you a call when I get back."

He started to hang up just as the TV cut to a car commercial for an SUV that could climb mountains at 60 mph.

"When are you going?" the voice on the other end quietly asked.

"What?"

"I said, 'When are you going?'"

"I . . . I'm not sure. Things are falling apart at work. I can't concentrate. Hopefully, Saturday, real early. I've got to get directions. It may take me another day to do the drive?"

"You're driving? You can't drive to Cuba!"

"No. I'm driving to Canada. It's only an eight hour trip to Toronto. I'll take I-80 into I-81 and follow the signs to Buffalo and Niagara Falls. Then it's just a little ways to Toronto's Pearson Airport. I'll make the reservation when I get there. If all goes well, I plan to catch a plane to Havana on Sunday."

"How are you driving? You're not planning to drive your car to Toronto, are you? It's a death trap!"

Cavanaugh loved his car. "Betsy" was an old battered, red, white, and blue former U.S. Mail truck. The letters had been painted over, but it was obvious what it once had been. He had bought it at auction complete with its rubber bumpers. Betsy had scraps, dents, and bullet holes in her just as he did. They had been through a lot together.

"Of course I am. Betsy and I are a team."

"Well, count me out of that team. I'll fly to Toronto and meet you there."

"What? You'll go? You still want to go after everything I said?"

"It's like I said last night. I don't know why, but I've fallen in love with you, too. You tell me you're a creep, but you're honest to admit it. You've never done anything to hurt me. You've treated me with respect. Yes. I am going with you."

Cavanaugh looked at the torn label on his beer bottle. She's amazing, he thought.

"Are you sure you don't want to fly up to Canada with me?" she asked.

"No. I want to leave as little a trail as I can. I'll drive." He added, "Why don't I call you when I get there?"

"I wasn't born yesterday, lover boy. So you can conveniently leave without me? No way. I'll meet you in Toronto Saturday night. Where are you planning on staying?"

"I found the Reisert Hotel on the internet. It looks like a nice enough place. It's close to the airport, and it's only for one night anyway." Cavanaugh became aware of a beep on the other end of the line. "I think someone's trying to call you, Fran."

"Whoever it is can wait."

"You'd better get it. It might be important. I'll call you tomorrow after I see a few people and get a few things set. You must be tired anyhow. Good night. And thanks. I really love you, you know."

"So I've heard. The feeling is mutual, Detective. Sleep tight. *Cioa*."

As Fran hung up and started to draw the water for her bath, her phone rang. She wondered who would be calling her at this time of night. As soon as she heard the voice, she knew, and, for some reason, she became frightened.

It was her grandfather, Vito Muscatelli.

* * *

V

Every truth has two sides;
and it is better to look at both,
before we commit ourselves to either.

Aesop

FRIDAY

34

Havana, Cuba

Jack Bennis lay in his bed motionless, eyes closed. He could feel the sun on his face. He had been asleep for a long time. He concentrated on the pain in his side until glimpses of the previous night started flashing before him. The first bullet whizzed by his head and ricocheted off the cobbled road and embedded itself in one of the concrete columns in front of an office building. It must have come from a roof nearby. He didn't see the second bullet as he accelerated around the corner. It wasn't until he arrived at Diego Velasquez's house that he realized his shirt was wet. The second bullet had embedded itself in his side. It wasn't deep, but it was there and he had lost a lot of blood.

He recalled limping into the house holding his side trying not to bleed on anything. His mind was racing. The shot had come from above. Probably one of the buildings across the street. Whoever it was, was waiting for him. They knew where he was. He had been careless in his "shopping spree" and had shown himself in public places. Or had someone tipped them off?

He concentrated. He knew he needed to stop the bleeding and to get the bullet out. And he needed help. Entering the house he found Diego busy at the kitchen table reading term papers on genetic mutations. When he looked up and saw the blood on Bennis' shirt, Diego jumped up scattering papers all over the room.

Diego called María Izabelle and they tended to him during the night. He told them what to do, and they did it. He apologized for using Diego's good Smirnoff "No. 57" 100 Proof vodka to sterilize the wound, but using a kitchen knife, a carving knife, and a spoon, they managed to dig the bullet out. It was a .22. Anything bigger, Bennis realized could have done more serious damage.

In his mind, he still saw María Izabelle staring at his half-naked body sprawled across the kitchen table. She saw the multiple scars from past injuries and other bullet wounds. Her eyes told him she realized he was not an ordinary priest.

"Who did this to you?" she had asked as she wound bandages around his waist.

"I don't know," he replied.

"We must notify the authorities," Diego insisted.

"No," Bennis had said sliding gingerly off the table. "That wouldn't be a good idea."

"But why not?"

"Trust me. I am fine. I am sure it was an accident."

María Izabelle examined the scars on his body. "Where did you get all these scars?"

He remembered telling her, "It's a long story. Once like the founder of the Jesuits, I too was a soldier."

"Enough talk for tonight. You need your rest, Jack," Diego said.

He recalled agreeing, "Yes. But I could use a good stiff scotch, too."

"You shouldn't be drinking," María Izabelle had insisted as her brother-in-law disappeared into another room. "You have lost a lot of blood. You should really see a doctor."

"No, precious lady, I don't need a doctor and there is no way in hell you could get me into that hospital of yours. What I need right now is a drink and a good sleep."

Diego had returned with a quart bottle of Riedel Vinum Single Malt Scotch and poured six ounces into a glass.

He smiled in his semi-sleep. "Diego, you are a man of many surprises," he had said. "This is good stuff. Single malt scotch. In Havana, Cuba, no less. Where in heaven's name does a college professor get a bottle of good scotch like this?"

"I save it for special occasions."

He remembered starting to laugh and then grabbing his side. He tilted the glass observing its consistency and placed his nose close to the glass to savor its aroma. "This very good scotch, Diego. I guess I should get shot more often," he coughed and then downed the scotch in one long gulp.

María Izabelle had held his arm and helped him into bed. "From the looks of your body, it looks like you have been shot more than enough."

Bennis had eased himself into the bed and closed his eyes. He didn't answer. He was asleep almost immediately. Turning slightly in the bed, he felt his side pull where the bullet had hit. But then he felt something else and opened his eyes. There next to him in the bed lay María Izabelle sleeping with her head resting on his arm.

* * *

35

Staten Island, New York

She hadn't seen her grandfather since her father's funeral. Now parking on the hill by the nursing home, she was nervous. Maybe this was a stupid thing to do. Why had she even called her grandfather? What did she expect him to do for her? Walking into the main lobby, she saw people parked in wheel chairs staring at nothing. A feeling of depression swept over her and the unmistakable odors of age and debility enveloped her.

When Francesca arrived at her grandfather's room she was surprised to see Dr. Benevento there. He was older now and fatter and for all his good clothes she wondered why he had never invested in a better hairpiece. Her grandfather sat in a leather lounge chair by the window. He looked older and frailer than she remembered him at her father's funeral. She reprimanded herself for not coming to see him more often, but life always seemed to get in the way. Now that she needed something from him, she came to see him.

Vito Muscatelli introduced Dr. Benevento and Gestas to her again. Gestas loomed over the room like a lethal cloud. Perhaps it was his size or his apparent absence of emotion which sent shivers down her spine. Looking at Dr. Benevento, she thought she saw fear in his eyes, too. But all about the room, although thin and wrinkled, her grandfather radiated a power that unnerved her.

"How you been, Francesca?" he almost smiled from his lounge chair. In his lap he held a little kitten. It wasn't the same one she had liked the last time she saw him, but then he always seemed to have a new cat when she saw him.

Fran told her grandfather about her planned trip and how she was going to meet Cavanaugh in Toronto because she wouldn't drive in his car. She talked fast and louder than necessary. She laughed when she told him what Cavanaugh's old Mail truck looked like, and he smiled while he gently stroked the kitten in his lap.

"Toronto is a long way away," he said. "How does this Cavanaugh plan to get there?"

Francesca spoke freely to her grandfather and proceeded to tell him the route Cavanaugh told her he intended to take and how he planned to leave at the ungodly hour of 2:00 in the morning in order to avoid traffic and get to Toronto before noon so he could make plane arrangements to get to Havana the next day. Vito listened intently as Gestas and Dr. Benevento stood like stone gargoyles against the wall.

"We are definitely going to need some help, Papa," Francesca finally said. "Can you help us? Please. I know there will probably be problems arranging for a flight. Our government has made it difficult to travel to Cuba."

"*Sì*, this is true," the old man said and motioned to Gestas to bring him paper and pen. "But I givea you name of travel agent up there I know. He will makea sure things go smoothly for you. You just tella him you are Vito Muscatelli's granddaughter. He will get you on plane." He scribbled a name and phone number on the paper and handed it to his granddaughter.

"When we get to Cuba, Papa," she added, "is there anyone we can contact there who you know who could help Tom find his brother?"

Suddenly, the kitten in Vito's lap screamed as if caught in a vice. The old man quickly recovered and stroked the kitten's belly. Gestas and Dr. Benevento remained motionless.

Vito Muscatelli smiled. "*Sì*, of course, I have close associate down there you musta see. He will helpa you contact your friend's brother." Again, he wrote on a piece of paper and handed it to Francesca.

"Thank you, Papa," she beamed and hugged him. "You're the best! This whole trip thing has made me a nervous wreck. I'm going to fly up to Toronto tomorrow and meet Tom there. I wouldn't drive in that car of his if my life depended on it."

The old man smiled again exposing his crooked teeth. "Francesca," he said turning up his Italian accent a few notches, "you remember Dr. Benevenuto here? We justa talking about how he used to hypnotize you when you were little. You remember?"

"Of course, I do, Papa. It was fun."

"Dr. Benevenuto here tella me hypnotize can relax a person, makea them feel good. You believe?"

"I don't know, Papa."

"You looka like you could use a little relaxing, Francesca. No?"

"You are right about that, Papa. To tell you the truth I think Tom is crazy trying to go to Cuba. I tried to talk him out of it, but he insists. He didn't want me to go and we've been arguing back and forth about it. I'll be happy when the trip is over."

Muscatelli motioned to Dr. Benevento. "You thinka you can relaxa my little granddaughter a bit? Makea her feel good."

Benevento moved forward with a forced smile. "It would be my pleasure, Mr. Muscatelli," he lied. "Would you like to try, Francesca?" he asked.

She laughed, "I don't know." She remembered the picnics when her grandfather had Dr. B hypnotize her brothers and her sister. They all did such silly things that they laughed until they cried. "Thank you, but I don't think so."

"It would take away some of your tension," Benevento said.

Then Vito spoke from his chair, "Francesca, you doa it for me. I wanta you feela better. It be good for you."

"It's just that it reminds me of when I was a kid and the good times we used to have." Her smile faded as memories of her father's death and her brother's arrest came back. Benevento seemed to read her anxiety and told her to take a deep breath and to sit down and relax.

Finally, she said, "Why not? I could use a little relaxation."

It didn't take Dr. Benevento long before he had Francesca in a deep sleep. When he finally brought her out of her hypnotic state, she did, indeed, feel better just as he had told her she would.

Walking back to her car, she felt she had accomplished a lot. She had a name in Canada of a person who could get them safely on the plane to Cuba and she had the name of someone in Havana whom they could contact to help them find Cavanaugh's brother. Her grandfather had even had the foresight to give her an international cell phone to use in case she needed it. Cavanaugh was wrong about her grandfather, she thought. He is a good man.

Up in his room, Vito Muscatelli watched his granddaughter approaching her car. She was beautiful. He was relieved she was flying up to Toronto and not driving with Cavanaugh. He did not want her hurt. She would be disappointed when the detective did not arrive, but she would get over it. Vito Muscatelli was thorough. A quick call to an associate and he would make the arrangement for someone to drive Cavanaugh off the road somewhere along Rt. 80 or 81 in the Pocono Mountains. But, just in case, Vito always had a contingency plan. If driving Cavanaugh off the road did not kill him, his associate in Havana would be a backup. And then, even in the conceivable chance he too failed, he always had Francesca and the subliminal thought Dr. Benevento had placed in her head to obey her grandfather's command when she received a call from him on the cell phone he had given her. Yes, Vito smiled to himself, Cavanaugh and his brother were not long for this world.

Fumbling for her car keys, Francesca dropped her Gucci purse, and one of the papers her grandfather had given her flew out. She caught it before the wind blew it down the hill. She smiled at her quickness. The note had the name of her grandfather's friend in Havana who would help them when they got there. "Wow! That was a close one," she said. "This must be my lucky day." She looked at the name on the paper: Francisco Santacruz.

* * *

36

Havana, Cuba

When Jack Bennis left the bedroom, he saw Diego sitting at the kitchen table drinking coffee and reading research papers from his class at the University. The professor looked up and casually asked, "How do you feel and how did you sleep last night?"

"What the heck happened?" Bennis asked. "How did María Izabelle end up in my bed?"

Diego smiled. "That, my friend, you will have to ask her. I think, however, she might have been worrying a bit about you. You had us both scared."

Bennis poured himself a cup of coffee and sat down. The coffee was strong, and the aroma mixed with the remnants of the alcohol odor of dried vodka coming from his side. "Excuse me if I'm a little confused here, Diego, but I'm not used to waking up with a woman next to me in bed."

Diego laughed. "There could be worse things to wake up to in your bed! I wouldn't knock it until you tried it . . . ."

They both looked up to see María Izabelle standing at the kitchen door. Her hair was disheveled, her dress wrinkled, and she looked tired. "What are you two talking about?" she yawned.

Bennis looked at her and said, "You! What happened last night? How did you end up sleeping next to me?""

María Izabelle's tan skin seemed to blush. "I was tired and worried about you. You had lost a lot of blood. You should have been in the hospital. I wanted to keep an eye on you. You fell asleep immediately, and the floor was hard. I should be asking you, what happened? Who shot you?"

Bennis realized the best defense is a good offense, but he also realized Diego and María Izabelle's lives might now be in danger because of him. "It's a long story, but I owe you an explanation. I came here from New York to get away from things and to see if I could start a new life here. I wanted to help. When I was in the military, I had a commanding officer a long time ago named Howard Stevens. His brother had been killed in the Bay of Pigs fiasco, and he blamed his death on Fidel Castro. Stevens wasn't in his right mind. He had a vendetta against Castro and wanted to kill him. He tried unsuccessfully many times. He even tried to kill me. Eventually, Stevens was killed by the police, but before he died he managed to get a list of names of people in Cuba who he thought could get him close to Castro. The person who gave him the names was a notorious New York mob boss."

María Izabelle sat next to Diego and listened.

"I ended up with that list, and came here to look around for myself. Part of me wanted to see if Castro had done any good, part of me wanted to help the people who were suppressed by Castro, part of me wanted to check on the names on the list, part of me didn't really know why I came." He stopped and took a drink of coffee.

"I didn't want to tell you any of this but over the last few days things have happened that made me realize my very presence in this house may have put the both of you in danger."

"What are you talking about?" Diego asked. He took his reading glasses off and leaned forward. "You are in my house. Nothing will happen to you here."

"I only wish that were true, Diego."

"What are you *not* telling us?" María Izabelle demanded.

Bennis rubbed his side and the pain radiated out like burning needles. Could they handle the truth? Could anyone handle the truth about Jack Bennis? Could he handle the truth about himself? And what good could come of the knowledge of the truth if there was nothing they could do about it? Discretion, not truth, he concluded, was needed.

"Last night when you saw the scars on my body, you said I wasn't an ordinary priest. You were right. I'm merely a man. A man who has been ordained as a priest, but still just a man. A man trying to serve God to the best of my abilities, but I seem to fall short too often." He hesitated and took another sip of his coffee. It was cold now. "I have made a lot of enemies because of things I have done in the past. Those deeds, like my shadow, seem to follow me no matter where I go. A few days ago some men tried to kill me. They were sent from that mob boss in the States."

"You must tell the police, Padre. They will investigate."

"No, Diego, I can't tell the police. They would ask a lot of questions."

"But those men! They must be stopped before . . . .""

"They have been stopped, María Izabelle. They won't be bothering anyone any more."

Silence fell on the room like a large blanket. Looking at each of them, Bennis said, "My point is there are always more like them out there. Yesterday, someone else tried to get me and almost succeeded. I let my guard down. And now I am afraid you are no longer safe as long as I stay here."

"Did anyone follow you?"

"No. I made sure of that. I weaved in and out of the streets and checked. No one followed me. But I have brought danger into your house and I must leave."

Diego stood, picked up his empty coffee cup, and brought it to the sink. He looked down at the dishes with his back turned to Bennis and María Izabelle. Finally, he turned. "You say you came here to help. I believe you. I saw what you did in the hospital. I am not a brave man, Jack Bennis, but I have seen things which I have told you about. And, whatever you have done in the past, I have seen you helping people here. You are welcome to stay here as long as you wish."

"But I can't put your lives in danger . . . ."

"We live in dangerous times, Padre. If we want to change things, we need to take a stand. I remember hearing about a minister in Germany during World War II who told how he sat by while the Nazi came for the trade union workers, then Jews, then the Catholics and did nothing. Finally, when they came for him, he said there was no one left to do anything." He looked over at his sister-in-law and she nodded. "We only have one question to ask you."

Jack Bennis looked from Diego and to María Izabelle. It had been a long time since he had trusted anyone. Fear gripped him like the pain in his side. He took a deep breath and asked, "What is it you want to know?"

They answered together, "How can we help you?"

* * *

37

Brooklyn, New York

Cavanaugh and Goldberg went over all the facts they had gathered on the case thus far. Results from Interpol and the F.B.I. came up with the name of a possible suspect, Cain Holland, a known assassin and suspected serial killer. Some of the killings linked to him followed a similar pattern. The female victims were apparently randomly selected and tortured before death. His victims like Crystal May and Luca Andrassy suffered wrist dislocations and their throats were cut. The victims were also missing one earring.

"What do you think, Tom?" Goldberg asked.

Cavanaugh stared at the papers on his desk and then stood up. "To tell you the truth, I'm tired of thinking. This case is too close to me. I have to get away. It doesn't add up. Nobody knows who this guy Holland is or what he even looks like. Why would he be doing this? Granted Holland kills in a similar manner, but the reports indicate he always takes the right earring. I'm not sure what it means, but both of our victims were missing their left earring. And then there are the notes. And why me? I don't know this guy. I never even heard of him before today."

"The maple syrup is a new twist, too," Goldberg added.

"It doesn't add up . . . ."

Their discussion was interrupted by Jimmy Monreale, a thin, serious lab technician, holding a stack of papers in his hand. "Good morning, gentlemen," he said. "I hope I'm not interrupting anything but I have the lab analysis of the hair found on Ms. Luca Andrassy. It is definitely human hair, head hair, not pubic hair. We were able to determine it is most likely of Caucasian origin. It is of medium coarseness, generally straight, and mostly dark brown with slight traces of gray."

"What else can you tell us?" Goldberg asked.

"Well," Monreale continued, "as you know the science of human hair is not exact. While without follicular tissue, sex is difficult to determine, the length of the hair and the lack of dyes, chemicals, or heat treatment suggest to me that the hair came from a white male."

"Great," Cavanaugh moaned, "that narrows the field down to millions!"

"Hair is not like fingerprints, gentlemen. Get me something to compare it with and I may be able to help more. Research has shown that human hair from two individuals is distinguishable and that accidental or coincidental matches don't just happen. Get me a comparison to work with and I can tell you if it matches."

"You've given us nothing, Jimmy, and you know it," Cavanaugh said. "Hair comparisons are not a means of absolute personal identification. Even if we get a match, it could get thrown out of court."

"Not true, Detective Cavanaugh. I can testify as an expert witness in court that clearly and without reservations the hairs I analyzed exhibit Caucasian characterizes, and, if you find me a match, that they are consistent with the hair of your suspect in microscopic appearance."

"For all we know, Jimmy, you've been studying the hair of a raccoon," Cavanaugh said.

"You just don't trust science, Cavanaugh. You are a Neanderthal. One of the first things I did in the lab was to compare the scale patterns of the cuticle and the medullary index. The shape and pattern of the medulla indicate whether a hair is human or animal . . . ."

"Easy, Jimmy," Goldberg interrupted. "He's just busting balls again. You did a good job here and thank you."

Monreale wasn't finished. "Analysis of hair will never be a sole indication of guilt, but it can definitely provide valuable information. Recent laboratory studies of Napoleon Bonaparte's hair showed that he may have actually been killed by arsenic poisoning . . . ."

"All right, Jimmy, all right. You convinced me." Cavanaugh stood and turned Monreale toward the door. He wanted to ask him if he knew Napoleon designed the Italian flag, but that would just prolong the agony. "Thanks for your efforts. I'm sorry I jumped at you. I guess I'm just having a bad hair day."

When he returned to his desk, he looked at Goldberg. "I wanted to tell him that the average scalp has 100,000 hairs and that redheads have the least at 80,000; brown and black haired persons have about 100,000; and blondes have the most at 120,000. And that both Napoleon and Hitler had one testicle, but I thought that would get him more riled up. What do you think about the hair as evidence, Morty?"

"The hair is not conclusive until we get a match." He hesitated for a moment. "You were there with me yesterday, Tom. We can't ignore it. You saw what I saw." Goldberg folded his hands and looked up at Cavanaugh. "What do you think about Officer Perez's involvement in this?"

"I don't want to go there, Morty. I'm too close to this thing. I have to get away from it. I'm serious. You saw how I jumped at Jimmy. I don't want to pursue this anymore."

He walked around his desk, reached in his drawer, pulled out his brush and unconsciously started brushing his hair. "I've been having nightmares about all of this. Last night I had a dream that woke me up in a cold sweat. It was my bother calling to me. I feel in my gut that he needs me, more than I need to pursue this thing. I know he's in some kind of trouble."

"Wait a minute, Tom, not this Cuban thing again. I thought you had gotten over that. There are a million and one reasons why you can't do it, not the least of which is we have a case to work and you're in the middle of it."

"You're a good detective, Morty. I don't know if I ever told you that. But it's true. I trust you. You will get this right."

"What are you talking about?"

"You don't need me on this one, Morty. I'm in the way. And I'm too close to it now, especially with Merry missing. I'm going to take a few days off . . . ."

"Hold on, Tom. You can't just walk away like this . . . ."

Cavanaugh dropped his brush in the drawer and hastily wrote a note that he placed in an envelope, sealed, and placed on his desk. "Some things are more important than others. With me out of the way, maybe this psycho will back off, the reporters will stop hounding me, and you will get a chance to find this killer. I'm in the way here."

"No, you're not. You can't just leave . . . ."

"Watch me, partner," Cavanaugh said heading toward the door. "I have some packing to do, Morty. *Hasta la vista*, baby!"

Goldberg watched Cavanaugh disappear and then turned to check the note left on his desk. It was addressed to him and it was printed—in all capital letters.

*   *   *

38

Staten Island, New York

Vito Muscatelli didn't waste time. After Francesca drove away and he dismissed Dr. Benevento, he dialed a number he kept in his head. Local police and federal investigators had tried for years to convict Muscatelli of crimes he had committed, but were unable. His residency in the Staten Island Nursing Home created the illusion he was old, feeble, and senile. While he was, indeed, old and feeble, he was not senile. His mind was a computer. He trusted no one and kept no written records. He knew who he wanted for this job.

Tony Healen was a low-level "wannabe" whom his son, Rocco, had used a few times. Healen was lazy and self-centered with delusions of grandeur and no conscience. He remembered Rocco laughing that if Healen thought it would advance him in the organization, he would kill his own mother. Vito knew Healen's mother and commented at the time that if he did kill her, it wouldn't have been a great loss to anyone.

Muscatelli's conversation on the phone was succinct. He had a job for Healen. He was to come to see him immediately to receive the details. Never make deals over telephone lines. There were always extra ears listening. Paranoia was a virtue and a valuable asset in Vito's line of business. Foolish people, arrogant people, careless people too often forgot. The papers were full of senators, congressmen, governors, ball players, Hollywood stars as well as common criminals who forgot and left a phone trail. Vito Muscatelli was no fool. He would tell Healen directly what he wanted done. He would give him a description of Cavanaugh's car, the route Cavanaugh was to take, the time he was planning to leave, and specific instructions to drive him off the road in the Pocono Mountains of Pennsylvania. It was to look like an accident. But Healen was to make sure when he left the scene that Cavanaugh was dead.

* * *

39

Havana, Cuba

That night, Jack Bennis and María Izabelle Melendez sat with Diego Velasquez in his small living room. An electric fan buzzed softly in the corner circulating the warm evening air. On the plain wooden coffee table before them there was a large map of the city of Havana.

All afternoon María Izabelle and Diego had tried to convince Bennis that he was safer where he was and that they were willing to help in whatever way they could. Bennis finally agreed. And now he reviewed again with them some of the details that led to someone trying to kill him. He explained there was only one name on the list the New York mob boss had prepared for Howard Stevens whom he was able to contact. The name was Frank Santacroce. The other names were of people who had died or he had been unable to contact.

"I never heard of Santacroce," María Izabelle said. "It's not a Cuban name."

"You're right," the priest agreed. "It's Italian. Literally it means 'holy cross.' He goes by the name Francisco Santacruz here. When I contacted him in an attempt to get to meet him, he hung up on me. I asked around a little about him and was told he is married to a tall blonde who wears too much make-up and too much jewelry."

"Careful, Padre," Diego warned. "You are venturing into uncharted female waters with opinions like that."

"You're right. Let me stick to the facts."

"Where does this Santacroce or Santacruz live?" María Izabelle asked. "And what does he do for a living?"

"I don't know what he does for a living, but he lives in what I would call a mansion. His house is a large well-kept three story white concrete house in Vedado. There is a black iron gate in front with two tall palm trees on either side of the entrance. At first I thought it was a bank or an office building. Maybe it was at one time. There are about seventeen concrete steps leading up to the front door. The portico in front of a large intricately carved wooden door is supported by two Romanesque columns on either side of the door. There is a small terrace over the tall front door jutting out from one of the upstairs rooms. I noticed bars on the bottom level windows, but none on the upper floors."

"Your friend Señor Santacruz lives in a well-to-do area," Diego said studying the map. "During the 1950's, the Vedado area was controlled by mobsters. They built the Nacional del Cuba Hotel and the Riviera. Liquor, gambling, prostitution were rampant. People like Meyer Lanski and Lucky Luciano ruled the area, and the casinos in their large luxurious hotels lured tourists from the United States and all over the world. When Fidel Castro took over he clamped down on them and most of them ran for their lives. The atmosphere in Vedado today is nothing like it once was. Now it is a peaceful area with tree lined streets, elegant homes, high-rise hotels, and commercial office buildings."

Bennis stood up and stretched. He felt the pull from the wound in his side. "Santacruz is not an old man. I doubt he was even born when Castro came to power. Would it be possible that the mob is trying to reestablish its influence in Cuba now that Castro is no longer president or commander-in-chief?"

"I have lived long enough and seen more than enough to say that nothing is impossible."

"Santacruz is the only one I know who would have contact with the man in New York who sent people to kill me. If I am to be of any use here, I will need to confront him."

"No!" María Izabelle exclaimed. "That would be suicide. He obviously has power and you are just one man."

Jack Bennis smiled. "Relax, precious lady. I do not plan to march into the jaws of the lion unprepared. All afternoon you both insisted that you wanted to help. Well, now you can—if you are still willing."

"What do you need, Padre?" Diego asked.

"Information. Can you find out for me details of who this Santacroce or Santacruz person is and what he does for a living? Can you check out the area around his house to see if he has established some security system? And, most important of all, can you do this without drawing attention to yourself?"

"I can use the research materials in the University library to check on Señor Santacruz," Diego offered.

"And I will check out the house and the area for you tomorrow. I know it fairly well. It is not too far from the Plaza de la Revolución where President Castro used to address hundreds of thousands of Cubans from a podium in front of the Memorial of José Martí."

"Thank you, my friends. That is all we need to do at this time. But please be careful." He extended his hand to Professor Velasquez and they exchanged strong handshakes. Then he turned his hand to María Izabelle. She ignored it and instead gave him a warm, wet, lingering kiss on his lips.

* * *

40

Brooklyn, New York

Morty Goldberg had worried about Cavanaugh all afternoon. Coming home to his wife and family did not relieve the concern. When the children were finally in bed, Goldberg tried calling Cavanaugh, but there was no answer. He let it ring and ring, but there was no answer and no answering machine to take a message. Cavanaugh's idea to go to Cuba was madness.

All afternoon people had been asking for him. One particular reporter kept calling asking to speak with him. He wanted to know where he was and what Cavanaugh knew about Meredith Perez. The calls kept coming throughout the afternoon from different newspapers and television stations. Someone had leaked information about the blood on Cavanaugh's jacket and the hair found on Luca Andrassy. None of this information had been released to the press, but they knew. Someone was obviously supplying tips to the media. Goldberg knew this was not a good time for Cavanaugh to suddenly disappear.

Before he went to bed himself, Goldberg decided to try calling Francesca Arden. If he couldn't convince Cavanaugh to change his mind, maybe Cavanaugh's girl friend could.

Francesca picked up the phone on the first ring.

"I'm sorry to call this late, Ms. Arden. This is Detective Morty Goldberg, Tom's partner."

"Yes, of course," she said. "I remember you. What's wrong?"

"Nothing really. It's just that Tom has this crazy idea about trying to find his brother in Cuba, and I've been trying to talk him out of it. I thought maybe you could do what I haven't been able to do."

"I wish I could, Morty. I've been talking to him all evening trying to do the same thing. He is as stubborn as a mule."

"Isn't there anything we can do to knock some sense into his thick skull?"

Francesca laughed. "You've got it right, Morty. He is impossible. I don't know how you work with him. But I finally convinced him that I should go along with him."

"You? No, Francesca. Please don't get yourself involved this *mish-mosh*!"

She laughed again. "*Mish-mosh*—that means a really fouled up mess, doesn't it? Tom always tells me how you throw in Jewish words."

Goldberg sighed. "It's Yiddish, not Jewish . . . ."

"I know. I know. I just wanted to see your reaction."

"Ms. Arden, is there anything I can do to prevent you two from going?"

"I'm afraid not, Morty. Except maybe say a prayer for both of us. I'm flying up to Canada tomorrow to meet Tom."

Goldberg saw how the two of them were so much alike. There was no sense talking anymore. He had tried his best. "I definitely will pray for you both. May you both go with God and may he deliver you from all evils. Please be careful."

"Thank you, Morty. We will. And you take care of yourself, too."

When Goldberg hung up, he felt a tiredness he had never felt before. God help them, he thought. They don't know what they are getting themselves into.

* * *

VI

That which does not kill us
makes us stronger.

Friedrich Nietzsche

SATURDAY

41

Brooklyn, New York

Cavanaugh traveled light. Some underwear, a toothbrush, toothpaste, razor, another pair of trousers, and some socks. Throwing a few extra shirts into a green duffle bag, he wondered if he were forgetting something. His gun and badge were locked in a metal box under his bed. He checked he had his passport. He didn't know how long he would be there, but he figured if he needed something else he could buy it. He checked his wallet. He hit the ATM the night before and withdrew as much as he could. He would find another one on his way to Canada just to be safe.

Walking out to his car, he thought about meeting Fran in Toronto. He didn't like bringing her along. It might not be safe. But he looked forward to being with her at the same time. He missed her already. He checked he had his passport again and then checked his watch. He was ahead of time. It was 1:55 A.M. Suddenly, he stopped. There was someone at his car. In the darkness it looked like the person was trying to break into "Betsy."

"Hey," he shouted, "what the hell do you think you're doing? Get the hell away from that car!"

"Or what?" the voice replied in silence of the night.

"Or what? I'll show you or what!" He tossed his duffle bag aside and rushed toward his car. Just as he was about to grab the figure at his car, it turned.

"Good morning, Detective."

Cavanaugh's mouth dropped as did his arms. "What the hell are you doing here?" he asked.

"I thought you might like some company," Francesca said.

"But you said you were going to fly."

"I changed my mind."

"I thought you didn't want to drive in my car . . . ."

"I don't, but I want to be with you more."

Cavanaugh stood stunned until Francesca finally said, "Well, are you going to kiss me or just stand there all morning. We have a trip to make. Unless, of course, you want to call it off."

He grabbed her with both arms and held her tightly. He couldn't believe it. There were tears in his eyes when Fran suddenly pulled away. "Hey, big boy, let's not get too excited now or we will never get to Canada. There will be time for this, this afternoon."

"And tonight," he added.

She smiled as he opened the door for her, "Promises . . . promises . . . promises . . . ."

Bouncing back to pick up his bag, he laughed, "Did you know a barnacle has the largest penis of any other animal in the world except, of course, for me in relation to its size!"

"Dream on, lover boy!" she giggled as she buckled her seat belt.

Neither of them saw the black 2006 Jeep Sportabout parked down the street with its lights out and its motor running.

* * *

42

Staten Island, New York

The phone rang in Vito Muscatelli's hospital room. He rolled over in bed and pretended not to hear it. As he moved onto his left side, pains in his back stiffened him and his right foot started to cramp up. Gestas quickly reached for the phone almost knocking the yellow plastic pitcher of ice water onto the floor.

"Yes," he whispered.

"I want to speak to Vito," the voice on the other end demanded.

"Mr. Muscatelli is sleeping right now. Can I take a message?"

"Wake him, numb nuts. I want to talk to him."

Gestas' voice rose and he straightened his massive body as if ready to engage in a fight with the voice on the other end of the phone. "Who the hell do you think you are? I told you he was sleeping!"

Vito turned slowly and opened his eyes. His neck was stiff and the dull, persistent pain in his back spread to his shoulders. His thin fingers grasped the hospital blanket and he tried to lift his head to speak, but his lips were dry and his swollen tongue caught the words like a dangling piece of flypaper.

"Don't get your balls in an uproar, stupid. Tell him Cain Holland wants to talk to him."

"And who the hell is Cain Holland?" Gestas almost shouted into the telephone.

When he heard the name, Vito emitted a sound somewhere between a burp and a cough and motioned to Gestas. "Give me the phone," he whispered hoarsely.

The huge attendant did as instructed.

"Hello. This is Vito. Who did you say you was?"

"It's Holland here. Like the dead fish said, Vito, 'Long time no sea.'"

"Spare me your humor, Cain. What do you want?"

"Man, you're a little testy now, aren't you? Just like the old Vito."

"I am an old and sick man; Cain. It is still dark out. What do you want?"

"I'm bored. There's not much business around anymore. The old guys are either dead or in jail."

"Most of the ones not in jail have you to thank for, how you say, their 'dirty sleep.'"

"I prefer 'dirt nap,' but as I remember it, you had a lot to do with that too."

"Why you call now?"

"I told you. I'm bored. I grew to like my old job. Now I have to go out and find my own business. It's like I'm free lancing now. But it's kind of boring. There's no real challenge. I enjoy the hunt and the chase."

"So why you call me?"

"You're one of the only ones left who may have need for my unique services."

Vito motioned to Gestas to raise the bed as the pain in his back worsened. He remembered Cain Holland well—a sadistic, cold-blooded killer with no conscience who enjoyed torturing victims before killing them. But Holland was truly the best Vito had ever hired, both reliable and efficient. Vito thought for a moment and then admitted, "You should have called me yesterday. I had a job for you. But I farmed it out."

Holland answered, "So I'm a day late and a dollar short, is that it? Have no fear, Cain's here if things don't work out as you planned."

Vito Muscatelli coughed and remembered the priest. If Tony Healen succeeded in killing Cavanaugh, there was still the priest. Bennis, he had learned, had proved to be a more difficult target than expected. "How can I get in touch with you? I just may need you."

"Is this really Vito Muscatelli? The old Vito I knew would know better than to ask that question. There are people who like to listen to other people's conversations. I think you need a good blow job to clear the cobwebs out of your head."

Vito smiled in spite of himself. No one else would dare talk to him like that.

"When will you know?'

"This afternoon if all goes well."

"Good. I'll be by to see you. *Cioa.*"

And the phone went dead.

* * *

43

Brooklyn, New York

When Goldberg came to work Saturday morning he realized he had forgotten his lunch. He almost always brought his own lunch. Cavanaugh's leaving bothered him. It was stupid, foolish, impetuous, reckless. But it was done. He looked over at his desk and saw the note Cavanaugh had left for him. He hesitated, but knew he had to get it over with and opened the envelope. There in neatly blocked capital letters Cavanaugh left his message.

> DEAR MORTY,
>
> I HATE DOING THIS TO YOU, BUT I REALLY HAVE TO GET AWAY. NO USE TRYING TO REACH ME. THE LESS YOU KNOW RIGHT NOW, THE BETTER THINGS WILL BE FOR ALL OF US. TELL THE LIEUTENTANT I AM TAKING SOME TIME OFF THAT I HAVE COMING TO ME. TELL HIM SOMETHING CAME UP AND I DIDN'T HAVE TIME TO GO THROUGH NORMAL CHANNELS (LIKE I EVER DO!). TAKE CARE, MORTY, AND GET THIS GUY BEFORE HE HURTS ANYBODY ELSE. I'M COUNTING ON YOU, PARTNER. I'LL KEEP IN TOUCH.
>
> TOM

Without Cavanaugh around to bother him, Goldberg felt a strange, unfamiliar, uncomfortable silence in the room. He needed to show the note to the Lieutenant.

"Goldberg," a voice called out to him. It was Lieutenant Bradley. "Where is Cavanaugh?"

"I don't exactly know, sir. Is there anything I can do?"

"Yes. The forensic report of the blood on Cavanaugh's jacket came back," he said walking toward Goldberg. "And it isn't that fat reporter's."

Goldberg frowned. "I don't understand, Lieutenant."

"Neither do I. Did any of you touch the body?"

"No, sir. We walked around it, but we left the touching to the lab boys."

"Was there blood on the walls?"

"No, sir. The blood was primarily on the victim's clothes and we didn't go near her except to get the note."

"Who found the note?"

"Officer Perez."

"What about Cavanaugh? Did he come in contact with the body?"

"No, sir. He came there late after the body had been found and the note discovered."

Bradley pounded the file in his hand into his other hand like a baseball player. He looked straight at Goldberg and said, "Then, Detective, can you tell me why the blood on Cavanaugh's jacket is that of the victim, Crystal May?"

* * *

44

Abington Township, Pennsylvania

It was still dark when Cavanaugh and Francesca pulled into a rest stop along the highway. Healen, who had been following them discretely since they left Brooklyn, pulled past their car and waited with lights off by the exit ramp. He figured they were stopping for an early breakfast and a cup of coffee. He came prepared. He looked at his watch. He didn't think old man Muscatelli would mind if he knocked the guy off a little early so he could make it back to Freehold for the afternoon races.

He didn't know who the broad was in the car with him, but that didn't matter. He didn't know who the guy was either. All he knew was that this was an easy payday. The guy was supposed to be alone. He wondered only briefly who the broad was. It didn't really matter. When he drove them off the cliff, Muscatelli would get two for the price of one.

Tony Healen scratched his head with one hand and shoveled half of a foot long tuna fish Subway hero with all the trimmings into his mouth with the other. Pieces of onion, pepper, and black olives fell on his lap while oil and vinegar dripped onto his shirt mingling with falling dandruff flakes. He didn't seem to mind. When he finished half of the sandwich, he tossed the wrapping in the back of his car, and it disappeared in a rubble of other trash.

He had parked his Jeep Sportabout at the end of the rest stop where he could get a good view of the cars exiting onto the highway. He reached down to the cooler he kept on the passenger seat alongside of him and pulled out a Budweiser. This job was going to be a pushover. All he had to do was force a car off the road and then make sure the driver was dead. Following the guy's car was a snap. How many old repainted U.S. mail cars were there?

After waiting by the exit ramp for fifteen minutes he began to wonder what happened to them. He opened another beer and laughed to himself, "Let the condemned man and his bimbo eat a hearty last meal." He checked the piece of paper on the dashboard with his intended victim's license plate number. This was going to be easy.

A half hour and two more beers later, a problem arose. He had to pee. He couldn't give up checking the car so he had to improvise. Never taking his eyes off the road, he reached into the back and felt around for a container. The best he could come up with was an old Starbucks coffee cup. It would have to do. This was an emergency. Carefully he unzipped his fly and made the necessary arrangements.

Keeping an eye on his side view mirror, he saw Cavanaugh's car leaving at the same time he realized the coffee cup was leaking and warm piss was flowing into his lap. "Shit!" he cried spilling the entire cup as a steady stream of seemingly unending urine showered down on his shoes and the brake pedal. "Shit! Shit! Shit!" he repeated, pounding the steering wheel with each expletive. He threw the empty cup out the window and accelerated after Cavanaugh and Francesca, vowing aloud, "This bastard is a dead man!"

* * *

45

Healen accelerated down the exit ramp onto Route 81 North. Traffic was light in the early Saturday morning darkness. An occasional tractor trailer would plow along the dark highway on its way to some unknown destination. Ahead of him he saw the beat up former U.S. Mail delivery car moving along at a steady 50 mph. It was still dark, but over the mountains in the distance the early morning sun was trying to make an appearance. Now was the optimum time to strike. They were climbing a long hill. When they reached the top, Healen would make his move. He shortened the distance between them. His wet pants felt cold and the car smelled of a combination of beer and urine. Healen cursed and hit the accelerator.

As they reached the crest of the large hill, Healen saw a steep, winding decline. He was only feet away from his intended victim's car now. He pulled out and side-swiped Cavanaugh's car. "Betsy" swerved to the right. Healen eased up and then accelerated again. He hit the left front wheel. Cavanaugh attempted to spin into a donut to try to avoid the Jeep Sportabout and hit the back right rear fender of Healen's car. Both cars spun around in the darkness heading straight for the edge of the road and a long drop into the trees along the side of the mountain. Healen cursed again and accelerated into the side of Cavanaugh's car. Pushed from the side, "Betsy" went over the side of the road and toppled down the hill bouncing off birch and maple trees as it went. But the force of the collision sent Healen off the road too. He hit the brake with his wet foot, but it was too late. He followed Cavanaugh down the steep embankment until he was stopped abruptly by a large oak tree.

When the dust settled, Cavanaugh found himself strapped upside down in a thicket of shrubs. He looked over at Francesca. She was conscious but her head was bleeding from a wound on the right side of her head.

"Are you okay?" he asked.

"What happened?" she said.

Cavanaugh loosen his seat belt and eased himself out to help Fran. "Some idiot hit us and drove us off the road."

"Was he drunk?" she asked climbing out of the car. "Betsy" hissed and sizzled and smoked.

"I don't know," Cavanaugh said looking over at the Sportabout which was bent around a tree. "Let's go find out. It looks like he took the worst of the ride."

When they reached Healen's car, it was on fire and he was unconscious. He wasn't wearing his seatbelt and his head had hit the windshield. The car smelled like a brewery. The force of the collision with the tree had exploded Healen's cache of Buds. The steering wheel had pinned him into his seat, and Cavanaugh had to pry him out as the flames increased. Reaching in over the steering wheel, he saw a piece of paper clinging to the broken dashboard. He stopped. It was Cavanaugh's license plate. He knew immediately, this wasn't an accident. Someone had deliberately tired to kill him.

Cavanaugh felt like leaving his attacker in the car to barbeque, but pulled him forcefully out. He had questions to ask him. "Call 911," he said turning to Francesca. And the memory of the shooting in the Deli returned.

Francesca found her phone and discovered it had somehow been preset. There was only one number she could dial. She dialed her grandfather—Vito Muscatelli.

* * *

46

Brooklyn, New York

Morty Goldberg's stomach was growling. He still had not shown the note to Lieutenant Bradley. Why was he hesitating? Suddenly, he heard his name being screamed from the Lieutenant's office. "Goldberg, get the f—in here right away!"

"Yes, sir," Goldberg said straightening his tie at the Lieutenant's door.

"Shut the f—in door and get in here!" Lieutenant Bradley's face was red and Goldberg could see a slight scar over his left eye. Standing next to him was Patrolman Bill Midrasic.

"Now, cut the bull shit! Where the hell is Cavanaugh?" demanded Bradley.

Goldberg handed the Lieutenant the note that Cavanaugh left. Bradley read it in silence. Then he put the note down and walked to his window. He stared out the window for some time without saying a word. When he turned, he spoke directly to Goldberg in a soft voice. "Detective, we have a crisis situation developing here."

Goldberg listened.

"Cavanaugh is suddenly gone. The blood on his jacket is the victim's who he supposedly never came in contact with. And, I don't know if you see what I see in this note, but it looks a lot like the same writing on the notes left on the two victims."

"Tom and I talked about that, Lieutenant. Handwriting is inconclusive. He even admitted it looked a lot like his writing. It doesn't prove anything."

"What about the hair on the victim?"

"It's human hair, but we don't have a match. Monreale says if we give him something to compare it with, he can tell us if it is a match."

"Why don't you check it against Cavanaugh's hair?" asked Bill Midrasic.

Goldberg ignored the question and Bradley glared at Midrasic. Midrasic looked down and shut up.

Bradley sat down. "I don't like the way this case is turning. I've got a bad feeling."

Goldberg squirmed in his chair. "We have a couple of other leads, Lieutenant. I left you our report on Officer Perez's apartment last night."

"I saw it, but I didn't get to read it yet."

"There are some items in the report which could be very significant."

"And have you questioned Perez?"

"Negative, sir. We can't find her. She didn't report for work and nobody seems to have seen her."

Bradley shook his head. "Two police officers disappear and we can't find them? What kind of a Mickey Mouse outfit are we running?"

"Cavanaugh didn't disappear, Lieutenant," Goldberg said. "He left the note. He'll be back."

Lieutenant Bradley leaned forward, "From your mouth to God's ears. I realize he's your partner and all, but did you realize the week after the Inquest into the shooting in the bodega, Cavanaugh took off. During that week, when he was not here, both Crystal May and Luca Andrassy were murdered. The blood of one victim is on his jacket and his writing looks pretty similar to that which was left at the crime scenes."

Goldberg stared straight ahead.

"I don't have to tell you, Detective, your partner is in deep shit! Now get the hell out of here and find something to prove he's innocent!"

* * *

47

Staten Island, New York

When Muscatelli received the call, he immediately called 911 and gave the operator the approximate location of his granddaughter. She wasn't supposed to be in the car. Why had she changed her plans? This wasn't supposed to happen. Now Healen not only injured his granddaughter, but he presented a possible link to him that needed to be eliminated. Now he had a job for Cain Holland. Cain would be able to "quiet" Healen and Cavanaugh at the same time. He threw the plastic picture of water against the wall. "Amateurs!" he swore.

Someone appeared at the door. "Is there something wrong?" a familiar voice asked.

Vito looked up and smiled. "You just in time," he said. "I have a job for you, Cain."

* * *

48

Brooklyn, New York

Goldberg went over and over the files on the murders. All bodies were found on Staten Island. All were female. One earring missing. Throats cut. Wrists dislocated. Maple syrup on the bodies. What did the murders have to do with Cavanaugh? Perez kept clippings of all the articles related to Cavanaugh's Inquest as well as the murders. Why? Did she still have love for him? Or was it hate?

He went back to the clippings and noticed the early ones before the murder weren't actual clippings. They were downloaded computer copies of articles from the newspapers. He stared at the papers before him. What made Merry Perez go back to old newspaper archives to pull up records of the bodega shootings and the Inquest? Something didn't fit. He was missing something. If Cavanaugh were here they could bounce ideas off each other. But Cavanaugh wasn't here.

Frustrated and hungry, Goldberg finally took his notes and went out for an early lunch. But it was Saturday and his favorite place to buy a sandwich, Mittleman's Supermarket on 16th Street was closed. He walked through Brooklyn's neighborhoods. He passed quiet streets with women in dark coats holding hands of little children whose curly side locks blew in the wind and men in black coats wearing big hairy round hats and white shawls decorated with black or blue stripes.

Crossing one street, he seemed to enter another country. Here he passed busy, crowded streets with Asian men and women rushing to and from fruit markets. Some women held umbrellas to block the morning sun. Brooklyn was an amazing place, he thought.

He remembered Cavanaugh asking why the Jewish men wore "rats on their heads" and the little boys all had long bangs, which he alternatively called "iskabibles" and "dingleberries." It made them look like girls, he said. Goldberg tried to explain that they were orthodox Jews from a Hasidic sect and they wore traditional clothing from the old world including the round fur hat which was called a *shtreimel.* He told him the long side locks on the children were called *payot* and they were part of the Holiness Code of the Torah which forbids shaving of the corners of the head. Cavanaugh, he recalled, shrugged his shoulders and said, "Whatever rocks your boat."

Resisting the temptation to go to Dunkin' Donuts or Burger King, Goldberg stopped in a grocery store on 65th Street and bought three apples, a banana, and a Diet Coke. Armed with his "lunch" he continued walking up 65th Street until he spotted Regina Pacis Roman Catholic Church. The doors were open and he decided to go in and use the quiet darkness to think and maybe even pray.

The church was dark and empty. Down the long aisle he saw a huge cross with a figure nailed into it. It made him nervous looking at a symbol of the atrocities man is capable of doing. Although he did not believe Jesus was the Messiah, he did believe he was a good man who deserved better than he got.

He settled himself in the rear of the church behind a large stone pillar and looked over his notes. The church was cool and the smell of incense and dampness prevailed. He took one of his apples out and began eating while reading. Something on Merry Perez's wall of clippings did not fit. He reviewed them again—one at a time. The shootings in the bodega. The obituary of Maria DeFillipo. The long, harrowing Inquest. The murder of Crystal May. The fight with the reporter. The murder of Luca Andrassy.

Something didn't fit. Looking back at the altar he noticed an assortment of flowers being removed by a young man. He wondered where he was taking them. There must have been a service a little while before he came in. He didn't see any rice or other signs of a wedding, so he concluded it must have been a funeral. The arrangements somehow looked more like funeral flowers than wedding flowers. He thought of Cavanaugh and their arguments about the merits of Jewish and Christian funeral services. Then it clicked.

"Hey, you there! What the hell do you think you're doing there?" The voice came from the darkness behind him. The man looked to be in his fifties and had blue overalls and a tool belt wrapped around a large beer belly. He carried a hamper in one hand which he pointed at Goldberg. "You don't eat in a God-damn church, feller!"

As the man moved closer he spotted Goldberg's yarmulke. "What the hell?" he exclaimed. "What the hell are *you* doing here? Don't you have enough of your own places all over the God-damn place? You don't belong here, you little Jew bastard! Now get the hell out of here before I call the cops or bash your beanie into your head!"

Goldberg picked up his bag of fruit and his papers and quietly moved out of the pew and into the bright morning sun. "So much for Christian charity," he thought as he headed up to Leif Eriksson Park where he could sit in the sunshine and pursue the path he imagined Merry Perez might have been following. The more he thought about it, the more convinced he became that Merry Perez was on the trail of the killer.

* * *

49

Carbondale, Pennsylvania

When they arrived at Huckvale Medical Center, Healen was taken immediately into their trauma center. Francesca and Cavanaugh waited in the emergency room for hours before a nurse, who appeared to be a Weight Watcher Failure, cleaned and bandaged Francesca's cut. It was close to noon when a gray haired doctor came out to greet them and examine them himself. He was thin, and older than the rest of the staff, but obviously in better shape than the rest of the staff, too.

"Looks like you two are the lucky ones," he began. "I'm Dr. Gianvito. Most people up here call me Dr. G. because they can't pronounce Italian names. How do you feel?"

Cavanaugh asked, "How is the other guy doing, doc?"

"I can't tell you that, friend. It's HIPPA regulations."

"Forget HIPPA. I'm a New York City Detective," Cavanaugh said.

"You're not in New York City now, son. You're in the Clarke's Summit area of Pennsylvania. Let's get you two looked at first and then we can deal with your friend in there."

"He tried to drive us off the road."

Dr. G. winked at Francesca. "Looks like he succeeded."

Fran smiled, and the doctor directed his attention to the cut on her forehead. "The cut on your forehead is small. It doesn't require stitches and it should heal nicely. But that's a nasty bump you took there, young lady. You probably didn't realize it, but you also have a large contusion on your belly caused by your seat belt. It probably saved your life, but I think it would be a good idea if you spent the night here in the hospital for observation."

"Well, I feel a little bit nauseous, but is it really necessary for me to stay in the hospital?"

"I'm a doctor, young lady, and I would prefer to be sure you're okay. You may have some internal injuries that aren't apparent right now."

She looked at Cavanaugh. "Maybe you'd better," he said.

"And what about you, big boy? How do you feel?" Dr. G. asked.

"I feel fine. Take care of her. When can I talk with the other guy?"

"He's in pretty bad shape. I think we had better let the police handle this."

"But I am the police!"

"You're the New York City police. Up here that counts for as much as deer crap."

"You don't understand, Doc . . . ."

"I understand perfectly, son. You're the one who doesn't understand. People up here don't take to city folk telling them what to do. Relax a bit. We may work a little slower than you are used to, but we get the job done. Your friend's not talking to anyone right now anyway. He's unconscious and in intensive care. Now how about me sending you for a few precautionary X-rays? You took quite a big spill back there."

Cavanaugh stood up and stretched. His back ached and his right knee hurt, but he said, "No thanks, Doc. Take care of Fran and I'll wait."

Dr. G. looked over at Fran and winkled again. "She's a fine looking woman, son. Do you trust me to take care of her?"

"Trust me, Doc. You better take good care of her!" He smiled at both of them. "I've got a few things to take care of now anyhow. I'll be back in a little while."

As Cavanaugh limped out of the room, Dr. G. turned to Fran and said, "Is he always this stubborn?"

"You haven't seen anything yet," she replied.

* * *

50

Brooklyn, New York

When Goldberg returned to work after lunch, his feet and back ached, but he thought he was onto a clue to catch the murderer thanks to Officer Perez. Entering the station house, however, he sensed a somberness, almost a sadness in the air. He looked around. Something was wrong. He could smell it as clearly as a clove of garlic or the incense in the church. Officers avoided making eye contact with him. When he arrived at his desk, there was a message there to see Lieutenant Bradley immediately. Walking into the Lieutenant's office he wondered what was going on.

"Have a seat, Goldberg," the Lieutenant said. He seemed calmer than this morning.

Goldberg sat.

"Where's Cavanaugh?" the Lieutenant asked again.

"I don't exactly know, Lieutenant. He said he was going to take a few days off."

"He didn't say anything to me."

"I gave you the note he left on his desk last night." Bradley looked at the note on his desk. Goldberg got up to leave. He looked back at the Lieutenant. There was something else. "Is that all, Lieutenant?" he asked.

Bradley stood, read the letter again, and then walked to his window. "You and Cavanaugh went to Officer Perez's apartment yesterday. What did you find?"

"It's all in my report, Lieutenant."

Bradley turned, "I read the report, Detective. I want to hear it in your own words. What did you see?"

"There were clippings taped to the walls from various newspapers about the two murders."

"Anything else?"

Goldberg clasped his hands. "There were some clippings of the incident with the reporter . . . ."

"What else?"

"There were clippings of Tom's shooting in the bodega . . . and clippings of the Inquest . . . . There were also clippings of the obituary of the woman who was killed in the shooting."

"What do you think about all of this, Detective?"

"We need to find Officer Perez and ask her some questions. She found the notes on the two victims and apparently some years ago she had a relationship with Tom . . . ."

"She had a relationship with Cavanaugh?"

"Yes, but that was a long time ago. They broke up years ago."

"Where is Cavanaugh now, Detective?"

"I told you, Lieutenant. I, er, I don't exactly know."

"Bull shit! You're his partner! You and he have been working this case. Where is he now?"

"I honestly don't know, sir. He told me he was only getting in the way in this investigation and he needed to get away. I think when we find Officer Perez we will be able to get some answers."

"We found Officer Perez while you were out."

"Great, Lieutenant. When can I question her?"

"You can't."

"But, sir, we need to find out why she was keeping those clippings and where she was?"

"She's not talking."

"Let me see her, Lieutenant, I think I can get her to talk."

Bradley sat down at his desk. "That really would be something. In fact, it would be an f—ing miracle, Goldberg. Officer Perez is in the morgue. She's our third victim."

Goldberg felt a sick feeling rising in his stomach. The more Lieutenant Bradley talked, the stronger the feeling became. Meredith Perez's body was found behind the dog run at Wolfe's Pond Park on the South Shore of Staten Island. Like the others, her throat had been slit, and her wrists dislocated. One diamond stud from her left ear was missing. There was maple syrup again. This time an army of red ants was swarming all over her body when it was found. And the note was different too.

TOMMY CAVANAUGH PUDDING N PIE,
KISSED BUBBLES AND MADE HER CRY
WHEN SHE CAME OUT TO PLAY
SHE JUST HAD TO DIE
AND TOMMY CAVANAUGH RAN AWAY.

When he came back to his desk, he read the preliminary coroner's report. Traces of hair similar to those on Luca Andrassy were found on Meredith Perez. But reading the bottom line of the report, Goldberg felt a nausea rising to this throat. "Bubbles" Perez was pregnant.

* * *

51

Carbondale, Pennsylvania

Cavanaugh limped down the corridor of Huckvale Medical Center looking for a pay phone. He had rummaged through the wallet of the man who had driven him off the road. Anthony Healen was his name. He lived in Brooklyn and weighed at least 250 lbs. But who was he? Why had he deliberately tried to run him off the side of the cliff?

It used to be that one could find a payphone almost anywhere. But not in our modern age when most people carried cell phones. But Cavanaugh wasn't most people. The midday sun was shinning brightly when he walked out of the emergency room exit. He walked two blocks until he saw a Mobil gas station and found a phone that took coins. He knew who he had to call.

"Detective Goldberg, Homicide, how can I help you?"

"Hi, Morty. I was hoping I would get you in today."

"Tom, where the hell are you?"

"I've had a little accident, Morty, and I was wondering if you could help me."

"All hell's broken loose around here. Everyone is looking for you. What do you mean you had a little accident?"

"Some clown by the name of Anthony Healen tried to run us off the road."

"Who's Anthony Healen and what do you mean 'we'?"

"That's what I'd like you to find out. He had my license plate number on his dashboard so it was intentional. I'd like you to check him out for me. Right now he's unconscious and in the hospital. They won't let me talk to him. As soon as he comes to, I want to ask him a few questions."

"Sure, Tom, I'll do that right away. Where are you and who else is with you?"

"Fran's with me. She hit her head on the side window and she's got a huge bruise from the seat belt. They're keeping her here overnight to check on her."

"I thought she was flying to meet you . . . ."

"Yeah, she told me you called. Apparently, she changed her mind. You know women. She showed up at my car this morning. I think she's going to be okay, but I just want to make sure."

"Where the hell are you, Tom?"

Cavanaugh looked out the gas station window. There was very little traffic. The smell of oil and gasoline surrounded him. "I'm in a little gas station in some small town someplace. It's probably better that you don't know."

The operator interrupted the call to ask for more money for more time.

"I've got to go now, Morty. I've got to make arrangements for another car and see how Fran is. I'll call you later to check on Healen. Thanks. Cheers."

"Wait! Tom, don't hang up. I've got to tell you about Merry . . . ." But the line had already gone dead.

* * *

52

Brooklyn, New York

"Detective Morton Goldberg?" two voices asked in chorus behind him as he sat staring at the phone in his hand. Goldberg flinched and then instinctively covered the files on his desk. He turned to see two people in charcoal gray suits standing behind him. One was a man and the other a woman although they looked androgynous with their matching suits and aviator sunglasses. He would have recognized them immediately as F.B.I. agents even if he had not met them briefly once before.

"Agents Hitchcock and Greene, I presume," Goldberg said rising to meet them and extending his hand.

They nodded in unison, ignored the offered handshake, and wasted no time. "We have reason to believe Vito Muscatelli has initiated a 'hit' on your partner Thomas Cavanaugh and his half-brother, Reverend John Bennis."

"What? What are you talking about? Why would he do that? How would you know?"

The man cleared his throat and then spoke, "The National Securities Act has given us some latitude in tapping phone lines. We've been taping Muscatelli's phone lines for some time now."

"Over the past two days," the woman added, "Vito Muscatelli has received calls in the nursing home in which he resides from two people. One was his granddaughter, Francesca Arden. The other was from a Cain Holland."

"Who the hell is this Cain Holland? I've just been going over a file I received from Interpol about him."

The man spoke this time. "Cain Holland is a known international assassin. No one has ever seen him. He has been rumored to be linked to murders of Muscatelli's associates in Brooklyn and to murders as far away as Sydney, Australia and Berlin, Germany."

"One of his trademarks seems to be slitting the throats of his victims after he has dislocated all their wrists."

Goldberg turned and looked at the files on his desk. He could feel his stomach tightening. "And he takes one earring from his female victims?"

"Correct," the woman agent stated, "and he places an earring at the scene of all his male victims."

"But why would he want to do in Tom and his brother?" Goldberg asked.

"We think Muscatelli believes Cavanaugh's half-brother was in some way connected to the death of his son."

The other F.B.I. agent added, "And so do we."

Goldberg scratched his head and felt his yarmulke. "What," he almost shouted, "are you both *meshuggeneh*! We closed that case." He added, choosing his words carefully, "All the evidence pointed to your old friend Howard Stevens. He had video and audio tapes of Rocco Muscatelli in his possession; his fingerprints were on the weapon used to kill both Muscatelli and his pal Malentendo. And we linked him to a number of other murders."

"We know what you said."

Goldberg looked over at Cavanaugh's empty desk. "But why Tom?"

"He's Bennis' half-brother. Muscatelli thinks the priest had something to do with his son's death."

"It's the old eye for an eye theme, Detective. You remember it, I'm sure. He killed my son. I kill his brother."

"And then, I kill him," added the woman as she adjusted her gold wired sunglasses. She hesitated a moment and then added, "We think Muscatelli may have already hired someone else to get Cavanaugh."

"You are full of surprises, Agent. Why don't you do something about it?"

"We can't. Three calls were placed from his room in the last forty-eight hours. One was to his granddaughter, Francesca Arden. One was to a Dr. Anthony Benevento, a respected psychologist with lingering ties to organized crime, and the other was to a Tony Healen, a small time wannabe. Healen usually makes his living as a bookie and is rumored to be involved in race track fixings. He was arrested once on a concealed weapons charge and spent some time in Rikers. He has also been picked up a number of times for intoxication and disorderly conduct."

"Why didn't you arrest him and this Holland guy?"

"Because we have nothing definitive to go on. The comments on the tapes are inconclusive. They both said they were coming to see Muscatelli in person. He would want to make the arrangements personally, and not over the telephone lines."

"Healen's already been to see Muscatelli. He came before we could fully set up our surveillance team. We lost him in traffic on the Verrazano Bridge after he left the nursing home."

"Beautiful," Goldberg muttered. "That's our government for you. I guess if you can send nuclear devices to Taiwan instead of helicopter batteries, we can't expect you to follow a car in traffic."

Hitchcock and Greene ignored the comment. The female agent added, "We have the nursing home staked out completely now, but other than the doctor, his granddaughter, and a variety of nurses and aides, no one else has been to see him."

"Hold on, you guys," Goldberg said raising his hands. "Let's take a step back. You're going too fast. We don't have any idea where Cavanaugh's brother is. After we apprehended Stevens, the priest just disappeared . . . ."

"He's in Cuba," the man stated.

"What? How did . . . how do you know?"

"Tapes, Detective. And Cavanaugh is planning on going there to meet him."

Goldberg suddenly became aware that his mouth was open. Slowly he brought his hand to his mouth before speaking. "And how did you learn that?"

The woman spoke first, "Tapes again, Detective. Francesca Arden called her grandfather to ask for help in getting her to Cuba. She's going with Cavanaugh."

"What? You can't be serious. Cavanaugh wouldn't let her go—even if it were true."

"We're not here to argue, Detective. We came to warn Cavanaugh. He's in danger."

"Where is he?"

Goldberg looked again over at Cavanaugh's empty desk and at the phone he had just replaced. He mistrusted the two androgynous federal agents and didn't want to give them any information. "Er, he had some vacation time coming. I think he took it."

"Where can we find him?"

"I honestly don't know. He said he would be calling in every once in a while." Goldberg smiled. "You don't know Cavanaugh, do you? He doesn't believe in cell phones. He has a beeper, but you'll probably find it in the top drawer of his desk over there along with his hair brush. When he goes away, he doesn't want to be disturbed."

The two agents looked at each other as if they had never heard of a person without a cell phone or a pager. Finally, the male spoke, "When he calls in, warn him." He looked at the woman and added, "We're done here."

Goldberg watched as Hitchcock and Greene turned and walked out of the office in step. Then he turned and sat slowly down. He stared at the files of Crystal May, Luca Andrassy, and now Meredith Perez without seeing them. "Some plan the two of them have," he muttered to himself. "They go through the lip service, but they're going to wait until somebody actually tries to kill Cavanaugh. Then they'll step in. Oh, that's a wonderful plan, Agents Hitchcock and Greene. Our government should be real proud of you. But you are a little too late."

* * *

53

Carbondale, Pennsylvania

Cain Holland made good time driving from Staten Island to Pennsylvania. The GPS system in Holland's car showed the fastest route to Huckvale Medical Center. Once there, Holland walked casually down the main corridor with a clipboard in hand. Holland smiled at a chubby security guard who smiled back as if they were good friends from grade school. A middle aged, heavy set nurse, however, stopped Holland on one of the halls and demanded, "May I help you?"

Holland looked around and saw no one else was in the hall and pulled out a knife. "Yes," Holland said directing her into a vacant store room.

Ten minutes later, Holland was walking casually down the corridors of the hospital in a slightly bulky nurse's uniform checking rooms for Tony Healen and Tom Cavanaugh. "Nurse" Holland found Healen first in a private room in the intensive care section of the hospital. Holland was in and out of the room quickly.

When Claire Sonnergren, the nurse on duty, checked her cardiac monitor, she saw the patient in room 137 was in distress. She quickly called a code and rushed to the room as another nurse left. "He's hemorrhaging," the nurse shouted rushing past her. "Call a code!"

The duty nurse responded, "I already did," and entered the room to find patient Anthony Healen covered in blood. When the doctors and other nurses arrived, Claire Sonnergren informed them what she had discovered immediately. Patient Anthony Healen's throat had been slashed through to the bone and a dangling earring had been place on his blood stained pillow.

The hospital staff looked for the mysterious nurse who had left the room as Claire arrived, but there was no trace of her. The chubby security guard, however, did discover something which sent the hospital into an immediate shut down. Another nurse was found in a vacant store room. She was naked and like Healen her throat had been cut. One of her earrings was missing—the right one—the same one found on Healen's pillow.

* * *

54

When Cavanaugh returned from calling Goldberg, he saw local police cars and state troopers surrounding the hospital. A local news team was there with cameras and crew. He stood in the crowd of onlookers wondering what had happened. Some of the hospital staff were in the crowd and had communicated by cell phone with staff inside. The word quickly spread that there had been two murders in the hospital. One of them was a beloved, old, no-nonsense nurse and the other a new patient who had been in a car accident. Cavanaugh's heart skipped a beat. "Who was the patient?" he asked, but no one knew.

He jogged back to the gas station again and called the hospital. It took awhile until someone finally answered. "Can I speak with a patient there named Francesca Arden?" he asked, adding, "It's an emergency."

"We have an emergency here already, Mister, hold your horses. I will see what I can do."

He counted the change in his hand and prayed as he waited for some news of Fran.

Finally, he heard her voice, "Hello. This is Fran Arden . . . ."

"Thank God," he said. "Fran, are you okay?"

"Yes, but there seems to be some problem going on here. There are police and all sorts of people walking up and down the halls and checking each of the rooms."

"You have got to get out of there, Fran."

"But the doctor said . . . ."

"Things have changed, Fran. Healen's been murdered. It's not safe there. We have to go."

"But . . . ."

"Trust me, Fran. Get dressed and sign yourself out of there. I'll meet you down the street at the Mobil Gas Station."

"But . . . ."

"Please, Fran. Just do it. Your life may be in danger and I can't get in there. There are police all over the place."

"But what if they won't let me?"

"Find a way, but get out of there. And hurry. Please."

Cavanaugh hung up and looked out the gas station window. Across the street was a used car dealership. It was a long shot, but he needed wheels. He checked his wallet. He had exactly $952.00. He knew that wouldn't buy him much of a car. Then there was the problem with registration and crossing the border. He needed a car now.

A garage mechanic came in to get a soda from the machine. He was young, no more than eighteen, with blond hair and grease all over him. He had a long thin face with freckles sprinkled freely alongside of the grease. He smiled a gap tooth smile at Cavanaugh as he hit the machine and a Mountain Dew spit out the bottom of the machine. The name stitched in red on his dirty blue shirt was "Larry."

"I see you know how to work machines," Cavanaugh said.

"No sense buying, what you can get for free."

"You're right about that, Larry." He hesitated. "I wonder if you could help me."

The blond mechanic took a long slug of the soda and looked up. "What can I do for you?"

"My car was in an accident and I'm going to need wheels. Do you know anywhere I could rent a car for a couple of days?"

"Not around here, Mister. We ain't a very big town if you haven't noticed."

Cavanaugh sized up the young man. "I'm really pretty desperate, Larry. It would only be for a couple of days. I'm willing to pay $500 cash just to borrow a car for a couple of days. I'd leave my old car here and my credit card."

"$500 cash for a couple of days?"

Cavanaugh reached into his pocket and showed the mechanic his New York City Police I.D. card. "I'm a homicide detective from New York," he said, "and I really need to get to Buffalo by tonight."

"$500 cash for two days?" Larry repeated. "That's a lot of money, Mister."

"Yes. In fact, if you could find a car for me, I'd throw in an extra $100."

"$600 for two days?"

"It's really important, Larry. It's the City's money anyhow," he lied. "I just need to get to Buffalo. It's a police matter. I wish I could tell you about it, but it's classified."

"I have an old car, Mister. It really ain't much, but it will get you to Buffalo and back again."

"Man, if you could help me out, Larry, I really would appreciate it. I think we could both help each other. It would only be for two or three days at the most."

Larry wiped his hands on his dungarees. "I don't know, Mister. My car ain't that much."

"It would just be like I would be borrowing it for a couple of days. I'd bring it back. You can trust me. I'm a cop. You can even keep my Police Benevolent Association card and my credit card as collateral."

Larry crushed the Mountain Dew and threw it in the trash can. Then he turned and abruptly walked back into the garage. Cavanaugh sighed and started to put his I.D. card back into his wallet, when Larry returned with the keys to his car.

"My car's out back, Mister. It's a 1992 Ford Pickup. Burns a bit of oil, but it should make it to Buffalo and back again."

Cavanaugh counted out $600 and handed his PBA card and the registration to "Betsy" to Larry. He kept his credit card. "You don't know how much this means to me. I'm going to try to get you a Good Samaritan Award from New York City for this."

Larry counted the money and handed the keys over to him. Together they walked to the back of the garage and Cavanaugh saw the car for the first time. It was rusted with dents in the front and rear. It looked like it had been blue at one time, but had been hand painted red. The tires were worn and the rear bumper was tied on with rope. He didn't think it was worth $300, let alone $600, but he needed a car.

"Registration's in the glove compartment," Larry said. "Just be careful with her. She does tend to shimmy a bit over 55 mph."

Cavanaugh got into the driver's seat and when he turned the ignition the Pickup backfired and a cloud of black smoke rose behind him.

"I've been meaning to work on that," Larry said.

"No problem," Cavanaugh said driving out of the gas station. He parked across the street and waited for Francesca. He realized he had just been robbed by a young blond mechanic in a small town in Pennsylvania. Larry would have a lot of stories to tell about the city slicker from New York who left him his PBA card and the registration for his car and paid him $600 to borrow his beat up Ford Pickup for a couple of days. What Larry didn't know was that Cavanaugh had another three PBA cards in his wallet, "Betsy" was totaled, and Larry would have to travel to Toronto if he wanted to get his truck back. All in all, Cavanaugh thought it was a good deal for both of them.

* * *

55

Brooklyn, New York

Goldberg studied the files on his desk again. Three murders. All bodies found on Staten Island. All women who had their wrists broken and their throats slit through to the bone. All with one earring missing. All covered with maple syrup. All with notes mentioning Cavanaugh.

Why Cavanaugh? What did he have to do with the murdered victims? He only knew one of them, Meredith Perez. At least, that was what he said. The blood on Cavanaugh's jacket was from the first victim whom he didn't seem to have touched. How did the blood get there then?

There was hair found on the last two victims. Whose hair was it? The Lieutenant had said Cavanaugh was in "deep shit," and Goldberg could clearly see a case developing against him. He looked over at his partner's vacant desk. Why had he left so suddenly? Why had he decided to leave the country in the middle of an investigation? It didn't make sense to Goldberg that Cavanaugh would risk his job and huge fines to try to go to Cuba to find a brother he hardly knew. Was he running away from something?

And now Meredith Perez was dead. She and Cavanaugh had been an item at one time. Could he have continued to see her? Could he be the father of her unborn child? Goldberg's head was pounding. The Lieutenant had said, "Find something to prove him innocent?" He stared at Cavanaugh's vacant desk. What was it he had said to the two F.B.I. agents? "You don't know Cavanaugh . . . . He has a beeper, but you'll probably find it in the top drawer of his desk along with his hair brush." Of course, he thought, the hair brush! It would eliminate Cavanaugh as a suspect and hopefully as the father of Merry's unborn child. He walked over to the desk. He felt a little like a traitor in doubting his partner, but he also felt he needed to clear him as a potential suspect so they could focus on the real killer. Opening the drawer, Goldberg saw Cavanaugh's beeper, a half eaten molding ham and cheese sandwich wrapped in wax paper, a little black notebook, two packs of Trojan condoms, and his hairbrush.

He moved the half-eaten sandwich to the side with his pencil and picked up the hairbrush and the little black book. Going back to his desk, he wrapped the brush in an evidence bag and called Jimmy Monreale in the forensics lab.

"Hey, Jim," he said, "this is Goldberg in Homicide. I wonder if you could do me a favor. I need a comparison of the traces of hair found on Luca Andrassy and Officer Meredith Perez with a hairbrush I found. Can you pick it up and do a fast comparison of it? I'd also like you to check the DNA on the hairbrush to see if it matches that of Officer Perez's fetus."

"Do you know how much work I have down here?" Monreale complained. "Do you think I have nothing better to do than run around as your personal errand boy?"

"I know how hard you work, Jimmy, but we need this information. It's really important."

"It will take some time for a mitochondrial DNA screening. I wouldn't know until I saw the hair if there are even any follicles to check. And then I would have to send the hair samples out for the DNA analysis. That could take weeks! Maybe months! We are not equipped for that here. You would have to get approval for that too because the process is very costly. And to be perfectly honest, I must warn you that it is sometimes not possible to extract DNA fully as there may not be enough tissue present to conduct the examination . . . ."

"Okay, Jim, I understand. How about if I bring the hairbrush down to you, and you just check the hair on it against what was found on the victims. You can do that, can't you?"

"Of course I can. That's no problem. I can microscopically compare the samples side by side. This way it is easy to distinguish hair from different individuals. However, again I do not want to give you false confidence. Although it is extremely uncommon to find hair from different individuals exhibiting the same microscopic characteristics, it is conceivable that . . . ."

"Fine. Thanks. I am bringing the hair brush down now. Do your best to see if it matches the hair on the victims. We'll worry about the DNA analysis later."

Goldberg hung up while Monreale continued talking about the intricacies of hair analysis. With the hairbrush in the evidence bag, he raced down the stairs and into the forensics lab. On the way down, he passed Patrolman

Midrasic on the stairs. Midrasic paused and murmured something under his breath, but Goldberg rushed past him without stopping.

Monreale was still on the phone talking when he entered the lab. "The average person believes that hair can be used as a source of DNA for a paternity test. This could be true, but in the case of hair samples from a brush or a comb, this would be impossible."

"Why?" Goldberg asked from the doorway. "I thought you could determine DNA from hair follicles."

Monreale continued, "Yes, that's what most people think, but unfortunately hair on a brush will not contain viable DNA because of the simple life cycle of hair. As hair ages, its nucleus deteriorates and its DNA becomes so degraded that the hair would be unusable for testing . . . ."

As he was talking he turned and stared at Goldberg at the door. "How did you get here?" he asked. "I'm still talking to you on the phone."

"I thought I could speed things up a bit, Jimmy, if I came straight down here. Can you show me how this microscopic hair analysis works?" Goldberg gently removed the receiver from Monreale's hand and hung it up while giving him the evidence bag with the hairbrush. He stood while Monreale retrieved the hair samples found on the last two murder victims and extracted hair samples from Cavanaugh's hairbrush for comparison.

"I don't like to be rushed, Detective. Microscopic analysis takes time and . . . ."

"I don't have much time, Jimmy. Look under the microscope and tell me if the hair is similar or not."

"Hair analysis can't be rushed, Detective . . . ."

"It's priority," Goldberg lied recalling Cavanaugh. "This came straight from the Mayor's Office."

Jim Monreale placed the hair samples under the microscope without another word. Moving the slides around a bit, he looked up after a few minutes.

"Well?" Goldberg asked. "Do they match or not?"

Monreale smiled, "Detective, I can say unequivocally they are a definite match!"

Goldberg felt his heart skip a beat. The blood of the first victim, Crystal May, had been found on Cavanaugh's jacket, and now his hair had been found on the next two victims, Luca Andrassy and Meredith Perez. Cavanaugh was truly in "deep shit."

* * *

56

Havana, Cuba

When Jack Bennis awoke that morning both Professor Velasquez and his sister-in-law were gone. He fixed a light breakfast for himself and cleaned his wound. Digging the bullet out had been more painful than the shot itself. But he was healing. He said his prayers and read from his breviary yet images of María Izabelle sleeping next to him and then kissing him the night before kept flashing back to him.

It had been a long time since he had slept with a woman. He had been a soldier then. And even now he could describe the room in perfect detail. The dried clay walls, the cracked windows, the dangling 40 watt bulb, the hard, splintered wooden floor. The dampness, the odors of gunpowder, lush forests, and lust. The sounds of that night so many years ago were as real now as the squeaky call of the killdeer bird he heard somewhere close by.

Somehow Bennis felt a kinship with the little olive-brown bird with a white belly and black stripes. The killdeer is a precocial bird and unlike other birds like the robin, it is able to move around right after hatching. It is independent and doesn't rely on its parents to bring it food. Bennis felt he had been on his own almost since birth. From childhood he assumed the role of a leader. Like the killdeer he had become a wanderer capable of blending unobtrusively into his surroundings. When the bird senses a predator to its nest, it tries to deflect attention and often pretends to have a broken-wing to lead the predator away. The killdeer, Bennis liked to think as he listened to its constant squeaky callings, was like him, an adapter and a protector.

But around María Izabelle he felt more like a newly hatched altricial bird—blind and helpless. He didn't know how to react to her. She was so affectionate, so kind, so loving. He had been in fire fights with enemy forces in different countries, he had fought in hand to hand combat, he had survived in deserts and in tropical rain forests, but he had little experience with women. Was it loneliness, or weakness, or human nature that drew him toward her? He didn't know. But in her presence he felt a feeling he never had in combat—he felt vulnerable.

He walked through the house looking for something to do, something to take his mind off thinking about María Izabelle. But like the constant chirping of the killdeer nearby, she kept coming back to him. Back in his room he sat on the edge of his bed. He thought he could smell her presence near him and imagined what might have been.

He turned abruptly back to his prayer book and opened up to Psalm 51 and read of David after his sin with Bathsheba. He vowed not to let that happen with María Izabelle, but he knew he was weak. "A clean heart create for me, O God, and a steadfast spirit renew within me . . . ," he read. "Give me back the joy of your salvation and a willing spirit sustain in me. I will teach transgressors your ways, and sinners shall return to you. Free me from blood guilt, O God, my saving God."

Suddenly, he got up and closed the book. "I can't sit around here any longer," he said aloud. "I must do something. Idle hands will only get me into more trouble." They were looking for him, but he was not going to stay in hiding. He would be careful. He couldn't go back to the church. They would be looking for him there. He knew one other place where he could do some good. He grabbed one of Diego's hats and eased himself out the back door. He headed back to Miguel Enrique Hospital. Tucked in the small of his back and held securely by his belt was the semi-automatic Makarov pistol he had taken from Leather Jacket. He would be prepared this time.

* * *

57

Carbondale, Pennsylvania

When he saw Francesca walking down the street, Cavanaugh beeped the horn. It didn't work. "Hey, Fran," he called from across the street. "Over here."

Fran didn't recognize him at first, but when she did she ran to the beat up truck. She was dressed in the clothes she had on when they left Brooklyn. Her white blouse was ripped and had blood stains on it. She cluchted her pocketbook like it was a football she was afraid of fumbling. "Where did you get this thing? What's going on?" she asked. "There are police all over the hospital. Something must have happened."

"Somebody killed Healen, the guy who ran us off the road. Hang on. We're getting out of here."

"We can't go. I have no clothes. They're in the back of your truck. We have to go back and get them."

"We can't, Fran. Whoever killed Healen may be looking for us, too." He turned down a side street and headed in what he hoped was the direction of the highway. The Ford Pickup belched and backfired when he accelerated. Driving along the road, he turned on the radio to get information about the murders in the hospital. The radio didn't work either.

"I don't understand, Tom. What is happening? Why is someone trying to kill us?"

"I don't know, Fran, but I'm not going to sit around and wait for it to happen." He looked at her and saw fear in her eyes. "I'm going to drop you off in Buffalo and you can fly back to New York. I told you this might be dangerous. I didn't think the danger would start so soon, however."

She sat silently next to him staring at the road ahead of them while trees seemed to speed past them in reverse. Larry the young mechanic had lied about the truck shimmying at 55 mph. It started to shimmy at 45. She held her hands tightly clasped in her lap and didn't say anything.

"I called Goldberg from the gas station and asked him to check on this Healen guy. He sounded nervous and said everyone was looking for me. The faster I get out of the country, the better I will feel."

Fran was silent.

Her silence made Cavanaugh nervous. He tried to get her to talk. "Did you know that a group of ravens is called a murder?"

Fran did not react and continued to stare at the road ahead.

He knew she hated it when he started talking trivia so he continued. "I suppose you knew the dragonfly has a life span of 24 hours?"

She stared at the road as if in a trance.

"How about the fact that lobsters have blue blood?"

Again silence.

"Well, okay. I give up. I tried. If you want to be quiet, so be it. I won't bother you. I just hope we can get to the highway before they set up any roadblocks," he said to himself.

Suddenly, Fran turned to him. He looked at the bump and the bandage on her forehead. "Did you do it?" she asked.

The noise of the engine and the rattle from a loose muffler made it difficult to hear. "What?" he said. "What are you talking about?"

"Did you kill that Healen guy?"

"No! Why would you think that? I wanted to question him, but somebody obviously got to him before I did."

"I saw that look in your eye. You were angry . . . ."

"Of course I was angry. I was pissed. That bastard tried to kill us. But he was hired by someone to do it. I wanted to find out who hired him. I had no reason to kill him."

"How did he die?"

"I don't know. I overhead some people talking outside the hospital about a nurse being killed also. I wanted to get you out of there before something happened to you. I paid some hick back there $600 for this heap of junk just so we could get away from there quickly!"

Cavanaugh gripped the steering wheel tightly. Now it was his turn to be silent. He checked the signs ahead and moved onto Route 247 and then followed the road till it merged into Route 81 and the signs indicated distances to Binghamton, Johnson City and Endicott. They drove steadily on in the rattling Ford Pickup until he pulled off the road in Cortland, New York to look for a gas station. Stopping at a Hess station he got gas, added two quarts of oil, and cursed Larry the mechanic again. He left Francesca in the truck while he took the maximum amount he could from the station's ATM machine, bought two cups of coffee, and looked for a phone to call Goldberg.

* * *

58

Havana, Cuba

Jack Bennis was careful traveling to Miguel Enrique Hospital. He took a camel bus. The camel was actually an eighteen wheeler tractor-trailer that hauled a homemade double-humped cabin made of two bus shells welded together. It was capable of cramming in 300 or more people, but often being twenty to thirty years old, the buses were unreliable and falling apart.

After purchasing fresh fruit at the plaza, he waited to avoid detection for over an hour with about 100 other people for the uncomfortable, hot, agony of the ride. Armed with two bundles of produce which he held in front of his face, he squeezed into the camel bus where bodies pressed against each other, and people pushed, shoved and cursed in the non-air-conditioned vehicle. The native Cubans complained bitterly about why there weren't more of the thousands of Yutong buses purchased from China being put to use in the streets of Havana. The Yutong buses were air conditioned, had two TV monitors for movies, and even had toilets. But for now, at least, they were being phased in primarily for the tourists and for long distance travel among the provinces.

With Diego's hat and the bag of bananas, mangos, papayas, and two coconuts, he looked like a tall, light skinned Cuban. He tried to diminish his height by bending over a little which also alleviated some of the pain in his side. He used the crowds, the groceries, and Diego's hat to maneuver himself toward the hospital.

When he finally exited the camel bus a block away from Miguel Enrique Hospital, his arms ached from the packages he held, and his shirt was drenched with perspiration. He watched the camel cough up clouds of black smoke as it lumbered away. He stood in the shade of a portico and scanned the area where he had been shot. He tried to figure out where the bullets had most likely come from. He found the faded blue column the first bullet had ricocheted off and studied the buildings across the street. From the angle of the bullet, he calculated the shots had come from one of those buildings. From there the shooter would have been able to see the hospital which was a block away and to have followed him as he rode his bicycle down the street. But was it just luck the shooter had spotted him? What if he had decided to go the other way? Could there have been another shooter down the other block? He couldn't be sure. All he knew now was that, judging from the angle of the shot, the person who shot him had most probably been on the roof of the four story building he was now looking at.

Bennis stood in the shadows for a long time studying the building. It was a four story Art Deco designed building probably built in the early 1950s which looked like it housed a number of different businesses. Shielding his face with the bag of fruit, he walked across the street and entered the lobby. He checked the directory. He was right. There were a number of different businesses, but only one stood out for him. On the fourth floor, he read Santacruz Importers, LLD. It could have been a coincidence, he knew, but he didn't believe in coincidences.

He was tempted to visit Santacruz Importers and to check the roof for possible empty shell casings, but the bags in his arms reminded him he was on another mission now. He was going to visit someone in the hospital. Santacruz would wait for another visit at a later date.

* * *

59

Brooklyn, New York

Morty Goldberg grabbed the phone on the first ring.

"Hey, Morty, about that info I asked for on Anthony Healen . . . ."

"Tom, listen to me. All hell's broken loose around here. You're in some deep shit."

"What are you talking about? The Lieutenant will get over my leaving . . . ."

"Listen to me, Tom. Merry Perez is dead . . . ."

"What?"

"She was murdered. They found her body on Staten Island just like the others."

"Shit! Why? Why would anyone kill Merry?"

"There's more, Tom. The blood on your jacket was Crystal May's."

"How . . . ?"

"The same hair found on Luca Andrassy was also found on Merry." Goldberg hesitated. "Tom, it matches your hair."

"But I don't understand how . . . ."

"I don't understand either, but you've got to come back here. Everyone is looking for you."

"I can't, Morty. You know where I'm going. I've got to see him. I know in my gut he's in some kind of trouble."

"Listen to me, will you? The F.B.I. was here today. They know your brother is in Cuba. They think he had something to do with killing Muscatelli's son."

"This is crazy. How could they?"

"They think Muscatelli hired some guy to kill you."

"That makes sense. That Healen guy tried to drive me off the road. But he won't be driving any one else off the road."

"What do you mean?"

"He's dead."

"What are you talking about? You asked me to get information on him for you. He's a small time hood who used to work for Muscatelli's son."

"Well, he won't be working for anyone anymore. Check the wires. Somebody killed him and a nurse this afternoon in the Huckvale Medical Center someplace in Pennsylvania."

"Tom, you have to come in. I haven't told the Lieutenant yet about your hair matching that on the victims. When they find out, they're liable to put an A. P. B. out on you."

"This is crazy, Morty. Somebody is trying to frame me. I had nothing to do with these murders. Steve told me someone was out to get me."

"Who's Steve?"

"He said some real psycho was going to taunt me and then go after me."

"Who's Steve?"

"He's my barber."

"Your barber?"

"That's right. My barber. Barbers hear a lot of things."

"When did you last see him?"

"I don't know. Sometime earlier in the week. It was after we found the May girl's body. I think it was Tuesday."

"This Steve might have been able to place your hair on the victims' bodies."

"No. Steve is a good guy. He keeps me informed about what's going on. The worst thing he ever did was probably wear sweat pants to a good restaurant."

"Well, I'm going to have to question him. But, Tom, you should know the F.B.I. thinks Muscatelli hired somebody else to get you and your brother. They think he may have hired that professional hit man Cain Holland."

There was silence on the other end of the phone. Finally, Goldberg asked, "Are you still there?"

"Yeah. I was just thinking. This Holland guy could have killed Healen and the nurse. I don't know how they were killed. Check on it." He hesitated for a moment and then added, "And check on those reporters at the scene of Crystal May's murder. Somebody knew too much about the details of the murder and the note. How did they find out? When we had the fight with that fat bastard from 1010 WINS, somebody could have dumped the blood on me."

"We didn't have a fight with the reporter, Tom. You did. And everyone else just seemed to jump in to try to separate you two."

"Yeah. Whatever . . . ." He hesitated again. "I'm sorry to hear about Merry. How did she die?"

"The same as the others, Tom. Broken wrists, slit throat, missing earring, and maple syrup."

"Shit!"

"There was another note, too."

"What did it say?"

Goldberg read from a copy of the note. "Tommy Cavanaugh pudding n' pie, / Kissed Bubbles and made her cry. / When she came out to play / She just had to die / And Tommy Cavanaugh ran away."

"Whoever it is knows a lot about me and Merry. Too damn much."

"One more thing I have to ask you." Goldberg hesitated this time. "Merry Perez was pregnant. Did you have anything to do with that?"

"Shit! No, Morty. I hadn't seen her in years."

"Are you sure, Tom? They are going to check."

"I'm sure, but can I ask you to do me a big favor? I guess you went into my drawer and took my hairbrush to make the comparison. It doesn't sound like you trust me very much."

"It's not that, Tom . . . ."

"It's okay. You've got your job to do. But could you hold off giving them the hair info for another day. You can check with Steve. He might know something. His address is in my little black book which you probably already have."

Goldberg was silent.

The last words Goldberg heard from Cavanaugh came over loud and clear. "Thanks anyway!"

And the phone clicked dead.

* * *

60

Havana, Cuba

María Izabelle Melendez was not working at the hospital when Jack Bennis entered through the emergency room. Maybe, he thought, she was researching Francisco Santacruz. He hoped she would be careful. He walked deliberately through the corridors carrying his two shopping bags of fruit. No one stopped him. He took the stairs to the second floor and moved directly to Manuel's room. When he reached the room, he looked in and found another man sitting on Manuel's bed. There were flowers on the window sill and the room looked and smelled much cleaner than it had when Bennis first visited it.

Manuel looked up when he saw the priest and smiled. "Padre," he called. "I am happy you came. Here is someone I wish you to meet."

The gentleman sitting on the bed stood. He was black, thin, and as tall as Bennis. The deep lines etched into his rough black features made him look a little like Mick Jaggert shrink wrapped in rhinoceros skin. But it was his eyes which struck Bennis. They were red and focused on him with the intensity of laser beams. The man extended his hand and Bennis shook it. It was cold and hard as freshly chiseled granite. He wore a multi-colored sports shirt and a white cowhide leather ivy cap. His smile revealed a number of missing teeth. His voice was deep and seemed to seep into one's soul. "Manuel has told me much about you, Padre."

Bennis looked to Manuel for an explanation.

"Padre," Manuel offered, "this is my Babalawo."

Bennis shrugged. "I apologize. Until I met Manuel the other day, the only 'Babalu' I knew was a song Desi Arnez used to sing a long, long time ago."

"I never liked that song," the tall man replied. "That song helped give the impression to people that Santería is like voodoo. A more accurate song might be 'Babau Alle' which combines the beat of the drums, dance, the orishas, and references to the African origins of Santería."

"I apologize again," Bennis said. "I am not much into music. I know music plays a large part in your Santería religious rituals, but . . . ."

"Sit down, Padre," the Babalawo said motioning to a chair in the corner as he sat on the edge of Manuel's bed. "Manuel tells me you can be trusted. My name is Hector. Some call me Babalawo, some 'Father Who Knows the Secrets,' some 'Father, Master of Mysteries.' I prefer 'Father in the Knowledge of Things Material and Spiritual.' Like you, Padre, I too am a priest. Babalawo is an African title that means I am a Priest of Ifa and a servant of Orumila. In my role as Babalawo, I humbly seek to counsel and help believers reach their highest good in any way that I can."

Bennis sat down and became completely engrossed in what the Babalawo was saying. He didn't hear the footsteps coming down the hall.

"And who is this Ifa and Orumila?" Bennis asked.

"Let me just say that Ifa is knowledge and wisdom and the highest form of divination. As a Priest of Ifa, I can communicate with Orumila, the god of wisdom, who knows the past, present, and future."

"Forgive me, Hector, if I seem disrepectful. I do not mean to be. I know when the Catholic Church tried to convert the early slaves brought here from West Africa, the slaves tried to keep their traditions and blended the Spanish saints with their traditional orishas which are something like our saints. Thus the orisha Obatala became Our Lady of Mercy, Babalu Alle I learned became St. Lazarus, Chango became St. Barbara, and . . . ," he said pointing to Manuel's statue on the table by his bed, "Manuel's devotion to Eleggua became symbolized in St. Anthony of Padua."

The steps in the corridor slowed as they grew closer. But Jack Bennis was too involved in discussing another man's religion to hear.

"From what Manuel told me the other day, and what I seem to be hearing from you now is you think you can see the future? That is a pretty good trick if you can do it. I can accept many of the concepts Manuel told me about Santería, but I have to confess I don't believe in fortune telling."

"I see you are a skeptic, Padre, but divination is not fortune telling. Indeed, it has been practiced by countries, cultures, and religions for thousands of years. In the Old Testament Book of Joshua, you can read how God used the casting of lots to find a thief. In the Book of Samuel, God uses the same technique to choose a king and to reveal it was Saul's son who broke the oath."

Bennis concentrated on the words of the Babalawo. He didn't hear the footsteps in the hall come to a stop outside Manuel's room.

"I have come here today to help counsel and guide Manuel. The special powers I have received come from my Orisha. I don't have to tell you, Padre, that people seem to continue to learn things the hard way. Too often we rely on our instincts and emotions and end up making poor decisions. I try to help my people avoid the mistakes that history and experience have shown us. Divination gives me the means to help believers at moments of crisis in their lives."

"And how do you accomplish this, what you call, divination?" Bennis asked.

Hector picked up coconut shells from Manuel's bed and showed them to him. "The use of the coconut oracle is known as Biague to honor the name of the first Babalawo."

Bennis looked at the four pieces of coconut shell in Hector's hand. "We believe the coconut not only gives us nourishment, but allows the orishas to pass their knowledge of the future . . . ."

Suddenly, Manuel shouted, "Cuidado!" and pointed toward the door.

Bennis turned in time to see a heavy set man in a flowery pink shirt aiming a pistol straight at his head. Instinctively, he grabbed the coconut pieces and flung them at the stranger. The man flinched and pulled back as Bennis leaped from his seat and knocked the gun out of his hand. The stranger turned and started lumbering down the corridor. Bennis picked up his gun and leveled it at him.

"No! No!" Hector shouted. "Don't shoot him!" Bennis felt the Babalawo's arms around him. They were like iron coils restraining him. "You gain nothing by letting your emotions rule your mind," he whispered.

Bennis watched the would-be assassin disappear around the corner and head down the stairs. The iron coils released their grip and Bennis lowered the gun. "Why did you do that?" he said to Hector. "That guy tried to kill me."

"And what would be gained by killing him? Our ancestors have long taught us that the key to success in this life and in the next is being of good character and acting in harmony with each other. Using your individual power for personal gain or revenge doesn't do anyone any good."

Jack Bennis looked at the old Spanish Campo-Giro automatic service pistol in his hand. Slowly he turned and placed the pistol on the small table next to Manuel's statue of St. Anthony of Padua. He felt his face flush. He needed to get away. "Sometimes in the excitement of the moment I react and forget Jesus' command to do unto others as we would have them do unto us." He looked down at Manuel lying in his bed and said, "Thank you. You saved my life. I owe you one."

Then he turned at Hector. "And thank you for reminding me of something I need to remember more often."

He turned and stared down the corridor he had scrubbed and cleaned only two days before. "I had better leave now," he said. "I've brought you enough danger. Keep the gun here. In case he comes back, you may need it."

Manuel reached up from his bed and offered Bennis his hand. "Thank you, Padre. You are a good man."

Hector looked at him and his red eyes seemed to penetrate Bennis's soul. "Do not be harsh on yourself, Padre. Manuel is right. I can see from what he has told me and what I have seen for myself that you are a man of strength and character."

Jack Bennis shook his head. "No. I am just a man," he repeated. "A man walking and stumbling through life like a wounded soldier."

Carefully leaving the hospital, he made sure he was not being followed. Slowly Jack Bennis weaved his way through streets and alleys toward Professor Diego Velasquez's house. Along he way, he thought frequently about the Babalawo's parting words to him. "As you travel your path, Padre, you may wish to recall an old Yoruba proverb that states it is easier to change a man's destiny than his character."

* * *

61

Brooklyn, New York

Goldberg knew what he had to do. The information that the hair on both Luca Andrassy and Meredith Perez matched Cavanaugh's had to be reported. But why was he hesitating? Did he really think his partner killed the women? Why would he? Unless he had lost it. Trying to go to Cuba to see his half-brother was evidence he might be losing it, but he had done crazy things before. What if someone was really was trying to frame him? But who? And why?

Look at the evidence. All victims had been found on Staten Island. Whoever was killing these women must know Staten Island. Cavanaugh lived in Brooklyn. He claimed the only trips he took to Staten Island were to go to Tugs Restaurant to get away from things.

The first victim's blood was found on his jacket. Could someone have put the blood on his jacket during the shuffle with the reporter? It was possible. Things had been crazy outside the old Staten Island Hospital that night.

Goldberg remembered Cavanaugh asking how the reporters knew about the note left by the body. Had one of the police tipped them off? Or had someone else tipped them off? The reporters seemed to know a lot more than they should have that night. How did they know?

And then there were the notes. Why would Cavanaugh mention himself in the notes if he were involved in the murders? Whoever wrote the notes, however, apparently knew a lot about Cavanaugh. The last note indicated they knew he had gone somewhere. "When she came out to play . . . Tommy Cavanaugh ran away." Who would have access to this information?

He took out a pad and began a list. Question the reporters and everyone else who was at the scene.

All the murders had followed the same M.O.—slashed throats, broken wrists, missing earring. The M.O. matched that of the known assassin Cain Holland. But Cavanaugh had never heard of Cain Holland, and Holland always took his victims' right earring. Crystal May, Luca Andrassy, and Merry Perez were all missing their left earring. And why was maple syrup poured over the victims? What was the significance of the maple syrup? Thus far, the police had been able to keep the maple syrup out of the newspapers, but it was only a matter of time before they would latch onto something like "The Maple Syrup Murderer."

The F.B.I. had warned him that Vito Muscatelli had spoken to Tony Healen and Cain Holland. They thought he had put a hit out on Cavanaugh and his brother the priest. Goldberg believed that. Cavanaugh had said his barber had warned him someone was after him. He looked at the notes he had taken while Cavanaugh talked to him on the phone. His barber's name was Steve. He opened his desk drawer and pulled out Cavanaugh's notebook. There printed in capital letters was Steve's address along with a number of other names and addresses.

Goldberg added to his list. Question Steve the barber.

He went back to the notes from Cavanaugh's conversation. He said Healen and a nurse had been killed. The hospital he mentioned was the Huckvale Medical Center somewhere in Pennsylvania. A few calls later Goldberg was on the line with the Cardondale Police Chief, Ralph Santoro.

"Chief Santoro," he began, "this is Homicide Detective Morton Goldberg from New York."

"What can I do for you, son?" the Police Chief said. "We're a little busy up here right now."

"Yeah. That's what I'm calling you about." Goldberg pictured a good old boy with a ten gallon white hat, a huge stomach, and a balding head smoking a cigar with his feet up on his desk. "I understand you had a couple of killings in the Huckvale Medical Center earlier today."

"Well, I'll be damned! You city boys sure do keep on top of things, don't you? But thank you anyway; we can handle our own problems. Have a good day, Detective Goldfinger . . . ."

"No, wait," Goldberg said. "I wanted to find out about those murders. We have had a few down here too, and I wonder if the victims had their throats slit and were missing an earring."

"Well, holy shit! What are you Karnack the Magician?"

"Chief, we have had three murders down here of women who have had their throats slit, their wrists broken, and their left earring taken."

"Well, I'll tell you, Goldfinger, the woman was missing an earring, but it was found next to the second victim who was a guy. Up here men don't wear earrings like they do in your city."

"Chief, can you tell me whether it was the right earring or the left earring that was missing from the female victim."

"Oh, for Christ's sake, Goldfinger, what the hell difference does it matter?"

"Can you check, please, Chief? It may mean something."

Goldberg heard Chief Santoro call to someone in his office. "Hey, Billy Bob, was that nurse at the hospital missing her right earring or her left . . . . Never mind why I want to know. Was it the right or the left? . . . . Well, God-damn it, look at the report!"

Goldberg waited patiently while he heard papers being shuffled and various voices shouting in the background. Finally, the Police Chief came back on the line. "Goldfinger, you still there?"

"It's Goldberg, Chief, and yes, I am still here."

"It looks like she was missing her right earring although I don't see what the hell difference that makes."

Goldberg avoided getting into a discussion. "One more question, Chief, were either of the victims covered in maple syrup?"

"What the fuck do you think we're running up here, an International Hospital of Pancakes?"

"I take it that is a no."

"You are f—ing right it's a no!"

"Thanks, Chief, you've been a great help."

Before hanging up, Goldberg added, "I guess you haven't found the killer yet, have you?"

"Don't give me any of your smart ass big city attitudes, Goldfinger. We're looking for the cock sucker. He was wearing a nurse's uniform which he took from his first victim. We'll find the bastard!"

"You might want to check with the F.B.I. Your killer is probably an international assassin named Cain Holland."

There was silence on the other end of the phone for a moment. "What are you talking about?"

"Check with the F.B.I., Chief. They'll fill you in on Cain Holland. Thanks for your help again, Chief. You really have been a big help."

With that, Goldberg hung up the phone and smiled. Now he was convinced. There were two killers out there. One was Cain Holland. The other was someone else.

* * *

62

Cortland, New York

When Cavanaugh returned to the pickup truck, he gave Fran a cup of coffee. She opened the lid and sipped the coffee. It was cold. "What took you so long?" she asked.

He stared ahead as if in a trance.

"What happened in there? What's the matter with you?"

"I called Goldberg." He hesitated. "Remember that woman I told you about? The one who found the notes at the murder scenes? The one I used to date that I said I took advantage of?"

Fran poured her coffee out the window. "We've been through all that . . . ."

Cavanaugh turned and looked at her. "She's dead, Fran. Goldberg just told me she's dead."

"What?"

"She's dead. She was killed just like the others."

"Oh, my God!"

"Somebody killed her just like he did those other girls. She didn't deserve that, Fran. None of them did."

He gripped the wheel tightly. "I'll drop you off in Buffalo like I said. I'm sorry I got you involved in this. Goldberg said the F.B.I. told him somebody hired the Healen guy and someone else to get rid of me and my brother." He didn't tell her the person who hired them was most likely Francesca's own grandfather, Vito Muscatelli.

He started the ignition and the truck backfired. Fran jumped.

"I'm sorry, Fran. I had no right to bring you along. This isn't your problem."

They drove along the road for a few miles before Fran spoke. "Tom, keep driving. Don't leave me in Buffalo. We started this trip together and we'll finish it together."

"I can't do that to you, Fran. Somebody is after me. I don't want you to get hurt."

"I'm not leaving, Tom," she said. "I'm sorry I doubted you back there, it's just that . . . ."

"I can't blame you, Fran. Somebody is trying to frame me. But I have to drop you off. It is too dangerous for you."

"I'm not leaving," she said. "You are not the only one who can be stubborn."

"No, you are leaving," he insisted. "I'm not putting your life in danger."

She touched his arm and tossed her long red hair back. "Tom, if you drop me off, I swear I will call the cops and tell them you abducted me and I'll give them the description of this piece of shit you are driving and you will never get to see your brother."

"You wouldn't do that!"

She folded her arms and looked straight ahead. "You know I would!"

"Please, Fran, listen to reason . . . ."

"Shut up and drive, lover boy, we have to get to Toronto tonight. We have some serious make-up sex we have to take care of."

He looked at her and smiled. He pushed the pedal to the metal and the truck started to shimmy like a belly dancer on crack. He didn't care. Make-up sex was the best news he had heard all day.

*   *   *

63

Brooklyn, New York

It was a puzzle, a big puddle of muddy water, but it was beginning to get clearer for Morty Goldberg. Whoever murdered Crystal May, Luca Andrassy, and Meredith Perez wanted it to look like they were killed by Cain Holland while at the same time implicating Cavanaugh. No one knew who Holland was or what he even looked like. The M.O., however, was distinctive—slit throat, broken wrists, missing earring. Using the same M.O. as Holland would send everyone searching in the wrong direction. It was a good idea, Goldberg had to admit, and it had worked too—except for a few things. The missing earring was from the wrong ear, and the real Cain Holland had come back into the picture.

It was slowly beginning to make sense. But then there were still the notes. Why had the killer mentioned Cavanaugh? What made the murders personal? The women had nothing in common. Cavanaugh did not know any of them—except, of course, for Merry Perez. She was different, and the note the killer left with her was different, too. What reason would the killer have to taunt Cavanaugh? How did he—or she—know so much about him? And how did he know about Cain Holland? Goldberg and Cavanaugh had never heard of Cain Holland before the Interpol report.

And then there was the maple syrup. It meant something. But what?

Questions, questions, more questions . . . .

Suddenly, the phone on his desk rang, and Goldberg jumped. It was Officer Michael Shanley, Merry Perez's partner.

"Goldberg, can I speak with Cavanaugh?"

"He's not here, Shanley. He took off for a while. I don't know when he'll be back. Can I help you?"

Shanley hesitated. "I was just wondering if you had any leads on Merry, er, Officer Perez's murder . . . ."

"You and she were really close, weren't you?"

"Yeah. She was like family to me. And she was a good cop. She had great instincts and would have made a great detective. I want to catch the bastard that did this to her."

"So do I," Goldberg said. Then he dropped the bomb like he was passing a piece of apple pie. "Did you know she was pregnant?"

"Sweet Jesus, no! She never said nothing. I thought she was putting on a little weight, but I never . . . ."

"Shanley, I know she was your partner and all, and partners get pretty close at times. I have to ask . . . ."

"No! I had nothing to do with that! She was like a daughter to me! I wouldn't."

"I'm sorry, Shanley. I had to ask. Do you know if she was seeing anyone?"

There was silence on the phone. Then Shanley spoke. "She had been seeing a few guys. There was one guy a while back, she spoke about a little. I think he may have been a reporter or something, but then I think they broke up."

"Did you ever meet this guy?"

"No, but something happened, and she broke up with him."

"She broke up with him?"

"Yeah. She didn't say much, but I remember her saying he had changed. He wasn't the same person anymore."

"What happened?"

"I haven't got a clue. She just said he had changed. I didn't ask any questions. It was her business."

"Do you remember when this happened?"

Goldberg thought he heard Shanley thinking. "I'm not sure. It was a while back. What does this have to do with her death anyhow?"

"I'm not sure. Maybe nothing. I'd just like to question his guy."

"If I can help in any way, let me know."

"I will, Shanley. Count on it. If you remember when she broke off with this guy or anything you can tell me about him, give me a call. He might be able to give us some more information about her."

Goldberg hung up and turned to his files. He spread out copies of the clippings found on Merry Perez's walls. She was on to something he felt sure. But what?

* * *

64

Staten Island, New York

The phone rang in Vito Muscatelli's room. He grabbed it before Gestas could reach it. He recognized the voice immediately. It was Cain Holland.

"Vito, I was able to take some beautiful pictures of the red-tailed hawk you wanted."

"Bene. How about the falcon?"

"I missed that one. The Peregrine Falcon flew away before I could photograph it. He was with a female falcon. What do you want me to do?"

"Do you have the address I gave you of my colleague. He will direct you to a good place to find and photograph the falcon?"

"Your friend the ornithologist?"

"The what?" Muscatelli was thinking of the travel agent Francesca would contact when they arrived in Toronto.

Cain Holland stifled a chuckle. "Your friend, the bird watcher."

"Si, of course. My bird watcher friend. He will tell you where to find the falcons."

"Do you want pictures of all the falcons?"

"Just the male falcons! Two of them. I don't need any pictures of the female falcon."

"This will involve some travel, Vito. Are you prepared for the expenses involved?"

Vito Muscatelli was tired of the bird charade. He wanted to tell Holland to make sure he killed both Cavanaugh and his half-brother, Jack Bennis. But he knew his line was most likely being tapped. The charade continued.

"Be careful not to harm the female falcon. I hear it is an endangered species."

Holland knew the "female falcon" was Muscatelli's granddaughter, Francesca Arden. "Don't worry about a thing. I would not think of harming the female falcon."

Vito gave the phone to Gestas to hang up. He was tired. He realized he should have hired Cain Holland in the first place. Holland was a professional. Healen was an amateur, a loser. He looked out the window. It was dark out. He felt a slight tremor in his hand. He closed his eyes and put his head on his pillow. It felt cold and good. But there was a frown on his face. Healen was a mistake. A younger Vito Muscatelli wouldn't make mistakes. He pulled the covers up and cursed under his breath. He hated making mistakes.

* * *

65

Toronto, Canada

Cavanaugh and Fran cruised into Canada without a problem—other than having to stop along the way for gas twice and oil three times. Each time they stopped he cursed Larry the mechanic.

"You needed a car. You paid for it," Fran said. "Now get over it." He looked over at Fran reading the map quest directions she had fortunately taken with her and noticed she was rubbing her side and her stomach.

"Are you all right?"

"Other than my side and my belly hurting, my head aching, and feeling nauseous, I'd say I felt like a truck ran over me."

"I'm sorry, Fran. Maybe the doctor back there was right. You should have stayed in the hospital, but there is a murderer out there gunning for me. I had to get you out of there." He knew the assassin was most likely hired by her grandfather, but he couldn't tell her that. Human life meant nothing to trained assassins like Cain Holland. If she stayed in the hospital she might get caught in the crossfire, no matter whose granddaughter she was.

"I'll be all right. I just hope this nausea goes away. I wouldn't want to mess up your friend Larry's luxurious vehicle."

Cavanaugh smiled. "Speaking of hospitals, do you know who the first U.S. President to be born in a hospital was?"

Fran shook her head. "Oh, no. Not this stupid ass trivial shit of yours again!"

"No. Seriously, you will never guess."

"You're right. I give up."

He wanted to reach out and touch her, but the Ford pickup's steady shimmying demanded his hands on the wheel. "No. You have to guess. You'll never guess who."

"If I'll never guess who, why should I try?"

"Oh, come on, humor me. It's been a rough day."

"Tell me about it." Fran sighed, thought, and then offered, "Howard Taft?"

"No. More recent."

"More recent?"

"Yes."

"FDR?"

"No. More recent."

"You're kidding me. Eisenhower?"

"No. More recent."

"Not Kennedy?"

"Nope. More recent than JFK."

She looked at him amazed. "It couldn't be Nixon."

"You're right. It's not Nixon. It's . . . ."

"Don't tell me it's the peanut farmer from Georgia!"

"You got it! Jimmy Carter was the first U. S. President born in a hospital!"

"You are right. I never would have guessed that. Now answer me one question, Mr. Trivial Knowledge Junkie. Of what practical use is that information?"

Cavanaugh's knee stung like his trousers were made of sandpaper. He embraced the pain and smiled again. "Well, it took up a little time, it kept us both awake, and we are almost there."

She looked up and saw the signs for the Toronto Pearson International Airport and just shook her head. Five minutes later they pulled in front of the Reisert Hotel. Fran eased herself out of the pickup and went in to register while Cavanaugh drove the truck to the Reduced Rate Parking Lot, located directly across from Terminal 3 on Airport Road. He could have left the truck at the hotel, but the airport parking would be easier and cheaper for Larry the mechanic to retrieve his truck if he really wanted it. He then went to the terminal and called the hotel's shuttle bus to pick him up.

When he finally arrived at the hotel and found their room, Fran answered the door wrapped in towel. She had just come out of the shower. She didn't look happy.

"What's the matter?" he asked.

"They said on the internet this place was 'comfortably unpretentious.'"

He looked around. "It looks like a typical hotel room to me—a bed, an air conditioner, a television. What more could you ask for?"

"The place is filthy, Tom. I heard a couple arguing in the lobby with the concierge that there was blood on their sheets, their carpet stunk, and there was mould in the bathroom."

"It looks okay to me. We're only going to be here for one night anyway."

Fran raised her hands and shouted, "You are impossible!" Her towel fell.

Cavanaugh stared at her naked body. "Holy shit!" he said. A huge bruise spread across her abdomen and breasts as if it had been painted indigo with a five inch paint brush. "Maybe we should see a doctor tomorrow. You really took some beating in that accident."

"No shit, Tracy." She smiled and added. "Go take a shower. If the sheets don't have stains on them, maybe we can find a position for that make-up sex we talked about."

"Are you sure?" he asked.

"Just shut up and go take your shower before I change my mind. You'll feel better."

Cavanaugh started throwing his clothes off as he headed for the bathroom. He didn't care if the place were dirty. The water was hot. It felt good beating down on his back. In the shower he checked his knee. It was scarped, but it didn't look that bad. He had a slight bruise on his chest, but nothing like Francesca's. The water felt so good he didn't realize the drain was clogged until the water rose passed his ankles. When he got out of the shower he quickly dried himself off and realized he had no toothbrush, no shaving gear, and no clean clothes. They would have to purchase new clothes at the airport terminal tomorrow.

Still drying himself off, he came out of the bathroom to see Francesca's naked, bruised body lying on the bed partially covered by the sheet. He smiled. She looked great.

Then he heard something. It was soft and low. He stopped and listened. Had Holland found them? He searched the room for something to defend himself with. Then he heard it again. Soft and low. It was coming from the bed.

He moved closer and saw what it was. Francesca had fallen asleep. He lay down next to her, smiled, and closed his eyes thinking of their make-up sex. Within a minute, with the lights in the room still on, Cavanaugh was asleep too. In less than sixty seconds, the long awaited, long anticipated make-up sex became the most effective form of safe-sex—no sex.

* * *

66

Brooklyn, New York

Detective Goldberg stretched his neck, yawned, and put on his glasses to read the clippings from Meredith Perez's apartment walls. They were from all different sources: *The Brooklyn Daily Eagle*, the *Staten Island Advance*, the *New York Daily News*, the *New York Post*, the *New York Times*, and even the *Brooklyn Paper* and the *Bronx Press Review*. Perez was thorough. Goldberg agreed with Shanley. She would have made a great detective.

When Tyrell Wallcot, 17, and Fernando Cardo, 18, tried to rob Samir Patel, 64, at the Quick Check on Park Place near New York Avenue in Crown Heights yesterday, they didn't realize off duty homicide detective Thomas Cavanaugh was in the store. The end result, after an exchange of bullets, was Wallcot, Cardo, and Patel all lay dead on the floor, while in the back of the store near the dairy products Maria DeFillipo, 28, lay mortally wounded. Ms. DeFillipo, who was six months pregnant, died later that night at Kings County Hospital.

Police reported both Wallcot and Cardo had criminal records and were associated with gang activities in the Dyker Heights section of Brooklyn. Roberto Martin, 68, a neighbor of Wallcot, said, "Tyrell was a good boy. He used to run errands for my family. He was not the kind of boy to do something like this." Deanna Diaz, 57, spoke on behalf of Cardo's grandmother who collapsed when told the news of her grandson's death. "Fernando was murdered by that cop. He had no right to shoot that boy. This will kill his grandmother."

Witnesses in the store had different versions of what happened. Cindy Ward, 28, a close friend of Ms. DeFillipo, reported hearing a number of shots as she and Ms. DeFillipo were shopping for items in the rear of the store. "Suddenly, we heard shots. We looked around, saw some boys in the front of the store and then there were more shots and I ducked behind some cases of soda. When I looked up Maria was next to me, but she was bleeding badly."

"This is the third incident this year involving innocent bystanders being shot by police," Councilman John Wolfe stated. "The police have to be more responsible in the discharge of their weapons."

A statement from Police Commissioner John Mullin's office indicated a full investigation would be conducted. Detective Cavanaugh was not available for comment.

Goldberg turned to the next story.

Two youths messed with the wrong delicatessen yesterday when they tried to rob a bodega on New York Avenue. Both Tyrell Wallcot, 18, and Fernando Cardo, 17, were shot to death by off-duty detective Thomas Cavanaugh after they allegedly shot the store owner Samir Patel, 63, in a botched robbery attempt. Detective Cavanaugh is a twenty-two year highly decorated veteran of the New York City Police force.

According to Michael Shanley, 38, who now works out of the 120 Precinct on Staten Island and is a former colleague of Cavanaugh's, "Those kids messed with the wrong guy." Councilman John Wolfe, however, had a different view on the shootings. "A police officer should use his weapon only in an emergency. There has to be liability here. We do not live in Dodge City. This is New York City, and we can't have the police running around killing people."

Mrs. Virginia Guma, 48, who had stopped by the Quick Check on her way home from work for some fruit and bread, commented, "I heard two shots and I turned to see Mr. Patel fall back. Then one of the boys turned and aimed his gun at another man. I ducked behind the cabbage. The next thing I knew there was a lot of gunfire and then when I looked up the two boys were laying on the ground."

Another shopper in the store, Maria DeFillipo (38) was severely wounded in the shooting and was taken to Coney Island Hospital. Detective Cavanaugh could not be reached for comment.

Two different news stories. Two different slants. Not even the facts were the same. Was it sloppy reporting or did the reporters just not care? No wonder the Coroner's Inquest took so long, thought Goldberg.

He turned to another story.

Homicide Detective Thomas Cavanaugh shot Tyrell Wallcot, 18, and Freddie Cardo, 17, after they had allegedly shot and killed Sam Patel, 65, of Carroll

Gardens, in a supermarketi on Park Avenue and New York Place yesterday. Also injured in the shooting was Ms. Maria DeFillipo, 28. According to sources, Ms. DeFillipo, who was seven months pregnant, was rushed to Kings County Hospital where she is listed in critical condition. Witnesses to the shooting told different versions of the shooting. The police are investigating the shootings in the light of strong political pressure, and Detective Cavanaugh has been suspended with pay until a full Coroner's Inquest has been conducted.

And so the stories went. There were human interest stories on Tyrell Wallcot who had dropped out of Boys and Girls High School, been caught spray painting graffiti along the Brooklyn Queens Expressway, arrested for shop lifting from Sears, and was the father of two illegitimate children. According to his neighbors, however, he was a model citizen who might have been an A student and an Eagle Scout to boot.

Fernando Cardo, the follow-up stories indicated, was a quiet kid whose hobbies were chess and reading. Neighbors described him as a "strange" and "trouble youth" who tried to avoid trouble, but trouble usually found him. He and Tyrell were close friends since childhood. They were both members of a street gang known in the area as "SS." Cardo had been expelled from Bishop Ford High School and dropped out of William Grady High School. The newspapers made no mention of the fact that Tyrell Wallcot was awaiting trial for assault and menacing a bicycle rider in Prospect Park with a tire iron or that Freddie Cardo had recently been charged with solicitation, aggravated unlicensed driving, and criminal mischief. The facts, Goldberg concluded, were what the press wanted them to be—even if they were wrong.

Goldberg noted the store owner, Samir Patel, who had been gunned down by the youths, didn't get much news coverage. He left a wife and five children, but the newspapers overlooked him. Perhaps their editors didn't think an immigrant trying to make an honest living for his family was worthy of news coverage. The stories were written to sell papers, and the most compelling story before the Inquest and the community demonstrations was the death of the pregnant Maria DeFillipo. Goldberg recalled the story he read about the artist sent to Cuba to cover the Spanish-American war. The artist cabled William Randolf Hearst that nothing was going on and asked if he should return home. Hearst allegedly cabled back, "Please remain. You furnish the pictures, and I'll furnish the war."

Goldberg studied the different computer generated downloaded news stories about Ms. DeFillipo. She was married to Jason DeFillipo, a groundskeeper at Yankee Stadium. This was to be their first child. She lived in the Westerleigh section of Staten Island and had been visiting her parents in Brooklyn while her husband worked a Yankee / Red Sox game in the Bronx. Her mother told one reporter how Maria and her twin brother, Tony, had gone to Brooklyn College and both graduated cum laude with Bachelor of Science degrees. Maria had been accepted to New York City Technical College's Department of Dental Hygiene in the fall. Her father was a retired Sergeant Major in the Army with a black belt in karate. Her friends told stories about her cravings for mocha chocolate ice cream, pancakes, dill pickles, and hot pastrami sandwiches. Despite her cravings, she exercised regularly and kept her weight under control. She and her family knew the baby was a boy and had already purchased a crib and decorated the baby's room.

Soon the stories of the dead faded to the back pages and the stories of the Coroner's Inquest took the headlines. There were pictures of demonstrations in front of the court house, stories of political activists rallying the community against "the rogue cop" who somehow became responsible for not only Wallcot and Cardo's deaths, but also Patel and DeFillipo's deaths. The rallies turned ugly. Cars were overturned. Garbage strewn over the street. A newsstand went up in flames. Angry men and women marched with placards demanding Cavanaugh's arrest for murder, a civilian board's review of the incident, and an end to the "blue wall of silence and protection."

Goldberg read the stories with distaste. He understood why Cavanaugh took off an extra week after he was cleared of all charges. In spite of in-store video taken at the scene which clearly showed the teens shooting the store owner and firing at Cavanaugh, the protests only faded when the ballistics reports confirmed that the teenagers had shot both Mr. Patel and Ms. DeFillipo. The only shots Cavanaugh fired were in self-defense and dead accurate. Goldberg thought how difficult it must have been for Cavanaugh to have endured all the abuse and hatred thrown at him. Now he regretted not calling him more frequently. They worked together, but their private lives were mostly private. And that was the way they both wanted it. They didn't need to hang around with each other at night. Goldberg was a family man, and Cavanaugh wasn't. Looking at the papers on his desk, however, Goldberg felt a pang of "Jewish guilt." He could have and should have reached out to him more.

Maybe, he thought, for the first time, Cavanaugh really did need to get to see his brother. The tensions from the shootings in the deli, the Inquest, the demonstrations, and now the serial murders were too much to endure. Cavanaugh's half-brother was the only family he had. They needed to talk for a lot of reasons. There was so much he didn't know about his brother, the soldier, the priest, and, they both knew, the killer.

Suddenly, a voice shattered his reverie. "Goldberg, get in here right away!" It was Lieutenant Bradley and his voice was drenched with anger.

"What is it, Lieutenant?" Goldberg asked entering the lieutenant's office.

"Shut the door after you and sit down!"

This wasn't going to be good news, Goldberg realized immediately.

"What's this bullshit I've been hearing from the press trying to confirm a story they have that Cavanaugh's hair was found on the last two murder victims?"

Goldberg looked to his right and then left. He should have told the Lieutenant immediately, but how did the press find out? No one but he, Cavanaugh, and, most likely now, the killer knew about the hair. Even Jimmy in forensics didn't know the hair he gave him was Cavanaugh's.

"I'm waiting, Goldberg. Speak to me!"

"I . . . I was going to tell you, Lieutenant . . . ."

"Bullshit! Is it true?"

"I asked Jimmy to check some hair from Cavanaugh's hairbrush . . . ."

"Is it true, Goldberg?"

"It looks like a match, sir," Goldberg admitted looking down at the floor.

"Out-fucking-standing! The first victim's blood is on his jacket, now his hair is found on the next two victims!"

"I think he's being set up, sir. He told me his barber warned him that someone was after him earlier in the week. It doesn't make sense that he would leave notes implicating himself . . . ."

"Where is he now?" Bradley almost shouted. "No more bullshit, Goldberg. I need to know. I hate surprises!"

"He didn't do it, sir. I know him. Somebody's playing with him."

"Read my lips, Goldberg. Where the hell is he?"

Goldberg swallowed. This was going to be hard. Finally, he said, "I don't exactly know at this moment, but he is on his way to Cuba to see his brother."

Bradley stood. His face was flushed and the little scar over his eye seemed about to burst. "On his way to where?"

"I know, sir. I tried to talk him out of it, but he thinks his brother is in some kind of trouble and he's going down there to try to find him."

Bradley sat down and seemed to collapse like a slow leaking balloon. Goldberg took advantage of the momentary silence and filled the lieutenant in on the accident in the Pocono's, Healen's murder, and his conclusion that there were two killers on the loose—Cain Holland, who had probably been hired by Vito Muscatelli to kill Cavanaugh, and someone else who was killing women and leaving notes and clues intended to badger and implicate Cavanaugh.

Finally, Lieutenant Bradley looked up and spoke. "So what are your plans?"

Goldberg took a deep breath and began. "In the morning we're going to question all the reporters on the scene of the first murder, and I'm going to question Cavanaugh's barber."

"Do you think the barber had something to do with this?"

"I don't know, sir. Cavanaugh trusts him, but he definitely knows something if he warned Cavanaugh someone was after him."

Lieutenant Bradley stood and moved toward the door. "Let's keep this hair thing between us for now. I'll stall the press. See what the reporters and the barber have to offer. With Cavanaugh out of the picture now, we may have some time to develop positive leads."

Goldberg nodded and added, "Thank you, sir."

Bradley hesitated before opening the door. "One more thing, Goldberg. Let's keep the Cuba shit between us, too. It would only muddy the waters more and be a distraction."

He looked Goldberg straight in the eye and added, "My Irish grandmother used to say, 'A silent mouth is sweet to hear.' Understand what I'm saying?"

Goldberg nodded again. "Yes, sir. You can trust me. My lips are sealed."

* * *

VII

How far can you go without destroying from within
what you are trying to defend from without?

Dwight D. Eisenhower

SUNDAY

67

Toronto, Canada

In the morning they were stiff. They ached in places they didn't know they had. Her bruise looked worse, but felt a little better. His leg looked better, but felt a little worse. When they looked at their clothes, she wanted to cry, he wanted to laugh.

"We'll have to buy some at the terminal," he said.

She picked up her blood stained, torn blouse she had bought on sale in Saks Fifth Avenue. "No shit, Tracy," was all she said.

He walked over to her and held her tightly.

"Ouch!" she cried.

He loosened his bear hug and gently kissed her lips.

The rest followed naturally even if a bit awkwardly because of their pains. Perhaps that made it even more special.

When their passions had been satisfied, they looked deep into each other's eyes. "Now what?" she said.

"You need to call that agent guy about getting us on a plane."

She found the number in her purse and dialed on the hotel phone.

"Thomas DiNotte Travel Agency," a man's voice answered.

"This is Francesca Arden," she began. "My grandfather told me you could get me and a friend on a flight to Havana, Cuba, today."

"Miss Arden, I am sorry. We don't arrange flights to Cuba."

"But my grandfather told me you could make all the arrangements."

"I am very sorry, Miss Arden. Since 9/11 we are cooperating with the United States Government and just do not arrange for flights to Cuba."

Francesca turned to Cavanaugh who was sitting naked next to her on the bed. "He says they don't book flights to Cuba anymore. What do we do?"

Cavanaugh said, "Tell him who your grandfather is."

She turned back to the phone. "I think you might know my grandfather."

"Your grandfather could be my brother, and I would have to tell him the same thing. I am very sorry."

Cavanaugh leaned forward looking at the bruise which ran across her breasts. "Tell him your grandfather's name."

She looked at him like robin red-breast spotting a human being coming closer and then told the voice from the Thomas DiNotte Travel Agency, "My grandfather's name is Vito Muscatelli."

There was silence on the other end of the phone. Then the man cleared his throat. "I . . . I'm sorry, Miss Arden, I didn't know. You didn't say you were Mr. Muscatelli's granddaughter. I apologize. If you will hold on for a minute I will see what I can do."

"Thank you," she replied as music began to play in the background.

They looked at each other. They were sitting naked on the edge of the bed. "This may take a while," Cavanaugh said. "Why not put the phone on speaker while we find something else to do?"

She smiled. "You're an animal!"

"I love you, Francesca Arden."

They fell back on the bed just as the man from the Travel Agency came back on the line. "You have a choice of flights, Miss Arden. One leaves Toronto Pearson International at 10:55 this morning and arrives in Havana, Cuba at 2:25 this afternoon. The other leaves at 6:25 PM and arrives in Havana at 10:00 PM."

He whispered to her, "We won't have time for the first flight, and the second is a little late. Ask him what other flights are available."

She asked, and he replied, "That's it for the direct flights. If you want to go to Nassau and then take a flight the next day to Havana we could arrange that . . . ."

Cavanaugh shook his head. "We need a direct flight. I want to get there today."

"Isn't there any other flight we could take that would get us there today?"

The voice on the phone hesitated. She heard him tapping a number of keys in haste. "There is one possibility I will check for you. There is a medical group that has chartered a Cubana Airbus for a tour of Havana health care facilities. The plane only holds 150 people and it might be all booked up. It leaves from Pearson at 1:15 this afternoon and arrives at José Martí International Airport in Havana at 4:05 . . . ."

Cavanaugh nodded yes. "That will give us time to get some clothes," he whispered looking down at himself and then at Fran's breasts.

She smiled. "I would appreciate it if you could check on that for us and try to squeeze us on that plane."

"Hold on, Miss Arden," he said, "I'll see what I can do."

The music came on again, but Cavanaugh stood and started searching for his clothes. "If we do get that flight, we are going to need some time to shop, eat, and go through customs."

"How do we get through customs?" Fran asked.

"I'm not sure. Maybe they won't bother with us." Then he added almost as an after-thought, "Why don't your ask your grandfather's buddy if he can help?"

"Don't get snippy, Tom. My grandfather is helping us."

Cavanaugh went to the bathroom. The water in the tub was still there. The drain was clogged. He washed his face in the sink and thought. He needed to check with Goldberg about how Healen and the nurse were killed back at the hospital. If it was Cain Holland how did he get to the hospital to silence Healen? The only way he could have known was if someone told him about the accident. When Fran tried to call 911, she got her grandfather instead. He must have told Holland to get rid of the evidence and Cavanaugh in the process. But he had taken off before Holland could get him. If Vito Muscatelli was behind this, he would soon find out what flight he was on. He might know already. He had recommended the travel agent. If Holland didn't make an attempt on his life here in Canada, he most likely would try to make one in Havana. Maybe that was what he was waiting for. Holland could get both him and his brother together. Muscatelli, "the kind, benevolent grandfather," had given Francesca the name of a man in Havana, named Francisco Santacruz, who supposedly would help them find his brother. Santacruz, Cavanaugh realized, must be another of Muscatelli's people. This wasn't going to be easy. He wondered what other tricks old man Muscatelli had up his sleeve. This definitely wasn't going to be easy. He would have to follow the path Muscatelli had laid out for them knowing all the way that he was walking into a trap. He felt like a Christian being thrown into the lion's den. He would have to watch his . . . .

Bang! Bang! Bang! Fran knocked on the door. "He did it, Tom! He did it!" she yelled. "The plane was booked solid, but there were three sudden cancellations this morning, and he said he is fitting us in!"

Cavanaugh frowned. He didn't like the sound of "sudden cancellations." "Did you ask him about getting through customs?"

"No," she said. "He's still on the phone, I'll ask him now."

Cavanaugh finished dressing and walked out of the bathroom to hear Fran shouting to the voice on the speaker phone. "What will we need to get onboard? We are both Americans."

"No problem, Miss Arden, go to the ticket agent at the far left in the terminal. His name is McClory. He will have your tickets and will tell you where to go."

"Thank you. Will you need my credit card number?"

"No. That won't be necessary. Just get to the airport at least three hours before scheduled takeoff. Goodbye and good luck."

With that the phone went dead.

* * *

68

Brooklyn, New York

It was Sunday, but Goldberg called in some homicide detectives to help him interview the newspaper and television reporters and photographers and camera crews who were at the scene when Crystal May's body was found. Barbara Palambo was a veteran cop. She took no nonsense from anyone. She was just as likely to call a spade a spade as she was to call it an f—ing shovel. He liked her. Mike Waters, on the other hand, was a short, burly veteran content to hang around eating jelly and chocolate cream donuts and telling jokes about different ethnic groups until he could collect his pension. He was putting his time in and little more. He didn't like being called in to work on a Sunday. But it was overtime, and Goldberg was supplying the donuts.

The list of people Goldberg compiled was extensive and none of them wanted to be interviewed. He gave Palambo and Waters two separate lists of names and addresses. Palambo's included the newspaper reporters on the scene that night: Clayton Shaffer, Daniel Feaster, Cornelius Carroll, Tony Yaccarino, Harry Joannides, Bob Boyd, Holly Siegel, Jerome Lipton, Adam Kulack, Carter Evans, Jim McCarthy, Frankie Funicula, and Dorothy Black. Waters' list included television reporters, photographers, and camera people: Jack Minutella, Dave Slattery, Jim Bolger, Gabe Pressman, John MacMullin, Joe Bocalla, Eugene Smith, Pablo Guzman, Mike Sheehan, Rita Nissane, Mike Gilliam, Greg Cerrillo, Tom Francis, Prentice Conte, Vanessa Lee, Bill Napolitano, and Fred Follabaluch.

Waters checked his list and started complaining immediately. "Why is her list shorter than mine? This isn't fair."

"Cry me a river, Waters. You sound like Ray Charles for Christ's sake."

"What are you talking about?" Waters said reaching for a chocolate jelly donut.

"Where the hell have you been all your life? Life ain't fair. If you think it is, tell it to the mosquitoes and the cows and the chickens."

Waters took a bite out of his donut and jelly slid down his chin like melting ice cream. He looked at Goldberg. "Hey, Goldie, what the hell is she talking about?"

Before Goldberg could respond, Palambo said, "If you don't like your God-damn list, give it to me. You can have my f—en list! Just stop whining like a cat in heat!"

Waters pulled his list back. "No. I want my list. I've got some heavy hitter names on my list. Maybe I'll get on TV tonight . . . ."

"Fat chance that will happen," Palambo stated. "They say TV makes you look ten pounds heavier. If that's true, you wouldn't fit on the screen."

Goldberg stepped between the two. "Hold it now, detectives," he said raising his hands. "We have a lot of work to do here. When Cavanaugh and I left the scene of the murder of Crystal May, there were news people and cameras all over the place."

"Yeah, that's when Cavanaugh slugged that radio reporter," Waters said. He reached for another donut.

"There was an altercation at the scene. The reporters there seemed to know too much about the actual murder scene which they had not seen."

"Someone tipped them off," Palambo commented.

"Exactly. And we want to find out who that was. They knew the victim was female, that there was a note beside her body, and that Cavanaugh's name was on that note. No one should have known those facts at that time."

Palambo looked intently at her list. Waters wiped sugar off his hands.

"I want you both to try to find out who tipped the reporters to some facts possibly only the murderer would know."

Palambo said what Goldberg was already thinking, "That's a long shot, Morty."

Goldberg nodded. "We've got to cover all the bases."

Waters asked, "And what are you going to do while we're out there busting our asses?"

Goldberg didn't want to answer him, but he did. "I'm going to interview Cavanaugh's barber."

Palambo and Waters looked at each other. Goldberg turned, straightened his tie and headed out to question Steve, Cavanaugh's barber, who had allegedly told Cavanaugh someone was after him.

* * *

69

Havana, Cuba

Father Jack Bennis said Mass in Professor Diego Velasquez's living room early Sunday morning. The congregation was small—Bennis, Velasquez, and María Izabelle Melendez. After Mass, the three moved into the kitchen where they sat around the small wooden table dunking *tostada* into their *café con leche* and discussed the results of their research into Francisco Santacruz. In the background the voice of Carlos Pueblo singing "*Hasta Siempre Comandante*" played on a blue plastic Motorola clock radio perched on top of the refrigerator.

María Izabelle chattered away like a group of parakeets on crystal meth. Diego and Jack Bennis listened while they occasionally sipped their coffee.

" . . . Santacruz is into real estate big time. He's been quietly buying up a number of buildings along the Malecón. The buildings are abandoned and dilapidated now. If the embargo ever ends, however, and we all believe it is only a matter of time, he is in position to make a killing . . . ."

"Were you able to find out where his money comes from?" Bennis asked.

"Nothing definitive. He pays for the buildings in cash—American dollars. I don't know where they come from."

Bennis put his coffee cup down and wrote on a sheet of paper, "Follow the money."

Diego spoke. "I checked old newspaper files and the Internet in the University library. He was born Frank Santacroce in Brooklyn, New York. His mother was an unwed stripper. He caused a bit of a commotion when he received probation after mugging an elderly woman. After three years probation, he apparently moved to Roseland, New Jersey, where he became involved in a concrete business. There was one small reference to his being questioned along with a number of others about a money laundering scheme. He never actually served time in prison. He disappeared from sight for a few more years and then surfaced here in Havana about ten years ago when he changed his name to Francisco Santacruz. Since coming to Cuba, apparently he has been a model citizen."

Bennis thought aloud, "I wonder if that's where his money comes from. He could be investing American dollars here as a way of laundering mob monies and of setting up a base for something else."

Diego studied the notes he had compiled from the library. "He's involved in practically every organization you can think of here in Havana." He started to read from a long list, "He is a member of the elite Central Committee of the Communist Party of Cuba, the Committee for the Defense of the Revolution, the National Association of Small Farmers, the Confederation of Cuban Workers, the Union of Young Communists of Cuba, the Federation of Cuban University Students. He is also a consultant to Alamar Associates which deals with hundreds of U.S. corporations and media outlets interested in establishing business in and with Cuba."

"That's some list," María Izabelle commented.

"That's not the half of it," Diego said. "He belongs to a number of professional groups including ProNaturaleza and the Cuban Society for the Biological Sciences as well as a number of different religious organizations."

"Why would he be so involved?" María Izabelle asked. "He must be a good man to belong to all those organizations."

"Or it could be something else," Bennis suggested.

"Padre, you might be right. Listen to this. He is also a member of the National Liberation Directorate, a group that supports revolutionary groups around the world and has set up a number of covert missions and terrorist training camps. And he is also an officer in the Latin American Solidarity Organization which is dedicated to fight what they call North American imperialism. And I happen to know he is a member of the Board of Trustees of the University of Havana."

"I see he is covering all the bases," Bennis whispered. "Back in New York, we would call him a Heavy Hitter."

María Izabelle smiled.

"What's so funny?" the priest asked.

She giggled like a little school girl. "I love your baseball allusions."

Diego redirected the conversation. "Why do you think he belongs to so many different organizations?"

"If he is laundering money from the States, he is trying to align himself with as many different groups as he can. It's good business sense. He works with the government; he works with businesses; he works with the churches; he even works with the revolutionaries. In the process, he has made himself a very powerful man," Bennis stated. Then he added, "And a very dangerous man, too."

"But didn't you tell us when you first came here, you were suspicious of Señor Santacruz?"

"Yes. I should explain. It's a long story. His name was on a list of contacts I obtained in a roundabout way from a notorious Brooklyn mob boss named Vito Muscatelli. Muscatelli is an old, but still very powerful mob boss who maintains ties with the Castro regime." Jack Bennis left out the details of how Howard Stevens, a former C.I.A. operative and his former commanding officer in covert activities had kidnapped Muscatelli's grandson and tried unsuccessfully to recruit Bennis to assassinate Fidel Castro. In a brief, but lethal shootout, his half-brother's partner, Morty Goldberg, shot and killed Stevens. In the ensuing confusion, however, Bennis slipped away with the list of contacts, a suitcase full of money, and a number of large Swiss bank account numbers. He had chosen to come to Cuba to get away from the crime and violence he witnessed around him in New York and at the same time to try to help in rebuilding a country ravaged by communism and religious suppression. He wanted to believe he could do this as a priest, but the crime and violence followed him like his shadow.

"What do you think, Padre?" Diego asked.

The question broke Bennis' reverie. "I'm sorry," he said, "what was that you said?"

María Izabelle repeated, "Why would he want you to hurt you if he never even met you?"

Jack Bennis paused and then answered. "I don't know for sure, but since I initially tried to contact him, some men have been trying to kill me. The shooting the other day was just one incident. A few days before, a couple of other men tried to kill me. And then yesterday at the hospital . . . ."

"At the hospital?" María Izabelle asked. "What were you doing at the hospital? You were supposed to stay here while we did research on Santacruz."

Bennis smiled and shrugged his shoulders. "I got bored."

"What happened at the hospital, Padre?" Diego asked.

Jack Bennis downplayed the fat stranger who almost shot him. "It was nothing really. I shouldn't have even said anything. I was doing a corporal work of mercy—visiting the sick. Manuel in particular. Manuel introduced me to his Babalawo and . . . ."

"You spoke with a Babalawo?" María Izabelle gasped. "They are the devil incarnate. He could put a voodoo curse upon you!"

"No, María Izabelle, he was a gentleman and we got along fine."

Diego cautioned, "It is said the powers of evil can betray us with honest trifles, Padre. You must be more careful."

"Actually," Bennis admitted, "Manuel saved my life and his Babalawo reminded me of a valuable lesson that could save my soul."

Both Diego and María Izabelle asked in unison, "What happened?"

Briefly, the priest related how someone had aimed a gun at him and after a brief struggle had fled down the hall.

"Did you know the man?"

"No. I never saw him before, but trust me, Diego, I will remember him. To paraphrase an old Irish saying, 'I try hard to forgive my enemies, but I never forget their names or their faces.'" He took another sip of his coffee which was now cold and added, "I did discover where the shot came from the other day, however. It came from a four story Art Deco building a block away from the hospital. Would you care to guess who has an office in the building on the fourth floor?"

María Izabelle and Diego looked at each other. They were puzzled until Jack Bennis answered his own question. "Does the name Francisco Santacruz ring a bell?"

* * *

70

Toronto Pearson International Airport, Canada

The terminal was busy. But there was an ease and a peacefulness to the busyness as people gazed about at the architecture and displays in the terminal. Cavanaugh and Francesca wandered around sculptures and art displays looking for Cubana Airlines. It didn't feel like a typical airline terminal. The artwork gave the airport an elegance that distracted them. Large neon tubing in the baggage area looked like someone had written script with bi-colored glass. Bright red, blue, yellow concentric bands flared out over the walls high above them like psychedelic waves spreading from a bull's eye. Transparent polycarbonate resin thermoplastic figures danced from stainless steel cables like multicolored naked astronauts swimming freely in space.

For a moment, Cavanaugh entered into a surrealistic world that absorbed his interests and diverted his attention. He became lost in observing sculptures and art work more reminiscent of a museum than an airport. It was the blue and black checkered acrylic and oil painting on wood by Ingelborg Hiscox, however, that snapped him back to reality. Obscure letters or formulas seemed to float on black checker boxes in front of blue skies and white cumulous clouds. The letterforms reminded him of the notes left by the bodies of Crystal May and Luca Andrassy. The letters on the notes were clearer, but their meaning as obscure as the writing on the painting before him.

"Fran," he said tugging her arm, "come on. We've got to find this guy McClory and get the tickets."

"Can you believe this art work, Tom? Everything, in one way or another, is a celebration of flight."

Cavanaugh suddenly became aware of passersby. He had the feeling he was being watched. "Come on, Fran. Let's get the tickets and then do some shopping for clothes."

The world "shopping" got Francesca's attention. Together they worked their way to the Cubana ticket counter. At the end of the counter, as the Travel Agent had said, stood a man in a blue uniform with a name tag that read "McClory." He stood about six feet tall. His face had an Irish sunburn that could have been caused by drinking. He had sad basset hound eyes and an angry pit bull mouth. He held an envelope in his folded arms.

"Excuse me, sir," Francesca began. "Would you be Mr. McClory?"

"That's what the name tag says, lady. What do you want?"

"The travel agent at the Thomas DiNotte Travel Agency told us to find you."

"I'm McClory. What do you want?"

"He said you would have tickets for us."

McClory stared at Francesca as if he were undressing her. Then he unfolded his arms and reached into the envelope. "What's your name?" he asked.

Fran told him. His expression didn't change.

"And him?" he said motioning to Cavanaugh.

"His name's Cavanaugh, Thomas Cavanaugh," Fran said.

"Does he have a mouth?" he asked.

Cavanaugh took a step forward. Fran stepped in front of him. "No, Tom, don't."

"Yeah, McClory, I have a mouth. Do you have the tickets or not?"

McClory checked the names on the ticket, handed them over, and said, "Follow me." He never checked for ID. He led them down the main corridor and then opened a door reading "Authorized Personnel Only," and they left the main terminal and entered a labyrinth of halls. The hallway was narrower and dimly lit. They continued following the man, who said his name was McClory, through a number of twists and turns. He used a key to open a few more doors. The smell of diesel fuel became stronger. They heard engines revving, some men cursing behind the walls, and baggage being bounced about. Occasionally an airport worker passed them, but they continued. Finally, they came to a door marked "Do Not Open." McClory used another key and turned to them.

"You are passed security now. There are some stores here where you can buy some clothes. You shouldn't have any problems from here on," he said.

Before he opened the door, he turned to Francesca. "Do you mind if I ask you one question?" His voice was softer, almost apologetic. "Are you really Vito Muscatelli's granddaughter?"

"Yes, I am," she said.

He opened the door slowly and motioned them to go through. "Have a nice flight, Miss Arden."

Cavanaugh and Francesca found themselves in what looked like a frequent flyer lounge. The door swung closed behind them and McClory was gone.

Cavanaugh looked around again. This was too easy. Much too easy.

* * *

71

Brooklyn, New York

Detective Goldberg checked the house number against his notes. According to the address in Cavanaugh's book, the house in front of him belonged to a Steve Impellizzieri. Tall stone columns stood on each side of the double entry doors. Seven stone steps led up to the door flanked by fat stone balusters supporting thick stone slabs. The white brick house contrasted with the other older homes on the block. The grass had been replaced with white gravel stones. A pink plastic flamingo clasped the mailbox in its beak with the house number emblazoned on it in gold letters. The number matched. This was the right house.

Goldberg wondered what the monthly mortgage payment on a house this large must be. It looked more like the home of a bank president or a Wall Street broker with tawdry taste, not a barber. He felt like he was on a movie set walking up the steps passed the two stone lions guarding the house. But when he rang the door bell and heard the chimes play *Volare*, he was confident whoever lived there must be a friend of Cavanaugh's with taste like this.

An elderly gentleman answered the door. He had stark white hair and blue-green eyes.

"Good morning, sir," Goldberg began showing the man his badge, "I am Detective Goldberg and I would like to ask Steve some questions."

"Why?" the man asked blocking the entrance and holding the door with a large muscular hand.

"I would just like to ask him a few questions."

"Why? What's he done?"

"Nothing, sir. I just have some routine questions to ask him about an incident we are investigating."

"What incident?"

Goldberg was growing impatient with the old man. "Listen. We can do this the easy way or the hard way. I just want to ask a few questions and then I will be on my way or I can come back with a warrant and bring everyone down to the stationhouse for questioning."

The white haired man thought for a moment and then made a decision. "Which Steve do you want?"

"Steve the barber."

"I'm Steve the barber. My son is Steve the barber. And my grandson will soon be Steve the barber once he gets out of barber school."

Goldberg straightened his tie. "I want to see the Steve who cuts Detective Thomas Cavanaugh's hair."

"Thomas Cavanaugh? I never knew his name was Thomas. I always just call him Cavanaugh. What trouble has he gotten himself into now? Did he slug another reporter? Is that what this is about?"

Goldberg stayed on target. "Are you the Steve who cut Cavanaugh's hair last Tuesday?"

"No. That was my son."

"May I come in and speak with him?"

"No."

"Excuse me?"

"You heard me. Do you have a search warrant?"

"Please, sir, I just want to ask him a few questions."

"Steve's having breakfast now. I'll get him and see if he wants to speak with you." With that comment, Steve the father and grandfather shut the door in Goldberg's face. Goldberg could feel his pressure rising. He wanted to ring the doorbell again, but he didn't want to hear the chimes playing *Volare* again. He remembered a joke Cavanaugh told about the two prisoners who were about to be executed. The warden granted them each one a last request. The first one asked them to play *Volare* once more for him. When the other prisoner heard this, he made his last request, "Kill me first." He was smiling at his partner's corny sense of humor when the door reopened. The man at the door this time was younger. He wore a white terrycloth bathrobe over what looked like blue and brown plaid flannel pajamas. His eyes were the same blue-green as the man in the white hair, but this man was balding.

"Sorry to keep you waiting, Detective. My father tells me you want to ask me a few questions."

"Are you Steve the barber that cuts Detective Cavanaugh's hair?"

"Well, actually I prefer to be called a tonsorial artist, but yeah. That's me. What did he turn me in for—a bad haircut?" Steve smiled and stepped out onto the steps. He did not invite Goldberg into the house.

"Did you cut his hair last Tuesday?"

"Guilty!" Steve said and held out his hands as if to be arrested.

Goldberg didn't laugh. "I didn't come out here to play games, Steve. I am investigating a number of homicides." He saw the expression in Steve's eyes change and he got right to the point. "Did you tell him someone was out to get him?"

Steve ran his hand through his thinning black hair. "Shit!" he murmured. "Is that what this is all about?" Then he suddenly looked at Goldberg and asked, "Is he alright? Did anything happen to him?"

Goldberg ignored the questions. "How did you come about this information?"

"Shit," Steve repeated, "tell me he's alright. I wanted to warn him. I didn't really believe it, but I thought I should tell him. He didn't seem to be too worried about it. I told him some psycho on the street was after him and that he should watch his back."

"How did you come about this information?"

"I didn't believe it. He's a good guy. We joke a lot when he comes in here. Tell me he's okay . . . ."

Goldberg nodded, "I spoke with him yesterday. He's okay. But who told you?"

Steve shook his head, "I should have told him the whole story, but I didn't."

"Tell me."

"I got a call in the shop from some guy. He had a deep voice. It sounded like he could have been disguising his voice. I don't know. He asked if I was the barber who cut Cavanaugh's hair. I told him I was. I thought the guy wanted a haircut like his. What an idiot!"

"Go on," Goldberg said as he began to take notes.

"The guy on the phone said he had a score to settle with Cavanaugh and that he was going to taunt him before he killed him. I told Cavanaugh I heard rumors on the street. I didn't tell him about the call. When I told him he just shrugged. He said something like the taunting had already begun."

"When did you tell him this?"

"It was the day after he slugged that news reporter. It was all over the papers. I remember my father teased him a bit about that. Cavanaugh was my first customer that day . . . ."

"When did you get the call?"

Steve thought for a minute. "Let me think. It was a couple of weeks ago, I think. Now I remember. It was right after Cavanaugh was acquitted by the Grand Jury. We were so glad to hear the news in the shop. Then the call came. I didn't make much of it, but I told him anyway. I told him to watch his back."

It was a Coroner's Inquest, not a Grand Jury, but Goldberg didn't correct him. "I have to ask you, Steve. Where were you Tuesday night?"

Steve looked down and then checked the door behind him. He hesitated. "I was in the emergency room," he said. "You can check."

"Why?"

"It's my father. He had a slight stroke. He's been having them more frequently lately, and it's affected him a bit emotionally and mentally. I guess you have to expect it. He's 89 and has smoked all his life. Physically, he's as strong and healthy as a bull, but he's slowed down in other areas, and I have to keep an eye on him."

Goldberg was curious. "He said he was a barber. Does he still cut hair?"

Steve shook his head. "He hasn't cut hair in about ten years. I watch him in the store. He reads the paper and talks with the customers. He usually forgets what happens during the day by dinner time." He stopped and looked at Goldberg. "I love him, Detective. It's not fair what's happening to him. Little by little, he's slipping away from us. I try to keep him active. He's my father. He took care of me and raised me. I have to take care of him. I know it's a losing battle, but . . . ."

They both heard dishes crashing inside the house and the white haired man's voice screaming. "I have to get back in there, Detective," Steve said.

Goldberg handed him his card. "If you remember anything else, please give me a call."

"I will," Steve promised opening the door, "and give my best to Cavanaugh when you see him."

"I will," Goldberg said. If I ever see him again, he thought.

* * *

72

Toronto Pearson International Airport, Canada

Cavanaugh and Fran surveyed the travelers' waiting area and worked their way to the gate where their flight was to depart. The departing schedule indicated their flight was on time. In the area by the gate they were to leave from a number of passengers had already assembled. Most of them were women. Cavanaugh imagined they were mostly doctors, physician assistants, and nurses. Their ages ranged from late twenties to early seventies. Most of them had carry-on bags. He and Fran had nothing but their dirty clothes.

"I think we had better get some new clothes before the plane takes off," he suggested.

Fran nodded covering her ripped and blood stained blouse with her arm. "Good idea," she said. "Then maybe we can change in one of the rest rooms."

"Why didn't I think of that?" Cavanaugh smiled. "Let's split up and get the clothes. It will be hot in Havana so think light stuff."

"Maybe we should each pick up a traveling bag, too, to put some toiletries and extra clothes in there. It might be difficult getting things in Cuba."

"Another great suggestion," he said. "Why didn't I think of that?"

She punched him in his arm. "Oh, shut up, smart ass! I'll meet you back here."

Cavanaugh's shopping was fast and furious. There actually wasn't much to choose from, but he purchased a few short sleeve shirts, a razor, a bar of soap, and a pair of trousers he would have never paid that much for back in New York. He shoved the clothes in a Toronto Maple Leaf hockey duffle bag and changed in the Men's Rest Room. Then he picked up a copy of the *Toronto Star* and went to the gate to wait for Francesca.

While shopping he had the distinct feeling he was being watched. He could feel it. Checking the other passengers no one seemed particularly interested in him. But the feeling persisted. Sitting at the gate, he turned to the sports pages of the *Toronto Star* as he eavesdropped on conversations going on around him.

"I can't wait to get to Cuba. I've always wanted to see it . . . ."

"We are scheduled to visit the University of Havana's biology department and the Insitituto Superior de Ciencias Medicas de La Habana . . . ."

"I don't speak Spanish. Will that be a drawback?"

"Don't worry. Our tour guide will interpret things for us. Plus Lisette speaks about six different languages. She will help . . . ."

"Do you think we'll see Castro?"

"I heard they have a great ice cream place in Havana. I can't remember the name of it though . . . ."

"I haven't seen the girls from Minneapolis we met last night at the Tryst nightclub . . . ."

"Didn't you love the Vault Room. It was so neat with all that snakeskin . . . ."

"I couldn't take my eyes off the spy screen where you could watch what was happening in the rest of the club rooms . . . ."

"It was great not having to worry about your purse . . . ."

"Where did you get those shoes? They look fantastic . . . ."

"Did you see the clothes Susan brought? You'd think she was going to spend a month there . . . ."

Cavanaugh turned the pages of the paper wondering when Francesca would return. He hoped it would be soon.

"Do you mind if I sit here, young man?" a short gray haired woman in a neat blue pants suit asked. Her accent was British.

"No," Cavanaugh said. "I'm saving this seat for my companion, but that seat is fine."

"Thank you so much. My back is killing me. You know when you get old your body seems to develop aches and pains all over."

Cavanaugh nodded and started to read the paper again.

"You sound like you are from the States. Am I right? I'm usually good at picking out accents."

He nodded again and said, "Yes. You are right."

"I'm originally from Great Britain. But I guess you could tell that, right?"

Cavanaugh nodded again.

"I've been looking forward to this trip to Cuba for some time. I could have flown straight from Heathrow, of course, but I wanted to see some of the churches here in Canada first."

Cavanaugh looked around for Francesca.

"Are you waiting for someone?" the woman asked.

"Yes. That's why I'm saving the seat."

"Oh, silly me. Yes, that's right. I'll bet it's a woman. Am I right?"

Cavanaugh checked his watch. The woman continued to talk. He stood up and looked around. "Maybe I'd better go look for her," he said.

"Oh, I'm sure she's all right. Probably shopping in those duty free shops. You know you can get some good prices on perfume there?" She laughed to herself, "But you don't use perfume now, do you?"

Cavanaugh reached for his bag just as he heard Francesca call, "There you are, Tom. I was looking all over for you." She wore a new red blouse and blue jeans and in her arms she held two huge shopping bags. She looked fantastic.

"What in the world did you buy?" he asked.

The woman from Great Britain chirped, "He was starting to worry about you, pet."

Fran looked at Cavanaugh as if to say, "Who is this woman?"

The woman stood and extended her hand, "Hello, dear," she said, "I'm Eloise. I'm going to Cuba, too."

"Nice to meet you," Fran said. They shook hands and Fran moved closer to Cavanaugh.

"You sound like you're from New York City . . . . Probably Brooklyn. Am I right?"

Francesca nodded.

"Oh, don't fret, dear. I'm good at accents. I've been around a long time so I have heard a few in my time," she giggled to herself and added, "I'm originally from Sunderland. Have you ever heard of it?"

"That's in England, isn't it?"

"Righto, dear. My father was a coal miner, but that was a long time ago . . . ."

Cavanaugh stretched and said, "If you'll excuse me, ladies, I have to visit the Men's Room." Fran gave him a dirty look and Eloise kept talking.

He headed in the direction of the Men's Room, but he was actually searching for a telephone. He wanted to check in with Goldberg before they left. Walking toward the bank of phones on the wall, he still had the feeling he was being watched. Maybe it was paranoia, he thought, but somehow he felt Cain Holland was watching him.

* * *

73

Brooklyn, New York

Goldberg got Cavanaugh's call on his cell phone as he was getting into his black Plymouth sedan from Steve's house.

"Hi, Morty. It's me again."

"Where are you, Tom? Everyone's looking for you."

"What did you find out about the killings in the hospital in Pennsylvania?"

"Almost the same MO. Slit throats. Missing earring from the female which was placed on the pillow of the male. It must be this sick bastard's signature."

"Was there a note?" Cavanaugh asked apprehensively.

"Not that I could determine."

"How about the earring? Right or left?"

"Right."

"And no maple syrup, right?

Goldberg hesitated. "Right, but how did you know?"

Cavanaugh spoke quickly confirming what Goldberg had been thinking. "We're looking at two killers, Morty. The one you have down there must be imitating this Cain Holland, but your killer is most likely right handed. When he reaches down to take the earring, he uses his right hand and takes the left earring. The one I think is following me is this Holland character, the guy nobody has ever seen. He's the professional, and he is probably left handed. He rips the right earring off his victims. Your killer has something personal against me, and the maple syrup means something. Find out what it is and you should be able to get him. He thinks he's pretty smart, but he might be too smart for himself. He obviously knows what is going on around the station because his last note indicated he knew I wasn't there.

My guess is Merry knew him and he killed her because she was onto him. It is someone who has access to police records."

"Shanley did tell me she was going out with someone and that she suddenly broke it off."

Cavanaugh still felt like someone was watching him. He heard the boarding announcement for his flight. "I've got to go now, Morty."

"What about the hair?"

"I don't know. You're the detective. Figure it out. I can't do everything for you."

"Where are you?" Goldberg asked.

"I'm about to board the plane to Cuba, amigo. *Hasta la vista*, Morty!" he said and hung up.

Goldberg drove back to the precinct slowly. He took time to stop at Mittleman's Supermarket for a corn-beef sandwich and a cream soda and ate in the park. The pieces were slowly coming together. They usually did. It wasn't like in the movies. It was more like digging for buried treasures. You didn't know where to look so you tilled and turned over all the stones you could and then dug and dug until you found something. And that something led to something else. Most of the time, however, you came up empty. Patience, determination, and hard work were what it took. The glamour and heroics were for the movies, he thought.

When he arrived back at his desk, both Barbara Palambo and Mike Waters were there waiting for him. They both looked tired after their interviewing of the reporters from the first murder scene. From the look on their faces, however, they didn't have much.

"That was fast," Goldberg stated. "How did you manage to interview all those people in such a short time?"

"It really wasn't that hard. We heard there was a shooting at Castleton Avenue and Broadway on Staten Island possibly involving a hostage situation," Palambo said. "We went there and pretty much found the whole crew."

"Yeah, we split up and got almost all of them," Waters said. "There were only a couple we missed who were assigned to other stories or just weren't working today."

"We can get them on Monday, but I have a feeling we're going to get the same story."

"You are probably right, Barbara, but let's check them out anyway on Monday," Goldberg commented. "You know the routine—cover all the bases."

"It was a total waste of my God-damn time!" Waters complained. "You dragged me in on a Sunday when I could have been home watching the Giants play New England to traipse around New York asking reporters for their source of information."

"Shut up and stop whining," Palambo said. "I swear you're like a freakin' broken record, for Christ's sake!"

Goldberg looked at them and asked, "Well, what did you find?"

"Not a God-damn thing," Waters said. "They all refused to give up their source."

"A few of them told me they heard it in the crowd and picked up on it. They had no real source, just the rumor that was spreading through the crowd of reporters. They jumped on it and ran with it, but Waters is right. They didn't want to give away their source—even if they didn't have one," Palambo said.

"Thanks anyway," Goldberg said. "I pretty much drew a blank, too."

His phone rang. It was Shanley. "Goldberg," he said, "I've been thinking about what you said about when Merry said her boyfriend changed. I've been racking my brain all day and then it hit me! It was right after the shooting in the deli with Cavanaugh and those kids. She said he changed and then a few days later she told me they had broken up."

Goldberg looked down at the paper clippings on his desk. The shooting must have had something to do with the murders. But what?

"Does that help, Goldberg?" Shanley asked.

"Yeah, Mike, I think it does. Thanks."

As he replaced the receiver, Waters asked, "Now can we go? My feet are killing me."

"One more thing," Goldberg said looking at the papers. "I want you to interview the immediate family of the two teens killed in the deli."

"What deli?" Waters asked.

"The bodega where Cavanaugh shot the two teenagers and almost caused a riot." He gave them the addresses of Walcott and Cardo. "Go together on this one," he cautioned. "I'm beginning to think the murders have something to do with that shooting. If you get anything, give me a call on my cell." He looked down at the obituary of Maria DeFillipo. "I'm going to visit Maria DeFillipo's parents, Mr. and Mrs. Yaccarino. She was visiting them the day she was shot."

A voice behind him startled him. "Need any help, Goldberg? I'm not busy. Maybe I could lend a hand."

It was Bill Midrasic. He was dressed in civilian clothes. Without his navy blue police hat, Midrasic's curly dark hair looked strangely out of place. Goldberg wondered why Midrasic was being so helpful. Probably trying to get some overtime, he figured. With the latest round of the city's draconian budget cuts, overtime was at a premium. Or maybe there were some personal problems. He had heard rumors about a possible divorce. Goldberg always found Midrasic to be a likeable guy, but he was well aware that there was no love lost between Midrasic and Cavanaugh. Neither man ever mentioned anything to him, but he could sense it in the air like sweat in a boys' locker room whenever the two were together.

"No thanks, Bill," Goldberg said, "but thanks for asking."

* * *

74

Toronto Pearson International Airport, Canada

Cavanaugh rushed back to Francesca. She was still talking with the woman from Great Britain. Or rather she was listening to Eloise who was going on about her favorite store in London, Alexander McQueen's on Old Bond Street. He excused himself and called Fran away.

"Does she ever shut up?" he whispered.

"Tom, she's nice. She's traveling by herself. It can be difficult when you are alone."

"Whatever," he shrugged and then added, "I just spoke with Morty on the phone. I think they're closing in on the serial killer down there." He didn't tell her there was still another killer on the loose chasing him and that her grandfather had probably hired this one to kill both him and his brother.

As they lined up for boarding, Cavanaugh checked the faces carefully. He spotted a tall man sipping a coffee looking in his direction. The man wore an untucked, orange black and white floral print tropical short sleeve shirt and a beige seagrass straw cowboy hat. With his thin face and black imperial moustache he looked like a Frank Zappa clone. He still had the feeling someone was watching him, but he couldn't be sure it was him. Two attractive middle aged women ahead of them were talking. Their name tags read "Rita Barnes" and "Rona Gecht" and indicated they were both from the Siteman Cancer Center in St. Louis, Missouri.

Rita commented to her friend, "I still don't see the girls we met last night. I hope they didn't oversleep.'

"They're big girls, Rita. I wouldn't worry about them," her friend Rona said.

"They were having a glorious time last night. I hope nothing happened to them.'

"They are probably checking their bags in now. Stop worrying, Rita. You worry about everything. We are on vacation. Relax."

"It's not a vacation, Rona. It's a convention."

Rona laughed, "Same thing!"

Cavanaugh looked around again. He couldn't believe he had gotten past security and was about to board the plane to Cuba. Behind him a tall gray haired man with gold wire glasses was trying to comfort a young, nervous blond who could have been his daughter, but was more likely his sweetheart. "Don't worry, Erica, everything will be fine."

"I can't help it, Albert. I have this terrible feeling that something awful is going to happen. I read on the Internet that Cubana Airlines has the worst safety record of all airlines."

"Now, now, Erica, how many times have I told you that you can't believe everything you read on the Internet. It is full of lies. There are so few people you can trust these days," he said kissing her softly on her forehead and fondling her breast with his left hand at the same time. Cavanaugh noted the wedding ring on his finger and the absence of one on hers.

The stewardess at the gate checked their tickets and welcomed them to Cubana Airlines with a smile. Rita Barnes and Rona Gecht turned and looked briefly behind them for the friends they had met the previous night, and then they disappeared into the ramp leading to the plane.

Following them, Cavanaugh held Fran's arm tightly. He too wondered what happened to the three women from Minneapolis. And why had there suddenly been three available seats on the plane. Coincidences? He didn't believe in coincidences.

Only one person on the chartered flight to Havana, Cuba knew what happened to the three women who were at that time piled naked, one on top of the other, in a blood filled bathtub of a hotel in downtown Toronto. Each had her throat slit, her wrists broken, and one missing earring—the right one. Cain Holland smiled remembering the pleas and the agony each of them had gone through before slitting their throats. The cleaning lady would have a surprise when she finally removed the DO NOT DISTURB sign and opened the door to Room 314. Holland would have liked to be there to see the look on her face, but by then Holland would be well on the way to Havana.

* * *

75

Brooklyn, New York

Goldberg sat at his desk for a little while after Palambo and Waters left. He read Maria DeFillipo's obituary again.

Maria DeFillipo 28
Expectant Mother Dies of Gun Shot Wound

Maria DeFillipo of Westerleigh, an expectant mother, died with her unborn fetus yesterday in Kings County Hospital, Brooklyn, of a gun shot wound received during an attempted robbery in Brooklyn. She was 28.

Born Carol Yaccarino in Bensonhurst, Brooklyn, she moved to Westerleigh after she and her husband, Mario, were married in Stella Maris Catholic Church in Brooklyn in 2006. Before moving to Staten Island, Mrs. DeFillipo had worked as a teller for a Chase Manhantan Bank in Bay Ridge, Brooklyn, and as a night waitress at the International House of Pancakes in Coney Island, Brooklyn.

She was a parishioner at Holy Family Catholic Church and a member of their choir and of the Staten Island Philharmonic. A graduate cum laude of Brooklyn College, she received her Bachelor of Science degree in 1999 and had planned to attend New York City Technical College's Department of Dental Hygiene in the fall. She was a graduate of Bishop Kearney High School where she ran cross country track.

Mrs. DeFillipo enjoyed jogging, cooking, singing, gardening, and helping others. Her sudden, untimely death is overwhelming to her family and loved ones. "She would go out of her way to help someone in need. She was a living angel," her twin brother Tony said.

Surviving Mrs. DeFillipo are her husband, Mario, her mother and father, Angela and retired Sgt. Major Joseph Yaccarino, and her twin brother, Tony Yaccarino.

The funeral will be Friday from Casey Funeral Home, Castleton Corners, with a mass at 9:45 AM from Holy Family Church. Burial will follow in Resurrection Cemetery, Pleasant Plains.

Goldberg recalled another article which mentioned her unusual cravings during her pregnancy for mocha chocolate ice cream, pancakes, dill pickles, and hot pastrami sandwiches. He also remembered her father had a black belt in karate.

Then he read the F.B.I. profile on the serial killer they were trying to stop.

The unsub is most likely a white, heterosexual male in his twenties or thirties who has low self-esteem and is sexually dysfunctiional. The analysis of his printing supports the theory of his insecure inner feelings which he attempts to hide from others by appearing outwardly confident. The methodical, ritualistic rage he exhibits in the torturing and killing his victims is likely sexual in nature. The killings may be part of an elaborate fantasy that culminates in the killing of female strangers. The breaking of the wrists to inflict pain is typical of serial killers' sadistic nature in watching others suffer. This killer, like many other serial killers, likes to involve himself in the investigation of the crime and enjoys taunting the authorities with the crude nursery rhymes and other carefully placed items of possible evidenes, such as the human hair and the maple syrup, that he leaves at the scenes. This serial killer most likely grew up in a viloent household, was a chronic bed wetter and as a young boy enjoyed torturing animals and setting fires. He may have a juvenile record. Some significant event may have triggered his rampage of killing and tortuing. He may see himself as an "Avenging Angel" who is trying to right some wrong.

Goldberg was folding the obituary and the F.B.I. profile to take with him to the Yaccarino home when his phone rang. It was Steve the barber.

"Detective Goldberg," he began, "I've been thinking. You asked if anything unusal happened the day Cavanaugh came in for a haircut. It may be nothing, but I thought I'd better tell you anyhow. You can decide."

Goldberg shoved the papers in his jacket pocket and asked, "What is it, Steve?"

"Well, Cavanaugh was my first customer that day. Right after he left, another guy came in. He sat in the chair and then grabbed for his cell phone.

As he was taking it out, it fell and he bent down to pick it up. He gropped around on the floor for a little while. When he came back up, he looked at his phone and said he had an assignment he had to go to and left."

"What was the assignment?"

"I don't know. He didn't say. He put his phone in his pocket and left. He said he would come back later, but he never did."

"Could you describe him, Steve?"

"Sure. He was a little taller than me. I'd say around six feet tall. He had black wavy hair. I notice hair. It's my business. His hair was course and naturally curly. It looked something like an Afro but it was longer and lacked any styling. I was wondering how he wanted it cut, but he never came back."

Goldberg wrote the details down.

"I probably wouldn't have called you about this, but the funny thing is, I never heard his cell phone ring or vibrate. I don't think it ever really rang."

"I know you're busy with your father and all, but if I send someone over with some pictures do you think you could identify the man."

"Definitely. I would know that head of hair anywhere. But I also seem to remember his face from somewhere, but I can't place it."

"Thanks, Steve," Goldberg said, "you've been a great help. I'll call you later about coming over with some pictures."

Heading out to his car to visit Maria DeFillipo's parents, Goldberg thought, "Patience, determination, and hard work do it every time, but sometimes a little luck helps too."

* * *

76

Havana, Cuba

María Izabelle laid the sketch she had made of Santacruz's house on the kitchen table. It was meticulous down to the shrubs and trees in front of the house. Jack Bennis studied the drawing like a surgeon examining an x-ray. He had walked by the house before, but had not been aware of the details he was now looking at. He looked up and smiled. "How did you manage to get this?" he asked.

Diego answered, "You don't know María Izabelle, Padre. When she puts her mind to something she can do anything."

Bennis raised his eyebrows and smiled again looking straight at María Izabelle. "You are beginning to scare me," he said.

María Izabelle reached into the large bag she had brought with her and pulled out more papers. There were floor plans for Santacruz's house. "I had a bit more trouble with these, but I finally discovered some interesting facts about his house. It was originally built by Meyer Lansky who was an American gangster and considered by many to be the brains behind organized crime in Cuba in the 40s and 50s."

Diego nodded, "I remember Lansky. He befriended Batista and then planned to build around fifty hotels with casinos along the coastal Malecón highway. One story has it that when Lansky spread out two suitcases with six million dollars in cash on a bed in a hotel room, Batista actually had an orgasm when he saw all that money. Lansky and his mob friends wanted to convert Havana into a Mecca for gambling, drugs, and sex. Back then it was a great place to go to lose your money, buy your dope, or see women having sex with animals. And for as long as Batista was in power, the mob and Lansky had their way."

"That all ended when Castro came into power," Bennis commented.

"Yes," María Izabelle agreed, "but Lansky used this house for a lot of different things. Originally, he supposedly built it for Carmen, his mistress, but when the American Mafia and Cosa Nostra leaders met here in Havana in 1946 he put some of them up there. In fact, after Castro took over and clamped down on the casinos, Lansky hid out in the house until he managed to escape with a phony passport."

Jack Bennis rose and went to the sink to make more coffee. "Lansky was a money man," he said. "He brought the mob organization and structure."

"I remember reading somewhere," Diego said, "how when Batista was in power he called on Lansky to reform the Montmartre Club. Lansky got rid of a lot of crooked dealers and croupiers in the casino. He was smart and innovative. He introduced dealing Blackjack from a six-deck shoe to increase the house's profit margin and minimize cheating dealers and players. He was definitely a shrewd businessman. He controlled the casinos in Cuba in those days. They say he personally deposited three million dollars in a Zurich, Switzerland bank for Batista and agreed to turn over fifty percent of the casino profits to Batista and his people for the monopoly he had on Cuban gambling."

"There is no telling what he could have accomplished if he were honest," Bennis added. "But like a lot of people his God was the Almighty Dollar. He believed there was never enough money a person could have. Supposedly, he left over $400 million dollars when he died. But no one knows where."

"With money like that," Diego stated, "people listen."

María Izabelle pointed to the floor plans she spread out on the table. "I tried to gather these from public records and visual recollections as far as I could," she said.

"Visual recollections? You were in the house?" Bennis asked.

She nodded. "I pretended I was looking for a job as a cleaning lady and they let me in. I told them a friend told me they were looking for a new person. I only got to look around the first floor before the wife came down and told me in no unspoken words I had been misled. The fat guy who let me in practically threw me out the front door."

Bennis recalled the man who had tried to shoot him in the hospital. "I thought you told me you were going to be careful, María Izabelle. These are bad people. They are dangerous. This is not a game. You could have been hurt."

She smiled and winked at him, "But I wasn't."

* * *

77

Skies over the Atlantic Ocean

Cavanaugh knew it was going to be a long flight when he saw Eloise, the loquacious lady from the boarding area, sitting in the seat by the window of his row. In front of them Rita Barnes and Rona Gecht had been joined by one of their friends. A few rows behind them on the other side of the plane, he saw the mismatched couple of Albert and Erica. As he was placing his duffel bag and Fran's shopping bags in the overhead compartment, another man abruptly bumped into him. Cavanaugh instinctively grabbed to check his wallet and inadvertently hit the man in the crotch.

The man doubled over in pain. "Excuse me," Cavanaugh said. "I didn't see you there."

The man stared at him. His eyes were steel gray and his face hard and pitted like buckshot on a NO HUNTING sign along Alligator Alley in Florida. He wore a dark blue striped suit which seemed somehow out of place on the plane of conventioneers. He straightened himself and grunted something illegible and hastened down the aisle. Cavanaugh noted his name tag read "Dr. Heinrich Boere."

After they were well on their way, Andres Passerio, the plane's captain, came over the intercom. He spoke in Spanish and then in an English that was almost incomprehensible. Fortunately, Lisette, the other woman in front of them, translated everything he said.

After one hour of listening to the women around him, Cavanaugh thought he was going to lose his mind. They worried about the three women they had met at the night club the night before. Maybe they overslept. Maybe they met some Canadian Royal Mounted Policemen and had decided to take a later flight. Maybe one of them got sick. The thought that they could have been murdered by someone on this plane never crossed their minds. But it did Cavanaugh's.

He glanced back in the plane. Albert was continuing to grope Erica. At this rate he would either have calluses on his hands or be dead of a heart failure by the time they reached Havana. Dr. Boere, on the other hand, buried his head in his newspaper when Cavanaugh looked at him. He had been watching him.

"Lisette, we were trying to think about the name of that famous ice cream place in Havana?" one of the women in front of him asked.

"You must mean Coppelia. It was the setting for the film *Strawberry and Chocolate*."

"I never heard of the movie."

"You are kidding me, aren't you? It was nominated for an Oscar."

"Never heard of it. It was probably before my time."

Eloise tapped the chair in front of her. "It was nominated for Best Foreign Language Film of 1995, and it also won honors at the Berlin International Film Festival and the Sundance Film Festival."

"Thanks," Rona's voice came back, "but I still never heard of it."

"It's about a really conservative guy and his flamboyantly homosexual neighbor," Eloise volunteered.

"It's about a lot more than that, Rona," Lisette said.

Cavanaugh checked his ticket to see how much longer he would be a prisoner on Cubana Airlines. He felt like he was in Purgatory. He almost hoped for an emergency to occur to stop the talk around him. Relief came in the form of a tall dark skinned stewardess with straight black hair that cascaded over her shoulder like the 5th Marine Corps Fourragere and a uniform that would make Mother Teresa look sexy. She was pushing a cart of drinks slowly down the aisle.

Lisette, Rona, and Rita all ordered diet cokes.

When the stewardess reached Cavanaugh's row, Francesca ordered a bottle of water and Eloise a double scotch on the rocks. Cavanaugh read the stewardess's name tag and asked, "Can I have a Becks beer, *por favor*, Marita?"

"I am sorry, señor," Marita said, "but we only carry Cuban beer."

"I should have known," Cavanaugh chuckled. "What are my choices?"

She smiled and read with a strong Spanish accent from a list on the cart. "Bucanero Beer, Cristal Beer, Hatuey Beer, and Mayabe Beer."

"Which one do you like, Marita?"

She smiled and Francesca poked him in the ribs. "I do not drink beer, señor."

“Good for you,” he said and turned quickly toward the rear of the plane. “I’ll try a Bucanero.” Down the aisle he saw Dr. Boere quickly duck behind the newspaper again. “Make that two Bucanero. It’s going to be a long flight.”

* * *

78

Brooklyn, New York

Retired Sgt. Major and Mrs. Yaccarino lived in a row of modest attached red brick homes in the Dyker Heights section of Brooklyn. Judging from the size of the trees, Goldberg estimated the homes had been built during the 1940s. They were neat and well kept. American flags and green, white, and red Italian flags were prominently displayed in windows. Statues of the Blessed Virgin Mary with outstretched hands and/or St. Francis of Assisi with birds perched on his hands and shoulders stood proudly on small patches of concrete in front of some of the homes or lurked ominously in windows looking out at the street.

Finding a parking spot on the block was like looking for pearls in oysters. Goldberg settled for parking on 86th Street at a meter in front of a French bakery with pies and pastries that looked too good to be real and Mario's Salmaneria with Oldani Genoa Salami and Prosciutto di Parma hanging like prisoners bound in fishnet stockings above Pepperoni links and Pecorino Toscano and Grana Padano cheese loaves. Across the street a Middle Eastern Travel Agency offered discount airfares to Asia and Russia and an "exciting" Siberian Express train ride. On the opposite corner, an Asian fruit stand displayed a colorful medley of apples, oranges, grapes, melons, and lemons that resembled a Jackson Pollack painting from the distance. Goldberg felt like he had been dropped into a United Nations shopping arena. Women with black burkas shopped beside Asian women who prodded and probed vegetables like C.S.I. investigators.

Turning the corner, Goldberg felt the silence of the Yaccarino's block fall softly down upon him. He missed having Cavanaugh with him. He could almost hear him slipping into his routine of wondering aloud why people would buy food from a store called "Salmonella." Goldberg never liked interviewing the parents of a victim. The fact that this victim had been young, pregnant, and accidentally shot in a botched holdup by a bullet meant for his partner made this even more uncomfortable for him.

Sgt. Major Joseph Yaccarino opened the door to greet him. The lines on the Sgt. Major's face seemed etched in a perpetual scowl. He wasn't quite six feet tall, but his broad shoulders and stocky frame reminded Goldberg of a fire hydrant. He wore a tight olive green t-shirt with the words "Death before Dishonor" in yellow letters surrounding a gray skull and cross bones. His dark brown hair was cut short and streaked with gray. His voice was raspy as if he were used to shouting and not taking orders. With one hand holding the door jam and the other the door knob, he commanded, "What do you want?"

Goldberg introduced himself, showed his badge and asked if he could come inside to ask a few questions. "You can ask your questions here," Yaccarino stated emphatically.

Goldberg shifted his weight and withdrew his note pad from his pocket. He wasn't going to argue with the man if he could help it. "We are investigating a series of murders of young women. You may have read about them in the paper."

Yaccarino stared. His expression didn't change.

"I would like to ask you some questions about your daughter."

"I read the stories about the women. My daughter and grandson were shot in the delicatessen up the block. They weren't victims of your serial murderer."

"Who is it, dear?" a woman's voice called from behind him.

Yaccarino's eyes never left Goldberg. "It's a cop," he said. "He wants to ask some questions about Maria."

"Invite him in," the voice answered.

The Sgt. Major looked up at the red maple tree in front of his house and then down at his spit polished shoes. He shook his head slightly and then stepped aside. "Come on in," he said.

Mrs. Yaccarino came out of the kitchen to greet him. She was thin with high cheekbones and a plastic smile. Her eyes were azure and looked like the sky on a clear summer day. She wore a simple white apron trimmed in red and was wiping flour from her hands. The lines around her eyes showed that life had not been a pleasant walk in the park for her, but she had endured, and the strength in her handshake told Goldberg she was strong and would continue to endure what life threw at her.

"Sit down, Detective. It is detective, isn't it?" she said motioning to a red and black flowered sofa in the living room. "Can I get you a cup of coffee or some tea?" she asked not waiting for an answer.

"No, no thank you, Mrs. Yaccarino," Goldberg said. He sat down and sunk deep into the sofa. On the walls around the room were pictures—pictures of various duty stations they had been in, pictures of family vacations, pictures of their children when they were young, pictures of Maria's wedding. On the end tables, there were pictures of Maria—Maria in her high school track uniform, Maria in her choir gown, Maria in her graduation gown. Goldberg could feel Mrs. Yaccarino's efforts to hold on to Maria for as long as possible and the Sgt. Major's efforts to do whatever he could to help his wife.

Before he could ask anything, Mrs. Yaccarino disappeared into the kitchen. There was a temporary awkward silence as the Sgt. Major with folded arms peered down at Goldberg who had sunk deeper into the recesses of the sofa. Mrs. Yaccarino quickly reappeared, however, with a tray of chocolate chip cookies and some napkins. "Here," she said, "try these. They came right out of the oven."

Goldberg took a warm cookie and a napkin to be polite and began, "This is difficult, Mr. and Mrs. Yaccarino, and I appreciate your help. I know how hard this must be for you."

"You don't know anything, Goldberg! Maria was a great kid. She was expecting a child, for God's sake!"

"Joseph!" Mrs. Yaccarino's voice cracked like a whip.

"He doesn't know, Angela! He has no idea. I have seen men die in combat. I have held onto bleeding men as they died in my arms. It's not the same. This was my daughter. This was terrible. It shouldn't have happened." He turned away and went to a wet bar in the corner where another picture of a smiling Maria with her husband in Yankee Stadium perched staring at them as a sad reminder of happier days. Next to the picture, in a brown leather frame, was a sonogram of Maria's unborn child. Goldberg watched the Sgt. Major pour himself two inches of scotch and down it in one gulp and then pour another and take a seat in a black ladder-back chair by the fireplace. He sat rigid, like his spine was a steel girder, holding the glass in one hand and his temper bottled up inside.

Mrs. Yaccarino smiled and turned to Goldberg. "So how can we help you, Detective?"

"I'm not really sure, Mrs. Yaccarino. One of our officers, Meredith Perez, was the last victim of this killer. On the walls of her apartment we found clippings of all the other murders." He omitted the clippings of the shooting in the deli where their daughter had been shot. "We think she may have been trying to solve the case herself."

Mrs. Yaccarino sat in a red Queen Ann's chair across from the fireplace. The Sgt. Major leaned a degree forward.

"I don't know why, but Officer Perez had a copy of your daughter's obituary on her wall. I am trying to figure out why."

"I don't know how we can help you, Detective. We never met this Officer Perez and we have no idea why she would have Maria's obituary on her wall."

"The papers said your daughter lived on Staten Island," Goldberg said. "What was she doing here in Brooklyn that day?"

"Since when is it a crime to visit your parents?" the raspy voice of the Sgt. Major asked.

"Joseph!" Mrs. Yaccarino snapped. She turned to Goldberg and spoke softly. "She often came to Brooklyn to visit us. This was the neighborhood she grew up in. We have . . . or . . . ," she corrected herself, "had a close family." She gazed at the pictures on the wet bar.

"I am sorry," Goldberg said, "but I have to ask these questions. Do you know why she went to the delicatessen?"

Mrs. Yaccarino started to shake. She pulled her apron up and began to cry into it. The tears started slowly, but they quickly escalated into an intense, uncontrollable sobbing. The Sgt. Major rose and came to her. He patted her back and then led her into another room. He was gone so long Goldberg thought they forgot about him. He rose and went around the room studying the pictures. On the wall behind the wet bar, an award shadow box with at least fifteen different military medals hung. Goldberg recognized the Purple Heart, the Bronze Star, a Silver Star, and a Distinguished Service Medal. On the mantel over the fireplace he saw a family picture of Maria's wedding. In the picture, the bride and groom stood in what looked like Brooklyn's Botanical Gardens. They were flanked by the Sgt. Major in his full military dress blue uniform. Mrs. Yaccarino wore a short sleeve aubergine bodice with pleated overlay decorated with beads and sequins. The groom was tall and thin. His black tuxedo looked like it could have been borrowed from someone twenty pounds heavier. He had short brown curly hair and a smile that proclaimed his love for Maria like a Time Square billboard. The lines in his face indicated he was either a chain smoker or a lot older than Maria. The bride was stunning in what appeared to be an ivory satin gown with a pick up skirt and beaded metallic embroidery on the bodice. Goldberg stared the picture. The man's face on the right hand side of the picture was an exact replica of Maria's. Aside from the tuxedo he wore, his height, and the full disheveled Afro-like hairstyle he sported, they were identical. Judging from the height of his father in the picture, he looked to be at least six feet tall. This must be Maria's twin brother, Tony, Goldberg surmised.

"Are you satisfied now, Goldberg?" the raspy voice stabbed at him from behind. "I had to give her a sedative. Now get the hell out of my house before I throw you out."

Goldberg recognized the look in the Sgt. Major's eyes and moved toward the door. "I'm truly sorry," he said. "I didn't realize she would be so upset. What did I do?"

Retired Sgt. Major Yaccarino pulled the door open. He looked straight into Goldberg's eyes and then softened. "You didn't know," he said slowly. "Angela blames herself . . . ."

"But why?" Goldberg asked at the door. "It wasn't her fault."

"I know that and you know that, but she thinks if she had only had some in the house, Maria would still be with us."

"I'm sorry," Goldberg insisted. "I don't understand. How could she have prevented the holdup?"

The Sgt. Major looked down. He was having a hard time saying it. Finally, he blurted it out, "Maria was having some crazy cravings. They say it happens in pregnancy. I don't know. She felt she should humor the cravings, that they meant her body was needing something. She kept fit. She was always an athlete. The both of them were . . . ."

Goldberg looked at him, but said nothing.

"She had one of those 'cravings' that day. There was no dissuading her. I had marinated a London broil and was preparing to barbeque it. She wanted no part of it. You know, red meat and all that shit. She wanted something else." He hesitated again. "She wanted to make pancakes. We had everything except one thing . . . ."

Suddenly, Goldberg felt an icy chill pass through his chest. He knew and he felt sick.

"If Angela had it, Maria wouldn't have gone to the delicatessen. She blames herself for Maria's death."

Goldberg glanced over the Sgt. Major's shoulder at the wedding picture on the mantel. The Sgt. Major's voice cracked, and he said softly, "She went to the store to buy some stupid fucking maple syrup for her pancakes, and she ends up dead. It's just not God-damn fair!"

* * *

79

Staten Island, New York

Vito Muscatelli sat in his brown leather recliner staring out his window. Gestas had given him word that they all were in the air: Cavanaugh, Francesca, and Holland. Muscatelli gently stroked a tiny white kitten with two blue eyes lying on the quilt of his blanket, his mind wandering to events in his past.

He smiled recalling how the F.B.I. always believed Meyer Lansky left over $400 million dollars hidden in bank accounts, but they never found any of the money. When Lansky died of lung cancer at 80 in 1982, he left a wife and three children and was worth practically nothing. In fact for the last years of his life he didn't seem to have much money at all. He lived modestly in his low-profile home in Miami Beach, Florida. He had very little property in his name. On paper, he looked like just another struggling old man worth almost nothing. There was a reason for that. And Vito Muscatelli was one of the very few people in the world who knew the reason. He was the reason.

Lansky had his day. He controlled the finances of the mob in Cuba during Fugencio Battista's reign from 1952 to Fidel Castro's final seizing of power in 1959. During that time Lansky made a lot of money for the mob, for Battista, and for himself. He considered himself a tough guy, all five feet of the little man. He once refused to pay Lucky Luciano protection money and told him he could shove his protection up his ass because he didn't need it. He was called "the business brains of the underworld" and "the Gangland Finance Chairman." Vito remembered him as a tough little Jew.

But Vito knew how to reach people and how to get things done. When over 100 members of La Cosa Nostra met on November 14, 1957 in Joe Barbara's house in Appalachia, New York, they had a lot of items to discuss.

Fidel Castro's Revolution had started in December of 1956 with a small boat load of only 82 people, but it had gained momentum, and the handwriting was on the wall. Battista's days in power were coming to an end, and with that end, the stranglehold they had on gambling, prostitution, and drugs in Cuba would also end.

More pressing problems for the mob, however, were Joe Kennedy's positioning his son Jack to run for President, and Jack's meddlesome brother Bobby's crusade against crime. As Chief Counsel for the Senate Committee on Improper Action, Robert Kennedy was unrelenting in his pursuit of Jimmy Hoffa on racketeering charges. Hoffa was then the President of the 1.3 million member Teamsters' Union. Kennedy claimed Hoffa worked with the mob, extorted money from employers, and raided the Teamster pension funds. Robert Kennedy was a real threat to the mob, and they knew it.

When the mobsters who assembled at Barbara's house noticed two police cars parked in front of the house, there was near panic and most of them tried to escape. They ran in all directions. It was like a scene from the Keystone Cops. In the end 62 people were arrested and identified. One of the major repercussions of this fiasco was that J. Edgar Hoover, who had previously denied the very existence of organized crime in the United States, acknowledged the facts and announced the "Tap Hoodlum Program" with which the F.B.I. began a concerted fight against the Cosa Nostra.

Meyer Lanksy was not present at the Appalachia Meeting, and his absence was noted. He claimed he was ill, but some felt he might have been the one who informed the police about the meeting because of his loyalty to Lucky Luciano and to Frank Costello in their power struggle with Vito Genovese. Costello had recently survived a bullet to the head in assassination attempt by Vincent "The Chin" Gigante as he was walking to the elevator in the lobby of his Manhattan apartment building. Lansky's informing the police was a way he could get revenge and keep his hands "clean" at the same time. It was typical of Lanksy's shrewd, calculating approach to "business matters."

When John Kennedy became President, Vito recalled Sam "Momo" Giancana's pillow conversation with Judith Campbell Exner who was alleged to be mistress to both Giancana and Kennedy. Giancana always had a big mouth. He bragged too much. In many ways he reminded Vito of his late son, Rocco. Giancana claimed if it weren't for him, Kennedy would never have been in the White House. He also claimed that he had been contacted by Kennedy regarding assassinating Fidel Castro. Poor Sam, Vito thought, he was always so impulsive, so unpredictable. You never knew what he would say. Poor Sam. He was supposed to appear before a Senate committee investigating C.I.A. and Mafia collusion in plots to assassinate Castro. Vito was younger then. He actually liked Sam, but business was business. If Sam had only learned to keep his mouth shut. He recalled the frying Italian sausages and peppers Giancana was preparing for them both in the basement of his home in Chicago. At least he didn't suffer. Vito made sure of that. The first bullet to the back of his head did it, but Vito flipped the body over and shot him six more times in the face just to make sure and to send a message. Silence is golden.

Giancana was easy, but Lansky was different. He was smart and shrewd. His bribes and payoffs had ensured the loyalty of many. When the F.B.I. and the police started to go after Lansky, he was forced to leave Cuba. He tried living in Israel, then Zurich, then South America. His running stopped, however, when Paraguay would not accept him and he was put on a plane back to the United States. As soon as the plane touched down, the F.B.I. were there to arrest him on racketeering charges. There was never a question Lansky would talk or cooperate with the government. But he still had all that money he had taken with him from the Cuban casinos. Vito decided to "free lance" this one by himself and undertook a secret mission to obtain that money.

He recalled how old Lansky looked then at 70. His skin was gray and drawn. The dark rings around his eyes looked like smudged mascara. The running around trying to avoid government investigations had taken their toll on his health and his heart, in particular. This was the time Vito made his move. As the government futilely tried to send Lansky to jail for contempt of court and tax evasion, Vito quietly came to him in the hospital and explained how, when he was a very young man, still in his teens, he had entered the backyard of Lanksy's old friend Bugsy Siegel's girlfriend's house and shot Bugsy through the window with an M1 carbine in the back of the head as he was reading the *Los Angeles Times*. Vito described in detail how Bugsy's eye went flying across the room and splattered off the wall. For emphasis, he told how he kept firing into him, much as he would do to Sam Giancana twenty-eight years later. There were others, but he didn't feel it necessary to belabor the point.

"I like to be thorough," Vito told Lansky. There wasn't much use in threatening a sick old man, so Muscatelli did the next best thing. "You have three children, Meyer. They look like good people. You wouldn't want anything to happen to them or their family, would you?"

Lansky looked at him with sunken eyes. "You wouldn't dare!"

"I didn't know Bugsy Siegel. So I used a rifle. It really made a mess. I know I hit him at least twice in the head and then I shot a white marble statue of Bacchus on the piano just for emphasis."

Lansky struggled to get out of the hospital bed, but Muscatelli ripped the oxygen tubes from his nose and slapped him firmly across the face. "Listen up, old man," he said. "I was friends with Giancano. He invited me to his home to eat, and I did—after I shot him." He paused a moment and then added, "He made great sausages and peppers. I should have asked for his recipe before I killed him."

Lansky was smart. He knew he could never use the money he had amassed and he wanted to protect his family, so he made the deal. The 400 million the F.B.I. thought Lansky had accumulated had grown by that time and through Vito Muscatelli's investments it now totaled over two billion dollars. But like Meyer Lansky believed, Vito felt there was never enough money. Money meant power.

Holland and Santacroce would be paid well for ridding him of the brothers. He looked out the window at the Verazzano Bridge in the distance. He thought back to a dinner he had had with Carlos Marcello in Muriel's Jackson Square in the French Quarter of New Orleans. It was a Monday night and he could almost smell the kidney beans and taste the rice, seasonings, spices and chunks of hot sausage. Funny how you remember things, he thought. Carlos ate a boudin rouge, a blood sausage mixed with onions, cooked rice, and herbs. He could almost hear Carlos's voice over the soft jazz in the background and the distinct aroma of Cajun food. "*Livarsi, na petra di la scarpa*!" It was the Mafia cry for revenge, "Take the stone out of my shoe!" Back then Carlos was talking about Robert Kennedy, the Attorney General, whose brother Jack was the President. Measures had to be taken to stop Bobby. But to eliminate him, they would have to eliminate his brother first. It was that simple.

Here, so many years later, Vito Muscatelli was planning the murder of two more brothers, Detective Thomas Cavanaugh and Rev. Jack Bennis. History, he thought, has a way of repeating itself.

* * *

80

Skies over Florida

Eloise Exeter never shut up. Her mouth seemed to be in perpetual motion. She sat by the window. Francesca was between her and Cavanaugh, but her shrill voice seemed to drill into his ear. She was "Miss Know-It-All." She told them and everyone else in hearing distance that she was born in Sunderland, England.

"Did you know Sunderland has a coal-mining heritage dating back hundreds of years?"

I don't care, Cavanaugh wanted to shout.

"At one time there were almost 200,000 miners employed in one county alone. When demands for coal dropped after the war, the mines closed causing mass unemployment."

Cavanaugh discovered whether he wanted to or not that the last coal mine closed in Sunderland in 1994. Cavanaugh closed his eyes.

"Did you know a person born or living around the Sunderland area is known as a Mackem?" she called over to him.

"Why would I care?" Cavanaugh said. Fran poked him in the ribs and he flinched.

"Your name is Scottish," Eloise went on oblivious of the sarcasim in his voice.

"How do you know?" he asked.

"You spell it with a C. If it were spelled with a K, it would more likely be Irish."

He always thought of himself as Irish. He hesitated and wanted to protest, but decided quickly not to encourage her. Instead, he unbuckled his seatbelt and asked to be excused for a moment. Albert, the tall gray haired man with gold wire glasses, had apparently fallen asleep with his hand resting on his trophy companion's right leg. Erica looked up at Cavanaugh as he passed and smiled what he called a "ID-10-T" smile—more commonly called an "idiot smile." He nodded and walked on. Dr. Boere now wore a pair of aviator sunglasses. He didn't move as Cavanaugh passed him. He could have been asleep or still watching.

At the rear of the plane, Marita, the stewardess who served him his Bucaneros, was talking with two stewards, Antonio and José. Judging from their good looks, their articulate voices, their well groomed appearance, their lack of wedding bands, and their professions, Cavanaugh immediately pegged them as being gay. He interrupted the three to ask them how much longer they expected the flight to take.

"We should be there in about an hour," Antonio answered.

"The Havana Airport is clean and pleasant," José offered, "but it doesn't compare to Toronto's Airport."

"It may take a while for you to get your luggage, so just be patient," Antonio suggested.

José smiled, "Captain Passerio, should announce the ground temperature when we get a little closer. He's a really nice guy. If he doesn't, I will find out for you as there is no air conditioning in the airport."

Cavanaugh nodded thanks and concluded Passerio was gay, too. Then Marita smiled and said, "Captain Passerio is a wonderful man. He is very special. He's how you say in the States, a hunk."

"You are not bad yourself," Antonio said and José nodded.

Cavanaugh turned and headed back to his seat. Maybe he was wrong about Passerio and maybe he was wrong about the stewards. He wasn't having a good day.

When he reached his seat, Eloise was still talking. Now Rita, Lisette, Rona, and Francesca were involved as well as a young couple on the other side of the aisle.

"I love to fly," Eloise said. "Did you know donkeys kill more people annually than plane crashes? It's a fact. And back in 1987, American Airlines actually saved $40,000 by eliminating one olive from each salad served in first-class. It's a fact . . . ."

Cavanaugh wanted to ask "Miss Know-It-All Jabber Jaws from Sunderland, Scotland" if she knew Venus is the only planet that rotates clockwise, that wet birds don't fly at night, or that butterflies taste with their feet and turtles can breathe through their butts, but he didn't want to encourage her—as if she seemed to need any encouragement.

Eloise directed comments like shotgun pellets in all directions. She seemed to know something about everything. "Lizette?" she called to one of the three women in front ot them. “That is such a pretty name. Did you know it means, ‘My God is a vow’?”

Lisette turned and thanked her. “How did you know that?” she asked.

“I love names. I believe they tell us a lot about people. And the stories behind the names are fascinating.” She motioned to Cavanaugh sitting on the end seat. “Take ‘Thomas,’ for example. Most people think of St. Thomas, the apostle who doubted Jesus’ ressurection and think it means ‘doubter,’ but it doesn’t. It is actually Aramaic and means ‘Twin.’”

Cavanaugh pretended not to hear. Lisette asked, “Do you know what Rita’s name means?”

Eloise seemed to have an answer for everything. “Rita actually means ‘pearl’ or ‘child of light.’ It comes from the Latin or Greek for Margaret.”

Cavanaugh thought of the killer who was hunting both him and his brother. He had the perfect name—Cain. The first recorded murderer who killed his own brother, Able. He felt somehow Cain Holland was on this plane or that he would surely be there to greet them in Cuba.

A head popped over the headrest in front. “Would you know what my name, Rona, means?”

Eloise rubbed her eyes with her left index finger and thumb for a moment. “I believe it is of Scandinavian origin, but I am not positively certain. I’m almost positive it means ‘mighty power.’ I get a bit confused. You see there is a Scottish island in the North Atlantic called Rona. The entire population of the island died in the late seventeenth century after an infestation of rats. The rats probably reached the island after a shipwrech and proceeded to eat all the food stocks of the people . . . .”

Cavanaugh understood now why Fran hated it when he started asking those “stupid trival questions.” He decided to close his eyes, block Miss Know-It-All Eliose out, and look forward to the dangers he could anticipate when they landed in Havana and he tried to find his brother.

* * *

81

Havana, Cuba

He had all the information he needed. It was time. Jack Bennis wanted it over. The shootings, the killings, the running, the hiding. He had had enough. He desperately wanted to help others, to make amends, if he could, for the damage he had caused when "following the orders" of his government and following the impulses of his emotions. He had caused the death of good as well as bad people. They may not have believed the things he did, but they believed strongly other things. When he had been on covert missions for the U. S. military, he and his squad had assassinated human beings with hopes, dreams, and families. It wasn't the answer. Killing never is. He had found that out over and over again.

After one of their covert assassination mission had been compromised so many years ago when he refused to shoot an eight year old girl who was crying over the body of her father whom he had just shot and killed, one of his men had been wounded. If he had killed the little girl, they could have escaped safely, but Lt. Bennis couldn't pull the trigger of the AR-15. She reminded him of his little sister, Theresa. But they were all someone's little sister or little brother or mother or father. It didn't make any sense any more. Maybe it never did.

When he tried to go back to rescue the wounded soldier, his commanding officer, Howard Stevens, ordered him not to leave, to let him die. Lt. Bennis refused and hopped off the helicopter and ran toward the trees where Sgt. Manny Rodriguez lay bleeding against a tree. Howard Stevens had been like a brother to Bennis. Why didn't he understand?

"Leave him!" Stevens shouted. "Get back here or I am going to shoot!" he warned.

Bennis couldn't leave his comrade on the field of battle. As the helicopter ascended into the night sky, Stevens kept his word and showered bullets down on him. He was hit and fell to the ground. The bullets kept coming. Stevens wanted to make sure Bennis was dead. He could still feel the impact of the bullets smashing into his bullet proof vest. After what seemed like an eternity, he heard the whirl of the Russian Ka-25 helicopter blades fade into the blackness above him and then he crawled to his wounded companion.

Lt. Bennis and Sgt. Rodriguez evaded the local militia by immersing themselves in the dense forest of tangled vegetation. They listened intensely for the cries of animals, the sounds of streams, and the snapping of twigs from possible pursuing enemies. Both men were wounded, but slowly, together they inched their way through treacherous terrain and a canopy so thick that little light could penetrate.

They ate almost anything that crawled, swam, walked, or flew that they could catch. They turned over rotting logs and ate ants, termites, beetles, and wood grubs. They dug worms in damp soil and after dropping them in clean water they ate them raw. They caught crayfish using their own feces as bait. Snakes became a source for protein that when cleaned and cooked became a delicacy they looked forward to. They pulled snakes from trees and feasted on fresh piranha and trapped iguana. They dined on all sorts of birds they caught in homemade nets. They found water in springs and rivers along their way. They cut water vines which grew throughout the jungle and drank the liquid that flowed out. They rubbed garlic and mud on themselves to ward off the bugs, especially the mosquitoes. They foraged for edible tubers, cashew nuts, berries, papaya, sugarcane, and yucca and even ate certain flowers. They relied on the sun and the stars more than their compasses.

Eventually, they came upon a remote village in the mountains and a visiting missionary provided medical and spiritual help to both men. They stayed in the village long after their wounds had healed and they had recuperated, helping the people, building homes, teaching the young people, and assisting the missionary in his duties. Finally, they moved on, each man changed by his experiences. Ironically, they both decided to abandon their weapons and continue the contemplative life style they had discovered. Bennis found himself drawn to a Jesuit seminary where he studied and prayed. For the first time in his life, he found peace.

When he worked his way back to New York and to Brooklyn, where he had been born, his mother was dead and his half-brother, he discovered, was a New York City homicide detective. He could have contacted his brother, but he chose not to. There were too many questions he didn't want to answer. Too many issues of the past he didn't want to confront. Instead, he tried to serve the people of his parish as best he could.

But Jack Bennis was always a doer. He never could look the other way. As a priest he heard things in the confessional that turned his stomach. Man's weaknesses of the flesh he could understand. But it was the other things that burrowed under his skin. One of the major mob bosses of New York had turned over the reigns of power to his son, Rocco Muscatelli. Rocco had absolutely no scruples. He tried to push drugs on younger and younger children. He promoted child pornography and recruited prostitutes from the high schools and junior high schools. Bound by the seal of confession, Bennis could not tell anyone about what he heard. He watched in frustration as the situation worsened. The police were powerless. Mob lawyers seemed able to bail even Beelzebub out of jail before the arresting officer had time to return home for dinner.

Finally, he decided to take matters into his own hands and rid the neighborhood of the devil he saw by the method he had been so carefully taught by the United States government. He decided to assassinate Rocco Muscatelli. And he did. He killed another mob boss at Muscatelli's wake. He may have continued, but his half-brother grew suspicious and confronted him.

Now here he was in Havana, Cuba, trying to start a new life, trying to help those in need, but the sins of his past had followed him. Vito Muscatelli, Rocco's father, now in a nursing home on Staten Island, had obviously put a "hit" on him.

Bennis wanted it over. He pictured a bloody Santiago in his nightmares asking him to help the man Bennis himself had pushed off the roof of a building. Santiago was a good man. He had a family. He was trying to do the right thing. Now he was dead. Bennis rubbed his forehead. "It's all my fault," he said softly. "It's all my fault."

It was time to end it all. He told María Izabelle and Diego his plan. He would call Francisco Santacruz and ask to see him tonight. There was no use postponing the inevitable. He could not function effectively with someone constantly trying to kill him. He needed to walk into the lion's den. He needed to face the devil. One way or another it would end tonight.

María Izabelle and Diego argued with him. "You can't go in there alone," María Izabelle pleaded.

"I must," Bennis said. "No one is safe around me now. I have to confront him. Maybe if I reason with him . . . ."

"You can't reason with people like him," Diego stated.

Bennis knew he was right, but he could no longer put other people's lives in danger because of him. Santiago had died because of him. Manuel in the hospital could have died. People in the street could have been hit by a bullet meant for him. María Izabelle and Diego were in harm's way as long as they harbored him. "It must stop tonight," he said.

María Izabelle left in tears crying that he was crazy, that it was insane to go there. Diego shook his head sadly. "I don't want anything to happen to you, Padre," he said quietly and then left the room.

Jack Bennis went to Diego's phone and dialed Francisco Santacruz. He asked if he could meet with him at his house around 9:00 that night. Santacruz seemed pleased. He would welcome a visit from the priest.

In his small bedroom, Bennis knelt by his bed and prayed. He didn't know what would happen that night, but he would be prepared. He only wished he would have had another opportunity to see and speak with his brother, Thomas. He was the only family he had left. There was so much he wanted to tell him. He closed his eyes in prayer and realized that he may never get that chance.

* * *

82

José Martí International Airport, Havana, Cuba

The plane landed roughly, bouncing a few times on the runway. Some of the luggage bins over the seats sprung open and bags tumbled out into the aisle and on top of passengers' heads. When the Cubana Airline Airbus rolled to a stop, the passengers and crew burst into wild applause.

Cavanaugh stood and opened the overhead bin. He looked down the aisle. Albert was foundling Erica's derriere as she reached back for a magazine on her seat. Cavanaugh concluded he must have taken one of those erectile dysfunction pills that had given him a perpetual hard-on and he was making the most of it. He must be popping them like jelly beans, he thought. Erica brushed her hair away and looked at Cavanaugh. She smiled and winked at him. He noticed, for the first time, her teeth were remarkably white and remarkably crooked. She had an overbite that should have been corrected in childhood. He imagined Albert was more concerned with what her mouth could do than he was with the state of her teeth.

A few rows behind them, pocked-faced Dr. Heinrich Boere smoothed out the wrinkles in his dark blue suit and straightened his tie. His eyes were concealed beneath his aviator sunglasses, but Cavanaugh felt he was still staring at him. He reached for his attaché in the bin above him. Cavanaugh noted he reached for the bag with his left hand.

"I hope we don't have to stand in a bloody long queue," Eloise commented. "I could go for some black pudding right now!"

Francesca turned to her and asked, "What's 'black pudding,' Eloise?"

"Blimey, I keep forgetting I'm with Yanks. It's delicious blood sausage mixed with sweet potatoes or, my favorite, oatmeal. I love it when it's mixed with cattle blood. You simply must try it, dear."

Francesca shook her head and grimaced. Rita pulled their bags from the overhead bin and asked Fran, "Where are you staying? We are staying at the NH Parque Central Hotel."

Fran gave Cavanaugh a quizzical look. She didn't know if she should tell them they were staying there, too.

"I simply adore the NH Parque Central. It's so elegant and majestic," Eloise interjected. "It's right in the heart of Havana. There's a fabulous outdoor swimming pool on the roof, where you can get a glorious view of the entire city. And it's close to the Grand Theater and the Capitol. It's a great hotel."

"We must all get together for dinner tonight," Rona said.

Cavanaugh thought he would rather shit through his mouth.

When they finally left the plane and reached the new International Terminal 3, Cavanaugh and Francesca thought they would avoid long lines at the baggage carousel because they were carrying their only luggage. But they were wrong. They first had their hand baggage scanned and inspected. The line seemed to take forever. Eloise who was behind them complained bitterly the entire time.

"You would think things would go faster," she said. "This terminal was opened in 1998 by Canada's Prime Minister Jean Chretien and Fidel Castro."

Behind them, Cavanaugh spotted Erica and Albert, but they were no longer together. Both looked serious and somewhat apprehensive. Maybe, Cavanaugh thought, Albert might be worried the inspectors would discover a cache of Viagra in his bag. The steward had been right. The crowds, the heat, the noise, and the lack of air conditioning made the wait extremely uncomfortable.

The airport was clean and starkly modern and utilitarian with steel beams crisscrossing across the ceiling forming what looked like a series of Vs. Cavanaugh looked up to see flags from different countries dangling from the end of the Vs.

"You won't find your flag up there, Yank," Eloise smiled. "Your bloody embargo and the fact that your planes bombed this place in 1962 a few days before the Bay of Pigs invasion took care of that."

"But why are all the signs in English as well Spanish?" Francesca asked.

"Your country is the only one that bans its people from coming here. Castro has been catering to people from the UK."

With their bags in hand, Francesca and Cavanaugh avoided the small, crowded baggage carrousels and headed outside to a queue of taxis. Walking quickly through the throngs of people in the airport, Cavanaugh spotted a man in a straw cowboy hat and a white floral short sleeve shirt for a second, but then the man slipped into the crowd and disappeared. Could it be the same man he saw in the Toronto Airport?

"I'm glad we don't have to get any luggage," Fran said. "From what I heard on the plane the wait can be up to two hours."

When they reached the taxis stand, they were about to get into a cab when they heard a familiar voice behind them. "Yoo hoo! Yoo hoo! Can I bum a ride with you to the hotel?" It was Eloise Exeter. She was trundling through the terminal doors with a small briefcase in her left hand and a large pocketbook in her right.

Cavanaugh looked at Francesca. "Where are we going?" he whispered.

"We're going to the NH Parque Central Hotel, Eloise," Fran answered quickly.

"That's beautiful," she said. "That's where I'm going, too."

Cavanaugh clenched his fists. He held the taxi door open for Eloise and Fran. Fran shrugged her shoulders at him as she climbed into the cab. Cavanaugh looked back into the terminal. Three more people were coming through the door. Dr. Boere, Erica, and Albert. Behind them he glimpsed a beige cowboy hat worn by a man with a dark moustache.

* * *

83

Brooklyn, New York

Before leaving the Yaccarinos', Goldberg tactfully asked a few questions about Maria's twin brother.

"All these young people," the Sgt. Major stated, "all they want to do is leave Brooklyn and move to Staten Island. And the young Staten Islanders all want to leave Staten Island and move to New Jersey. It doesn't make sense, but when did youth ever make sense?"

Goldberg nodded.

"At least Tony moved there to be closer to his work."

"What does he do?" Goldberg asked.

"He's a reporter for the *Staten Island Advance*. He lives in Grasmere. It's not far from where he works."

Driving back to the station house, Goldberg felt like a hound dog pursuing a fox. He sprang into action when he returned to his station house. He needed a picture of Tony Yaccarino to show Steve the barber. He hadn't asked Sgt. Major Yaccarino for one. The family had been through a tremendous tragedy. He didn't want to cause them the added trauma knowing that their son might be a serial killer. Sometimes police work was a dirty business and innocent people could needlessly get hurt in an investigation. He recalled innocent people who lost their jobs, who lost their reputations, some who even lost their marriages.

Goldberg knew he was a cop on the trail of a vicious killer, but he didn't have to inflict needless pain on others when there were other ways to obtain information. He hadn't asked Sgt. Major Yaccarino for his son's picture because he didn't want to worry the family possibly needlessly. Plus, he knew as sure as Adam must have known he had made a mistake when he bit into that apple Eve gave him, that there was no way in hell, Sgt. Major Yaccarino would give him a picture of his only surviving child without a court order.

There were other ways.

He checked with the Motor Vehicle Department and made a couple of other discrete calls and within the hour he had both the employee photo and the driver's license photo of Tony Yaccarino.

Things were happening quickly now. Steve the barber and Steve's father the barber both made tentatively positive IDs on the picture of Tony Yaccarino. "It sure looks like him," Steve said.

Office Mike Shanley recognized Yaccarino as one of the beat reporters who hung out around the 120 Precinct. He remembered him as "a good guy." He recalled how he and Merry Perez seemed to "hit it off together." He didn't know if he was the one Merry had been dating, but he agreed it was a possibility.

It was all fitting together. Cavanaugh's hair could have been collected by Yaccarino at the barber shop. Steve was almost positive he was the one who dropped his phone and fumbled around for it on the floor after Cavanaugh had his hair cut. Steve would make a good witness. His father, on the other hand, was totally unreliable and could just as well deny he had ever seen Yaccarino before.

Shanley's statement proved Yaccarino had access to police information. He was a reporter. Checking the list of reporter's on the scene when Crystal May's body was found, Goldberg found Yaccarino was there. He could have spread the rumor about the note and then he could have dropped a vial of her blood on Cavanaugh during the scuffle with the WINS reporter.

The F.B.I. profile indicated the unsub killing spree might have been triggered by a traumatic experience. What could be more traumatic than the death of your twin sister?

And then there was the maple syrup. Maria DeFillipo went to the bodega to get some maple syrup for the pancakes she was craving. Could Yaccarino be blaming Cavanaugh for the death of his sister and her soon to be born child?

In some sick, twisted way, had Yaccarino snapped after his twin sister's death and started his killing spree?

Goldberg looked over at Cavanaugh's empty desk. He wished he had his partner here to bounce his theories off. Cavanaugh had an instinct for this, a feeling he got, a hunch based on facts. And he was usually right. Goldberg, on the other hand, was a plodder. He didn't trust hunches. He needed the facts. He had uncovered a lot of evidence, but he knew the evidence was all circumstantial. He needed more concrete evidence.

* * *

84

Havana, Cuba

Jack Bennis lifted the mattress and removed the Makarov pistol he had taken from the man in the Leather Jacket whom he had kicked off the roof. He stared at the pistol in the palm of his hand. It was old. It had a history he could only guess. He knew it had been the Soviet Union's standard military sidearm from the 50's through the 80's. How many times had it been fired, he wondered? How many people had it killed? How much misery had this rusty weapon caused? How much more would it bring?

He tossed the pistol from hand to hand feeling its weight, getting familiar with its touch. He placed the gun carefully on the bed and released is clip—eighteen rounds lined up like soldiers in a close order drill—or like a line of second graders lined up to receive their first Holy Communion.

He closed his eyes and pictured the innocent seven and eight year olds, hands clasped, in white suits and dresses. He could almost smell the flowers on the altar, the incense in the air.

Then he looked down at his hands. He thought back to the day Bishop Coppolino anointed the palms of his hands and sent him out to love and serve his people. He thought back to the first child he had baptized, Benedict Anthony. He saw little Benedict with his scrawny legs peeking out from the white Christening dress and his proud parents smiling, apprehensive, wondering what the future would bring for their tiny son. He thought of all the other babies he had baptized and the children he had prepared for First Communion and Confirmation. How many times had his hands given blessings and forgiveness in the sacrament of Reconciliation? His hands which had killed and taken bread and wine and transformed them into the Body and Blood of Jesus Christ. His hand had married people, anointed the sick, brought hope, comfort, encouragement, and death.

Then he reached further under the mattress and found the Nagant 7.62 revolver he had picked up from the man who killed Santiago. He examined it and checked that it was loaded. It was scratched and the handle cracked. Had it once been aimed at American soldiers in WW I and WW II? What countries had it traveled through? How had it changed the lives of those it came in contact with?

Ripping one of his t-shirts into stripes, he carefully tied the pistol to his right ankle and then pulled his trouser leg over it. Next, he stuck the revolver behind his back under his trousers, next to his coccyx bone and secured it by tightening his belt. Pulling his black shirt out, he checked himself in the mirror. He nodded. The guns were concealed. He didn't know what he would find in Santacruz's house, but now he felt better prepared.

He knew revenge motivated Vito Muscatelli. But what motivated Francisco Santacruz? Why was he following the dictates of an old man in a nursing home thirteen hundred miles away on Staten Island? What power did Muscatelli still have which led people to murder for him? He would find out tonight. Patting the guns, making sure they were secure and hidden, a part of him knew violence was not the answer, but another part of him knew, "For everything there is a season . . . . A time to live and a time to die."

* * *

85

Havana, Cuba

Eloise Exeter seemed to have a motor mouth. On the twenty minute ride from the airport, she pointed out historic sights and regaled Francesca with stories of her childhood, her trips through Europe, Asia, Australia, and New Zealand. Cavanaugh looked out the taxi cab window at the countryside, the people, the eclectic architectures of a physically tired city with a still vibrant energy pulsating through the streets and market places. Eloise's chatter about her love of vegetables, her belief in the China Study, her conversion to vegetarianism, became elevator music to Cavanaugh.

He had other things on his mind. If Vito Muscatelli had hired Tony Healen to kill him, Muscatelli knew where he was now. And that meant Cain Holland was somewhere nearby. If Muscatelli had given Francesca Santacruz's number to help find his brother, Santacruz must be dangerous. He glanced over at Francesca who actually appeared interested in Eloise's babbling. Muscatelli would not do anything to endanger Fran. As long as she was with him, he didn't think Holland would try anything. Then again, Healen had driven them both off the road in Pennsylvania.

This wasn't safe for Fran. She had to know the danger she was in. But how could he tell her, that his half-brother had murdered her father? How could he tell her, that her grandfather was plotting both his and his brother's deaths?

As the taxi bounced along the uneven road, Cavanaugh saw the city of Havana ahead. A dull haze seemed to cover everything a pastel blue. His brother was in danger. He was as sure of this as he was of anything. He looked to the dark clouds above. A light rain began to fall. For the first time in years, he started to pray. He didn't remember the words anymore. But that didn't really matter. He wasn't sure there was anyone up there even listening to him. After all the things he had done, there wasn't any reason to believe He would help him now even if He was there. But it was worth a chance. It was like they said, there aren't any atheists in foxholes. Passing a huge picture of Ernesto "Che" Guevara dangling over the entire side of a building, he realized that prayer was pretty much the only chance he had left now.

* * *

86

Brooklyn, New York

Morty Goldberg stood in front of the squad room carefully laying it all out for Lieutenant Bradley and the District Attorney, J. R. Coyle. Sitting around the room, Palambo, Waters, Midrasic, Prince, Roland, Balossi, Foxell, and Coco listened. Goldberg went through the steps deliberately.

Tony Yaccarino had motive. Somehow, he blamed Cavanaugh for the death of his twin sister.

He had allegedly visited Steve's barber shop and had opportunity to collect samples of Cavanaugh's hair.

As a reporter, he had access to police information.

He was present at the fight between Cavanaugh and the 1010 WINS reporter and had opportunity to place Crystal May's blood on Cavanaugh's jacket.

He lived and worked on Staten Island where all the bodies had been found and knew the area well.

The maple syrup poured over the victims' bodies could be a reminder of his sister's going to the bodega to buy maple syrup for her craving for pancakes.

According to Patrolman Shanley, Merry Perez broke her relationship with her boyfriend shortly after the shooting in the bodega claiming he had suddenly changed.

His personnel record at the *Staten Island Advance* indicated he had a temper.

Tony Yaccarino fits most of the F.B.I. profile of the killer. He is a white, heterosexual male in his twenties or thirties who grew up in a violent household. Yaccarino's father is a no nonsense military man. The death of his twin sister may have been the significant event which triggered his killing and torturing rampage. Indeed, he may see himself as an "Avenging Angel" who is trying to right the wrongful death of his sister.

The obituary of Maria DeFillipo, Tony Yaccarino's twin sister, on the wall of Merry Perez could indicate she could have been suspicious of Yaccarino. The way Goldberg saw it, Officer Perez was getting too close to uncovering her ex-boyfriend and therefore he silenced her.

District Attorney J. R. Coyle, a tall, red headed man with gold wire glasses leaned against a water cooler in the rear of the room listening. Palambo busily took notes. Waters munched on a chocolate cream donut. Midrasic scratched his dark curly hair which looked like a messy Afro. His legs quivered up and down as if he were having an orgasm. Prince absent-mindedly picked his nose. Finally, Goldberg stopped. He looked at the Lieutenant and asked, "What do you think?"

"Have you brought him in for questioning?"

"Not yet. I was hoping we could get a search warrant and check out his apartment. I didn't want to tip our hand and possibly spook him."

Suddenly, a voice from the back of the room spoke in a deep, commanding voice. It was Coyle. He was a political animal. Rumors flew like papers in the wind that he had eyes on running for Mayor in the future. He prided himself on his high conviction rate and held press conferences and managed the media more deftly than a Hollywood diva. "It doesn't work that way, Detective, and you should know that," he said. "All you have is circumstantial evidence. No judge in New York City would grant a search warrant on the circumstantial evidence you have."

"How many more people does this guy have to kill before we stop him?" Goldberg answered.

"Get me solid evidence, Detective, and I can do something. All you have here are theories. A good defense lawyer would rip your case apart like a hungry tiger on a three legged lamb." J. R. Coyle pointed at no one in particular with both index fingers. "Get me concrete evidence, not half assed theories." He turned and made a dramatic exit.

A silence fell on the room for a few seconds. Then the Lieutenant spoke. "Good work, Goldberg. I think you're on to something. Coyle's running for office, but he's right. We need more evidence. Check this guy's school records. Question his neighbors. See if anyone can place Merry Perez and him together. Check his phone records. See if they called each other. He will probably give some reason for calling her, but it will establish a link between the two and then we can hopefully get that search warrant."

"Should I bring him in for questioning?" Goldberg asked.

Lieutenant Bradley thought for a moment. He knew he was playing with fire. It was a difficult call. Finally, he answered, "No. Let's keep this among ourselves for the time being until we get something we can hold him on. I think we are on the right track, but with Cavanaugh out of the picture right now I think we have a little time."

Goldberg looked at the Lieutenant. "I hope you're right, Lieutenant."

Lieutenant Bradley lowered his head. "I hope so, too. I hope so, too."

* * *

87

Havana, Cuba

Francesca made the call from their hotel room in the NH Parque Central. A man's voice answered.

"Hello. My name is Francesca Arden. My grand . . . ."

"Ah, Miss Arden. Yes. Yes. I have been expecting your call." The voice on the other end of the phone spoke English with a strong Brooklyn accent. "Your grandfather called. How can I help you?"

Cavanaugh sat on the edge of the bed. The room was neat and roomy with tangerine walls and gold and scarlet drapes. A simple wooden desk faced a king sized bed with a yellow and green checkered bedspread. Looking out the window he could see the park. He rubbed his hands together. His palms were sweating.

"I am here with . . . ," she hesitated. She glanced at Cavanaugh and smiled. "I am here with my fiancé."

Cavanaugh gripped the bed spread. He shook his head and smiled back.

"He is trying to locate his brother. His brother is a Jesuit priest. His name is Father John Bennis. Do you think you could help us locate him?"

"Padre Bennis?" Francisco Santacruz laughed. "But of course. I know Padre Bennis very well. He said mass in my house."

Francesca covered the phone. "He knows your brother, Tom. He says he said mass in his home."

Cavanaugh felt his chest tighten.

"Could you tell us, Señor Santacruz, where we could locate him?"

"I can do better than that, young lady," Santacruz replied excitedly. "Padre Bennis is coming to my house this evening. Let me send a car to pick up your fiancé and bring him here."

Francesca turned to Cavanaugh. "Your brother is coming to his house tonight. He says he'll send a limo to take you to him."

This was too easy, thought Cavanaugh. "What time?" he asked.

Arrangements were made quickly. A man would pick Cavanaugh up in the lobby at 8:30 and drive him to Santacruz's house. It didn't give him much time.

Fran was bubbling with joy that things had worked out so well. Her grandfather had helped make this all possible. Once this was all over, she would make Tom apologize for all the bad things he had said and intimated about her grandfather.

Cavanaugh surprised her. "Let's celebrate, Fran," he said and called room service. He ordered champagne, cheese and crackers. He might have thought of the condemned man ordering an expensive, if skimpy, last meal, but he was planning. He knew the danger he was walking into was real. Things were going much too easily.

"I'll call you from Santacruz's house when I meet my brother," he said as they waited for their champagne. "Then maybe we can all go out and celebrate together at a good restaurant."

"What do you mean?" Fran asked.

He smiled. "Just what I said. After we meet maybe we can come back and meet you and go to a good restaurant and really celebrate."

Fran looked him in the eye. "What are you talking about? I'm going with you!"

"No, Fran! You are not! That's final!"

"I'm going with you!" She stood and folded her arms like an angry female Mr. Clean.

Those unanswered questions sprung back at him. Was this the time to tell her? But how could he tell her that her grandfather had ordered a hit on both him and his brother? How could he tell her that her grandfather was a murderer? How could he tell her there was an international killer somewhere out there preparing to kill him and his brother? How could he tell her that his half-brother, the priest, had murdered her father?

And even if he did tell her, would she believe any of it?

What had been going along too easily suddenly became much more complicated. And he still hadn't met the danger he knew was lurking somewhere ahead.

* * *

88

Brooklyn, New York

They needed more evidence. Morty Goldberg kept his thoughts to himself, but Barbara Palambo was outspoken as usual. "Who does that arrogant son of a bitch think he is? He's nothing more than a God-damn politician. He'd sell his mother for a freakin vote!"

Waters reached for a jelly donut. "Who ate all the chocolate cream donuts?"

"You did, you garvone!" shouted Palambo.

Goldberg raised his arms. "Focus, people. Focus. We have to stop this guy."

"We don't even know if it's him," Waters said. "You heard Coyle. All you've got are theories."

"That's why we need evidence, asshole," Palambo stated.

Lieutenant Bradley looked around the room. His face was red. "Listen up, everyone. Cut the bullshit. You're acting like a bunch of ADD pre-schoolers. Goldberg, put a tail on Yaccarino. Waters, check to see if he has a juvenile record . . . ."

"Are you kidding, Lieutenant? The kid was an Army brat. It will take me forever to check that out. The kid was probably in a half-dozen states and another half-dozen countries."

"Stop complaining, Waters, just do it!" Bradley turned to the group and continued. "Palambo check his phone records. Prince, check with motor vehicles. I want to know every ticket this guy ever got from parking to failure to put his seatbelt on. Midrasic, check his credit card statements. Foxell, check his bank statements . . . ."

Lieutenant Bradley proceeded to give out concrete assignments to everyone. He concluded with, "You heard what the D.A. said. We all know what his motivation is, but we want to catch this guy and make it stick. I'm going to contact the F.B.I. to enlist their help and close support. This is no place for jurisdictional arguments or disputes. We need to catch this guy. If Yaccarino's the guy, let's nail him. If he's not, let's find who is killing these people out there."

Patrolman Midrasic murmured, "I still say we pick up the bastard and sweat it out of him."

Goldberg looked back at Midrasic standing in the rear of the room. He wanted to tell him to quiet down, but he stopped. He hadn't realized it before, but with his black curly hair, Patrolman Midrasic looked a lot like Maria DeFillipo's twin brother, Tony Yaccarino.

* * *

89

Havana, Cuba

When Cavanaugh and Francesca walked down the winding steps of the NH Parque Central Hotel into the humid night, a heavyset man wearing a loose short sleeve multicolored shirt was leaning against a 1955 India white and skyline blue Chevrolet waiting for them. Cavanaugh noticed the man's shirt partially concealed a weapon he had tucked beneath his belt. The man pulled himself off the car and opened the front door.

"Señor Cavanaugh?" he asked. "My name is Geraldo. I am your driver."

Cavanaugh nodded, and Francesca moved forward toward the open door.

Geraldo put his hands up. "No, Señor! Only you!"

Francesca stepped forward. "I'm going, too."

"But, Señorita, I have my orders. Only Señor Cavanaugh is supposed to come. Señor Santacruz was most specific about this."

Francesca replied in an angry voice, "Consider your orders changed. Either I come too or neither of us comes."

The man's face flushed, and he looked to Cavanaugh. Cavanaugh held his hands up and shrugged his shoulders. "No use arguing, Geraldo. I haven't been able to talk any sense into her yet. Be my guest."

The man looked confused. "I'm only supposed to take one. Señor Santacruz said only one. You, Señor Cavanaugh, not her."

"I'm not a *her*," snapped Francesca. "I have a name!"

Cavanaugh smiled and placed one hand on the fat man's shoulder. "Let me make this easier for you, Geraldo." Then in a sudden move, he reached under the man's shirt and pulled his weapon from his waistband. Geraldo pulled back and tried to grab Cavanaugh's hand, but Cavanaugh's other hand pinched a nerve in his neck while the hand with the gun pressed the muzzle of the gun deep into his flaccid stomach. The gun sunk in like a pencil into Play-doh.

Cavanaugh whispered, "This gun is so far into your gut no one will even hear the shot. Do yourself a favor and get in and drive. I'll explain things to Mr. Santacruz."

"But . . . ," Geraldo began to stammer.

"No buts," Cavanaugh said. "You don't need this. If all goes well, you'll get it back later." He pushed the fat man into the car and slid in next to him. Francesca got in the back. Holding the gun steadily on the driver, Cavanaugh reached into his jacket pocket and pulled out a sharpened dinner knife. "Here, Fran, hold this. If he tries anything push the blade into his neck. He should have a little trouble trying to apply a tourniquet to his neck to stop from bleeding to death."

Francesca stared at the knife. "Where did you get this, Tom?"

"Compliments of the room service I ordered when we arrived. I sharpened it in the bathroom before we left." He smiled, "I just wanted to be prepared."

As they pulled away from the curb, Cavanaugh saw Albert and Erica enter a taxi in front of them. He didn't see Dr. Heinrich Boere in a red and white 1954 Ford a block away slowly move into traffic and start to follow them.

* * *

90

Francisco Santacruz lived in a modest section of Central Havana. As Jack Bennis casually rode around the block on his bike surveying the area like a recon specialist, he reviewed events in his mind. Santacruz's name was on the list of names Vito Muscatelli had sent to Bennis' former commanding officer Howard Stevens. The priest had taken the list along with a suitcase filled with unmarked bills and a variety of Swiss bank accounts when he abruptly left New York.

Francisco Santacruz, from all outward appearances, appeared to be a modest Cuban businessman with a deep devotion to his adopted country. Bennis had faced danger before. It had an odor he was familiar with. He had crawled head first in narrow Viet Cong tunnels, he had defused time bombs in dimly lit places, and he had narrowly escaped ambushes in Mozambique, Serbia, Panama, Uruguay, and Brooklyn. He knew that the night of Santiago's death his small apartment at the church was fire bombed. He knew someone had tipped Muscatelli that he was in Cuba. And that someone was most likely Señor Francisco Santacruz.

It was with these thoughts that Jack Bennis approached the concrete steps leading to the ten foot high Art Nouveau doorway of the Santacruz's house, armed with knowledge, hope, and a revolver tucked in the small of his back and Leather Jacket's pistol tied around his ankle.

Now it was time to meet the man who Jack Bennis was convinced was carrying out Vito Muscatelli's orders.

He had circled the block three times on his bicycle looking for signs of potential hazards. The streets were eerily empty. There was a silence in the evening air that smelled like danger. Even the night birds were quiet.

Pausing momentarily at the front of Santacruz's house, Jack Bennis took a deep breath. He patted the Nagant 7.62 tucked into the rear of his trousers and brushed his foot alongside of the Makarov PM he had tied to his ankle.

He didn't want it to go this way, but if it did, he was prepared. He looked up into the night sky and slowly made the sign of the cross like a college basketball player at the free throw line with his team losing by one point facing a one and one with one second to play. But his thoughts weren't on basketball, or winning or losing.

"Lead us not into temptation," he prayed silently as he climbed the steps, "but deliver us from evil." As he knocked on the door, he thought of his brother and all the things he would never get to tell him.

* * *

91

Cavanaugh bound and gagged the driver and left him in the trunk of the Chevy three blocks away from Santacruz's house, and slowly he and Francesca walked to the house. A block and a half from the house, they saw a man on a bicycle pull up in front of the house, stop and then walk up the stairs.

"Who's that?" Fran asked.

"Probably the pizza delivery man," Cavanaugh snapped. "Santacruz probably ordered pizza for us for dinner." He looked down at her and added, "Your grandfather probably told him we might be hungry after the flight."

She poked him sharply in the ribs. "Very funny, wise guy. Just remember—without my grandfather's help we wouldn't be here right now."

"You're right, Fran," he said. "That was a cheap shot. I apologize." But that was the very point that he was worried most about. Without Vito Muscatelli's help they wouldn't have a killer on their trail and be walking into what most probably was a trap. Much as he hated to admit it, having Vito Muscatelli's granddaughter with him now was more helpful than the beat up 9mm Italian Glisenti he had taken from Geraldo and tucked beneath his shirt.

When they reached the house, the bicycle lay unattended next to the stairs. Cavanaugh looked around quickly. "Maybe Santacruz's real name is Hannibal Lector and he's having the pizza man for dinner tonight!"

He never saw the man and woman getting out of a taxi on the next block. The man was older than the woman. Both turned in the shadows and moved behind a tangled fragipani tree and watched Cavanaugh and Francesca knock on the large doors of Santacruz's house.

Cavanaugh's mind was focused on the possibilities that faced him behind the massive doors. What surprises had Francisco Santacruz planned for him? If Cavanaugh had been more vigilant, he might have seen a well dressed man walking nonchalantly with a cane from the opposite direction and a man with a large straw hat squatting in an abandoned stucco building across the street.

The street in front of Francesco Santacruz's house remained morbidly silent as Francesca and Cavanaugh waited for the doors before them to open. Only occasionally the faint sounds carried by the evening breeze of drums, music, and song drifted in and out like waves on a beach from a group of people assembling many blocks away.

* * *

92

A tall blonde woman in a tight red dress revealing more cleavage than a Playboy Bunny had answered Jack Bennis' knock. She wore almost as much jewelry as she did makeup. She looked up at the priest as if surprised to see someone taller than she.

"My name is Jack Bennis," he said. "I'm here to see Señor Santacruz."

She smiled like the Cheshire cat. "You must be the priest," she said. "Come this way. My husband is expecting you."

Cautiously, he followed her tracing in his mind the floor plan of the house María Izabelle had detailed to him. They passed a large room with a massive mahogany table surrounded by twelve chairs and preceded into a smaller room with two sofas, a plain wooded desk and two arm chairs.

The home was modest, but well kept. The floors were covered alternatively with random brown and white tiles, the walls were a light coffee, and the furniture was plain wood and looked like it came from a storage lot for a 1920's motion picture. There were no pictures in any of the rooms. The only signs that Santacruz might not be a typical Cuban businessman were glass bookcases, well stocked wine ranks along the hallway wall, and the zaftig blonde American wife who worn her dresses tight, her jewelry sparkling, and her makeup thick.

Mrs. Santacruz stopped. "Take a seat, Padre. He'll be right with you."

Bennis quickly surveyed the room. Clearly Francisco and his Amazon trophy wife were no interior decorators. There were bars on the outside of the window behind one of the sofas. On each of the other walls, there were doors. The one they had come in from was open, the other two closed. There were no pictures on the walls and little decorations. The walls were painted red and a large ceiling fan hummed noisily above him. Bennis moved to the side of the room and stood where he could view all three doors and waited.

When Francisco Santacruz suddenly opened the door on Bennis's left, instinctively, the priest reached his hand behind his back to the revolver concealed beneath his shirt.

"So," Santacruz said munching on a Cuban cigar as he talked with a distinct Brooklyn accent, "we finally meet." Behind him the blonde who answered the door appeared. She towered over her diminutive and disheveled husband as she closed the door loudly behind them.

Francisco Santacruz was not what Bennis had expected. He wasn't a big man in stature. He was built like a fireplug with white and chestnut straggly whiskers which made him look more like a vagrant than one of the wealthiest and most influential men in Cuba. His real name, Frank Santacroce, fit him better than the Francisco Santacruz he now went by. Bennis had learned from Diego young Frankie Santacroce's hair was short and red when he was raised in a tenement in the Red Hook section of Brooklyn. His mother, Rose Santacroce, had worked in a local bucket of blood which doubled as a clubhouse for some of Brooklyn's wantabes as a stripper and waitress. His father was unknown. Frank drifted into local petty crime eventually being a bookmaker and then an enforcer. After a couple of minor scrapes with the law and a period of probation, he had moved to Roseland, New Jersey, where he set up a concrete business. After a few years, however, he drifted out of sight only to turn up one day in Havana as the head of an import-export company with a lot of money, and slowly began to buy up the crumbling buildings along Avenue Antonio Maceo and the Muro de Malecón.

Jack Bennis looked at the scruffy little man. He had never seen him before. What could Santacruz or Santacroce have against him that made him send people after him to kill him? He could understand Vito Muscatelli's wrath if he believed the priest had been responsible for the deaths of his son and his best friend. He had left New York to get away from people like him. As much as he had wanted to stay and reestablish ties with his brother Thomas, Bennis knew his presence in New York meant trouble for both of them. Vito Muscatelli was a smart, ruthless, revengeful old man even though he was in a nursing home.

"I've heard a lot about you, Padre." Motioning with his hand he said, "Please, have a seat. You're my guest."

Bennis remained standing. "I'll get right to the point, Santacruz. Why are you trying to kill me?"

Santacruz laughed and bit down on his cigar. "Can I offer you a drink or maybe a cigar? They're genuine Cuban cigars, you know. Or maybe you'd like a scotch? I've got some good single malt. I hear you clerics like scotch."

"Why are you trying to kill me, Santacruz?" Bennis repeated.

The little man sank down into the sofa opposite the priest. His legs barely touched the bare wooden floor. His wife stood behind him like a bodyguard, her diamond necklace and earrings glistening blue and yellow in the room's lighting. Somehow they reminded Bennis a little of Dagmar and a scruffy Mory Amsterdam.

Santacruz snapped his stubby fingers. "Get me a tall Grateful Dead cocktail on the rocks, babe, and leave us along for a few minutes." Señora Santacruz silently disappeared out the doorway she had led Bennis in.

"Sit down, will you, Padre? You're making me fuckin nervous standing there. I ain't got no beef with you."

"You've sent at least three people after me to kill me, Santacruz. I want to know why."

The little man crossed one of his fat legs and farted. "Opps!" he laughed. "You never know what will come out of me," he laughed. "All things in their time, Padre. But first I have a surprise for you."

Jack Bennis stared into the beady dark eyes of Santacruz.

"Remember your brother? Maybe I should say your half-brother. Same mudder, a different fadder." He laughed again even louder.

Bennis's eyes narrowed.

"Yeah, you remember him, don't you? Well, he's going to be here in a few minutes. I thought you two should get together—at least this one last time."

"What are you talking about? My brother's in New York."

"No, Padre. You're wrong. He landed here in Havana a few hours ago and is on his way here right now. Trust me, Padre, I wouldn't lie to a priest." He added, "Even if he did kill my brother."

Bennis moved closer. "What are you talking about? I never killed your brother."

Santacruz took the cigar out of his mouth and smiled. "Don't sweat it, Padre. I never liked the fuckin bastard anyway. You and me are a lot alike actually. You really did me a favor. Now all his shit's going to be mine."

Bennis's brow furrowed. "I don't know what you're talking about."

A loud knock echoed down the hall.

"That must be Mr. Thomas Cavanaugh himself now, Padre. This is going to be like a grand old fuckin reunion." He turned toward the open doorway and shouted, "Hey, babe, get that fuckin door will you and bring our other guest in here."

"What in God's name are you talking about, Santacruz? My brother's a New York City detective and I never met your brother."

"Actually, Padre, like I said, we're a lot alike. He's really my half-brother. Only we shared the same fadder, not mudder. When you shot Rocco Muscatelli in Brooklyn a while back, you killed Vito Muscatelli's son. But you didn't kill his *only* son. I'm old Vito's bastard son—the one he never wanted to acknowledge."

Jack Bennis' eyes widened.

"Yeah, Padre, old Vito Muscatelli figured it out. He's a shrewd old cock-sucker. When you called me about your fuckin church thing, I told him and he put two and two together and figured you had the sheet he faxed to that guy Howard Stevens. He never believed the shit the cops said about the killing. He always suspected you had something to do with it."

Santacruz put his feet up on the sofa and smiled again. "I have to confess, Padre, you were right about one thing. Old Vito gave me my orders to kill you and being the obedient little bastard that I am," he laughed, "I always follow Dad's orders. After all, now that Rocco the Prick is dead, I'm all the loving family the cock-sucker has. Plus, I'm going to get the old bastard's loot when he checks out."

Santacruz farted again and laughed. "I have to admit, Padre, you didn't make this job easy for me. You're quite an elusive son of a bitch yourself."

Behind him in the doorway, Bennis saw the big blonde appear in front of two people whom he recognized immediately, Francesca Arden and his brother, Thomas Cavanaugh.

Both brothers locked eyes. Bennis's eyes jumped from Cavanaugh to Francesca. Santacruz saw the shift in his eyes and turned. "Francesca?" he shouted. "What the fuck are you doing here? You ain't supposed to be here!"

Just then, the two closed doors on either side of the room opened and a man appeared in each doorway with a gun pointed at the priest and the detective.

"Freeze," Cavanaugh said. "I've got a gun pointed at your wife's back, Santacruz. Drop your guns. We are all going to leave here peacefully."

Santacruz slithered off the sofa with a smile. "Fuck you, copper. I can replace her as fast as I got her. Shoot them all," he ordered, "but don't hit the broad behind him."

Bennis grabbed the pistol from his back and dove behind the couch as shots rang out from both sides of the room. He peered up to see the shapely blonde in the red dress bounce back as blood splattered from a shot to her head from the right. Another bullet ricocheted off the door jam by his brother's head as he dropped down and pushed Francesca back into the hallway. Bennis aimed first at the shooter on his left and placed a bullet neatly in his temple. Another shot rang out from the other side of the room smashing a vase of artificial flowers on the desk alongside of him. Turning toward the shooter, he heard two more shots in rapid succession and watched the shooter at the other door fall back suddenly and collapse to the floor.

It was all over in seconds. On the floor lay Mrs. Santacruz and two unknown would-be assassins. Francisco Santacruz knelt on the floor shaking like he was suddenly afflicted with palsy.

"Please, please," he begged, "don't shoot me. I didn't mean nothing." Beads of perspiration ran down his blood splattered forehead into his tangled beard.

Jack Bennis moved forward and leveled his gun at Santacruz's head as Cavanaugh lifted Francesca to her feet.

"Are you alright, Fran?" Cavanaugh asked.

She stood frozen in silence looking at Jack Bennis who now held his gun directly against Santacruz's head.

"Who is that man? How did he know me?" she asked.

Cavanaugh looked up and saw his brother. "No, John! No! Don't do it!"

"He tried to kill us both, Thomas," he answered. Santacruz wept like a baby and a small puddle formed beneath him.

Suddenly, they heard the beating of drums, the sounds of music, and chanting voices from the front of the house. Francesca moved to the window.

"There's a group of people outside," she said. "They're building a fire and it looks like they're going to roast some chickens!"

The rhythmic beating of the drums increased and people started dancing around the flames. A loud voice shouted out over the music.

Bennis turned his head. He recognized the voice. Cautiously, he moved to the window to see for himself. There he was—the Babalawo whom he had met in the hospital. He looked back at Santacruz who was now weeping uncontrollably on the floor in the midst of three dead bodies and a puddle of his own urine.

"Let's get out of here," Bennis said. He tossed his gun to Cavanaugh. "Here, Thomas, take this one. Wipe your prints off your weapon and leave it here."

Remembering María Izabelle's sketch of the downstairs floor plan, he added, "Quickly, we can leave through the kitchen and exit the back way." Francesca and Cavanaugh followed the priest as he led them through the house and out the back into a vacant lot and away from the noisy group in front. In the back yard, they scaled a low cinder block wall and moved quickly across the lot. As they ran, they heard the sound of chanting and drum beating slowly fading. Two blocks down, just as Diego had promised, was an old 1953 brown Chevy Bel Air two door hardtop with the ignition keys in it.

Bennis opened the door and pulled the front seat forward. "Quick," he ordered, get in and get down." Cavanaugh and Francesca flew into the back seat while Bennis climbed into the driver's seat and eased down the darkened street. "We are going to drive around for awhile to make sure we're not being followed. Then I'm going to take you to the home of a friend with whom I've been staying. We should be safe there—at least for a little while."

* * *

93

When Cavanaugh, Bennis, and Francesca were gone, Santacruz slowly regained his composure. He got off the floor, wiped his tears away, and reached for the gun Cavanaugh had dropped.

"I wouldn't if I were you," a voice from the open doorway on his right warned.

Santacruz turned. He squinted in confusion.

"You don't know me, Frankie. Your father, you know, the 'cock-sucker' you so highly spoke of sent me to do the job he knew you would screw up."

"I don't know who the fuck you are," the little man said as the figure in the doorway leveled a Walther P22 with a silencer half the size of the gun directly at his head and moved slowly forward to pick up the dropped weapon.

"The name's Cain. Cain Holland. You might have heard of me. Maybe not. It makes no difference. I'm a hired killer and a damn good one at that."

Cain looked at Santacruz and nodded back and forth. "Your dad's going to be disappointed in you, Frankie. But then again he always has been, hasn't he? Too bad you're never going to get to see his money."

"What the fuck are you talking about? I don't even know you." Francisco Santacruz flared his arms like an out of control marionette. Standing in the midst of three dead bodies, he shouted, "Get the fuck out of here before I hurt you!"

Cain smiled, totally ignoring Santacruz's rambling. "I think old Vito will understand. After these two intruders broke into your house and killed your dear sweet wife over there, well, you shot them. Then when you realized what you had done, you killed yourself in a fit of despair. Yes, he'll understand."

"What the fuck are you talking about?" Santacruz snapped. "I'm not going to kill myself . . . ."

"No, of course not, Frankie," Cain said placing the gun from the floor under Santacruz's chin. "I'm going to kill you."

"Wait a minute. What are you talking about? Why?" Santacruz stammered. "Why would you do that? I don't even know you."

"Why?" Cain smiled. "It's really simple. Because I like to kill people, Frankie. I guess it's my nature. I actually prefer a knife. It's more up front and personal, but this will make things easier to explain to your loving dad. I somehow doubt he'll be too distraught, however."

Francisco Santacruz or Frankie Santacroce as he known back in Brooklyn felt only a cold chill as the bullet entered beneath his jaw and sped directly up into his brain. The slight sound of the gunshot was further blunted by the chanting, the music and the drums outside. Santacruz's eyes rolled back in his head, and he flew back against the sofa.

Cain calmly reached down and placed the gun Cavanaugh had left into Frankie's lifeless hand and just as calmly disconnected the silencer from the Walther P22 and put it away. Looking around the room at four dead bodies, Cain thought of the last act in Hamlet and grinned. Approaching the door to leave, however, something caught Cain's eye. It was the beautiful diamond earrings Frankie's wife wore. "It would be such a waste to leave them. I'm sure she wouldn't mind if I took just one," the killer whispered and proceeded to pull out a 3.5" talon sheath knife and with one swift swipe, slit the dead blonde's throat. Cain then reached down and viciously pulled one of the diamond earrings through her right earlobe.

"No sense letting a pretty thing like this go to waste," Cain said placing the earring in a pocket.

* * *

94

In the dim, wavering light of a dangling 60 watt bulb, Jack Bennis, Tom Cavanaugh, and Francesca Arden sat around Diego Velasquez's kitchen table while he busily prepared coffee for them. Francesca was pale and shaking. Reality had quickly settled in when they climbed out of the car and walked up the steps to Diego's modest home. Both Bennis and Cavanaugh tried to comfort her.

"I don't understand," she kept saying. "What happened back there? Who was that little man?" She looked at her hands and then her blood stained blouse. She started to cry. "How did this happen? I don't understand? I don't understand . . . ."

Bennis reached out and held her hand. He looked at his brother. Cavanaugh patted her other hand gently. "Relax, Fran. It's over. Try not to think about it."

"They shot that woman right in front of us!" she sobbed. "How could they? How can I not think about it! And then the shots . . . the shots . . . you shot them. You both shot them! How could you do that? You killed them . . . ."

Diego brought three cups of coffee over to them. "Here, Señorita," he said. "Have something to drink."

"I don't understand," she murmured. "Who was that man? Why did he try to kill us? I don't understand."

Bennis cleared his throat and glanced at his brother. He began slowly, "He didn't want to hurt you, Francesca. His name is Francisco Santacruz . . . ."

"He's the man my grandfather told us to see," she said looking up at Cavanaugh.

"Yes, Fran. That's why I wanted you to stay home and not come along. I told you it would be dangerous."

"But why? Why would he try to hurt us?" She ran her fingers through her long red hair.

"He didn't want to hurt you, Francesca," Bennis began. "He is your uncle."

"No, that can't be. I don't have an uncle. My father was my grandfather's only child!"

The priest stood and walked to the sink. Cavanaugh looked up at him. "What do you mean, John? Santacruz is Fran's uncle? How could that be?"

"Before you came," he began, "Santacruz told me he was the illegitimate son of Vito Muscatelli." He hesitated for a moment and then turned to Cavanaugh. "He said he was told to kill both of us, Thomas."

"No! No!" Francesca cried. "That's a lie! My grandfather wouldn't do that! That's a lie!"

Cavanaugh reached over and put his other arm around her. "It makes sense, Fran. I tried to tell you, your grandfather isn't the nice guy you think he is. I called Goldberg when we were in Toronto and he said the F.B.I. suspected he sent someone to kill me."

"No! No! You're both lying!" She pulled away from him and knocked over her cup of coffee. "He wouldn't do this! He loves me! You're lying!"

"That Healen guy who drove us off the road in the Poconos had my license plate number on his dashboard. Somebody must have given it to him. Did you by any chance tell your grandfather where I was going?"

"This is crazy! Yes! I told him when I asked him to help us get here. But he wouldn't try to kill us!"

"Did you tell him you were coming with me?"

Francesca walked back and forth holding her head.

Cavanaugh answered for her. "You didn't, did you? You told him you were flying to Toronto to meet me there. You changed your mind at the last minute, and he didn't know."

"Stop it! Stop it!" she cried.

"When we had the accident, you tried to call 911, but you got your grandfather instead. You told him where we were. That was how he was able to hire Cain Holland to come after me and Healen."

"Who's Cain Holland?" Bennis asked.

"He's a hired assassin, a killer, we initially thought might be involved in a series of murders back in New York. I was investigating the murders when I left to come here. Holland's MO is similar to our murderer, but there were slight differences."

"I think I need a drink!" Diego said. He rose and went to the cupboard and pulled out a bottle of Havana Club rum and some orange juice from the refrigerator. "Would anyone like a Havana Loco?"

"Holland killed Healen to make sure he wouldn't talk. He probably followed us down here to get the both of us," Cavanaugh said looking directly at his brother.

Suddenly, the front door swung open and a woman followed by a tall thin man rushed down the dark hallway into the kitchen. Both Cavanaugh and Bennis reached for their guns.

The woman ran to Jack Bennis and threw her arms around him. "Are you alright?" she asked. "What happened? We heard the shots . . . ."

The priest gently pushed the woman back. "Err," he began, "this is María Izabelle, Diego's sister-in-law."

Diego threw some ice cubes into a glass and downed his Havana Loco in one long slug.

The tall thin man stood motionless in the doorway. His skin was rough and black and he wore the same multi-colored sports shirt and a white cowhide leather ivy cap Bennis had seen him in the last time they had met. "Hector," he said, "that was you outside Santacruz's house tonight? How did you get there?"

"María Izabelle called me to help," he replied in a deep, resonate voice. "I am sorry we arrived too late."

Bennis thought back to how he had almost killed Francisco Santacruz. "No," he replied. "You arrived just in time to save me from doing something very stupid."

Cavanaugh got up and went over to Francesca who was sobbing. Diego made himself another Havana Loco.

"John," Cavanaugh asked, "what the hell is going on here?"

Bennis sighed. "It's a long story, Thomas. Let's just say I met Hector at one of the hospitals here. He is a Babalawo, a Santería priest. He and some of his followers were beating the drums and chanting in front of Santacruz's house. They created a diversion which allowed us to escape."

"We were praying for your safety, Padre," Hector corrected. "Orumila, the god of wisdom, works in mysterious ways at times."

Bennis looked at María Izabelle. "But," he asked, "how did you get in touch with Hector. I thought you were afraid of him."

"I knew you were going to need help so when I left here I went to see Manuel in the hospital, and he told me how to contact the Babalawo. And you were right about him. He is a kind and good man."

"We had hoped we could prevent the violence that occurred," Hector said, "but we were too late."

"We appreciate your help, Hector. As you probably heard, there was some shooting in the house. Two men tried to kill us. They shot and killed Señor Santacruz's wife, and we had to shoot them. I don't know what's going to happen now. We left Santacruz crying on the floor. I pray he doesn't send more people after us. But he probably will."

María Izabelle looked at the Babalawo and then at Bennis. "He won't be sending anyone after you," she stated flatly.

"How do you know?" Cavanaugh and Bennis asked.

"Because we went into the house to check on you. We counted the four bodies."

"You must have miscounted. There were three bodies when we left," Cavanaugh corrected. "His two men and his wife."

"No, Señor, four bodies. Señor Santacruz was dead also. I recognized him," María Izabelle said. "It looked like he killed himself."

"That can't be!" Bennis said. "He wouldn't kill himself. He may have been a coward, but he was too arrogant and egocentric to kill himself."

Cavanaugh stepped toward María Izabelle. "I'm John's brother, Thomas. I'm a New York City Homicide Detective. Can I ask you a couple of questions?"

"Of course," María Izabelle smiled. "Your brother has spoken much about you."

"When you went into the house, did you get a good look at Señora Santacruz?"

"There was a lot of blood around. She was lying in the doorway. I reached down to feel for her pulse. There was none."

"What did you notice about her?"

"She had been shot in the head and her throat was cut."

"Her throat was cut?" Bennis asked. "No one cut her throat."

"No, Jack, I am sure. I saw her. Her throat was cut clear through to the bone. Now that I think of it, there wasn't much blood coming from that wound though. It looked like it may have been done after she died."

Cavanaugh said slowly, "Think carefully. This is important. I know it was a horrible scene, but did you happen to see if she were wearing long sparkling diamond earrings?"

"Leave her alone, Thomas. It was an ugly scene. Don't make her dwell on it," Bennis said.

"This is important, John," Cavanaugh replied. "Think carefully, María Izabelle. Did Mrs. Santacruz have earrings on?"

Hector spoke up. His voice seemed to echo through the room. "She had one earring on," he said. "I remember I thought it was strange."

"Yes, that's true," María Izabelle said. "Now that you mention it, I remember, too. She was missing her right earring."

Cavanaugh turned to his brother and the others in the room. "Cain Holland is here in Havana. It looks like he killed Santacruz to make it look like a suicide, but couldn't resist taking an earring as a trophy."

"What does that mean?" Francesca asked.

"It means we have trouble. There is a professional killer out there trying to kill my brother and me," Cavanaugh said.

Diego poured the bottle of Havana Club rum straight into the orange juice container and took a long gulp.

Cavanaugh added, "We don't know what this guy even looks like, but he knows us. To put it bluntly, we're in deep shit!"

* * *

VIII

Sometimes in our confusion, we see not the world as it is,
but the world through eyes blurred by the mind.

Anonymous

MONDAY

95

Brooklyn, New York

It took a lot of hours, regular and overtime, but everyone from NYC Police Commissioner John Mullen and Lieutenant Thomas Bradley to the Mayor and the entire City Council had given the green light—even in the fiscally strait times which seemed to perpetually plague the Big Apple like an infestation of hungry green fruit worms.

Pressure from politicians soon softened District Attorney J. R. Coyle's position and when the police received an anonymous tip that Tony Yaccarino had rented a storage shed in the Travis section of Staten Island and one of his co-workers at the *Staten Island Advance* recalled Yaccarino's saying at one time he was dating a policewoman, Coyle reassessed his position and called a press conference demanding to know why the police had waited so long to seek a search warrant.

Morty Goldberg was assigned lead detective on the investigation, partly because of the information he had gathered on Yaccarino and, partly because his partner who could not be located, was still a possible suspect. The Police Department was subtly covering its own ass. If Goldberg couldn't clear his partner and save the Department more unwanted publicity, nobody could.

Goldberg took the Staten Island Ferry again, this time with Detective Barbara Palambo and Police Officer Bill Midrasic. Officer Mike Shanley met the three at the foot of the ferry in Staten Island and drove them out to a section known as Travis.

"Looks like you've got this one nailed up in a bag," Shanley said driving steadily along the Staten Island Expressway. "It's all over the papers."

"You can't believe everything you read in the paper, Shanley," Goldberg answered. "We still only have circumstantial evidence. Hopefully we'll find something in the storage shed."

"What did the creep have to say when you brought him in?" Shanley asked.

Goldberg took a deep breath. D.A. Coyle had played this like a chess master. He leaked the news to the press to show the success of his office while at the same time giving himself a lot of room to question the integrity and efficiency of the police force. Now that the press had information about a suspect, Goldberg had lost his advantage.

"He disappeared before we could question him," he replied.

"Oh," Shanley moaned, "that doesn't sound too good."

"They should have let me bring him in yesterday like I wanted to. I'd have gotten a confession out of him," Midrasic shouted from the back seat.

"We'll get the bastard," Palambo stated. "Don't sweat it. Having the press involved this early, however, just makes it more difficult. I wish I knew the bastard who leaked this thing."

Goldberg sighed again. He thought he knew. "Politics is a dirty business," he murmured as they merged onto the Pearl Harbor Expressway more commonly known as the West Shore Expressway. When they exited at South Avenue, they proceeded slowly down a winding road that could have been a toxic waste area at once and probably still was. Less than a mile away, what once was the largest dump in the world now held bits and pieces of the Twin Tower Massacre. The side of the road was covered with patches of wild grass, yellowed newspapers, weeds, abandoned flower bouquets, empty cans and beer bottles, and the occasional skeletal remains of an old car left to rust beneath the sun.

Behind the assortment of tall weeds, wild flowers, and mangy shrubs, a group of blue and white aluminum storage sheds came into view. They gave Goldberg the illusion of attached sterile mausoleums of the future or the largest group of cabanas he had ever seen.

When they got out of the patrol car, Goldberg got the key to Yaccarino's storage bin from a gray haired man in his late 60's named Bernie who sat in a shabby air conditioned office watching a Giants-Eagles replay on a 12" television while reading an old Playboy magazine and drinking a can of Colt 45. Bernie didn't seem too interested in getting up or even questioning what was going on. Maybe it was the beer or maybe it was his wooden leg which rested in his lap. There could have been a rock concert going on down one of the rows of storage bins and Bernie wouldn't have cared and probably wouldn't have noticed.

Walking down one of the long row of storage sheds, Goldberg couldn't help wonder what was in them. Furniture? Unused equipment? Files? Family treasures? Each storage facility had a history. Turning down another row, he saw four police officers standing guard in front of one of the sheds in the distance. As they grew closer, he saw a fifth figure dressed in blue. Approaching the men, Goldberg recognized Officer Rhatigan. They had worked together in Brooklyn before Rhatigan and Shanley had transferred to Staten Island. Rhatigan looked concerned. He walked quickly toward Goldberg, Palamba, Midrasic, and Shanley.

"We've got a problem, Morty," he said motioning back to the shed where three other officers, who looked to Goldberg like they were still in high school, stood facing a man with folded arms in front of the shed. Goldberg recognized him immediately. It was Sgt. Major Yaccarino dressed in his full military dress blues.

"What do we do?" asked Rhatigan. "He's got a chest full of medals including the Purple Heart and the Silver Star. He says the only way we'll get into the shed is over his dead body."

* * *

96

Goldberg stood for a moment staring at Sgt. Major Yaccarino. What the hell was he doing here? Surrounded by two detectives and six police officers, the Sgt. Major stood his ground like a stone statue.

Suddenly, Patrolman Midrasic pulled his 9 mm Smith & Wesson service pistol and pushed forward. "Out of the way, old man," he demanded pointing the gun at him. Before Goldberg had a chance to stop, the Sgt. Major swung his right leg up and over knocking the gun down the row of sheds. He then used Midrasic's forward motion and propelled him into the shed leaving a large dent in the blue aluminum door and Midrasic lying dazed on the ground.

"I didn't come here for any trouble, men. But you're not going to pin this rap on my son. I lost a daughter and I don't intend to lose a son. I know you're looking for a cop killer and you think my boy's the one. I know what I would do in your situation, but I'm not about to let you railroad my son!"

"No one's trying to railroad anyone," Goldberg said stepping forward with both hands up. "Stand down, everyone," he said and motioned to Shanley and Rhatigan. "Secure Officer Midrasic and make sure he doesn't get his weapon back until we leave here. Take him to the squad car and keep him there."

The Sgt. Major stood like a Marine recruiting poster. Goldberg slowly lowered his arms. "How is Mrs. Yaccarino taking all this?" he asked.

"I sent her to her sister in Florida. She doesn't need this right now."

"Neither do you, Sgt. Major."

"You're not taking my boy away from me."

"We are just trying to find the facts. There is no proof Tony did anything. What's in that storage shed could be nothing."

The Sgt. Major could have been a miniature Sequoia tree. He stood motionless.

"We have a court order, but that's not the point," Goldberg said. "What happens if we have to arrest you? How do you think Mrs. Yaccarino will react? She needs you now. Now is not the time to play John Wayne or Rambo."

The Sgt. Major could have turned to stone. He didn't move a muscle.

The three remaining police officers and the two detectives stood silently waiting for the Sgt. Major to react. Minutes passed and they all stood there in silence waiting.

Finally, Goldberg broke the silence. "Okay," he said. "You win. I'm going to give you the key to the storage bin. You open it and I follow you in. It will just be you and me. Everyone else will stay outside until you give them the word to enter."

Goldberg looked at the Sgt. Major intently. "It's the best I can do. It will prevent any of us from planting a bloody glove or any other so-called evidence. And it will give us all a look at what your son has in there."

"It could be he has nothing in there," he continued, "but then again it could be he does. Either way we need to find out."

Goldberg flipped the key to the Sgt. Major. "I think you need to know, too," he added. "Your call."

Sgt. Major Yaccarino stared at the key in his hand. The only sounds were the tracker trailers rushing by on the West Shore Expressway. No one moved.

Finally, he looked at Goldberg and said, "Only you."

"Agreed," Goldberg nodded.

Palambo and the three teenage police officers backed off.

The retired Army NCO turned and unlocked the shed. He slowly raised the door. The first thing that hit Goldberg was the smell. It hit Yaccarino, too. He backed out as the sunlight shone into the dark shed.

There on a table lay the body of a young woman. Her nude body was strapped to the table. Both her wrists were twisted like slinkies in awkward shapes and her head hung over the side of the table like a broken bobble head doll.

The smell was nauseating. Goldberg gagged and turned. One of the young police officers started vomiting while the other two held handkerchiefs to their noses as they backed even farther away. Detective Palambo screamed. Goldberg looked for the Sgt. Major.

He was gone.

* * *

97

Staten Island, New York

It was early evening in the nursing home. Vito Muscatelli's dinner of cauliflower and broccoli pasta lay untouched by the side of his bed. No one made pasta like his mother. The sticky toffee pudding with butterscotch sauce dessert had not been touched. When Gestas returned from tapping his kidneys, he would send him to Carvel's for a vanilla thickshake and a frozen brown bonnet. To hell with what the doctor's said.

Suddenly, the phone rang. He picked it up immediately. This might be the news he was waiting for.

"Vito," the voice on the phone began, "I wanted you to know right away. I almost had the pictures of the two male red-tailed hawks you were looking for, but they flew away at the last moment. I'm camped out now at their nesting ground where they're bound to return."

Muscatelli gripped the phone. His hand was shaking. Had he underestimated Holland? Had Cain Holland lost it? Or had Muscatelli underestimated the brothers? Either way, he still had an ace in the hole.

"Vito, are you there?"

Cain's voice jarred him back. "*Sì. Sì*," he said. "Can that friend I told you about help in any way?"

"Negative, Vito. Frankie's dead. Apparently, he killed himself before I got here," Holland lied. "They say there was a robbery or something at his house, and the robbers killed his wife. Frankie lost it, and, according to what I heard, he shot the intruders and then turned the gun on himself in a fit of despair." The story sounded weak even to Holland, but Muscatelli would find out soon enough about his good for nothing bastard son. Holland elected to get the bad news over right away. "I can look over matters here for you for awhile, if you want."

An image of Frankie's mother flashed before him, her naked body hanging from an extension cord over his desk in his old office in the Red Hook section of Brooklyn. "Like his mother," Vito said, "he was a worthless piece of shit from the moment he was born."

Holland smiled. This bogus story just might work. People tend to believe what they want to believe. "What do you want me to do now?"

"Stay where you are and get those pictures when the birds come back to their nest. Be patient and careful."

"I hear you. I'll call you to tell you when I have the pictures. Trust me, Vito, Cain Holland always gets the job done!"

Vito Muscatelli ended the conversation abruptly with a warning. "Make sure you don't send me any female bird pictures."

On the other end of the line, in the NH Parque Central Hotel in Havana, Cuba, Holland smiled again. "The old bastard is a sly one. He loses his accent when he wants to."

Back on Staten Island, Muscatelli sat up in bed and began to dial a number. Suddenly, he stopped. It could wait till the morning. He would give Francesca the call in the morning. If Dr. Benevento's post-hypnotic suggestion worked, Francesca would save Holland the trouble of eliminating the two brothers. Once he gave her the signal, she herself would avenge the death of her father and his son. It was fitting to end it this way. Yes, Vito Muscatelli's mouth curved upward in his version of a grin. Tomorrow he would make the call, and Francesca would be sent on the mission he had planted in her brain before she left for Cuba. Tomorrow Francesca would be sent on her mission to kill Bennis and Cavanaugh.

* * *

98

Brooklyn, New York

It was as official as it could be. The police and the F.B.I. were now looking for Tony Yaccarino. His picture was all over the newspapers and the television. C.I.S. discovered a small plastic bag containing Cavanaugh's hair clippings, vials of blood from Luca Andrassy, Meredith Perez, and the latest victim, as yet unidentified. There were candid shots hanging on the walls of Cavanaugh and Francesca Arden. A trophy case, similar to the one his father kept his medals in, hung on the back wall. In the case, carefully lined up, was one earring from each of all his victims, and video tapes of all of them, except Meredith Perez, pleading with him and of their futile screams as he slowly broke their wrists and ultimately slit their throats.

The decomposing body found in the storage shed had undergone a degree of savagery not seen before in the other murders. In addition to her wrists being broken, her facial skin had been pared layer by layer with a surgical scalpel. To prevent the victim's inevitable screams, the killer had cut her tongue out and glued her eyes open so she would see what he was doing to her.

Watching the videos made everyone present horrified. They had seen murder victims before, but the fiendish pleasure this killer obviously got out of his sadistic torturing of his victims was sickening to watch. After viewing the tapes everyone went to the phone to call home and check on their loved ones. Everyone except Patrolman Bill Midrasic.

Midrasic sulked in a corner of the squad room glaring at Goldberg.

For his part, Goldberg had the urge to leave the station house and go home and hug his wife and children. Knowing Yaccarino was still out there sent a chill through his body. But there were other things that troubled Goldberg, too.

The Sgt. Major like his son had disappeared like the Invisible Man. It was as if Mandrake the Magician had gestured hypnotically and they had both vanished into the breeze.

And then there were the nursery rhyme notes. The police found two hand printed nursery rhyme notes at the scene. One was written for the victim on the table. It lay on top of her neatly folded clothes in the back of the shed by the "trophy case" together with a vial of her blood, and a sparkling multi-colored handmade butterfly earring. The note was longer than the others. It read:

Little Maureen used to be a happy soul,
A happy soul was she.
But when I peeled her skin away
She so desperately tried to flee.
You should have seen her gurgle so
When the blade slit through her throat.
Her tears and blood like a river they did flow.
Little Maureen wasn't happy anymore.
Cavanaugh would have loved to see her float.
Someday soon he too will pay the toll.

But there was a second note, too. It was even longer. It read:

Hickory dickory dock.
I have this to say—
It's time to make Cavanaugh pay.
Hickory dickory dock.
Even dead, doesn't she look so good
With her hair so red?
Hickory dickory dock.
I'll bet you never thought I would!
Hickory dickory dock.
You should have heard her squeal.
Hickory dickory dock.
Now, Cavanaugh, you know how I feel.
Hickory dickory dock.

The awkward nursery rhyme was pinned to a picture of Francesca Arden.

* * *

99

Havana, Cuba

They stayed up all night talking. For the moment they were safe. No one else knew where they were. When Professor Diego Velasquez passed out on his kitchen table, Bennis and Cavanaugh carried him into his small room. Diego felt eerily sticky and smelled like a basket of over ripened fruit after drinking a full bottle of Havana Club rum and a quart of orange juice. There was no question he would have a hangover when he awoke, but that wasn't on either of the brothers' minds. They were safe for the moment. They were below the radar. It was a matter of time, they both knew, however, before they would have to leave Diego's house and become walking targets for the enigmatic and lethal Cain Holland.

The brothers tucked Diego in his bed and then sat on the floor of his room and talked softly in the dark.

"What do we do now, John?" Cavanaugh whispered at one point.

"We can't stay here forever, that's for sure," Bennis stated. "The longer we stay here, the more danger we place Diego and María Izabelle in."

"Speaking of María Izabelle," Cavanaugh began, "she's a hot looking chick. What's the story between you two? I saw the way she ran to you. It's none of my business, but what do you two have going?"

"You're right, Thomas. It's none of your business. But to satisfy your curiosity, there's nothing between us."

"As my lieutenant back in New York would say, that's bullshit!"

"Get serious, Thomas. If what you say is true, we have a hired professional hit man after the both of us. Muscatelli must have sent him when the others failed."

"The others? What others?"

"There were at least three others. One came a little too close for comfort." Bennis patted his side. "The real question now is how do I get you and Fran out of this?" He rubbed his side again embracing the pain and added, "What does this guy Holland look like?"

"That's part of the problem. No one knows. Apparently, he's a real sicko. He likes to torture his victims by breaking their wrists before he slits their throats. He usually takes an earring from his female victims and sometimes leaves an earring as a sign of his work next to his male victims. We were investigating a copycat of this guy back in New York when I left."

"So we don't know what he looks like, but we do know he's out there someplace looking to kill us."

"That about sums it up," Cavanaugh admitted. "I think we have to stick together until we can get out of here. There are three of us against one. If we watch each other's backs we should be okay."

Bennis looked over at the snoring Diego. "There are only two of us, Thomas. I can't involve Diego in this. He's put himself in enough danger already for me."

"You're forgetting Francesca. She wanted to be a part of this and she can help. Do you have a weapon she could use?"

"Are you crazy? Do you think she'd help if she knew I killed her father?"

"She doesn't know, John, and she doesn't have to know. Some things are better left unsaid."

They sat in the darkness of Diego's bedroom in silence. Only the deliberate ticking of the clock on Diego's dresser, his intermittent snores, and the low murmur of Francesca, María Izabelle, and Hector's voices from the kitchen were heard. Finally, Bennis reached down and unwrapped the Makarov PM pistol tied to his ankle. He examined it in the somber shadows and then handed it to his brother. "Whatever happens to me, I want you two to be able to get out of here and start a new life together. Fran's had a hard time after what her father put her through." He added, "I hope she's a good shot."

Cavanaugh grasped the gun, and replied. "I hope she doesn't have to use it!"

* * *

IX

Do not worry about tomorrow,
for tomorrow will worry about itself.
Each day has enough trouble of its own.
Matthew 6:34.

TUESDAY

100

Brooklyn, New York

Morty Goldberg was the type of man who liked to dot all his i's and cross all his t's. Sitting at his desk, he reviewed the evidence collected from the latest crime scene. The renter of the storage bin was listed as Tony Yaccarino, but the rental agreement was unsigned. Old Bernie apparently wasn't much of a stickler on paperwork. He couldn't describe Yaccarino. All he knew was the guy paid cash.

The crime scene investigators found no fingerprints in the storage bin. Even the latest victim's finger tips had been flayed and burned. Identification of the victim was going to be difficult. This murder was more vicious and sadistic, dental records wouldn't help either. All her teeth had been removed—while she was still alive.

Goldberg rubbed his eyes. This was definitely a crime of deliberate, savage passion. The killer savored this kill. He exhibited a new level of torture and cruelty. He had to be stopped. Who was this Tony Yaccarino? Could the killing of his twin sister have turned him into New York's version of the Marquis de Sade? He felt sick to his stomach looking at the pictures of the dead woman.

"You should have let me get him when we had the chance," Bill Midrasic muttered at him from the corner. Next to him, Mike Waters bit into a foot long Subway hero.

"Do you ever stop bitching?" Barbara Palambo asked. "I swear to God you're worse than Waters."

"His father's in on this, too. Mark my words," Midrasic said. "You should have locked him up for assaulting an officer, Goldberg! I'd like to get my hands on that prick one time!"

"Yeah? And what are you going to do?" Palambo asked. "He kicked your ass once already!"

"You stupid bitch! What do you know? You're just like all the rest . . . ."

Palambo stood up and started walking toward Midrasic. "And just what is that supposed to mean, Dick-head?"

Waters looked up from his half eaten hero and asked, "Does anyone have any ketchup?"

Palambo stopped and turned. "Ketchup? What the hell do you need ketchup for?"

"I like it on my tuna fish," Waters responded like a third grader.

The telephone rang, and Goldberg answered it.

"Detective Goldberg?" a man's voice asked.

"Speaking."

"This is Sgt. Major Yaccarino."

Goldberg motioned for someone to put a trace on the call. Midrasic and Palambo reached for extension phones. Waters continued eating.

"You don't need to trace this call," the Sgt. Major said. "I'm in the Bronx with my son. He didn't do it. I want to talk to you about it. I don't want him railroaded. He didn't do it!"

"Mr. Yaccarino," Goldberg began, "no one's going to railroad your son. We have a legal system in our country. Everyone is innocent until proven guilty . . . ."

"It was a setup," the Sgt. Major continued. "My son never rented that storage locker!"

"Why don't you bring him in to the station so we can talk?"

"No! You think he's a cop killer. He doesn't stand a chance if I bring him in."

"We need to talk, Sgt. Major. You are both in a lot of trouble right now."

There was a long period of silence on the other end of the phone line. Finally, Sgt. Major Yaccarino spoke. "He's innocent, I tell you. He's innocent! You've got to believe me!" And then he hung up.

Goldberg looked up. "He's innocent my ass," Midrasic volunteered immediately. "Just like the prisons are full of innocent people and the graveyards are full of indispensable people."

"We got a trace on the call, Morty," Palambo said. "It's from a bar on East Tremont Avenue in the Bronx."

Goldberg stood and straightened his tie. "Let's go and see if we can find them there. Maybe we'll get lucky."

Waters looked up from the last bite of his sandwich. Pieces of lettuce, black olives, mayonnaise, ketchup, and tuna fish were splattered over his face, his hands, and his chest. "Why don't we just call the Bronx and have them pick him up?"

Goldberg stopped and checked his Smith & Wesson service pistol. "Because the Sgt. Major is right. They don't know him up there. All they are looking for is a psycho serial killer / cop killer. I want to bring the son in for questioning. I think his father trusts me."

Waters wiped his face with the sleeve of his shirt. "If you think he trusts you, then why are you checking your gun?"

Goldberg didn't answer. He buttoned his jacket and headed for the door. Midrasic, Palambo, and Waters followed him.

* * *

101

Havana, Cuba

How do you tell the girl you are in love with that your brother killed her father? How do you explain to her that her grandfather, even in his retirement, is still one of the most powerful mobsters on the East Coast? Do you even try? What's the use? Cavanaugh thought as he looked at the loaded Makarov PM pistol in his hand.

Most of his adult life had been a series of escapades like a picaresque novel. Joining the police force had let him exercise and partially excuse his dark side. He always threw himself headfirst into life like an Acapulco diver whether it was writing out speeding tickets, investigating a murder, or making love. Over the years he had written a lot of tickets, investigated a number of murders, and made love with all sorts of women. But Francesca Arden had been different. Was it her familial ties to the mob? Was it the feeling that he was walking on the edge with her? Or was it the desperate loneliness he recognized in her green eyes whenever he looked in the mirror? He didn't know.

For everything there was a season. Maybe this was not the season to tell the truth? It could wait until they were home and safe again.

Francesca sat at the kitchen table staring out the window at a small Bananaquit bird perched in a papaya tree. Her red hair seemed to glow in the early morning sunlight. She was beautiful and, he believed, as delicate as the bird singing innocently in the tree. Could she really not have known what her father and grandfather did for a living? Was this too much to believe? Did he believe it because he wanted to believe it or because it was true? He shook his head. He didn't want to think about it.

She turned as he approached. "Where were you?" she asked. "You and your brother took the Professor off to bed and we never heard from you again. I tried to wait up for you, but I fell asleep at the table. María Izabelle went home."

"We were talking, Fran. It's been a rough night and there was a lot to catch up on."

He sat across from her. He stared at her, not saying anything.

"What is it, Tom?" she asked.

"Someone is trying to kill my brother and me. You saw what happened last night."

"I kept waking up thinking it might have been a dream. And then I would look at that woman's blood on my blouse . . . ."

"We've got to get out of here. My brother doesn't want to leave, but I'm going to try my best to talk him into coming back to New York."

"Why does he want to stay if someone is trying to kill him?"

"He says there are a lot of good things he can do here. He's been reaching out into the community to help people." He hesitated for a moment. "There was a lot going on in New York when he left. Your father was killed . . . ." His voice tailed off.

"But what does that have to do with him? He was there to help my mother and my brother and sister. We needed him and he was there. Here someone is trying to kill him!"

Cavanaugh held the gun in his lap. It felt cold. His hands were sweating. What would she do if she found out Father Bennis had killed her father?

"Did you give it to her, Thomas?" The voice came from Professor Diego's room. He turned and saw his brother standing there. "Did you?"

"Not yet. We were just talking."

"Give me what?" Fran asked.

Cavanaugh swallowed hard. Maybe he should take the bullets out of the gun. But then it would be useless. She might need to use it. Slowly, he brought the Makarov pistol from his lap and placed it on the table. "My brother wants you to have this in case you need it."

"What are you talking about? I don't need a gun!"

Bennis moved forward and pushed the gun toward her. "Do you know how to use a gun, Francesca?"

"Yes. Of course I do. My grandfather taught me to fire a gun when I was eight years old."

Her God-damn grandfather again, Cavanaugh thought. He had mental glimpses of Vito Muscatelli teaching his grandchildren to shoot. Could Fran really not understand who her grandfather really was? He never knew his own grandfather. He had learned from his mother that her father worked as a laborer in Edinborough and may have worked on the London Bridge. He had come to the United States in the 1920's. It was a hard time. They had struggled and survived. He never asked anyone for a dime. Working three jobs, he raised his family. He died trying to break up a fight in Greenwich Village when two thugs from the local bookie tried to put pressure on his neighbor, Gerry Gilmartin, an Irish immigrant with a slight drinking problem, a more serious gambling problem, and a heart of gold to go along with a silver story-telling tongue. Cavanaugh's father died of a massive cerebral hemorrhage brought on by a hammer to the skull. Gilmartin suffered a broken arm. In the end the bookie got his money, and Cavanaugh's grandmother lost her husband. It didn't seem fair to Cavanaugh. But he learned early in life that life isn't fair.

Jack Bennis saw the look in his brother's eyes and placed the pistol in Fran's hands. "Be careful, Fran, it's loaded. I want you to have it because we are going back to your hotel. We want you to be able to defend yourself if need be. Look at it this way, there are some people out there trying to kill Thomas and me. We may need help. Please take the gun, put it in your purse, and only take it out in an extreme emergency. More innocent people have been accidentally killed by hand guns than intended targets."

Francesca reluctantly took the pistol. She looked at both men. Each had killed someone the night before. They talked about it like they had bought a loaf of rye bread at the supermarket. How could they be so callous, so unfeeling?

It was as if the priest read her mind. "Fran," he began, "no one in his right mind wants to kill another human being. It's a horrible feeling, believe me. I am not asking you to kill anyone. Just having a weapon is often enough to dissuade someone. If Thomas did not have that gun last night he or I or maybe both of us wouldn't be here this morning. We talked a lot last night in the dark by Diego's bed. I know Thomas feels the same as I do. He still has nightmares over the young girl who was shot in the bodega back home. It wasn't his fault and he didn't fire the shot that killed her, but he regrets it and it burrows a hole in his insides. I have similar dreams. Believe me, Fran, no one is asking you to shoot anyone. We want you to be able to protect yourself in case . . . ," he hesitated, "in case neither one of us is around to help."

Cavanaugh looked out the window and saw the little grey, black and yellow Bannaquit with its white eye stripe blissfully chirping in the tree. He looked back at Francesca.

"I don't want the gun," she said flatly.

"For God's sake, Fran, take the stupid gun!" Cavanaugh snapped and pounded the table knocking over a cold cup of coffee. "I'm tired of this shit! Take the gun! Those people last night were not playing games! This is serious. I told you it might get dangerous and it has. Now take the God-damn gun and let's get back to the hotel!" He stood up abruptly and knocked the chair over.

Jack Bennis said nothing. He watched his brother storm out of the room.

Francesca slowly took the Makarov PM and placed it in her purse. Her face was red.

There was a strange silence in the room.

The Bannaquit in the tree had stopped singing and flown away.

* * *

102

Bronx, New York

It took them a little more than an hour to drive from Brooklyn to the Bronx even with the siren on and lights flashing. Sgt. Major Yaccarino' call came from a pay phone in the Manor House, a bar and sometimes grill in the Parkchester section of the Bronx. Goldberg let Midrasic, Palambo, and Waters out at the Motor Vehicles Office across the street and then circled back and pulled down the cul-de-sac by the bar. The long plate glass window facing East Tremont Avenue would give the Sgt. Major a clear view of them. In all likelihood, Goldberg thought, the Sgt. Major would be watching the bar from somewhere else anyway. He wasn't a fool.

Midrasic watched the front door. Palambo and Waters the side door. Goldberg walked in to a large semi-circular bar with tables on one side and booths on the other. Three men in their sixties sat together at one end of the bar. A well dressed man in a blue pinstriped suit sat on a barstool near the door reading a newspaper. A leather attaché sat next to him on another bar stool. In a booth near the pay phone in the rear of the bar, two more men sat with their backs to Goldberg. One had curly dark hair and the other a gray crew cut. They were studying a paper on the table.

"Can I help you, fella?" the bartender asked. He was tall, probably six four or five. His ruddy complexion, bibulous nose, and barrel-like belly indicated he may have enjoyed a slight libation on the altar of friendship with his clients a few too many times.

"I'm looking for someone," Goldberg said.

"Why don't you try the synagogue?" one of the old timers from the other side of the bar laughed to the amusement of his buddies.

The two men in the booth turned. They weren't the Sgt. Major and his son.

Goldberg flashed his detective's shield. The three men stopped laughing and reached for their drinks. "I'm looking for a man and his son. The man is a retired Sgt. Major in the Army. He may be wearing his military uniform."

A silence fell over the bar. The three men sipped their beers and avoided eye contact. The two men in the booth returned to whatever it was they were looking at.

"Have any of you seen them?" Goldberg asked.

More silence.

"I know one of them called from this pay phone a little over an hour ago."

The bartender braced himself on the bar and glared down at Goldberg.

"Is your name Goldberg?" a voice asked from behind him. It came from the man in the blue pinstriped suit.

"That's me," Goldberg said.

"The men you are looking for were here about an hour ago. They left after the older one made a call. He asked me to give this to you if you showed up." He reached over and opened his attaché.

As he did, Midrasic barged in the front door with his service revolver out. "Freeze, mother fucker!" he shouted. Two of the gomers on the other side of the bar fell off their bar stools. The other one with the big mouth ducked so quickly his head bounced off the bar.

The man in the suit froze in midair with one hand on his bag.

"I thought I told you to stand guard at the front door," Goldberg said to Midrasic.

"I saw him reaching for a gun."

"Lower your gun and stand back," Goldberg ordered. Then he turned to the well dressed man. "Open the bag please—slowly."

Goldberg saw that the man was reading the help wanted pages in the *New York Times*. Slowly the man removed an envelope and gave it to him. Palambo and Waters quietly came in the side door and each walked up a different side of the bar. Palambo stopped to help the two men who fell off their bar stools. Waters spotted a bowl of pretzels and peanuts on the bar and reached over for a handful. He noticed the bartender had a thick baseball bat in his right hand. "Take it easy, big fella," Waters said. "I'm hungry."

Goldberg opened the envelope and read the letter enclosed.

> I hoped you'd come, but I had to be sure you were alone. If you're not alone, don't bother looking for me because I'm

history. But please do your homework. My son never signed any documents for that shed on Staten Island. Check it out. Somebody is setting my son up. Tony did date Meredith Perez, but after his sister was shot they broke up. He tells me he was in love with her and I believe him. If you knew Tony you'd know he's not capable of murdering anyone. I may be capable, but he's not. And trust me, Detective, if I find the murderer of those girls before you, I will kill the sick bastard! That's a promise.

* * *

103

Havana, Cuba

When Cavanaugh and Francesca arrived back at the NH Parque Central Hotel, they went straight up the winding staircase in the lobby. Fran was hungry. Cavanaugh just wanted to take a shower and get ready to meet his brother a little later at the Colón Cemetery, as they had planned, to discuss how they would get out of Cuba.

"Are you alright here, Fran?" he asked.

"I think I can order something to eat without your help," she snapped. She hadn't like his shouting at her in Diego's house, especially in front of his brother. They hadn't spoken very much on the ride to the hotel. Diego had a huge headache, but he drove them in silence from his house to the hotel. The silence was awkward, but Diego didn't mind because of the tremendous hangover he had. "Don't ever let me drink like that again," he repeated over and over again in the car.

Cavanaugh looked down at her. There was a special beauty to her, he thought, when she was angry. "I'm going to go up to the room to shower and change clothes. Do you want to come up, too?"

"I told you, I'm hungry. When you come back, I'll go up and change out of these bloody clothes."

When Cavanaugh had left, she ordered a cheese omelet from an over solicitous waiter whose eyes seemed to gravitate toward Francesca's breasts. Tall and dark skinned with a thin black moustache, the waiter lingered at the table trying to make small talk while mentally undressing Francesca. His lecherous staring was only interrupted by a familiar voice.

"Good morning, dearie," Eloise Exeter cheerily said pulling up a chair and plopping down next to Fran. "And I'll have a Shepard's pie, *muchacho*."

"A what?" the waiter said.

"Oh, I keep forgetting where I am. Make it a bowl of bran flakes, a glass of orange juice, and a cup of American coffee."

"We don't serve American coffee," the waiter said.

"Then give me the best continental coffee you have. And make it pronto. We have a tour bus to catch."

Fran looked up appreciating her loquacious plane companion's interruption. "Where are you going?" she asked.

"We have a tour of the city, dearie. Aren't you going?"

"Er, no," Fran hesitated. "We're going to the cemetery this morning."

"Oh, my God, are you going to the Colón Cemetery?"

"Yes, I think so."

"You're going to love it. Of course as cemeteries goes, that is. It's always better to visit them than to stay in them. The Colón Cemetery is beautiful. Wait till you see all the headstones and sculptures. It's like an outdoor museum. You won't find cemeteries like this one in the States. Make sure you see the tomb of Amelia Goyri. She's known as *La Milagrosa*. Apparently, the story goes that she died in childbirth, and they buried her stillborn child at her feet. Well, they dug her up a few years later, and there she was holding the baby in her arms!"

Eloise rambled on non-stop. "I hope our tour takes us there. I have to check. I love cemeteries. There's a tombstone there with a double-three domino tile on top. The story goes that the man buried there died of a heart attack playing dominoes when he realized the double-three in his hand was the winning tile. Oh, you're going to love the cemetery. It's a beautiful place. If you plan on walking, look for the statue of John Lennon in the park on your way there. He's sitting cross-legged on a bench in Rockers Park. At first Castro was dead set against those Liverpool boys, but he came to like Lennon's revolutionary spirit and had a statue of him put in the park. It really looks like him, too. The only problem is his eyeglasses. Apparently, they keep getting stolen by tourists. I think they may even have some old retirees there now guarding the statue to prevent people from taking the glasses from poor old John's statue."

"And, dearie, don't forget to have some ice cream at that place Rita and Rona spoke about on the flight. It's a tourist trap, but the ice cream is good. Oh, I wish I were going with you."

Francesca smiled politely, but thanked God Eloise was not coming with them. Still, she was glad she had arrived when she did and managed to chase the young oversexed Lothario away. When the waiter brought them their orders, he quickly made his exit. Eloise Exeter, Fran noticed, had that "try to get away from her as fast as possible" affect on a lot of people including Cavanaugh.

Fran marveled at how well Eloise could speak with a mouthful of food. She ate as quickly as she talked and fortunately left for her tour just before Cavanaugh came back. Fran finished her coffee and started up to their room as the waiter brought Cavanaugh his usual breakfast of buttered English Muffins and a diet coke. The only thing he said to her was, "We have to meet my brother there at 10:30." She said nothing.

As she reached their room and was opening the door, her cell phone rang. She fumbled with her purse, dumping her makeup kit, some tissues, keys, and the loaded Makarov pistol on the bed before she found the phone.

When she answered it, she heard the familiar voice. "*Buongiorno,* Francesca."

It was her grandfather.

* * *

104

Brooklyn, New York

Returning to his precinct, Morty Goldberg felt like he had been on another frustrating wild goose chase. It was like trying to catch a fly in the dark. The Sgt. Major was calling the shots, and he was protecting his son. He believed his son was innocent. Most fathers would. And most fathers would defend their children to their deaths. What made matters more complicated, however, was that most fathers wouldn't have the skills to avoid capture when the entire New York City Police Department and the F.B.I. were looking for them. Sgt. Major Yaccarino was a trained professional. If he didn't want to be found, he wouldn't be. Unless, of course, he made a mistake.

Sitting at his desk, Goldberg reviewed the facts. Steve the barber gave a positive I.D. to Tony Yaccarino, but as Goldberg discovered on further investigation, Steve suffered from the early stages of dry eye macular degeneration. His father wasn't absolutely certain. The tip on the storage shed had been from an anonymous caller. The Sgt. Major was right about the paperwork. It was incomplete and unsigned, and Bernie, the gray haired storage shed manager with the wooden leg, was a totally unreliable alcoholic.

But the motive was plausible and the maple syrup tied in perfectly. Maria DeFillipo had gone to the store for maple syrup and been killed. Tony Yaccarino admitted dating Meredith Perez. But why the notes implicating Cavanaugh? Did he blame Cavanaugh for the death of his twin sister? Goldberg closed his eyes and shook his head. The headaches were coming back.

And then his cellphone rang.

"Detective Goldberg, homicide," he said absent mindedly.

"You should have stayed out of this, Goldberg," a digitally altered voice sounding like a cross between Darth Vader and Mickey Mouse warned.

"Who is this?"

"You took my office away, Goldberg."

"How did you get this number?"

"Now I'm going to modify my plans."

"Who is this?" Goldberg demanded.

"Now you've given me a challenge. I'm going to have to take my operating room on the road. Where might that be? Why not use my victim's house? As long as they're home alone."

Goldberg knew the phone his caller was using was probably a throw away phone, but he'd have to check it out. "Why are you calling me?" he asked.

The voice on the other end chuckled. It suddenly switched to a nursery rhyme rhythm.

> "Oh where, oh where can Cavanaugh be?
> It doesn't seem like he's even looking for me.
> Goldberg, you have kids at P.S. 25.
> Right now, they're safe and alive.
> But your dear, sweet wife,
> The love of your life,
> Is home and alone.
> I wonder how much she'll cry
> Before I finally let her die."

"Who is this?" Goldberg shouted. "What are you talking about?"

The voice's parting words were slow and deliberate. "I hope your wife likes maple syrup!"

When he heard the click of the receiver, Goldberg immediately called his house.

No answer.

He checked his Smith & Wesson Model 64 .38 special service revolver and called Lt. Bradley. "Lieutenant, the killer just called me. He's going to kill my wife. I'm on my way there now . . . ."

"Slow down, Goldberg. What are you talking about?"

"No time, Lieutenant. I'm leaving. Notify all patrol cars in the area to go to my house. Notify the Feds, too."

He shut his phone and ran to the motor pool. Bill Midrasic was leaning against a patrol car talking on his cell phone.

"Out of the way, Midrasic. I need that car!"

"Bull shit, Goldberg. You go through procedures like everyone else. File the paperwork."

"No time to argue," he said pulling out his service revolver. "The killer's got my wife."

"Shit!" Midrasic said and threw him the keys. "I didn't know. I'll go with you. Maybe you'll need help."

Goldberg flew through the streets of Brooklyn, lights and siren on all the way. As he approached his apartment house, he saw the police had already arrived. Police cars lined the block along with a Police Medical van and the Emergency Service Unit vehicle. A cold chill raced through his body. He pushed his way through the crowd of curious onlookers and ran up the front steps two at a time.

The door to his apartment was open. Two grim police officers from the NYC SWAT team stood guard. Goldberg felt his heart pounding. Walking into the apartment, his legs were shaking and felt like they had turned to rubber.

Then he saw her.

She had a towel wrapped around her head and was wrapped in the pink terrycloth bathrobe she loved.

"What's going on, Morty?" she asked.

"Are you okay, Sara?" he answered rushing to her.

"Of course, I am. I was taking a shower when these goons of yours broke down the door."

Goldberg turned to the police officers Sara was pointing to.

"We knocked. When we got no answer . . . ," one of them began.

"No need," Goldberg said. "Thanks."

"What is going on, Morty?" Sara repeated.

"I got a call," he began and then turned back to the officers. "Did you find anything unusual?"

A tall thin officer with crooked teeth and a square face pointed to a package lying next to the shattered front door. "We found this after we entered. I didn't actually see it at first. I almost tripped over it when you guys arrived. It's addressed to you, Detective."

Another officer with the body build of a plump tomato offered, "We called in the bomb squad to check it out. Your wife refuses to leave."

Goldberg knelt and read the label. He recognized the printing. It was all in capital letters, slightly slanting to the left.

"I think I know what it contains," he said. "There's probably no need for the bomb squad, but have C.S.I. check it out for everything from fingerprints to fibers."

"What's going on, Morty?" Sara asked again clutching her bathrobe tightly around herself.

The bomb squad and the crime scene unit seemed to arrive on the scene together. The room was crowded with blue bodies. Goldberg took Sara by the arm and led her into their bedroom and closed the door. They sat on the edge of their bed. "I got a call from the serial murderer this morning," he began. "He threatened to hurt you . . . ."

She hugged him tightly and began to cry. "Oh, Morty, why can't you leave this job?"

"I can't, Sara. We've got to stop this guy before he hurts anyone else." He added, "Now he's made it personal."

He stood and looked down at her. "You'll be alright, Sara. There will be someone here to make sure of that. I'm going to check on the kids now. They'll be alright, too. I promise." He didn't wait for her response, but turned and went outside to speak with the first responders. They were sure the package was inside the apartment when they entered. It definitely wasn't outside. That meant the killer had been inside his apartment.

Goldberg made sure there would be a twenty-four hour guard on the apartment and on his wife. Together with Midrasic, he drove to his kids' school to make sure they were okay. Along the way he fantasized about catching the psychotic serial killer. The Sgt. Major may not want to admit it, but he could be wrong about his son. This was personal now for Goldberg, too.

He clutched the steering wheel of the patrol car tightly. Bill Midrasic looked at him. "Are you alright, Morty?" he asked.

Goldberg ignored the question and drove on in silence. His heart was racing again. He knew what was in that package. He didn't need the bomb squad or C.S.I. to tell him. They wouldn't find a bomb, and they wouldn't find fingerprints, or fibers, or anything else. The killer was too smart. All they would find was a bottle of maple syrup.

* * *

105

Havana, Cuba

The plan Jack Bennis had come up with during the night was simple and, he hoped, effective. Cavanaugh, Francesca, and he discussed it and agreed to it. They all realized their staying in Havana was potentially injurious to their health and the health of others. He would make plans for their escape from Cuba and meet them at Christopher Columbus Cemetery, just south of the Plaza de la Revolution.

Fran and Cavanaugh would take a taxi from their hotel to Parque Lennon. There they would mingle among the tourists and music lovers around the realistic bronze statue of John Lennon relaxing on a park bench. Then they would casually slip away and move slowly down Calle 8 for two blocks, then make a right onto Calle 23 for another two blocks. There they would turn right and proceed until they ran into the Necropolis Cristóbal Colón, Cuba's largest and most famous cemetery. Colón Cemetery is a mini-city for the dead, spread out symmetrically like a Roman military camp in perfectly square lots forming a large cross. Along the way, Cavanaugh would have ample time and space to check to see if he were being followed. If all went well, Bennis would meet them at the tallest monument in the cemetery, the Firemen's Monument, a pantheon dedicated to the victims of an accidental fire in a hardware store in 1890.

During their ride in the taxi and their walk through Lennon Park, Francesca was unusually quiet. Cavanaugh frequently asked her if she was alright. He thought her silent treatment was the result of his losing his temper the night before. He apologized again for his outburst, but insisted they were in a potentially dangerous situation. There was an assassin out there somewhere on the streets of Havana trying to kill both him and his brother.

Francesca simply nodded, clutched her Gucci handbag tightly under her arm, and walked silently on as if in a trance.

There were a lot of visitors in Lennon Park, and tourists from Canada, the U.K, and Europe crowded around the statue of John Lennon. An old man in his 80's with a red beret kept an eye on the crowd to make sure no one stole John's glasses. Cavanaugh saw Castro's tourist trade had not been crippled by the United States' embargo and its policy of prohibiting American tourists going to Cuba. How long the embargo and the sanctions would last, he realized, was a political decision on the part of the U.S. Unfortunately, he had seen how long conflicts and even wars with other countries lasted and didn't hold out hopes for a quick end to the embargo. The fact was the U.S. had barred trading with Cuba for close to fifty years with no positive effects for United States' exports and little positive influence on Castro's reign of power. The only ones adversely affected seemed to be the innocent people of Cuba.

When they left the park, Cavanaugh frequently checked and double-checked to see if they were being followed. Francesca walked steadily on in silence clutching her handbag under her arm.

They entered Colón Cemetery at the main gate on Avenue Zapata. On top of the three huge Romanesque-Byzantine arched portals was a Carrara marble statue of the three theological virtues—Faith, Hope, and Charity. In the vastness of the "whited sepulchers" gleaming in the sun before him, Cavanaugh recalled Joseph Conrad's *Heart of Darkness*. Welcome to "the City of the Dead," he thought. In front of him in symmetrical block forms lay close to a million graves. The white concrete shocked his eyes at first. Mausoleums, monuments, and statues sprung up in majestic tribute to the dead. Wherever he looked there were marble and granite angels, saints, gargoyles, temples, crypts, chapels, and pantheons. He and Francesca wandered silently among the graves of the famous, the unknown, and the forgotten.

"This is unbelievable," Cavanaugh commented. "It's like an outdoor art museum for the dead."

Fran remained silent.

They wandered to the left passed what looked like a miniature Egyptian pyramid. They walked passed mausoleums and family vaults decorated with metal wreaths, griffins, and saints. To their left they saw a crowd gathered around a tall statue of a woman holding a cross in one hand and an infant baby in the other. Cavanaugh moved closer to get a better look.

Two young guards riding bicycles stopped by them. They wore white shirts with epaulets on their shoulders and loose gray ties. One of them spoke to Cavanaugh in hesitant English. He explained the people were gathered around the gravesite of Dona Amelia Goyri who died in childbirth. When they buried her, they placed her still-born infant at her feet. Years later when they dug her grave up, they found her perfectly preserved and cradling her dead baby infant in her arms.

"There are always people praying and placing flowers at 'The Miracle Woman,' '*La Milagrosa*'s' grave," he explained.

A cold chill ran through Cavanaugh as he looked at the dark eyes of the female statue holding the baby. An image of Maria DeFillipo crying on the floor of the bodega flashed before him asking for her baby.

"Tradition has it," the guard continued, "that people who wish to have children knock three times on her grave and then walk backwards from her gravesite like her husband once did."

Cavanaugh blinked hard trying to get the image of the bleeding Maria DeFillipo out of his mind. "What do you think, Fran?" he asked. "Want to knock three times on the grave?"

Fran ignored the question and looked at the guards. She asked in perfect Spanish, "Where is the Monument for the Firefighters?"

Both guards smiled and pointed back to their left. "You can't miss it," one of them answered. "It's the tallest monument in the cemetery."

His companion spoke in English and told Cavanaugh, "The Monument for the Firefighters was built to remember the victims of a fire in a hardware store back in the late1800's in which twenty-seven volunteer firemen were killed when gunpowder in the store exploded and the walls fell down on them crushing and killing them."

Again, Cavanaugh's mind flashed back to the bodega.

"You look like an American," the guard said. Cavanaugh flinched. "Don't worry. I have an uncle in Miami, and I wish I too could get away." He pointed back toward the Firefighters' Monument in the distance. "I know you had 9/11, and I read about how over 340 New York firefighters died that day. That was horrible. To you, twenty-seven may not seem like a lot, but it was back then. The men killed that day were volunteers, and they came from the best, most prosperous families in Cuba. They were prominent people in the social life of Havana. We didn't have many tall buildings back then. Most were under four stories and the firemen did not have to climb much and fear the danger of falling walls. Their deaths affected all of Cuba."

Cavanaugh thought about the two teenagers who shot Samir Patel and Maria DeFillipo and her unborn child. It was another accident. More deaths. More sorrow. There wouldn't be a monument for Samir or Maria or her dead child, however. They were nameless, faceless victims, few would remember except their families, some friends, and Thomas Cavanaugh.

The English speaking guard kept talking. "Not far from the Firemen's Monument is the Students' Monument. It recalls an ugly part of Cuban history. Back in 1871, a class of medical students at the University was charged with scratching the glass ornament on the grave of a Spanish volunteer officer who had been killed in a duel by a Cuban at Key West during a political quarrel. The Spanish volunteers garrisoned in Havana used the supposed defacing of the tomb to get back at the Cuban people whom they hated. Even though no desecration of the grave was actually proven, the Spanish soldiers threatened to mutiny unless the students were put to death. A court-martial chose eight students at random and ordered them to pay the penalty of the indignity to the gravesite with their lives. Two of those chosen were the only sons of a widowed mother, and because of this the court-martial showed mercy to her and named another student in place of one of the brothers."

Cavanaugh listened in disbelief.

"No, Señor," the young guard continued. "It is hard to believe, but it is true. The parents of one of the condemned boys even offered his weight in gold if his son's life would be spared, but their pleas and prayers went unanswered. It is said the boy's parents died of a broken heart and are buried close to where the Students' Monument was eventually built. On the front of the monument you will see the names of the students in whose memory it was erected. They were eight young boys, none over the age of twenty. They were shot to death because no one would tell which of the medical students, if any, had actually desecrated the grave. Their bodies were thrown into a cart, buried crisscrossed in unconsecrated ground in a filthy ditch, as was the custom in those days for burying traitors. Some time later, their bodies were exhumed and transferred to the Colón Cemetery where their bones now rest beneath the beautifully sculptured monument erected to their memory by the Cuban people."

"Thanks," he said to the guard and started moving in the direction the guards pointed. He didn't notice Fran following him, still clutching her Gucci pocketbook, and staring straight ahead as if in a trance. He didn't notice if anyone else was following him. His mind was on Maria DeFillipo and her child whose blood he felt was somehow still on his hands, and on his own brother.

Walking through Colón Cemetery, he passed the graves and monuments of politicians, generals, artists, revolutionaries, wealthy landowners, writers, and intellectuals. But he didn't notice. Another day he would have liked to wander aimlessly among the splendid sepulchers, ornate tombstones, magnificent mausoleums, ossuaries, crypts, and pantheons of the deceased, but today he was focused on meeting his brother again and arranging for transportation back to the United States. He had no idea how that would be accomplished. His brother promised to make the arrangements. And he trusted his brother completely.

The cemetery had been designed in the form of a huge cross with rows and blocks set in clear-cut large squares. Somehow, the precise arrangement of blocks reminded him of a trip he had once taken to Pompeii, Italy. Here, as in Pompeii the Roman influence could be felt as clearly as rain drops on a golf course. Suddenly, Francesca let out a short squeal, almost like a cat's scream. He turned and saw her looking down at the charred remains of a chicken.

"It's just a burnt chicken, Fran. Probably one of those Santería ceremonies or something John spoke about last night."

She lifted her head up slowly and proceeded forward without another sound. There definitely was something going on with Francesca, he thought. It was more than her just being annoyed with him.

"Did you know that emus and kangaroos can't walk backwards?" he called after her.

There was no reaction. His delight in repeating inane facts usually got her to fire back at him. But not now.

"That's why they are on the Australian coat of arms," he added to her back.

Still no reaction. Beyond her, however, he spotted his brother. He was dressed in a loose colorful flowered sport shirt and khakis and his favorite Yankee cap. From the distance he looked like he had put on some weight he hadn't realized in the excitement of the night before. He would have to tease him about his weight on their way back to the States.

At the Monument to the Students, Jack Bennis motioned for Francesca and Cavanaugh to follow him under a tall Ceiba tree, not too far away where it was more isolated from passersby.

"Were you able to make the arrangements?" Cavanaugh asked.

"Leave it to me, little brother." Fr. Bennis smiled and held out four plane tickets. "These will get you to Cancún. There you will catch a flight to New York . . . ."

"Wait a minute, John. What about you?"

The priest hesitated a moment too long. "I . . . I have a few things I have to straighten out here first. I'll be along, but I can't leave right now."

Out of the corner of his eye, Cavanaugh noticed Francesca reach into her leather bag and pull out the Makarov pistol he had given her. It happened so fast, he didn't react.

"What are you doing, Fran?"

"He killed my father. I must kill him." She hesitated a moment, then added, "And you, too." Her voice was staccato, almost robot-like.

"What are you talking about? Put the gun down, Fran. You don't want to kill anyone."

Jack Bennis remained motionless behind his brother. His hand never reached for the revolver tucked beneath his shirt.

"I must," she said. "He told me I must."

"Who told you, Fran?" Cavanaugh asked. He had to keep her talking. She was in a trance. It was like she was hypnotized. But how? "Who told you?"

"I must," she repeated. Her hand was shaking.

"Fran, this is all wrong. You don't have to do anything. You don't have to shoot anyone."

"I must," she said. "He told me I must. Father Bennis killed my father."

Cavanaugh noticed beads of sweat on her forehead. Maybe it was the hot Havana sun. Maybe she was fighting some hypnotic suggestion she had been given.

"But why would you want to kill me?" Keep her talking, he thought. "I love you. I thought you loved me, too."

"I . . . I do love you," she stammered. There were tears in her eyes. "But I must. I must," she repeated.

Cavanaugh stepped forward. "Put the gun down, Fran. You're not going to shoot anyone."

"Stay back, Tom. I don't want to shoot you, but I must. He told me . . . ."

"You don't have to shoot anyone, Fran," Cavanaugh said reaching out to her with both hands. Instinct told him Vito Muscatelli was somehow behind this. He recalled her telling him how he used to have someone hypnotize them when they were small. "Your grandfather can't make you kill anyone. You can't do something your conscience tells you is wrong. You control your actions. Not him."

He moved slowly forward between two concrete slabs on top of tombs. She lowered her hands. Tears ran down her cheeks. Her whole body shook like she was having a seizure.

And then he heard a soft puff. It came from behind him. A flock of white winged doves nesting in a nearby tree scattered in a flutter of wings. Cavanaugh recognized the sound immediately. It came from a silencer. He turned and saw his brother fall back against a white grave in front of a large statue of Jesus with outstretched arms. Bennis' head hit the gravestone and his body slid between the gravestone and a three foot cement urn attached to the marble slab covering the grave.

From behind a family mausoleum close by, a figure emerged holding a Walther P22 with a silencer. Both he and Francesca recognized the figure immediately.

"Eloise," Fran asked, "what are you doing here?"

"I'm here to finish the job your grandfather sent me here to do, dearie," she said.

"Who are you?" Cavanaugh asked.

"Well, I surmise you have figured out I am not the Eloise Exeter you expected, Mr. Detective. All you really need to know," she added, "is I'm your executioner."

Cavanaugh looked over at his brother lying motionless on the grave of Hubert de Blanck. The half wreath on the headstone appeared to be growing out of his head. Cavanaugh turned and looked at the chatty annoying woman he had known as Eloise Exeter. His eyes narrowed. He stared at the Walther P22 held steadily like a marksman in her left hand. Then he smiled. "You had them all fooled, didn't you? They were looking for you in all the wrong places. You're good. Real good. I should have suspected. In the taxi you pointed out sights with your left hand. But why do you break their wrists?" he asked.

The woman with the gun chuckled. "You're a smart cop. Vito warned me about that."

"You're going to kill me anyway. Just tell me why the broken wrists? I can almost understand the earring thing, but why the torture bit?"

"What is going on?" Fran asked. "If you aren't Eloise Exeter, who are you?"

"It's best you don't know, pretty lady," the former Eloise said.

"Her real name is Cain Holland," Cavanaugh explained. "She is a pathological assassin who is known for torturing her victims before usually slitting their throats. In the case of women, she usually tears one earring from them. The right one, if I am correct, Ms. Holland."

"Impressive, Detective Cavanaugh. You have done your homework. It is a little late for that now, but still I am impressed."

"Cain? I don't understand. That's a man's name. He's the one that killed Able in the Bible, didn't he?" Fran asked.

"Yes, Cain was the first murderer, exiled to the land of Nod for his killing his brother."

"Your range of knowledge is wide, Detective. My useless, incompetent parents thought it a bloody fantastic name because it means 'beautiful' in Welsh. Little did the idiots know how fitting the name would become."

"But why the broken wrists?" Cavanaugh asked.

Cain Holland smiled again and moved closer. "It all goes back to one of my ancestors, John Holland, the second Duke of Exeter. He was in charge of the Tower of London back in the 1400's and invented a rather unique instrument back then. You may have heard about it. It was the rack. They called it most appropriately, the Duke of Exeter's daughter. It was most effective in getting confessions from people—whether innocent or guilty. I took the principles, in the true tradition of my ancestor and devised a smaller version of the rack which can be snapped onto a wrist in the matter of moments and with the help of a handle, a ratchet, and a pulley, it can quite effectively snap the cartilage, ligaments and bones in the wrist. It really is quite interesting to hear the loud popping sound as my little Duke of Exeter's daughter is applied. I dare say, it gives me great pleasure to see the excoriating pain my little machine can produce. I would show you how it works, but alas, your screams would attract a crowd, and we wouldn't want that now, would we?"

"Oh, my God," Francesca exclaimed.

"You are a sick bastard, Holland," Cavanaugh blurted out.

"Now, now, Detective," Cain Holland smiled aiming the gun directly at his head. "Sticks and stones may break my bones, but names will never hurt me. But they may just cause you a bit more pain in dying."

Cavanaugh recalled the Eloise Exeter who sat with them on their plane ride from Toronto. Think, think, he told himself. She was boastful, talkative, egocentric. How much of it was an act? He didn't know. If he were to have any chance of escaping, however, he knew he would have to keep her talking. "Holland, they're been looking for you all over the world," he said.

"But they haven't found me now, have they?"

"How have you managed to elude them all?"

"Who would suspect a middle aged woman to be a professional assassin? I had you fooled, didn't I, Detective?"

"But how did you find us?" Cavanaugh asked. Out of the corner of his eye, he saw his brother move slightly. "I made sure we weren't followed."

Holland smiled again. She was enjoying the conversation. "You can thank your girl friend here for that, Detective. She told me where you were headed. She was so trusting. How could poor, sweet Eloise be a threat? She told me where you were headed like an innocent lamb. I never thought the hypnotic suggestion Muscatelli planted in her head before she left New York would take. You need a professional like me for getting things done. I took care of his incompetent bastard son Frankie last night right after you left. If it hadn't been for that bunch of screaming maniacs burning chickens and singing and dancing on his front steps, I may have finished you off then, too. But today's another day, isn't it? I got your brother, and now it's just you."

"My grandfather hypnotized me to kill Tom and his brother?" Fran almost screamed.

"Yes, dearie, but he never intended for you to be hurt." She leveled the gun at Cavanaugh. "Now it's time. It's been a pleasure, Detective."

"Hold on a second, Holland. I know how much you pride yourself on little known facts. I marveled at the breath of your knowledge on the plane. Let me ask you one last question to try to stump you, if I can."

"Give it your best shot, Detective," she said, "because it will be your last one."

Cavanaugh's mind raced. Stall, stall, stall. "Let's see," he began, "you probably know the children's nursery rhyme 'Ring-around-the-Rosy' was actually about the Black Death which killed almost thirty million people around the time your sadistic ancestor was torturing people in the Tower of London . . . ."

"Careful, Detective," Holland warned.

"Most Englishmen and women would probably know Winston Churchill was born in a ladies' cloakroom during a dance at Blenheim Palace . . . ."

"Get to your question, Detective. I grow weary of your inane chatter."

"Okay, here goes. My life is on the line. How many people signed the Declaration of Independence on July 4th, 1776?"

"I think you could have done better than that, Detective. There were fifty-six signers of that traitorous document. The largest signature, of course, belonged to John Hancock."

"Is that your final answer?"

"It's your final question."

"But you may want to know that you are wrong."

"What do you mean I am wrong? I can name most of your traitorous gang of cutthroats. Edward Rutledge was the youngest at twenty-six, Benjamin Franklin the oldest at seventy . . . ."

"True, Holland," Cavanaugh interrupted. "But you are still wrong. There were only two men who signed the Declaration of Independence that day."

"Balderdash!" Holland spat at Cavanaugh.

"Check it out for yourself. John Hancock and Charles Thomson were the only ones that signed the document that day. Most of the rest of them signed in August, and the last signature wasn't added until a full five years later. You lose, Holland. I win!"

Cain Holland leveled her pistol. She took careful aim. "And your prize, Detective Cavanaugh, is death!"

The shot shattered the peaceful atmosphere of the cemetery.

* * *

106

Brooklyn, New York

Morty Goldberg couldn't sleep that night. The doctor gave Sara a sedative to calm her down and get her to sleep. She was more angry with Goldberg than she was with the police who had barged in on her coming out of the shower or the serial killer who had threatened her life.

"Why do you keep this *paskudne* job?" she demanded. "It threatens all of us. You are killing us!"

Morty reviewed his children's homework, cooked their dinner, and put them into bed over his wife's constant kvetching. When everyone else was finally in bed and hopefully asleep, he sat at the living room table and opened his computer.

At this moment, no matter what his father believed, Tony Yaccarino was their prime suspect. Goldberg decided to get a better idea of who this Tony Yaccarino actually was. He Googled Yaccarino on the computer and up popped 1504 hits. Apparently, Goldberg discovered, Tony Yaccarino was a prodigious writer. In the six years he had worked for the *Staten Island Advance*, Yaccarino had written articles and stories on elementary, high school, college, and professional basketball, football, baseball, track and field, soccer, golf, and swimming. He had covered significant horse races at Pimlico, Churchill Downs, Aqueduct, Belmont, Yonkers and Freehold. But he had also written about hospital scandals, the financial crisis, bitter political races, crime, local gossip, and food, book, and movie reviews. Starting with his earliest writing, Goldberg meticulously read one article after another. He soon discovered Yaccarino grew to more than just a reporter of facts. He developed into an investigative reporter, digging beneath the surface for more information. Over the last two years, most of his investigative reporting involved crime families and police corruption on Staten Island. He reported on a local referee who allegedly accepted bribes to influence C.Y.O. elementary basketball games. He reported on the trial of a woman accused of killing her husband in his sleep. He uncovered a million dollar illegal football lottery run in a local dry cleaners. Goldberg read with particular interest Yaccarino's investigation of the assassination of Rocco Muscatelli, the son of the retired crime boss Vito Muscatelli. Yaccarino's writing suggested there was more to the story than the police were admitting. Goldberg knew from personal experience he was right. His most recent articles concerned alleged payoffs by Staten Island businessmen to crooked cops.

His eyes became bleary from reading from the computer screen. He leaned back and rubbed his eyes.

"Daddy," a voice behind him said softly, "I can't sleep."

He looked down to see Aaron, his three year old son. His cheeks were wet as if he had been crying. "What's the matter, little man?" Goldberg said.

"I can't sleep, Daddy," Aaron lisped. "I keep having bad dreams."

"What are they about? You can tell, Daddy."

Aaron looked up at his father. The blue rockets on his pajamas pointed up toward his shaggy red hair and freckles. "I keep thinking of those big policemen. Why did they take us home in their car?"

"Well," Goldberg replied turning from the computer to Aaron. "It's a long story, but those men are my friends and they want you to be safe."

"Nathan says someone is trying to kill us."

Goldberg took a deep breath. "Nathan likes to exaggerate. No one is going to hurt you. I promise."

Little Aaron reached up and Goldberg pulled him into his lap. Aaron was soaking wet. He needed to be changed. But Goldberg held him gently in his arms and patted his head and back. In a few minutes, Aaron's relaxed breathing told him he was asleep. Still Goldberg held him in his arms and cherished the moment. He would deal with big mouthed Nathan in the morning. Right now Aaron was his concern.

A few minutes later, Goldberg rose slowly to change Aaron's diaper. His knees cracked, but Aaron didn't hear. The three year old slept through the changing of his diaper and being carefully tucked into his bed. Goldberg then checked on Sara and the rest of his family. They were all asleep. Peering out the window, he saw the police car parked in front of his building.

He thought for a moment about going to bed himself. He was tired. In a few hours it would be morning and time to get everyone off to school. The computer screen had taken a break and turned black when he returned to it. He nudged the mouse and slowly the screen woke up and came to life.

That's when he saw it. It was an article written a few months ago—before the shooting in the bodega, before the Inquest, before the demonstrations, before the murders. Reading it carefully, he realized it was an article that might explain the murders.

* * *

107

Havana, Cuba

In José Martí International Airport that night, Francesca Arden sat quietly sipping a tasteless cup of coffee and waiting for the plane to Cancún, Mexico.

Thoughts of the afternoon in the cemetery whirled through her mind like a cyclone. After the first shot there was another and another. She watched Cain Holland's head explode and blood and skull fly in all directions. As Fran kept shooting, she saw blood spurting from her chest and her neck. Holland's body flowed into the ground still clutching her weapon. When her head hit the concrete grave, her eyes rolled back and the gun slipped out of her hand with the gracefulness of a ballet dancer. And Fran kept firing until the gun was empty, and he grabbed her hand and took it away.

"It's over, Fran. It's all over," Cavanaugh said.

Now she was crying. She couldn't stop herself. "I killed her!" she cried. "I killed her!"

Father Bennis rose slowly from the tomb he had been laying on. He rubbed his head. It was bleeding. A hole in his shirt, chest high, showed where Cain Holland's bullet struck him. "We've got to get out of here," he said. "There will be a crowd here in a short while." He motioned to Cavanaugh. "Help me drag her behind this tree."

Francesca looked down at Cain Holland, a.k.a. Eloise Exeter. Her large straw bag had flown open and strewn across the marble and concrete gravesites there were now a vast collection of earrings. Francesca recognized one particular diamond earring that Francisco Santacruz's wife was wearing the night before. And then she realized. "Oh, my God," she said. "They're all different!"

Cavanaugh came back from the tree and held her tightly. "They're just part of the horror this woman inflicted on others. They're some of her 'trophies.' I'm sure she had a couple picked out for John and me."

Stepping from behind a nearby mausoleum, Cavanaugh recognized the lecherous Albert, the gray haired man with gold wire glasses, and Erica, the young, attractive blond bimbo, he was traveling with on the flight from Toronto. Instantly, he reached for his gun.

"Put the gun away, Thomas," Fr. Bennis said. "You won't need it."

"Quick!" the man whispered just loud enough for them to hear, "this way."

Bennis pushed Cavanaugh and Fran ahead of him. His head was bleeding, but he didn't seem concerned.

"But . . . ," Cavanaugh began, "I don't understand. Who are they? They were on the plane with us. And you . . . ," he said talking to his brother, "she shot you. I saw it. You should be dead."

"Don't worry, little brother, it's not a miracle. I made arrangements with Agents Reilly and Francis. Once you told me about this Holland character, I knew he would try again. I wanted to be prepared. Reilly and Francis fitted me with this rather bulky bulletproof vest. It makes me look a little fat, but it saved my life."

"But I saw them on the plane. They were a couple. He couldn't keep his hands off her."

"They're C.I.A., Thomas. They can be very convincing when they want to be."

They hurried around and over an assortment of graves as Bennis talked. "When you told me Cain Holland was after us, I thought I'd make a call to someone I know in Guantánamo. He still owes me a couple of favors. They'd been looking for her for a long time—only they thought 'she' was a 'he.' They followed you down from Toronto hoping to find her. They did find an old hit man from the Nazi Waffen SS squad during WW II, but they couldn't find Holland. After I contacted them, they gave me this vest. The rest is history."

"History, my ass!" Cavanaugh exclaimed. "Those bastards used us as bait! They could have gotten us all killed. What the hell were they doing?"

Bennis smiled. "Thomas, when are you going to learn? That's the way governments work. It's all for the 'greater good'—at the moment. And 'the moment' changes at the flick of a leaf. We are all expendable to them."

"Well, I'll tell you something, John," he said tripping over a dead chicken on the path, "I think it sucks!"

"Look on the bright side, Thomas. We're all alive."

Cavanaugh clutched Francesca's arm. "Not because of those bastards. It's only because of Fran. If she didn't shoot that psycho bitch back there I'd be a dead man now."

Approaching the main entrance, Cavanaugh saw the backs of the statues of Faith, Hope, and Charity looking out on the city of Havana. Reilly and Francis had a 1958 Chevy there waiting for them. The man behind the wheel wore a large straw hat and a black moustache. For some reason, he recalled the King of Hearts is the only king in the deck without a moustache.

"I almost killed you, Tom," Francesca murmured. "I almost shot the both of you." Her voice quivered. "I almost killed you," she kept repeating.

The two C.I.A. agents abruptly pushed Bennis, Cavanaugh and Francesca unceremoniously into the back seat. As the car moved away from Colón Cemetery, Cavanaugh stared for a long moment at Francesca. Finally, he said, "He hypnotized you, Fran, and you still couldn't do it. You can't hypnotize a person into doing something they believe is wrong. Your conscience is stronger than his hypnotic suggestions."

"And besides," he smiled looking into her moist green eyes, "*almost* only counts in horseshoes and hand grenades."

* * *

X

If everyone is thinking alike,
someone isn't thinking.

George Patton

WEDNESDAY

108

Brooklyn, New York

Jimmy Monreale was in his lab early. He prided himself on his work. The fact that they had not yet identified the body of the woman found in the storage bin on Staten Island troubled him. There were no fingerprints. Her teeth had been extracted. The skin on her face, hands, and feet had been scrapped off and burned. He wondered how long she had been tortured. How long did it take for her to die? He was only a lab technician, but the way this woman died bothered him.

The police artists came up with possible sketches of what she looked like before. But no one had reported her missing, and District Attorney J. R. Coyle wanted to withhold the sketches for a few days. He claimed he wanted to wait to see if anyone reported her missing.

Jimmy looked at the pictures he had taped to the walls of his lab. Who was this woman? Why would anyone want to torture a person like this? Whoever did this, Jimmy thought, was a sick bastard.

"Good morning, Jimmy," a voice behind him said.

He turned to see Detective Goldberg there with two cups of coffee and a bag of donuts. "Mind if I come in for a few minutes? There are some questions I'd like to ask you about the last victim."

"What am I supposed to do? I'm only one person. It's not like the TV shows. I do what I can . . . ."

Goldberg came forward, pulled over a lab stool, and handed Monreale a cup of coffee and the bag of donuts. "There is some milk and cream in the bag."

Jimmy took the coffee and the bag tentatively. "Why are you being nice to me?" he said as he looked into the bag of donuts.

"This whole mess has been bothering me. We're looking for Tony Yaccarino as the prime suspect in the murders. His father claims he's innocent."

"Every father believes his child is innocent."

"You're right. But some things don't add up. I need someone to bounce ideas off of. If Cavanaugh were here, I'd ask him. I trust you. Do you mind?'

Jimmy Monreale sat down and bit into a powdered jelly donut. "I'm no detective, Detective."

"I know, but you are intelligent, dedicated, and objective."

Jimmy wondered how anyone could be objective after seeing what had been done to the last victim of the "Maple Syrup Murderer." "Why don't you ask Midrasic, or Palambo or Waters?"

"They might be too close to it," Goldberg said and then added, "I have my reasons."

It was cold in the lab and everything smelled of chemicals. He looked around and saw the sketches of the victim. "What can you tell me about her?"

Jimmy added cream and two sugars to his coffee. "Well," he began, "she was about your age. I'd guess in her mid forties. We haven't gotten a definite on that yet, but that's my guess. She was a natural blonde. Her lungs were clear suggesting she was a non-smoker. Judging from her liver and kidneys she was definitely not a heavy drinker. In addition to the broken wrists, she had a number of broken ribs. Some had healed. This would suggest he had been beaten over a long period of time. Possibly she was being abused by someone."

"Did she have any children?"

Jimmy reached back for his report on Jane Doe. "I don't think so judging from her hip size. She wasn't a virgin, however. There were signs of vaginal and anal sex. Because of the vaginal cavity's acidic level, semen tend to degrade rapidly. Although I doubt we will be able to find anything, I did send samples off to check on the possibility of anilingus."

"Ana who?" Goldberg asked.

"Anilingus. It is a form of oral sex with the perineum or anus of one person and the mouth of another. On the street it is sometimes referred to as it rimming, salad tossing, butt licking . . . ."

"Enough!" Goldberg held up his hand. "I get the picture. Why would you check for that?"

"Possible DNA and since the anal and vaginal passages were severely damaged the suggestion is that something other than a penis might have been used—like a baseball bat or a broom. Since this murder was extremely vicious, I didn't want to rule out analingus as it is sometimes used as a form of erotic humiliation."

"Do you think this Tony Yaccarino we are looking for could have done this?"

"Anything is possible, Detective Goldberg, but from the damage done to this poor woman I would think the murderer was more emotionally involved with this woman than with the other victims. Most of the damage done to her was done while she was alive. The first two victims suffered from the broken wrists, but they did not undergo the torture this woman did. Officer Perez's wrists, interestingly enough, were administered post-mortem. She died the quickest of all the victims."

"Interesting, Jimmy. You have been a great help."

"I have?"

Goldberg smiled. "Yes. I came across something on the Internet last night that made me think those other killings might have been decoys for the real thing—the murder of the woman in the storage shed."

"You know for all the evidence we found there relating to the other murders there were no fingerprints of Tony Yaccarino or anyone else. That's kind of strange isn't it?"

"Strange or smart? I don't know." Suddenly, Goldberg's cell phone started beeping. He fumbled with his pockets until he found it. It was Midrasic.

"I think I've spotted Yaccarino. He went into his house. I think he's alone."

"Stay there. I'll be right over. Don't go into the house alone."

Goldberg turned to Jimmy Monreale. "Thanks again, Jimmy. We just got a call that we may have spotted Tony Yaccarino going into his house on Staten Island."

"*Sholem aleichem*," a familiar voice called from the door of the lab.

Goldberg turned. He couldn't believe his eyes. It was Cavanaugh.

"Aren't you supposed to say something like '*aleichen sholem*' or something like that which means 'peace be with you, too'?"

"What are you doing here?"

"I just got back. I've been hopping planes and hailing taxis just to get here to see your smiling face. How are things going? Did you miss me?"

"You look terrible," Goldberg said.

Jimmy Monreale studied Cavanaugh. His shirt and pants were wrinkled and dirty. He needed a shave. There were dark lines under his eyes. Jimmy added, "He's right. You look horrible."

"Sorry, guys, but I haven't slept in a couple of fun-filled days." He motioned to Goldberg, "Let's go get a cup of coffee and a bagel, and I'll tell you all about it."

Goldberg stood. "Can't, Tom. We just got a call that Tony Yaccarino was spotted going into his house. I've got to go."

Cavanaugh glanced beyond Goldberg. His eyes became fixed. Both Monreale and Goldberg noticed the look in his face change.

"What is it, Tom?" Goldberg asked.

"The sketch on the walls. Why is she there?"

"That's our latest victim," Jimmy offered. "We found her in a storeage shed on Staten Island on Monday. We've been trying to identify her, but haven't had any luck."

Cavanaugh moved forward and took the picture in his hand. "Did she have a birth mark on her upper left thigh?"

Monreale checked the notes in his folder. After a few seconds, he looked up surprized. "Yes. She did."

"Oh, my God," he said.

"Do you know her?" Goldberg asked.

Cavanaugh folded the sketch carefully and placed it in his pocket. "Yeah. I knew her. Her maiden name was Maureen Donnelly. We went to school together. I had a serious crush on her in the eighth grade." He turned and looked at Goldberg. There was the sparkle in his eyes Goldberg recognized. "Yaccarino didn't kill those women."

"That's what I've been thinking, too," Goldberg admitted.

"It was all a cover up for Maureen. He thought by implicating me he'd give me grief, deflect the investigation."

"The maple syrup and the other clues were meant to lead us in Tony Yaccarino's direction. I read last night how Yaccarino was doing some intensive investigative reporting on police corruption that could be related to the murder of Merry Perez."

"Throwing suspicion on him and me would stop Yaccarino's investigation and get me into a lot of trouble. Merry may have suspected that."

Goldberg looked at his watch. "I've got to go, Tom."

"I'm going with you!" Cavanaugh said.

"Wait a minute, guys!" Monreale called. "What's Maureen's last name?"

Cavanaugh looked at Goldberg. Goldberg nodded, "It's okay, Tom," he said. "He can be trusted."

Cavanaugh and Goldberg responded together, "Midrasic."

* * *

109

Staten Island, New York

Bill Midrasic moved slowly out of his vehicle. He held his 9 mm Smith & Wesson under his jacket. The neighborhood was quiet. Kids had gone to school. Parents had gone to work. Now was his chance.

He had accomplished most of what he wanted. Cavanaugh and his girlfriend had disappeared. He couldn't find them. He would repay Cavanaugh at a later date. Now he would tie up the loose ends. Killing Yaccarino in a "shoot-out" would probably earn him a meritorious ribbon and maybe even a promotion. He tapped the Saturday night special in his left pocket which he had been saving for this. He smiled. He had played them all like pawns in a chess game. Eliminating Yaccarino would be check-mate. He wouldn't be able to link him to the bribery investigation the noisy reporter had started. He wouldn't be able to identify him as the father of Merry Perez's unborn child. Yaccarino would go down as "The Maple Syrup Killer." Case closed. And he had gotten rid of his wife in the process.

He stood looking for a moment at Yaccarino's house. It was a simple two-story 1920's era blue wood sided house. Midrasic thought how Yaccarino had brought this on himself. Had he minded his own business this whole thing might have been avoided. Well, not exactly. One way or another he had decided to kill Maureen. The others were fun. He actually enjoyed killing and torturing those women. But planting the blood on Cavanaugh and scooping up some of his hair from the barbershop—that was pure genius.

Midrasic heard another car pull up. Shit, he thought, another police car. It pulled behind Midrasic's car, and a tall, thin young patrolman with a big shinny shaved head pulled himself out. His bald head and bushy mustache, which he probably grew to make him appear older, made him look somewhat like a walrus on a stick. The officer adjusted his uniform and carefully placed his police cover on his bald head. "What's up?" he asked.

Midrasic read the officer's name tag—Gill. "I was just going in to check," he said.

"I got orders to stay here until backup arrives."

"I saw him drag a woman in there," Midrasic lied. "If we wait, it may be too late."

"I don't know," Gill said. "My orders were to wait. I think we should wait."

"I'm going in," Midrasic answered. "You can either stay here or be my backup. I'm not going to let that bastard torture another woman to death." He started walking toward the side of the house.

"Wait up!" Gill called following after him.

Midrasic tried the side door. It was unlocked. He carefully opened it and moved into the shadows.

Gill whispered behind him, "We don't have a search warrant."

"A woman's life is at stake," Midrasic said. "My conscience won't let me sit around and wait for stupid paperwork while someone is tortured and the Task Force is finishing their coffee and donuts."

Quietly, he moved up the three steps which led to the kitchen. There were sounds coming from the living room. Midrasic's left hand gripped the Saturday night special in his pocket. In the living room, he saw Tony Yaccarino sitting in a worn red and blue checkered lounge chair watching the news on CNN. He had what looked like a bowl of Cheerios with sliced banana and strawberries in his lap. A cup of coffee sat on the table next to him.

Midrasic burst into the room. "Freeze, Yaccarino, you're under arrest."

Gill followed and started checking for the woman Midrasic said Yaccarino had brought into the house. "Where's the woman?" he asked.

Midrasic turned, pulled the pistol from his pocket and fired. "Here she is, Gill!" The officer's face exploded like an overripe tomato as two quick shots from the Saturday night special hit him in the face. Officer Gill fell back and slid down the wall like melted butter leaving a trail of blood behind him.

Yaccarino stood. The bowl of cereal splashed all over the floor. He raised his hands. "What are you doing? Who are you?" he asked.

Midrasic smiled. "You don't remember me? I'm the guy you were investigating for bribery and selling cocaine."

Yaccarino backed up. His hands were high in the air. "You," he said, "you're Midrasic? But why . . . ?" His head tilted in the direction of the fallen officer.

"Because it gives me a perfect reason to knock you off right now. You shouldn't have shot Officer Gill over there. But you did. And I had to shoot you in self-defense. Too bad I was too late for Gill."

"You're crazy! What are you talking about?" Yaccarino said. "I didn't kill anyone."

"Of course not," Midrasic smiled. "I did. But everyone else thinks you're the 'Maple Syrup Killer.'" He hesitated a moment, then added, "I made sure of that."

"You!" Yaccarino exclaimed. "You killed those women? You killed Merry?"

"Yeah. That was my kid she was carrying. Did she tell you that? I figured it would only be a matter of time before she told somebody. She said she wouldn't, but I've never trusted a woman. But that wasn't the real reason I killed her." He moved toward Gill's motionless body and reached down to check for a pulse. There was none.

"No," he continued, "the real reason was she started investigating the murders and began asking a few too many questions. She was a good cop. She picked up the maple syrup thing right away. At first, I think, she might have thought it was you, but when she dug deeper she discovered you were working on your undercover story about police corruption. She came to me and figured out you were investigating me. I had to silence her. Too bad, too. She was a good lay."

Yaccarino started toward him. "You bastard . . . ."

"Easy now, lover boy," Midrasic said. He tossed the gun he had shot Gill with on the floor by Yaccarino's feet. "Why don't you try to go for it? It will save me the effort of putting your fingerprints on it."

Yaccarino stepped back. The weather forecast came on the TV. Tomorrow would be cloudy with a slight chance of precipitation in the afternoon. "Why did you take that storage shed out in my name?" he asked.

"Establish a chain of evidence, Mr. Reporter. You should know that. I didn't plan on doing it so soon, but my damn wife started to stink up the place. I thought an anonymous call would seal things up. If your God-damn father didn't show up, things might have been easier."

"But why would you want to kill your wife?" Yaccarino asked.

"Obviously, you were never married. You know why there are so many battered women in the world? It's because they don't fucking listen!" He laughed and then became dead serious. "Her stupid friend she went to grammar school with told her to rat me out the next time I hit her. What was I supposed to do? She found out I had forged her signature and emptied the bank and stock accounts her grandfather had left her. She threatened to turn me in."

It felt good telling someone how smart he was. Even if the person he was talking to he was about to kill.

"That old friend she went to school with was Detective Tom Cavanaugh. If he didn't disappear suddenly, I'd have killed him and his girlfriend, too. But that will have to wait."

In the distance Midrasic heard approaching sirens. "Well, kid, it looks like it's time. Any last words?"

"Yes!" A raspy voice came from behind him.

Midrasic spun around to see Sgt. Major Yaccarino standing in the doorway with an M 16 A4 assault weapon aimed right at him.

"You! How did you . . . ?" Midrasic glanced at the gun he had tossed on the floor. He backed up.

"Didn't you wonder why my son would come back to his house alone and leave the door unlocked?"

"You . . . you set me up!"

"You might say that," the Sgt Major said moving closer. "Check that vase on the bookcase in the corner. There's a miniature camera in there recording everything. It got you shooting Officer Gill. It got you confessing to the murders. There's a second camera in here, too. Just to make sure."

Midrasic stood still, his head weaving back and forth around the room as if he were watching a tennis match. He could hear his heartbeat over the sirens which were louder now. Car doors were opening and closing.

"Drop the gun, Midrasic," the Sgt. Major commanded. "It's over."

"Fuck you!" Midrasic said and spinning around suddenly. "I'm taking your son with me!" he screamed as he fired at Tony Yaccarino.

The room was suddenly filled with the sounds of gunfire. Tony fell behind the chair. The Sgt. Major emptied the thirty round clip in bursts of three into Midrasic. The bullets tore through his clothes splattering blood, flesh, bone, and cloth in all directions. Midrasic bounced off a 55 gallon fish tank in the corner sending angelfish, guppies, bleeding heart tetras, black mollies, and red devils flapping furiously on the floor.

Six police officers with flack jackets and assault weapons burst in the front door and the side door. "Police! Drop your weapon!" they ordered.

The Sgt. Major obediently dropped his now empty M 16 A4 and directed the police to his son who was bleeding badly from a wound to his shoulder.

A short time later, Goldberg and Cavanaugh arrived along with Waters and Palambo. The Sgt. Major stood at parade rest with his hands behind his back—handcuffed. Tony Yaccarino had already been taken away in an ambulance. "The whole shooting was recorded," he informed them. "He admitted everything. You have it on tape. He shot the officer in the corner and tried to kill my son. Tony was investigating police corruption involving him. He killed his wife because she threatened to turn him in for embezzling and physical abuse. He shot the poor officer over there before I could do anything. He planned to kill Tony and probably thought he'd get a commendation for it."

"He probably would have," Goldberg agreed.

"Over my dead body," Cavanaugh answered quickly. "The guy was dirt!"

They looked over at the shattered remains of Bill Midrasic. A giant upside down Asian catfish jerked slightly on his left eyeball and an enormous pleco lodged in his open mouth.

"Nice shot," Goldberg commented. "I see you keep your promises."

"I was so close, it was a no brainer," the Sgt. Major conceded. He added, "He was shooting at my son. I had no choice."

Cavanaugh knelt down beside the lifeless Bill Midrasic and whispered in his ear, "Too bad you didn't suffer more."

* * *

XII

In life as in golf, it's the follow through that counts

Anonymous

THURSDAY

110

Brooklyn, New York

Goldberg and Cavanaugh sat in Lt. Bradley's office. "So, Cavanaugh," the Lieutenant began, "you deigned to grace us again with your presence."

"Come on, Lieutenant, I was only gone for a few days. I was just getting in the way around here anyway. Besides, Morty handled things just great. He got your killer for you."

"The word I hear from the F.B.I. is that someone got Cain Holland, too."

"Is that so, Lieutenant?" Cavanaugh said.

"I think you know it's true. But I can't do anything about it because you weren't where I know you were."

"You can't believe everything the F.B.I. tells you, Lieutenant. They're less reliable than the press."

Bradley got up and went to the door. He locked it and then returned to his desk and opened the bottom file cabinet. "By the way, whatever happened to your brother, the priest?" he asked pulling out three plastic cups and a quart bottle of Johnny Walker Black.

"He said he had some business to attend to and that he would be returning soon."

Bradley nodded and then offered a toast. "I know it's kind of early, men, but this calls for a celebration for solving the case and a tribute to Officer Gill who gave his life trying to serve and protect."

"I usually don't drink before 5:00, Lieutenant," Cavanaugh stated, "but it must be 5:00 someplace in the world now."

The Lieutenant poured two inches for each of them and they drank in silence. As they started on their second cup, Goldberg asked, "So what's going to happen to the Sgt. Major?"

Lieutenant Bradley rubbed the scar over his eye. "It's a crock of bullshit if you ask me. In 1993, the Federal Government passed a law about buying assault weapons like the one Yaccarino used. They also let it expire in September of 2004. More political bullshit! It probably wouldn't matter anyhow as the Sgt. Major claims he was given permission to bring the weapon home with him from Iraq. Whatever the case, our illustrious D.A., J. R. Coyle, would sooner arrest his mother for prostitution than pursue prosecuting a war hero in an obvious case of self-defense when he is positioning himself to run for Mayor."

"So he'll go free?" Cavanaugh asked.

"There's nothing to hold him on. There will be an Inquest, of course, but it won't be a long, drawn out deal like yours. I think everyone wants this mess to end."

"That M16 sure made a mess of Midrasic. It shredded him up like a piece of lettuce. Thirty rounds! I don't think the Sgt. Major missed his target once."

Goldberg leaned forward in his chair. "I couldn't understand how the killer got into my house with the door locked. I realize now that he didn't. Midrasic drove home with me that day and probably placed the package there after we arrived. The first responders didn't remember seeing a package there when they broke through the door. He most likely brought it with him and dropped it during all the confusion."

"They found a voice distorter in his locker along with a throwaway cell phone and the pad he used to write those notes. The impressions were still on the pages."

Cavanaugh stared at the wooden letters on the Lieutenant's desk. "Sometimes I wonder what makes people do things like Midrasic and Holland did. Then I think about how all our lives are interconnected. My being in the bodega that night . . . , my chance meeting with Maureen in the supermarket . . . . We never know how our actions affect others."

Bradley looked at Goldberg. "Does he always get philosophical when he drinks?"

"Be grateful, Lieutenant," he said. "It beats his constant asking trivial, arcane questions."

"Hey, that saved my life . . . in the place I can't mention."

"Well, in Brooklyn it could cost you your life."

"I'll bet twenty dollars neither of you know who each king in a deck of cards represents?"

"Let's see the color of your money," Bradley said.

Cavanaugh reached into his pocket and pulled out a crumpled pile of bills. One by one he counted out twenty singles.

Bradley leaned over and counted the bills slowly, then with the money in his hand, he said, "The King of Spades represents King David. The King of Hearts represents Charlemagne. The King of Diamonds, Julius Caesar. And last but not least, the King of Clubs represents Alexander the Great."

"How did you know that?" Cavanaugh asked.

Bradley smiled, "That's why I'm a lieutenant and you're a detective." Then he put the cap on the bottle of scotch and placed it back in the cabinet. He looked at both men and added, "And besides, you asked me the same question last week."

Cavanaugh and Goldberg looked at each other and started to rise. "Thanks, Lieutenant," Cavanaugh muttered turning toward the door.

"Wait a minute," Bradley asked suddenly. "I almost forgot. What about Vito Muscatelli?"

"What about him?"

Goldberg answered the question, "He hired Healen and Holland to kill you, Tom. He should be brought to justice."

Cavanaugh shook his head slowly, "You sound like Martin Luther King, Jr. What was that he said about justice denied anywhere diminishes justice everywhere. I guess he's right, but how are we going to prove Muscatelli hired someone to kill me? The old man is smart. He didn't leave a paper trail. Everyone that may have been involved in this is dead. All we have is hearsay. And the people who said something are all dead. I'm sure our illustrious, publicity junkie D.A. J.R. Coyle, would love to prosecute him, but for all the time, effort, and, most of all, money we would have to put into preparing a case, the old man would probably be dead by the time it reached trial.

Cavanaugh shook his head. "No," he said, "it's probably better we let Nature take her course. From everything I hear, old man Muscatelli isn't long for this world anyway."

* * *

111

Staten Island, New York

The sun had started to set and the sky was a beautiful pallet of colors. High in the sky, the moon began to peek through the clouds. Vito Muscatelli lay in his hospital bed stroking another kitten. He hadn't heard from Holland or anyone else in a couple of days. It seemed longer. He had tried calling Francesca again, but the message he got was that the phone was no longer in service. He hated waiting. It was the uncertainty about it. It was like death, but he could block out death. He didn't have to think about death as long as he had other things to think about.

"Gestas," he called.

The huge bodyguard/nurse quickly lumbered to his side. "Yes, Mr. Muscatelli."

"Are you sure you haven't heard anything from Cain Holland?"

"Positive, sir."

"Have you tried reaching Francisco Santacruz's associates?"

"Yes, sir, but there is no answer."

Muscatelli was worried. His stomach rumbled. He realized he hadn't eaten anything for lunch or dinner. Now he had a sudden, unexpected craving for a Carvel vanilla thickshake. His stomach continued to talk. He looked up at Gestas and said, "Get me a Carvel vanilla thickshake."

"Sir?"

"You heard me. A vanilla thickshake. And not one of those watered down things they pass off in the cafeteria. I want the real thing."

"But, Mr. Muscatelli, I would have to leave the building for that."

"I know. Tell the nurse on duty. I will be alright. It's after visiting hours anyway. Just get the damn thing and hurry back."

Gestas slowly backed out of the room. He would do as he was told.

Muscatelli pulled the covers closer and watched the moon brighten in the darkening skies. His eyes grew heavy and he closed them for a moment.

When he awoke the room was dark and there were stars in the evening sky. But where were Gestas and his vanilla thickshake? "Gestas!" he called out.

The door to the room opened and light from the corridor flew in. A tan skinned nurse in a white uniform appeared. Her long black hair was pulled back and tied in the back with a blue ribbon. He had never seen her before. Even in the dark, however, he could see she was beautiful.

"Who are you? I've never seen you here before. Where is Gestas?"

"I'm your new nurse, Señor Muscatelli."

"I don't know you. Where is Gestas?"

"My name is María Izabelle, Señor Muscatelli. I have brought you a priest."

"I didn't ask for a priest!" he almost shouted. His lips were dry and his hands cold.

The nurse moved aside. Behind her, Muscatelli saw a large figure in black. He walked slowly up to the bed. There was something familiar about his walk, his face. Muscatelli couldn't quite place it. "Do I know you?" he asked. His thick pseudo-Italian accent had vanished.

"I think you do," the priest smiled.

Muscatelli's hands were cold and shaking. "Who are you? Where's Gestas? What are you doing here?"

The priest leaned down close to Muscatelli and whispered, "You should remember me, Vito. My name is John Bennis, and I've come here to give you your Last Rites, your *very* Last Rites."

* * *

ACKNOWLEDGEMENTS

Writing a novel can be a lonely, isolated process. But, as John Donne once wrote, "No man is an island, separate unto itself." There are so many people I need to thank for helping me in writing this novel I will never be able to thank them all. Along the way, there was the encouragement and excitement from readers of my first novel. Their influence helped motivate me in my efforts to complete this sequel.

But there were others whose concrete assistance helped produce the book you have read. In particular, I would like to thank my cousin Anne Reisert who diligently reviewed the manuscript entirely and corrected many of my lapses; Bob Muir, a man I have only met a few times, but who has become a trusted friend in communicating with me by e-mail and offering constructive criticism on different parts of the book; Robert Boyd, a teacher and former colleague, who also read parts and offered constructive help; Anthony Guma, a friend since childhood, who, despite being separated by thousands of miles, has given me encouragement and more importantly true friendship; Larry Arann, whose simple comment that if I wrote only one page a day, by the end of a year, I would have written a complete book spurred me to action; my special writing workshop members at the Noble Maritime Museum on Staten Island—Albert Balossi, Jean Roland, Ray Coco, Carolyn Clarke, John Foxell, Evelyn Palambo, and Dawn Daniels for allowing me to share their writings and for their comments on mine—hopefully we all have become better writers and, more importantly, lifetime friends. And, I could not forget my wife, Diane, and my entire family, who "endured" my writing this story.

I also have to express a special thanks to my doctor, Dr. Louis Gianvito who supplied me with medical advice for my characters and has managed, thus far, to keep me alive. For both, I am very grateful.

And to the "Silver Schertoes," the "social/athletic club" of my youth, and to "The Stockton Club," the "social/not-so athletic club" of my later years, both of whose camaraderie, wit, honesty, and friendship I cherish.

There have been many, many others whose influence and encouragement have left indelible marks on me and on my writing. As they read this book, they will know who they are. But above all, please remember, this story is fiction and the characters are all creations of my imagination. There has been no intention to portray actual events or actual people.

If you enjoyed this book, you may want to read its predecessor, *Blood Brothers*, a fast-paced mystery/suspense adventure novel, which relates events leading up to *Collateral Consequences*. *Blood Brothers* is available at Xlibris.com, Amazon.com, and Barnes and Noble.com, or it can be ordered from your local bookstore.

I sincerely hope you enjoyed this story and welcome your comments. You can reach me at my e-mail address: *Hopkins109@aol.com*. I promise to get back to you.

Sincerely,
George R. Hopkins